Mended

Mended

by

D.S. NASS

Copyright © 2021 by D.S. Nass

All rights reserved. No part of this publication may be reproduced, distributed, or transmitted in any form or by any means, including photocopying, recording, or other electronic or mechanical methods, without the prior written permission of the author, except in the case of brief quotations embodied in critical reviews and specific other non-commercial uses permitted by copyright law.

Contact the publisher at DSNassauthor@gmail.com

ISBN: 978-1-7373113-0-0 (paperback)
ISBN: 978-1-7373113-2-4 (ebook)

Cover Art by A. Osh Designs: www.alekseyosh.com
Interior Design by M.V. McLaughlin

Printed in the United States of America

This book is dedicated to: Don and Joyce Brown.

From the very beginning you have always seen the best in me. Kids don't get to choose their parents, but in this case, I was the luckiest one of all. Together you shaped me into the person I am today, a child of God. You both showed me what love can do and taught me a strong faith.

I will be forever grateful. Love you always!

Acknowledgements

This book came together with the help of many.

Stefani Milan – author of *This Side of the Dream*
We met at my first author event working at a library many years ago. Stefani helped me through every step of the writing process and editing process. Sometimes it was painful, yet other times we laughed so hard. This book truly exists because of her dedication to the craft of writing and her love of helping others realize their dreams. Stef was not only my mentor and my editor in this process, but I'm honored most of all to call her a friend.

Megan Starbuck – author of *Packrat to Clutter-Free: How I Cleaned Up My Life in Less than a Year and Surprised by Marriage: A Cynic's Guide to Believing in Love*
Megan and I met in a Facebook group. Her books inspired me, and her writing group kept me writing when I wanted to give up. Megan was a true inspiration and an intricate part of my writing process. Thank you for being there when I need you the most.

Melissa Drake – author of *TransenDance* • www.uncorpedinfluence.com/

There are times when people come into your life when you need them most. She shared her book format with me when I need to organize my book the most. Melissa encouraged me to set a date to finish my first draft. *July 4, 2020*. She continues to inspire me to this day, and I can't wait to meet her in person.

Jane Babich – awellcraftedlegacy.com • fireborninspirations@gmail.com

I loved being a part of the original writing group with you. Your inspiration kept me writing and accountable to finish the novel. For this, I'm so ever grateful for your input and guidance.

Anna Marie – Wisdom2Heal.com • angelsrwhispering@yahoo.com and **Carol Harkavy** – author of *Rosie (And Me): A Memoir*

The saying about it taking a village is accurate. Your encouragement weekly in our writing group kept me not only accountable but looking forward to each week. Knowing you both were in my corner helped me to create what the book has turned into today. Thank you again for your enthusiasm and kindness.

Carol: Thank you for the final proofread!

Dru Hopkins

My best friend who taught me how to navigate life while raising five children. You are the friend that I laugh and cry with. Thank you for your unconditional love.

Julie Bunucci
We started as co-workers and now we walk the trails together. Just like the Julie in the story, you really have been there for me during some of the greatest transitions in life. Thank you for being a dear friend.

Karen Holmes – Clarity Coaching • www.knowtrustgrow.com • Karen@knowtrustgrow.com
Karen continues to be an amazing asset to my personal growth. Thank you for reminding me that Jesus will calm the storm!

Melissa Biggy – www.mythirtyone.com/mbiggy
My dear friend who has cultivated my love for reading! Your encouragement has helped me through the most difficult times putting this book together. Just like the nurse in the story, you have been by my side always. I love you like a sister and your faith is inspiring. Thank you for being my biggest fan!

Julie Schutz, Barbara Nass
Thank you for being the first of many readers. Your thoughts and insights were invaluable. Thank you for being part of my team and bringing these characters to life.

My family
None of this could have been possible without the help and support of my family. My granddaughter Daisy filled my days with light and laughter. My children Nic, Zak, Skylar, Creed and Erick. You all inspired me to be a better person. There are nods to each of you throughout the book as some of the characters carry your name. I love you all so much and I am excited to see what life unfolds for each of you. You bring meaning to my life. I love you to the moon and back.

Jason

We have seen many miracles together since we were kids, and I am blessed to have married a man of faith. After more than two decades of marriage you are still the one for me! Through life's ups and downs you helped me see the big picture and enjoy the adventures. God has blessed us with five children and grandchildren. Your dedication to your work inspired me to create this book. I could not have made this book without your support, and I appreciate all that you do. Love you always and forever.

Author's Note

I'm honored that you chose to read my first book! This book and the characters are entirely fictional, even if it may have character names similar to my real life. The *Mended* story idea began when I wanted to have an older woman advising a younger woman how to navigate life. I am fascinated with the wisdom that comes from past generations. The last five years writing this book, I saw it take on a life of its own. Grace's message will show that no matter what happens, women can lift each other up and become stronger than they thought possible. Erick's theme is forgiveness, hope, and second chances. The title was inspired by Matthew West's song, "Mended." No matter what your faith is, the universal story of hope can touch your heart during the current times. Our past scars hurt, but through them we all can tell our story and extend hope to others. I hope you will enjoy this tale of transformation, and may it inspire you, give you pause, and set you on a path to discover your true self. I sincerely hope this story will provide you with the courage to reach for the dreams you never thought were possible until now.

"Sometimes, you need to lose yourself in the middle of nowhere, and sometimes in the middle of nowhere is where you find yourself."

– Author Unknown

Prologue

The Finn brothers arrived at Lance Cohen's high school graduation bash in their classic, shiny black Chevelle. Dominick Finn, who most people simply referred to as Finn, handed the valet the keys. Erick stepped out of the car's passenger side as soon as they arrived at the party. Erick opened the door for his little brother, Daniel, who was fifteen. Students from Kings Oxford High School crowded every part of the sprawling manicured lawn and equally magnificent house. Of course, the party of the century would not be complete without a professional D.J. who played loud music. The music was blasting outside. The three Finn brothers stood at Lance's long walkway entrance, each having a different reason to be there. Daniel smiled as he thought about being at his first high school party. Finn looked over at his brother Erick and rolled his eyes, and frowned. Erick's eyes darted around while he shoved his hands into his pockets. He just wanted to set things right with his girlfriend.

Finn smiled as he slapped Erick's back. "Let's do this!" Just then, Daniel was surprised when a Junior named Blair approached them.

"Oh my God! It's *you*!" She jumped on Daniel and kissed him.

A wide grin spread across Daniel's face. "Later!" he smiled and took off with Blair.

"Dude! Did you see that girl?" Finn asked Erick as they walked through large double doors into Lance's house.

"Yeah, what the heck? Didn't you date her?" Erick half-shouted. The music was drowning out his voice.

"Yes, and most of the Lacrosse team at Kings Oxford." Finn shrugged and made his way to the bar. He pointed to a large bottle of vodka and shouted, "Let's drink!"

"I'll pass." Erick was focused on scanning the crowd. Many people had red Solo cups in their hands. The music pumped in his ears, making them throb. Finn handed him a cup, and Erick shook his head, realizing either Finn did not hear him or he had ignored him.

"You made it!" Tall, blonde, beautiful, and popular, Brooklyn Becker squeezed her way between Finn and Erick.

"Have fun you two!" Finn winked, handing Brook a now filled cup and getting lost in the crowd.

Erick could barely hear or move, for that matter. He hated these kinds of parties—full of superficial people whose only goal was to get wasted. Some people were well on their way to that already, he noticed.

Brook got close to his ear and whispered, blowing warm breath on his neck that sent shivers up his spine.

"Let's dance and enjoy our last night of freedom," Brook said. "Before our family makes us work for a living. Her blonde hair was pulled tight into a long high ponytail braided and held together with a diamond clip. Her hips swayed back and forth, and Erick suspected that she had been drinking way before he got there.

"I thought you said Grace was going to be here?" He had to find Grace, his girlfriend, and explain why he had not returned any of her calls. He scanned the crowd for anyone with long red hair with no success. *Where was she?* Meanwhile, Brook moved seductively around him, her intentions clear.

"She will be! I promise. Don't worry so much. Here," she said, exchanging Erick's cup with hers. "*Drink this.* I promise it will relax you, and when Grace comes here, I will make sure she finds you."

Erick took a sip. It was candy-sweet and barely tasted like alcohol. He finished the cup and felt better immediately. Soon Erick felt the music change, and he started to relax. He stopped scanning the crowd and took his eyes off the door as his body began to move to the music. Feeling dizzy, Erick closed his eyes and leaned on Brook. The room spun. He felt Brook as she placed her mouth on his. Erick no longer remembered why he was at the party or how long he and Brook stayed in that embrace.

"Oh, my God!!!" A shriek came from somewhere in the room.

Erick's heart stopped, and he pulled away from Brook, assessing the danger. The music had stopped, and everyone was staring at them. Then the crowd parted like the Red Sea to reveal a young woman standing by the door. Erick blinked. His vision was blurry, but he had seen that face before and the red hair with loose curls. Now, they seemed more like Medusa's snakes and were about to turn him into stone.

"Grace?" Erick squinted and stumbled.

"*How could you?*" Grace turned her hair flowing behind her like flames as she ran out the door.

"*Grace!*" Erick pushed past Brook and stumbled through the crowd. He made it out the door and fell flat on his face. He looked up just in time to see the headlights on Grace's silver Honda Civic drive away into the night.

Erick picked himself up, leaned his head on the stone column on the porch, and was thankful to hear his own thoughts. Away from the crowd. Away from the music. Daniel came over and sat by him. He felt sick.

"You okay, dude?" Daniel sipped from a plastic cup. "What happened?"

"What are you drinking?" Erick's hand hit the cup sending the contents splashing onto Daniel's shirt. "I told you no alcohol." His words slurred.

"Hey! That was my drink. You're the one who is wasted!"

"What happened to Blair?"

"She was only interested in our money. I should have known better. I wish people would like me for me, not my name." Daniel examined what remained of the liquid and dumped it onto the ground. "I think I had enough anyway." The night sky opened, and a heavy summer shower soaked the boys.

"Let's get out of here." Erick stood up in the steady rain as he saw the car pull up, "Daniel, when you find the right one, it won't be for money."

"How will you know?" Daniel looked down at his shoes as the valet pulled up with the car and the keys.

"You will know because she makes you a better person. When it's gone, you feel empty inside." Erick took the keys and stared off in the distance.

"We should find Dom," Daniel said.

"I'm not sure where he went." Erick stumbled off the curb, dropping the keys.

"You okay to drive?"

"I only had one drink, and that was hours ago."

Erick did not remember what happened next. He woke up in the Chevelle, steam rising out of the car, the engine wrapped around a large oak tree that lined the Finn driveway. Red and blue lights flashed continually and illuminated the raindrops on the windshield. Erick looked over at Daniel, slumped over the dashboard. The cracks formed in the windshield in circles around the top of Daniel's head. Blood was splattered on the window and all over the seat. Erick wiped his eye with the back of his hand. Warm liquid ran down his head and onto the leather bracelet on his wrist. *Where were they? What is happening?* He saw something shiny like small twinkly diamonds on the seat next to him; *What were diamonds doing here?* His eyes tried to focus, but the more he concentrated, the shiny object blurred even more. Erick fell into the blackness.

PART 1

One

Ten years later

Grace felt a cold chill as it wormed its way up her spine. Next, a high-pitched shrill sound filled her ears. All at once, she realized the sound was coming from her. Wide-eyed and gasping for air, her body jerked back. It was like watching a movie in slow motion as cobalt blue eyes burned into Grace's, and she could not look away. She wondered how she ended up here, what was happening to her? As her breath became shallower, her vision blurred.

Smash! Grace turned her head to see an explosion of glass against a wall. Shattered and broken pieces slid down next to her.

Grace gasped for air and awoke with a start. The blue light poured into the New York loft. It was just a dream; she breathed in a long deep breath and looked at the clock. 3 am. Grace laid her head back on the pillow and gazed at the empty side of the bed. Finn did not come home again. *He couldn't possibly be working this late.* She didn't want to believe that the rumors that were circulating at the office were true. He didn't mean to throw the glass at the wall that night. He was just under a lot of pressure at work. The signs were there. Finn did not love her anymore, and she did not feel safe. The arrangement they made after high school was not working. It was then Grace realized she had nowhere to go. Her parents were not an option. Not how she left things between them. An idea began to form in her mind. Grace would call her aunt when she got to the office. Aunt Raven would know exactly what to do.

Unable to go back to sleep, Grace made her way to the shower. She let the warm water flow through her jet-black hair. She remembered the first time she colored her hair when she started school at NYU. It was an attempt to reinvent herself to remove her fire-red hair and become someone new. Grace would no longer be the second-class daughter of a carpenter; she was with New York's most eligible bachelor. Changing her hair color would change her look on the outside, and she hoped it would have changed how she felt on the inside. Looking at the water as it ran through her long dark hair, she knew now she had made a terrible mistake.

Erick froze as his ears filled with a loud, piercing sound that screeched into his consciousness. Rain pummeled onto the broken windshield, and rhythmic drops splashed onto the windows in time with the sound of his heartbeat. It was dark, and the spider-web-like cracks caused an eerie kaleidoscope effect. Each splinter sent a shudder down his spine. It made a horrific popping noise as the glass separated into longer and longer cracks as if they were in some sick race to reach the edges.

Where am I? Erick closed his eyes. It was so quiet. Erick's nose filled with the acrid smell of gasoline and burnt metal. Through the rain, he noticed white steam billowing from somewhere. The blood pounded in his head, and his eyes tried to focus on something shiny on the floor. His memory returned in pieces slowly at first, then faster. The party. The drinks and knocking Daniel's cup from his hand. The music, the red hair that flowed behind his girlfriend as she ran through the door. The rain poured down as he and Daniel jumped into the 1970s Chevelle. What happened next is a blur. Where was Daniel? *Oh, God, Daniel!* Despite the searing pain in his head, Erick forced his gaze over to the passenger seat.

"Daniel!!" Erick screamed. Blood poured down over his face.

"Hello, Erick!" Daniel smiled as blood dripped from his face and filled up every space in the car. Erick held his breath—he began gasping for air until he closed his eyes, and went under the sea of red liquid.

"It's okay, babe," a woman's voice from far, far away broke his thoughts. Erick awoke with a start and wiped icy, cold sweat from his forehead. He sat up straight. "Did you have a nightmare?" A young blonde woman began to trace her fingers on his arm. Jace, his yellow lab, was right there licking Erick's other arm.

Erick got up from the bed, taking his sweat-soaked shirt off, leaving him in just his soft navy pajama pants. Without looking back, he selected a clean white t-shirt from the drawer. "Brook, I don't want to talk about it." His back now turned from her.

"I know you better than anyone else, Erick. When will you give me a chance? Let me in."

Erick looked at her and tried to look beyond her beautiful exterior. His gaze fell to Jace, his beloved Golden Labrador Retriever who wagged his tail, pressing his body against Erick's legs. "I just need time to work things out." Erick focused on Jace's soft vanilla fur.

"I don't understand why you keep shutting me out. After

all these years, we should, at the very least, be living together. Being together has been our destiny since our fathers went to school together. You can't deny the history!" Brook slid herself out of bed, still wearing her slip. Making her way over to Erick, she put her arms around him. Jace stood there wedged between them.

Erick closed his eyes and pushed down his reservations about the relationship. "If you must know, the nightmares started ever since my dad got sick," Erick confessed. He took a deep breath. "I *do* care for you, Brook. I'm just not ready to take the next step. I have to deal with my past before we can have a future."

Brook studied Erick's face, "Your father appointed *me* to run the Tabitha Finn Foundation, your *mother's* foundation, Erick. Our family *wants* us to be together." Brook moved back enough to hold her gaze to his. "*I* want us to be together. We will change the world, just the way our parents always envisioned. Both of our families want us to take the next step. You know our fathers aren't getting any younger. Dad would love to see his daughter finally married." She kissed him just then on the cheek, then pulled away to look directly into his eyes, "*You* are the only one who doesn't see it."

Erick could not look away. Brook had a point and bringing up his mother was his Achilles heel. He pleaded with her. "We are so . . . different, Brook. Since we were kids, I always admired your ability to know who you are. You take life head-on. But I'm not like you. I still carry the guilt of the past. You were there for me my whole life; you know what happened senior year. I get it if you don't want to wait around." He dropped his arms from her, and the space between them grew more significant.

"I was there for your entire life, Erick. *You* kissed me all those years ago. *I* stood by your side after the accident. It was an *accident*. Stop blaming yourself." Brook broke her intense stare and looked around the room. "It was a mistake coming here," Brook spoke with an edge in her voice. She picked up her blue dress from the chair and put it back on.

"I don't want to hurt you." Erick stood there helpless, looking away from Brook.

"If we are going to be together, you need to make an effort, Erick. What's a girl supposed to do to get your attention?" She gathered up her shoes and bag, eyeing the door for an escape to get out of this losing situation. "Where is my phone?"

Erick left the bedroom without answering her. Erick made his way to the front door. Jace followed him outside. With the door still open, Erick felt the morning chill air reach him. He could finally breathe again. Jace and Erick walked out onto the porch. Jace came back after a few minutes and sat at Erick's feet. He had never really told anyone about the nightmares, which seemed to be more frequent in the last few months. Erick wasn't ready to share that with Brook or anyone. He rubbed his beard and stood on the deck remembering their conversation from last night.

He attempted to drive her home last night and even tried to break it off without success.

"You are always trying to break up with me!" Brook rolled her eyes over her wine glass. He had lost count of how many she had consumed without touching her dinner. "I know you aren't ready to propose, but it has been ten years!" Brook pushed a small light blue box tied with a white silk ribbon towards Erick. "Maybe you will consider *my proposal*."

Erick slowly untied the ribbon with a shaky hand and a pit in his stomach. He opened the blue box, revealing a velvet box. Erick carefully opened it and saw a shiny silver key. He quickly closed it and slid it across the table to Brook. She was smiling with a sense of satisfaction. Erick collected his thoughts, "What makes you think I want to live with you in the city? You haven't even been to the cabin."

Brook, stunned at the lack of his enthusiasm, drained the red wine from the glass she held. "Fine, I will come out to your cabin, but only if you consider moving in with me."

In the car and then back at the cabin, things moved fast. "You had too much to drink. I don't think we should . . ." Brook had threatened to leave again, but in the end, she promised to sleep it off and talk more in the morning. All he could think about as they both went to bed, their backs to each other, was how far apart their worlds were. They'd known each other their whole lives, and after some convincing, dated after college. Over the years, the canyon of their differences began to divide them. Her life's work kept her in the city. In contrast, Erick's life was simple. He lived in the woods with Jace and spent his time helping others at HigherGround, his physical therapy office.

Erick looked into the woods and took a deep breath, shaking off the remnants of last night's fiasco. It was early, and the dark blue sky surrendered to the sun's break into dawn. The final legs of summer stood unsteady in Connecticut, and the morning was cooler than usual. Inside, a rage started to build. It began as a burning in his chest that made its way up through his neck, threatening to choke him. He immediately moved to the wooden chair and sat down. The porch was the length of the cabin, long and rectangular. It was not enclosed, but it had a roof overhead so Erick could enjoy sitting there even in the rain. The porch held only two wooden Adirondack chairs that he had built himself. As Erick sat down in one of the chairs, Jace sat by him. He prayed for Brook to leave.

Erick gazed out to the white oak and red maple trees as far as the eye could see. A few leaves caught in the morning wind swirled around as the night sky gave way to more morning light. He took another deep breath. *God, help me to forget what happened that day. I cannot let it defeat me. Please give me the words to say to Brook.* He stood up and filled his lungs with the New England air. What to say became clear in an instant and he went back inside. Brook had her fancy shoes on now and her Louis Vuitton bag and met him in the living room with her eyes on the phone in her hand. He noticed that she wore the same dress from last night, further proof she had not planned on coming there to stay for any actual length of time. He took in her beauty. Brook's blonde hair was brushed and swept back into a fresh long ponytail. Her eyes were as blue as sapphires. Her perfect bone structure did not outdo her tanned arms and toned legs. *Get it together, man!* Erick said to himself.

"I'm sorry, Brook. I need to be alone. I can't do this anymore. I'm not any good to anyone right now. It is all too much. People around me usually end up hurt. You're better off without . . ." he trailed off as she kissed his cool lips. He knew if she stayed any longer, he might change his mind for all the wrong reasons.

She pulled away first and opened the front door. "My driver is here. I won't wait forever, Erick. Eventually, you have to stop chasing ghosts."

His family had always seen things differently. Other than his brother Daniel, he had successfully avoided his family all these years for the most part. He wanted nothing to do with them, and perhaps Brook was still the bridge between him and his family. How long could he avoid the truth? He just wanted to be set free from this relationship, once and for all.

Erick quickly changed into his running clothes and trail shoes. Jace wagged his tail, and Erick walked out of the cabin and onto the porch watching the red taillights as Brook's driver pulled out of the dirt path. Erick patted Jace's head, "Let's go, buddy!" The two of them were off, and they ran fast through the woods. The sun was now making its pink and gold entrance through the trees. Away from that terrible night long ago, that he couldn't seem to forget. With only the wind at their backs, his feet would carry him far, far away. Away from Brook's narrow eyes. Away from his disappointed family. Away from the inescapable pain, he held inside. Away from that terrible night long ago, he couldn't seem to forget.

Two

Grace was in the office washroom looking at her hair and makeup on Monday morning. She had a very important meeting today. Her black hair was straightened and pulled into a capable long ponytail. She smoothed her lips together with lipstick and smiled wide.

Grace had to give credit to Finn, her boyfriend and boss. She felt she owed him everything. Over the last ten years, he was generous and provided this extravagant lifestyle, and it was everything she ever wanted. Finn extended this offer during one of the most challenging times in Grace's life—high school. She remembered it like it was yesterday.

Nearly a decade ago, her life changed entirely, and it all started when Lance Cohen, a popular senior, threw a huge graduation party. Grace hadn't even planned to be there that night. She got into New York University and the University of Connecticut. Erick, her high school sweetheart, wanted to live with her off-campus and go to UConn together. He was going to study business while she studied journalism. A twist of fate brought Grace to this party. She needed to sort things out with Erick, who hadn't returned her calls or texts for over a week. Seeing him kissing Brook that night was the last straw, and she knew he would never fight against his family to be with her.

Grace remembered she couldn't run fast enough to get outside that night. She handed the valet the ticket for her car. It was dark except for the tiny lights down the driveway. She could smell a faint scent of cigarette smoke as the memory unfolded like it was yesterday. She looked over, and a lopsided smile and dimples were smiling back at her. Finn. She had met Finn first, after all, on her first day at Kings Oxford High School in the principal's office. How he graduated was still a mystery to this day.

"This party is a drag!" Finn dropped the cigarette and had stomped it out with his leather loafers that Grace was sure to cost more than her car. Right on cue, the valet brought her old silver car to the front as Grace tried to conceal her embarrassment.

"Yes, you want to get out of here?" Grace's heart was racing as Finn jumped into the passenger seat, and she slammed her door shut. Her tires squealed, and as she looked in her rearview mirror, Grace caught a glimpse of Erick stumbling down the front steps.

Grace drove into the night, wanting to forget the scene she saw.

"You know, Grace," Finn said, "my brother, Erick, isn't the one for you. Brook had her claws in him since they were babies. You never stood a chance."

"Your *family* never gave us a chance." Tears ran down her face.

Grace furiously drove around for a while and parked her car out on Red Hill Lookout point.

"My dad will come around and see it my way," Finn continued, "but not with Erick. He is too much like my mother. Too soft for the business world."

"You give someone your heart . . . I trusted your brother. With everything." Grace swallowed a sob. "What is wrong with me? I can't help that I don't come from money. Did he even love me at all?"

Finn put his hand on her arm. "My brother doesn't know what he wants. That's why my dad wants to keep him close. Brook, she always gets what she wants."

"I will never forgive him for this." Grace could feel her anger rising.

"You are going to rise above this, Grace. I know you will! I know you applied to NYU." Finn looked at her, the moonlight shining in the car. "I'm going to New York as soon as possible. My dad is fast-tracking me to be the CEO of FinnLondon."

"Your dad will never change!" Grace hesitated. "How did you know I got into NYU? I didn't even tell Erick because he, um, we were going to . . ." Grace pinched her eyes shut, and she was not going to cry again.

"I have my connections. I think you'll be happy there away from this town, away from *Erick*. I also know Erick will never go against the family. Me, on the other hand." Finn looked straight into Grace's eyes. "I never follow the rules. I suspect you don't like rules much either." Finn's face was inches from hers. "NYU gave you a full scholarship, right?"

"What do you mean *full scholarship*?" Grace looked directly into Finn's eyes.

"Maybe a little birdie put in a good word for you . . ." His breath was warm on her face as his lips brushed hers. He sat back suddenly. "I never take it slow with women. But you are different, Grace. You are worth waiting for, and from what I heard, you have what it takes to be a best-selling author and journalist. If you want it bad enough."

Breathless, Grace asked, "*You* helped me get a scholarship? Why would you do that?"

"Guilty as charged, but it really was all you. You impressed the scholarship committee with your essay. I just put a recommendation in that you are an up and coming journalist. I'm in publishing, after all. Honestly, you can have all your dreams come true. Money never will be an issue for you again, Grace." Finn leaned against the window. "So what will it be? Do you want to pine after my brother Erick, who will never stand up to his family? Or be with a man like me, Grace? Together we can show the world that Grace and Finn are a force to be reckoned with."

"What about your father?" Grace asked in disbelief. This opportunity was too good to be true.

"Once I take over the family business, my father will be eating out of the palm of my hand. He will see you. Grace, a famous published author. Not Grace, the daughter of a carpenter."

"What's the catch?" Grace was skeptical now.

"No catch. Let me do something nice for a change. I will take care of everything. You can stay with me at the loft. Before you get the wrong idea, it's a large space with *two* bedrooms. Your scholarship allows you to stay on campus if you prefer a better roommate." Finn shrugged. "I can offer you a job at FinnLondon publishing once I get things set up. I will be the perfect gentleman, and if you want, we can go out on a proper date, or we can just be friends. No pressure. I have always admired you from a distance. What do you say?" He looked directly at her. "On second thought, never mind, don't give me an answer right away." He opened the car door and leaned down, his hair falling over one eye. "I'm going to walk the rest of the way to give you time to think. When you decide you want a different life, then you call me." He picked up her phone and put his number in her contacts. He winked at her and closed the car door.

Grace started the car and drove the short drive home. She thought about Finn's offer that might be too good to be true. She was free to do what she thought was best, even if it meant a life without Erick in the picture. Now, Grace could finally get out of her house and live the life of a writer. A *published* writer. It seemed foolish not to take the offer. Erick wasn't going to fix anything, and even now, a decade later, he was practically engaged to Brooklyn Becker after all.

Nowadays, Grace carefully managed to avoid the spotlight while Finn was on the covers of magazines. She was no longer the assistant, and Grace had her own corner office and title of chief editor. Grace had almost everything she had ever dreamed of with Finn by her side. He always took care of her, and up until recently, he treated her reasonably well. Her book wasn't published, but she couldn't press Finn because he was working long hours. The stress of Finn's father being sick had caused severe problems for their relationship. Terrible things she could conceal from the world. No one would ever know.

Now, Grace shook off the terrible memories and looked at her reflection in the washroom at work. Grace plastered on a fake smile and was now ready to start her day. Grace left the restroom and walked confidently with perfect posture back to her glass office.

"Good morning, Miss Evans!" Finn's newest assistant headed into the ladies room in a hurry avoiding her gaze.

"Morning, Athena." The door closed behind her, and Grace made her way through the glass offices to her own.

"Hi Miss Evans, looking beautiful today as always," chirped the male intern who sat by her office.

"Hi, Ryan."

Grace opened the glass door of her corner office and walked to the window. The floor-to-ceiling windows overlooked a busy Manhattan. The city seemed to breathe on its own as if it was alive. She looked down on the tiny people who were out walking the streets and breathed it all in. New

York was her home now, and she owed Finn everything for he made it all possible.

Grace sat in her white leather chair behind her desk. *Funny how things have changed*, she thought. *It was so good back then, and maybe it can be even better now. Perhaps she could be better. Maybe she could make it all better.* One thing Grace knew, she owed Finn, and he had been with her since the beginning, and *he* was her family now. It was Finn and her against the world. The voice in her head continued. *Then why was there an empty bed again? What about the broken glass?* His behavior was erratic and possibly dangerous. Uncertainty filled her as she picked up her cell phone and called the one person who could help.

Erick took a sip of his green tea as he looked out the window. He heard a rumble of thunder in the distance. His watch read 5:15 am. Erick managed to sleep past 4 am for once. It was nearing the start of fall in Connecticut, and he watched the birds greet each other at the bird feeder. *They must be discussing bird events*, Erick thought as he sipped the warm liquid. He hoped the storm would pass soon so he could go for a run. He could feel the tension rising in his shoulders and took a deep breath to settle himself.

"*God*, another masterpiece in the making," he whispered to the red bird, who whistled in delight. Erick smiled at the birds' simplicity, moving about as the grey and dark blue clouds rolled into view.

Erick sipped his tea, remembering when he was in medical school and moving into the rustic cabin with detailed woodwork. He thought about Brook and all the years he and her family had been together. He remembered how she was always there for him after the accident and during the grueling hours of school. Erick wasn't quite sure if his mother would approve if she were alive today. He had overheard her once talking to his dad about the Beckers. She always thought James Becker was reckless because he never took care of himself. His wife couldn't stand him and ran off with his business partner. Regret filled him as he thought of his mother and how she had never met his first girlfriend, Grace. No longer in his life, and he had accepted that his high school sweetheart had moved on, even if it was with his brother.

Erick pondered his love life since high school. He failed at an attempt to date a fellow medical student who was allergic to dogs. That was a deal-breaker, especially when he just brought home a puppy in his last semester at school. Then, Brook always seemed to turn up at school with a picnic basket lunch or tickets to an off-Broadway show.

Despite all their differences, Brook was beautiful, and their fathers were best friends. She wanted him to move into the city, but he was content here with the birds. To him, this was life, and he liked Brook, but they were worlds apart. After the accident, he didn't want to be around anyone. Brook disappeared for a few months after that night. Erick was thankful to be alone, but then she just started coming around the house again. He let her in because they had known each other their entire lives.

Erick wanted more than anything to escape the past and choose a life of helping others and make a difference. It would never erase what he had done, but it was his life sentence, and he was willing to serve that out until his last day. It was his penance for not obeying his dying mother's wish at the age of eight to look after Daniel. All the money in the world would not bring his mother back, and her loss weighed heavily on him.

Tears dared to leak from his eyes as he remembered the

night before she passed. She had been his whole world as a little boy. Erick was a small boy who loved to climb up into her bed and burrow his way into her neck. Her honey-colored hair smelled like honeysuckle.

    She whispered in his little boy's ear. Her voice was soft and hoarse, "My son, you are the heart of the family. I'm counting on you to take care of Daniel. Promise me you will . . ." She coughed and strained as she spoke the words louder as if she demanded it. His mother's dark eyes were wild with desperation. "Promise me!" His little brother, Daniel, was only five, and he was fast asleep at the foot of the bed. Finn stood at the doorway with his arms crossed that night. Erick would promise her the world if it meant she would stay in his one more minute. Her grip tightened, "Promise me!" She was hoarser now. "I promise you, Mommy . . ." It was that night a little boy's promise took root. A promise that would haunt him the rest of his days, and Tabitha's final words she would ever speak. Even now, when he would be heading to the physical therapy office where he did his most remarkable work, it would still not be enough.

    It was days like this when thoughts of his mother would come into his mind, and he wanted to run. Run far into the woods, far away from his thoughts. Thoughts of how he had not honored his promise. Beliefs about how he was not good enough. Not good enough to keep his mother alive. Not good enough to keep his brother safe and not good enough to earn his father's respect. And certainly not good enough for the girl with the hair like a late August sunset.

Three

Grace dialed her Aunt Raven's number and waited to hear her aunt's bubbly voice. Aunt Raven always picked up the phone when Grace called, so when she heard the voicemail, Grace felt disappointed. Aunt Raven was probably hiking and had no cell service. As she left a message, her assistant Ryan walked into her office. He waited for her to hang up.

"Sorry to interrupt Ms. Evans, but Mr. Finn is waiting for you in the conference room."

"Thanks, Ryan." Grace headed to the meeting, excited to hear her novel would finally be approved for publication.

The meeting ended sooner than expected, and Grace's mouth was gaping open as the fellow executives exited the conference room. She could feel disappointment filling her body. They voted on her novel, and Finn's vote would have been for her as planned, but his vote was the one against it. He pulled her aside at the end of the meeting. She felt his hand pressing tight on her forearm. "You're hurting me." Grace grimaced.

"I'm sorry, I believe in you, Grace. We just have to wait a little longer. We are behind on already approved books . . ."

Grace couldn't hear anymore and started to walk away. "Unbelievable."

"Declan still runs the shots, and he is counting on me to take this company to the next level."

"So, your father is preventing you from publishing my book?" Grace was stunned. "Have you even *read* my novel?"

"He is the one who has the final say. When my father hands off the business to me, I can take a look at your book. I have another meeting across town right now. I will catch up with you tonight."

"Where have you been, Finn?" Grace dared to ask.

"Keep your voice down." Finn gripped her arm tight against him this time. "I ask the questions around here, *not you*. Remember, if it weren't for me, you wouldn't be here right now." His eyes blinked, and he released her. "I will see you tonight."

Grace walked back to her office without saying a word. It felt like a punch to the gut. She sank into her white leather chair behind her desk, her head slumped over and resting on her hand.

Breaking through her thoughts just then, her phone buzzed, and her intern Ryan's voice came over the phone intercom. "Sorry to interrupt Miss Evans. I have a Robin Evans on the line. He said it's urgent."

She had not spoken to her family since she left in a hurry all those years ago. She hesitated and stared at the blinking light on the phone. *What could he possibly want after all these years? Why now?*

"Thank you, Ryan."

She pressed the button and picked up the receiver.

"*Dad?*" Grace braced herself for the answer.

"It's your Aunt Raven," Robin spoke quietly.

"What?" Grace asked as her heart broke into two. She missed her father's voice more than she wanted to admit.

"She fell, hiking in California." Robin stopped trying to stifle his tears. He choked on his words, "She . . . she didn't make it. Can you come home for the service? Please, it would mean a lot to me. The funeral is this afternoon. I didn't want to bother you. I tried calling last week, but they said you were in meetings. I had to try . . ."

Grace could hear him muffled and sobbing.

"Of course," Grace assured him as she felt her heart break for her dad. She missed him. "I didn't get the message. I will leave as soon as I can." Robin thanked her, and he hung up. Grace collected her things and asked Ryan, "Why didn't I get any messages from my dad until today?"

Ryan looked up from his desk and nervously around the office. "Sorry, I was told you were not to be disturbed," he lowered his voice so no one could hear.

"Well, if my father calls again, make sure you let me know. I have to go to a funeral now, so make sure you take my messages. Please don't tell anyone, but if anyone asks, just say it was a family emergency."

Grace would call Finn later from the road since he was in meetings all day, and after his angry exchange with her earlier, he would most likely try to prevent her from going at all. It was raining when she arrived at the loft for her things. Back on the road, Grace dialed Finn.

"Grace? I can't really talk right now," Finn spoke in a low voice.

"My Aunt died. I'm going home to attend the funeral."

"Now isn't the best time for *me* to leave." Finn sounded exasperated as his voice rose.

"I can go by myself. It's fine. I will be home as soon as I can."

"I don't want you to go alone. Are you still mad about the meeting this morning?" Finn's voice was low again, "Let's talk tonight. You can tell your parents we have plans."

"*Plans?*" Grace shrieked. "My aunt is *dead!*" Tears would have to wait. She could barely see the road. "I have to go.

It's raining, and I need to pay attention." Grace insisted. "I will be home tomorrow." A car swerved in front of her. Grace had to slow down to avoid a collision. A horn sounded behind her.

"Please don't go. Your parents were never there for you! You should be with people who actually love and care about you. I'm your family now!" Finn protested.

"I'm sorry, Finn!" Grace winced as she did the unthinkable and ended the conversation by hanging up the phone abruptly. The one thing that Finn hated most in the world. No one hung up on Dominick Finn.

Within a few hours, she was in Connecticut. The cemetery was near her childhood home, and she was the last to arrive.

Grace pulled her jacket closer as she walked up the hill and found her place in the back of the crowd, but in view of the casket. The minister held a large black umbrella as he delivered his message. Grey clouds rolled over a hill where the Evans' family stood. The weather looked as dismal as everyone felt, and the sky released its emotions alongside them. About a dozen opened black umbrellas all joined together to honor and respect Raven.

"We came to earth with nothing, and we leave with nothing . . ." The minister held a small Bible and was reading about the transition from this life to the next. "Raven Willow Evans' life was a celebration of freedom, and she is sure to be finding adventures in the next . . ."

Grace barely listened as she held onto her umbrella. The priest's words about *freedom* caught Grace by surprise.

"Psalm 23:4. Even though I walk through the valley of the shadow of death, I will fear no evil, for you are with me; your rod and your staff, they comfort me."

Grace wasn't sure if there was a God, but she knew one thing for sure, there was a way to live life. She learned from her Aunt Raven's stories that were full of passion and freedom. Her aunt always talked about being free and open to adventure. What if that was *precisely* what Grace was missing in her life? She had never considered it until now.

"Raven lived her life by embracing every moment. She did not hold back her love for others, and when doubts came, she stood in the face of fear and stared it down. Raven was always travelling and experiencing all that life had to offer. She lived a full and abundant life. We are all called to live a life in this way . . ."

As the minister turned the page of his small black leather book. Grace remembered that the last time she saw her aunt was at her graduation party. Grace would have asked her aunt for advice if she knew that would be the last time she would see her. Grace had meant to call, but she had been so busy. She sighed as she looked over at her parents and realized how much time she had lost with them as well.

Grace smiled as she recalled her favorite memory of Aunt Raven when she was about four years old. Her aunt's house was like a tiny cottage in the woods set back on acres of the property, complete with an arched door right out of a children's fairytale book story. Weeping willow trees and fields of wildflowers surrounded the tiny hidden house.

Aunt Raven had opened the door and Grace's father, Robin, walked in holding Grace's tiny hand. Grace was amazed at all the vibrant colors of the furniture and rugs. Pinks, greens, and purples. Grace recalled her mother's absence in this visit. Aunt Raven placed two yellow cookies in front of Grace on the coffee table and then brought over two cups of tea for the adults.

Grace looked at her dad and placed her small hand on his leg. "Daddy, this is your sister?"

"Yes." Robin patted her hand. "This is your Aunt Raven."

"How do you do?" Raven reached out to shake Grace's hand. Grace hesitated but extended her hand.

Grace's eyes widened, and she smiled when she looked into her aunt's green eyes. Grace noticed they were the same emerald shade as her dad's. Grace carefully took a bite of the cookie and felt the taste on her tongue. The delicate cookies tasted like flowers and melted in Grace's mouth. With crumbs tumbling from her mouth, Grace chattered. "You and daddy were little once?"

Robin took a sip of tea and laughed. "Yes, Pumpkin, we were. Actually, we are twins." He smiled over the cup, "Of course, I was born a few minutes before she was."

"Robin! Always pointing that out."

"What are twins? Where are *your* mommy and daddy?" Grace brushed the crumbs off her face with the back of her little hand.

"Twins mean we look alike even though we aren't identical. Sometimes we know what the other is thinking. That's a story for another time." Robin patted her head.

"We may as well share it with her. It is *our* family story," Raven insisted. "Stories are what life is."

Grace could not help notice her aunt's wild red hair trying to break free of the bright fuchsia pink silk scarf containing it.

"It was a hot summer June night, much like tonight," Robin had a faraway look on his face. "Your grandmother, Alo, was part of the Sequin tribe of Native Americans. A white man with red hair visited the tribe long ago, and they fell deeply in love. But your grandmother's tribe did not approve. When your grandmother became pregnant with twins, she and your grandfather were only allowed to stay in the camp until she gave birth." Robin took a breath.

"Your grandma went to sleep after Robin and I arrived. She never woke up."

"Never? Did she d-d-die?" Grace whispered the words and decided she did not like this story after all.

Drums and Native American flutes filled Grace's ears, breaking through her reverie. Three Native American men began to pray and sing over her Aunt Raven's grave. It was a death song lament, haunting and uplifting at the same time. Grace wondered what it was like, to cross over into the afterlife.

Her thoughts once more drifted back to the memory of that night she visited her aunt. Her father, Robin Wren, and her aunt, Raven Willow, were born on June 11, 1965. Grace realized she had never got to meet her grandfather. She had heard very little of the story, and she did not even know her grandfather's name or if he was still alive. Surely her grandfather would have attended his own daughter's funeral. Wouldn't he? Perhaps he did not even know.

Grace noticed the clouds as they tumbled over the sky in various shades of grey and black. The rain fell harder now as the service continued. Tender sprigs of fresh lavender were placed on the casket by each person paying their respects. As more people passed through, the scent grew stronger and more intense.

The smell of lavender brought on another memory. Grace could not have been more than three years old. She remembered sitting on a high bar stool at the kitchen table.

Behind the sink, on walnut-colored wooden shelves, were several colorful and unusual-shaped jars. At the time, Grace had imagined all the jars contained magical potions and that her aunt was a real-life fairy godmother. The jars were (as she found out later when it was tea time) indeed filled with magical, healing herbs and mostly tea leaves. After taking a chubby handful of sweet cookies, she was allowed to take a sip of lukewarm golden liquid from a beautiful porcelain cup. After tea, Aunt Raven scooped her up, and they went outdoors to a wide field of hundreds of wildflowers. Grace ran around free, her arms wide open, her white sundress twirling around her as she spun in circles. Dotted pinks, purples, yellows, and white filled the yard. The wildflowers grew up to Grace's waist; she danced along the path surrounded by the rainbow of wildflowers and imagined her favorite fairytale, complete with unicorns and a young prince riding in on a white pony to whisk her off to a castle of her dreams.

On other occasions, she'd stay with her aunt several days at a time if her parents were travelling. They'd lay in the lush green grass looking at the clouds letting their imaginations run free.

"What do you see, my Raya sunshine?" Her aunt's nickname made Grace smile. Grace's hair, a light, strawberry blonde in loose braids, touched the top of her Aunt Raven's wild red hair, untamed and curling around. The bluest sky above had set the stage for all the animals in their cloud imagination zoo parade. They had had front row seats to the wonder.

The clouds faded with the memory as thunder rumbled in the distance. The sky was ominous and looming. Under the sea of black umbrellas, a canopy of grief, Grace stood next to her dad. It felt natural as she reached into the crook of his arm. She saw a flicker out of the corner of her eye. Suddenly, a black raven appeared in the heavy rain and then perched on a gravestone a few yards away. *What did the bird want with her?* Grace grew uncomfortable under its stare. Next, the bird let out a squawk and spread its wings, taking to flight, higher and higher. In that next instant, Grace felt something shift—as if just the mere act of watching the creature take flight left her forever changed. The feeling was slight, hardly noticeable at first, but Grace knew that one thing was sure. Her life would never be the same after today.

Erick arrived at work an hour early, as he often did. He loved to show up before everyone else. It gave him a moment to gather his thoughts and pray over each patient's files that he would see that day. Erick did his best work when he was focused, and God helped him see what he needed to see in the most challenging cases. Erick unlocked the door and turned on the lights. *This was what I was meant to do,* he thought.

Erick looked around and smiled, his eyes landing on the expertly laid-out equipment.

He looked out over the sizable expansive studio. In his mind's eye, he could see the years pass by of rehabilitating people. Some had even been small children who lost hope when they were given the devastating news that they could never walk again. Seeing the look on the parent's face and the tears of joy on the child's face when he took his first small careful steps brought pure joy to Erick. He remembered the look on one little boy's face when he took his first steps after three years of being in a wheelchair. He recalled another one of his first patients, a Navy man in his early twenties who had seen more battle than most people would ever have to face. The man was on a mission one day and lost both of his legs when he fell on a grenade. With prosthetics and Erick's help, the man learned to walk well enough to complete a full marathon before his twenty-fifth birthday.

Once, he treated a mother who lost her husband and child to a drunk driver. Even though she had lost everything, Erick helped her regain her mobility. He walked down the hall to his office. The floor was light wood, and the wall was lined with framed photos of his patients smiling and with drawings from the children he had helped learn to walk again over the years. Erick built this building from a dream and with the help of a contractor four years ago. He also designed the apartment where Daniel lived now. Erick knew this was a sacred space. God was the architect, and he was simply the instrument to carry out His miracles. Erick looked up and whispered, "I give all the glory to you . . ." He truly was humbled by the joy in his patient's faces. He removed his shoulder bag, stepped around his desk, and brought his computer to life. As his schedule popped up, he reviewed the list of people he was going to see today.

Just then, his phone buzzed with a text from Brook.

Sorry about the other night. Things got crazy. Let me make it up to you. I have an important meeting with the CEO of Stamford Hospital this afternoon. Will you meet me at 7 pm at LaRue for drinks?

Erick didn't text back.

"*Drinks . . .*" Frustrated, Erick shook his head. "Really?"

After being together all this time, how could Brook even suggest that? Erick felt his stomach churn. He had not touched a drink in over a decade, not since that night of the accident. He took a deep breath, realizing that this was the problem in their relationship. She didn't know him. *No*, he thought. What Brook wanted was for him to get over his issues, to swallow his feelings, and to be the fast-paced city boy she wanted him to be. But that was never Erick, not really. And it never would be.

It angered Erick that Brook would rather spend her time under bright lights in fancy restaurants with fake people who only talked about superficial things like vacations and not aging and visited a plastic surgeon for entertainment. Rumor had it that even Brook had undergone in some elective surgeries. City people, including Brook Becker, spent so much time climbing some imaginary ladder of success, all the while missing out on what was most important. Erick wanted other things like Love. Family. Happiness. Erick knew all about the fake life. He saw it firsthand watching his family when he grew up. His father always wanted him to run the family publishing business with his brother, but he saw what it did to their *character*. Cocktail parties, fundraisers, and conferences were part of that life and always had drinks flowing. Erick didn't care for it. He loved to be in the air around the trees and away from the cars. Erick chose this spot to build HigherGround, keeping the location outside the city but close to the bird-filled woods he called home.

Just then, Erick had a realization. Maybe it wasn't that Brook didn't accept *him* for who he was now, but perhaps it was *he* that wasn't accepting of who *she* was. Perhaps *he* was the problem, not her. Erick felt defeated and texted Brook back that he would meet up with her.

You're the best. I couldn't love you more. She replied immediately.

Brook Becker did not take no for an answer. Not in business or her personal life. She had high standards that no one could ever live up to. He should be glad a woman of her caliber was interested in him. He knew how things could change in an instant. Erick remembered being excited to start his life at eighteen. After walking in his cap and gown, shaking the teachers' hands, beaming at him with great expectations, he thought his future was going to be extraordinary. A decision he made that night after graduation changed all that—the night he lost everything and hurt those he loved the most.

"Dr. Erick?"

Joyce, Erick's office manager, appeared at the door. She had short curly dark brown hair and pale green eyes. She had been with Erick since the beginning when they started up. He had interviewed many people for the job, but this woman had a spark about her. She was in her early 70s, and something about her reminded him of his mother. She also would not put up with him being behind schedule. He always pictured her over the decades, chasing him around well into her 100s, making sure he not only took care of the patients but was taking care of himself as well.

"Now, don't you make me drag you by the ear, dear. Sally Jennings is here, and you know how she gets if you don't give her the royal treatment!"

With a twinkle in her eye, she looked right into Erick's face like only she could and smiled. Erick was glad for the distraction from his thoughts. He followed Joyce out to the waiting room, which was alive with people. People who looked up to him. People who wanted the very thing that Erick had embodied since he started this journey. *Hope.* And by God, he would give it to them if it was the last thing he ever did.

Four

Grace found her father in the foyer of her childhood home. After the service, her parents had invited her to stay the night instead of driving home in the dark. Robin Evans was not a tall man, but even as he stood there looking at Grace, he seemed smaller. She noticed the silver hair around the edges of her father's temples and the brownish-red color that peeked through his beard. His eyes, a warm green hazel, looked at Grace with compassion. Outside, the storm whipped tree branches around , and the rain hit the roof in a rhythmic pattern. Flashes of light illuminated the window causing intermittent shadows over Robin's face making his expression seem even more weathered.

Robin held out a thin handmade wooden box about the size of a small book. The initials RWE were carved on the top piece. "I was supposed to give this to you when you turned eighteen, but then you left suddenly . . ." he trailed off, seeing Grace look away. "There is something I've wanted to talk to you about. All this time . . ."

"Dad, if it's about me leaving, I don't want to talk about the past."

"Grace, please just listen. I'm sorry I didn't support you all those years ago. I regret everything I said to you the night you left. I also regret what I did not say to you as well. I hope you will forgive me. I'm so proud of you."

He handed her the box, which seemed a bit worn, and she looked at it.

"Read it when you're ready," he pleaded. "I want you to know that I always wanted the best for you. I always loved you, and always will. No matter what. I hope you can forgive me one day. For everything."

Grace felt the connection with her father again after all these years. She reached out and hugged him tightly. He wrapped his arms around her, and his embrace was like a balm healing an old wound for Grace.

"Pumpkin, I'm glad you are finally *home* . . ." he breathed into her ear with all sincerity. She was glad too.

When they pulled out of the embrace, she could see the tears in his eyes. Her father's face seemed to have aged, and Grace knew the loss of his sister was not going to be easy for him. She remembered the last time she saw her dad so distraught. It was the day Grace decided to go to New York with Finn. No one could stand in her way. How ambitious and free she had been then. But now she was in Finn's world, which made her feel less like herself. Grace did not want to admit to anyone that things were strained with Finn, least of all her parents. What had happened to that spirited woman she used to be? Back then, Grace thought her parents were between where she was and where she desperately wanted to be. Now, Grace was unsure.

Faith walked in slowly and carefully, looking pensive. Grace braced herself for what she suspected would undoubtedly be a difficult conversation.

Faith Evans was a petite woman with a sleek, ebony blunt bob. She had met Grace's father over three decades ago when she was on the UConn Debate team. Faith was now one of the most sought-after family lawyers in New England.

"Grace, sweetheart, what did you do to your hair?" Faith moved in for a light hug that felt like she was trying not to break the glass. "It looks like *my* hair color." Her approval was vaguely apparent. "Anyway, we are so glad you could come home. Your father and I are hoping you'll stay the week and, well, catch up." Faith quickly added. "It would mean a lot to your father."

"Mom, I can't stay long. Finn is . . ." Grace trailed off as she noticed her mother roll her eyes at the mention of Finn's name.

"You are old enough to make your own decisions now. I just think you should make family a priority. We haven't heard from you since you ran off to New York and all. Your father and I wanted you to become *whatever* you wanted to be. We just didn't want you to follow after a man. Especially not Dominick Finn." Faith spat his name out like a bad taste in her mouth. Even Robin, uncomfortable, squeezed his wife's arm softly. Faith continued, "They are shady as they come, that Finn family! You have no idea what they get away with . . ."

"You have no idea, Mom!" Grace interrupted. "You didn't know me *then*, and you certainly don't know me *now*. No matter what I do, it is never enough. You have to accept that I'm with Finn now, and he is the reason why I'm in the publishing world now." Grace opened the door to her bedroom, planning an escape from the uncomfortable conversation.

"Oh, so your book is *published*?" Faith never asked a question that she didn't know the answer to already.

Grace did not need to explain herself to her mother. She turned to her dad, who looked uncomfortable as he averted his eyes away from the scene. "I can stay tonight. For *Dad!*" Grace ignored the statement about her book still not being published. The truth nagged at her heart about how Finn had not kept his word about publishing her book. She remembered Finn's words that morning when he admitted his father had the final say. It wasn't the first time Declan stood between her and what she wanted most.

"It's been a long day," Grace finally said, exasperated again with her mother's interrogation. "Good night, Dad."

Grace went into her room and closed the door behind her. She had felt the walls closing in on her, the same walls she felt before she left for New York. She closed her eyes and sank to the floor. Grace hugged her knees to her chest and took a deep breath. Suddenly, she remembered the box her father gave her still in her hands. She carefully opened the box; inside was a brown leather book with a compass etched on the cover and brown leather ribbons tying it closed. A dried iris lay there wilted on top. Grace lifted herself off the floor and put the book and the box on the bed.

Her room wasn't different from the day when she'd left in a hurry. Grace's eyes landed on some pictures left on her old cork board from her high school days. A black cord hung from a thumbtack with a golden compass charm on it; a gift from Erick on her seventeenth birthday. Grace carefully lifted the necklace, unclasped the cord, and put it around her neck. She needed all the help she could get, especially now when she felt lost.

Next, she noticed a faded picture of Finn and his brother Erick. Erick's face had a large thumbtack through it. "I guess he deserved that!" Grace winced, thinking *if he could see me now!* She ran her hand down a few ribbons from her writing awards, which hung from a clear pushpin there as well.

Grace sat on the pink quilt on the bed. Looking down at the book, *Aunt Raven, what did you do?* Grace felt drained to the core, physically and emotionally. After travelling, attending the funeral, dealing with her mother, and thinking about how angry Finn might still be with her, she was totally exhausted.

It was too late to turn back now. What was done is done. Grace laid back on her childhood bed and shuddered at the memory of the last conversation she had with Finn. She removed her hair tie, and as her rain-dampened black hair fell free, she ran her hand through it.

She knew she needed to call Finn and apologize. She would let him know she was okay, and perhaps he would be relieved. Grace pulled her cell phone out of her pocket, and pressed his number. A familiar voice came on.

You have reached Finn of FinnLondon. Leave me a message, and I will get back to you.

Grace decided not to leave a message. She knew she needed this time to be with her family and say goodbye to Aunt Raven. Grace was in trouble with him either way. When she got back, she would make it up to him. She planned to fix everything after the funeral. Grace leaned back in her bed, opened the journal, and began to read.

If you are reading this, then you have become the woman I knew you were meant to be. I asked Robin to give this to you when he felt you were ready. My hope is that you will find all that you are looking for in this world.

This story is dear to my heart, and I want to share it with you because things are never what they seem, my child, and be careful my darling Raya Sunshine. Be careful who you trust and let in your heart. You will learn in time that every woman must take a journey of rediscovery at least once in her lifetime. A journey is necessary to find out who you are and to rediscover your voice and your free spirit. Like a Phoenix, you will rise again, even when you think all is lost. I took this journey years ago and learned some valuable lessons on the Freedom Trail. The answers you seek will be found there and in your heart. That feeling inside that things are not right is a voice inside telling you to awaken and see. Honestly, my sweet Raya Sunshine, I fear your life may depend on it.

Erick stated simply, "Hello, my name is Erick, and I'm an alcoholic."

A small group of men murmured "hello" back. They sat in a circle on a Tuesday night after hours in a church basement in the town center. The room was quiet except for the chairs' metal screech as the men adjusted their postures to lean in to hear what Erick had to say. "It's been ten years since I started this journey."

Erick was interrupted by an eruption of clapping.

"You would think I have figured this out by now, but I'm still struggling. Just the other day, my girlfriend invited me out for drinks. It's like she doesn't know me or just doesn't accept that recovery is a significant part of me. Every day that goes by, I wonder what am I doing with someone who . . ."

Erick trailed off and, with his right hand, stroked his thick beard thoughtfully.

"Is it too much to ask for someone to really *see* me, to really accept me, flaws and all? I feel like I'm constantly at war with who I am and who people think I should be. I know God has a plan for me, but I wish I knew what it was. I don't want to hurt my girlfriend, but it's becoming clear that she isn't the right girl for me. Just the other day, she came out to my cabin for the first time since I bought the place. I realize now that I'm better off being alone. This way, I can be me, and no one will get hurt."

His voice wavered as he tried to keep back the tears. He continued. "I can forgive others, but for some reason, I cannot forgive myself." Erick took a deep breath. "The worst part is the nightmares. They keep me up at night. I can't remember what really happened all those years ago. What I do know is I hurt the two people I love most in the world. Alcohol cost me everything. Sometimes I think about drinking again. Drinking so much might temporarily allow me to forget about the nightmares. Sometimes I just want to be someone else. The nightmares are getting worse these last few months. They now come every night, almost like I'm trying to remember something about that night. Honestly, I just want to forget."

Erick put his hand in his back pocket and pulled out a chip. He held it up for the men to see. He moved the coin through his fingers and said, "But this reminds me to take it one day at a time. I will walk through the fire and come out the other side, sober. I won't let alcohol win."

The other members at the meeting thanked Erick for sharing, and Erick sat back down in his seat. He examined the inscription on the sobriety coin.

On one side of the coin, engraved around a triangle, was the quote, *"To Thine Own Self Be True."* On the other side of the coin was the serenity prayer. He pressed the coin into his palm as if burning the words into his brain through his palm.

When the meeting ended, Erick headed over to a table with a spread of tea in all varieties, coffee, doughnuts, and muffins. Erick opened a green tea bag and placed it in a paper cup. He picked up a carafe of hot water and filled the cup. He looked at the tea as it began to steep as if hoping the answers he needed would appear.

Erick was in deep thought when his friend Joe slapped him on his back. Erick moved the cup to avoid spilling the hot liquid. With his other hand, he gave Joe a firm handshake.

"Good to see you, Joe!" Erick smiled at his friend.

"That was some heavy shit you are going through, my

friend." Joe picked up a doughnut and took a bite. "Do you have someone like a sponsor to talk to? It might help you work some of that shit out." He shrugged and took another bite of doughnut.

"Not in a long time. I will try to get one soon. Hey, how is the family, Joe?" Erick carefully took a sip of the hot beverage.

"My youngest just started college a few months back. The wife and I are trying to navigate the whole empty nest thing. It is harder than it looks. I miss both of my kids. I miss going to all those years of soccer games. Who would have thought I'd say that?" Joe chuckled.

"I can't imagine, man. I hope to be married one day and have a few kids. Just haven't found the right woman yet."

"Enjoy your time as a free man, my friend." Joe slapped him on the back again. "I gotta run. Catch you at the next one."

Erick moved on to greet some of the members and told them a little bit of his story. Part of being in recovery was giving back and helping others to find their healing.

Erick was one of the last to leave. He hopped into his jeep and made the long, lonely drive back to his place. Erick had turned the radio off to think. He knew he had to break up with Brook for good this time. It was time to move on before someone, likely himself, would get hurt. After all these years, he could not afford to hurt anyone else again.

Five

"I came so far on the road home. The price was higher than I wanted to pay. The heart always finds a way. It compelled me to keep going even though it cost me everything. It's a force I'm powerless to control. Something inside me won't rest until I know you are safe. You might be in danger! Somehow, we must also save ourselves."

– *Raven's Diary*

Grace closed the journal and hugged it tightly to her chest. Her eyes were heavy with sleep. She had driven for hours through heavy traffic and rain to get to West Hartford in time for the funeral today. Now, the moon cast a glow through the window, and Grace felt a presence as it loomed over her. A shiny black bird perched on the window tapped the glass pane, startling her. The cawing seemed so loud, and she couldn't tell if the bird was inside the room or just outside the window. The cawing continued as if the bird was giving her a message or a warning or an omen. Grace's mind recalled the sentence that she had read in the journal. *"You might be in danger."*

Grace reached over to turn on the lamp. As the light filled the room, the bird vanished. Still tired, she turned the light off and closed her eyes. The sound of the raven's wings rhythmically flapping filled her mind until it faded into nothing.

Did she dream up this black bird? Or could it be that her aunt had sent her a raven? After all her aunt's name choice was after the ominous bird. One time Grace remembered she had edited a book from a writer who wrote about folklore and birds.

A raven meant danger in most folklore and mythology, she thought. Her next thought made her shudder. *What if I really am in danger? From what or whom?*

One hour later, Grace was still wide awake, thinking about the potential danger she might be in, and her heart raced. Her thoughts drifted then from the raven to Finn. He sounded so disappointed with her when she brought up the trip home. Grace had seen him disappointed before. It only happened a handful of times. Finn would always apologize and buy her something the next day. It was like dealing with two different people. The fact that he wasn't calling her began to worry her. She thought about how he had changed so much in the last year. Ever since his dad's health declined, Finn took on more responsibility at Finn-London, and his behavior became even more erratic.

She looked out at the moon and scrunched down under the covers. His father, Declan, became ill earlier that year and had to seek treatment that made him too weak to be at work every day. He still came in for meetings. They had three locations, New York, Connecticut, and London. Lately, when Finn did come home, he returned late at night and sat in the chair, silent at the end of the bedroom drinking whiskey—one glass after another. Grace pretended to sleep, but she could hear the ice cracking and the bottle clanking and the sound of the liquid filling the glass. Finn had reminded her that she was nothing without him and replaceable.

Grace distinctly remembered that Finn came home angrier one night and blamed her for losing a contract with a new author. He said she was unfocused, and he could find someone else to do her job at any time. Finn pointed out that the only reason she had her prestigious job in the first place was because of his family. He made it clear that she would not have a job if she didn't work harder to exceed his expectations.

Her phone buzzed just then, interrupting the memory. It was Finn.

"Hello?" Grace picked up the phone, realizing it was quite late.

"Grace? Why did you leave me?" Finn sounded defeated.

"I will be home tomorrow. The funeral was beautiful, by the way." Hoping this would jog his memory of why she was there in the first place.

Silence. Grace could hear the sound of swallowing.

"I'm here. Where are you at?"

"I'm at my parents' house."

"Grace, we left them for a reason. I can't believe you would ever go back there. They do not love you."

There was a ring of truth in what he said that she could not deny about her parents. They did leave them for a reason. It all seemed behind her now—the reason muddled over time.

"My aunt died, Finn," Grace whispered into the phone reminding him.

"Besides," Finn ignored her, his voice louder now. "You can't leave work in the middle of the day like that. What would people think?" Finn kept on. "I'm sure your boy Ryan will be happy to cover the slack. I have seen how he looks at you. I should just fire him now, honestly. I don't need the stress of him in the office. I feel bad letting him go. It will be your fault if he loses his scholarship." Finn strained to speak in a hoarse whisper. "You should have chosen me over your family."

"Finn, it's not like that!" Grace pleaded with him.

"I don't care, but as far as your boy Ryan goes, he is done at FinnLondon. Make no mistake about that," His words slurred as he spoke into the phone. "And one more thing, Grace!" His words were exact and measured. "Don't. Ever. Hang up on me again, ever." The phone clicked, and the call was over. She cringed because she knew Finn fired people for less. He could punish her, and young Ryan was collateral damage. It was her fault. Again. Guilt wrapped its hand around her neck. Poor Ryan. She had to try harder with Finn when she returned.

Grace put the phone on the side table and tried to fall back asleep. One question loomed in her mind: What if Finn fired her too? Then what would happen to her? Would he throw her out of the loft also? She had to get back before it was too late.

Consider the trees, tall and robust. They do not need to compare themselves to the other trees. They offer me shade, beauty, and warmth. The forest is where I'm alive and born again. All paths in nature lead you to the truth, and all answers lead you back to yourself. Be careful of those who promise you the world. They are like snakes in the grass. You will be able to see through the lies. The trees will help reveal your true nature. The trees will light your path and show you the way. And I will always be with you.

– RAVEN'S DIARY

Erick came home after the AA meeting and texted Brook that he could not make it after all. He was relieved when she did not text him back. He was not up to another fight. Not sleeping more than a few hours each night was taking a toll on his body.

Erick awoke the following morning as the nightmare dissolved from his memory. Erick and Jace left the house for his daily run just as the strokes of oranges and pinks began to break through the clouds. Night after night, the nightmares relentlessly plagued him. Always the same. The night of the crash. His brother, covered in blood. The agony of reliving the crash over and over was becoming unbearable. Each morning his prayer to take the nightmares away went unanswered.

When he ran for miles on the trails, Erick's feet hit the earth in sync; his heartbeats and his rhythmic breathing allowed him to glide effortlessly over the trails that morning. A memory drifted into Erick's mind as he ran.

He remembered the day he told his father he wanted to be a doctor instead of being in the family publishing business. That was the plan that fall after the accident. Erick postponed college that semester to take care of Daniel.

"Dad," Erick remembered the confrontation in his father's office like it was yesterday. "I need to talk to you."

"Son, we can talk later. Everyone is waiting for us in the conference room." Declan Finn was not going to be late when he had something important to announce.

"It can't wait." Erick moved closer to his dad behind his desk, who did not look up from the laptop.

"Son, I'm sorry about what happened to Daniel that night. He tells me you enrolled in school with some nonsense about being a doctor. You have more than enough money, son."

He peered over his reading glasses. His blue eyes did not conceal his dismay as Declan shut the laptop.

"Dad, please. I was there for Daniel through all of the physical therapy and doctor visits. I know I have money. That is not what this is about." Erick took the seat by the large oak desk, looking away from his father's penetrating gaze.

"You have so much potential, son. Your loyalty to this family business is all I require. And I would think it's a small price to pay for all I have given you. Of course, you are free to decide in the end since you do have your mother's money. You should know this is what she always wanted for you, Erick. Security with the family. No struggles in life. Please don't do it for me, Erick. I would hope you would honor *her* wishes. Your mother and I always imagined all of our boys running the family business."

Declan took his glasses off, picked up a cloth, cleaned them, and finished the conversation.

Erick cringed under the guilty weight of the last sentence his father carelessly threw out there. It was like an arrow to his heart. What his *mother always imagined*, he couldn't give her then, but maybe he could now. Swallowing his grief of her loss and how he'd potentially let her down yet again, he took a deep breath, and the words tumbled out.

"Dad, I know this is what you have always wanted, but I know that I need to do this. I think I can help Daniel. Help him to *walk* again."

Erick searched his dad's eyes for something. Anything. A sign that his dad cared even a little, but his dad was looking off to some faraway place. Was his father lost in a daydream, picturing his older two sons standing by his side as he accepted awards for numerous accomplishments? Erick felt like he was crushing his father's dream and his chances for his father's elusive approval.

"Family is important, Dad. This is why I want to help

Daniel and do something more. I made a promise to Mom to always take care of Daniel. And after everything that's happened, I owe Daniel. If there is even a chance, he could . . ."

The phone on the desk rang, interrupting Erick.

Declan replaced his glasses and answered the phone. "Yes, we are on our way." He spoke to his assistant and hung up the phone.

Erick ran faster on the trail as he remembered what happened next—his father's announcement around the black leather conference table. Glass walls lined each office, including the conference room.

"The day I have been waiting for has arrived here at FinnLondon. I always hoped to build a legacy here. Today starts the day where my two older sons will join our team. Together, side by side, we will be the number one publishing company in the world!" Declan's booming voice and his big smile captivated the audience.

Erick heard the words and the resounding applause from the staff, all dressed in their stuffy suits and flashy ties. His brother, Finn, embraced his father as Erick just stood there stunned. He could hear the clicks of the cameras as the press took photographs. Flashes of light from the camera could not hide the crimson blush on Erick's face. He felt trapped like a small fish about to be eaten by a shark in this fishbowl conference room. His stomach began to churn, and sweat began to bead on his forehead, and if that wasn't enough, the tie he had on began to strangle him.

Erick reached to loosen the tie that was around his neck. It was a noose slowly getting tighter, threatening to choke the life from him. Spots danced before his eyes, and he ripped off the tie and threw it down.

Erick ran out the door, the clapping fading as he distanced himself from the room. Declan would be furious, but he didn't care. Erick was finally free. All he could remember were the words whispered across his soul before everything got so crazy. Words that came to him before that fateful night Erick tried to forget. The night when he lost everything. The night when he lost *her*. The girl with the fire in her heart. He remembered one night they spent talking about life and looking at the stars from their rooftop place when she said, *"The world is dark, but you are like a firefly in the night. Follow the light, and most of all, follow your heart."*

Even now, as Erick ran harder, the leaves crunching under his sneakers, he wondered how she was doing. It was no longer his right to worry about her. She made it clear that she was with Finn now, and she was happy. After the accident and after that day, he had chosen a new life. He walked out of FinnLondon all those years ago and never looked back.

Six

"The worst of all the lies told are the ones we tell ourselves."

– Raven's Diary

Grace left her parent's house quietly before dawn the next day, to avoid any confrontation. Traffic was light, and it only took her two hours to get to the office in Manhattan. She parked her car in the parking garage below the Finn-London offices. Grace grabbed her purse and her laptop, nearly dropping her car keys as she attempted to juggle the items while using her foot to shut her car door. She grabbed her phone and texted her dad that she had made it to the office. She wouldn't want him to worry about her. It was better this way. She was back at her office where she could work, and she could figure out a way to make it up to Finn.

Grace quietly slipped into her office, careful not to make eye contact with anyone who might alert Finn that she was back. After shutting her glass door, she hung up her long raincoat on the hook by the door and dropped her bags next to her desk. She settled in her white leather chair and looked out the window. It was after 6 am now.

The grey clouds had rolled back, and the sun was shining, rising over the taller buildings. She rolled her chair back around and reached into her purse to remove the soft leather brown journal. Grace opened it and started reading.

> *I hope one day you will truly understand some choices that you get to make, and some choices make you. It all started years ago. I was captivated at first sight. He was everything I thought I wanted. It started out so exciting and carefree. Over time I began to disappear into the relationship. Things changed, and I was in way over my head. It was too late. I had all but given up. Then a miracle happened, and I decided to fight back. Not just for me, but for you. The signs were there; all you have to do is open your eyes and see the world as you once saw. It was too dangerous, and the secret was going to be exposed. I had to do something.*

Suddenly, the door burst open. Grace flinched at the sound and quickly replaced the silken ribbon bookmark and put the book into her desk drawer. Finn stood six feet tall, his presence filling the room, demanding attention. Today he wore tailored dark grey pants and a white shirt. He loosened his maroon tie. His appearance today reminded her of when they had met that first day at Kings Oxford. He had come a long way from being a delinquent student. He didn't like ties then, and today his tie looked as if he never finished putting it on, and the buttons on his white shirt were open at the top.

Grace was accustomed to Finn barging into her office, and there wasn't any point in mentioning anything about privacy. With Finn, she had none. However, Grace was not ready to show him the journal for fear he may take it or destroy it. His behavior had been so unpredictable lately, and Grace thought the less she told him, the better. Instead, she took a deep breath and braced herself for the inevitable explosion. Finn glided over to the glass desk, leaned over the edge and stared at her. Grace met his gaze and waited.

"Yes, Finn?" Grace finally broke the silence. She hoped he didn't notice her heart racing. She fidgeted slightly by reaching up to make sure her ponytail was still straight.

"How was your trip?" Finn asked as if there wasn't a care in the world and placed a quick kiss on her lips. He acted as though it was any other ordinary day. Sometimes Finn had two personalities, one at work where he was more professional, the other at home that was more intense and fueled by alcohol. Grace held her breath as she waited to see if he would say anything else, but he didn't.

She exhaled under his intense gaze. "The funeral was beautiful. My parents are doing okay, I guess."

"I'm sorry I was a jerk on the phone. I just hate being without you. Is it a crime to care that much about my girl? I'm only guilty of loving you *too* much. I don't want to be without you." He shrugged.

Grace thought about what Finn said. He was persuasive, but his actions told a different story. They would be spending more time together, not less if he was speaking the truth.

"How is your father doing?" Grace changed the subject.

"They are doing more tests at the hospital. It is going to be a long road." Finn ran his hands through his hair. His playful demeanor faded, and he frowned. Finn looked agitated to be talking about his father. "Until then, I can't let my father down, and he is counting on me. Sorry, I could not go to the funeral. I'm under a lot of pressure right now. My dad is not easy to please." Finn stared out the window to the offices. He looked like a king looking over his kingdom that was burning. "I just have to show my dad he made the right choice." Finn glanced back at Grace, his blue eyes sparkling now. "It has been some time since we had dinner together. Are you up to going out?" His hands covered hers. "Dinner at the new place uptown. It's called The 101. 7 pm?"

Finn fixed his tie and smiled his big flashy smile now as he gazed down at Grace. With a swift and determined motion, he started towards the door. Finn moved like a well-choreographed dance that demanded that one take notice. He winked at Grace as he opened the door.

"See you at 7 pm. *Don't* be late." Finn spoke so powerfully that it felt like a warning more than an invitation.

Stepping out the door, he nearly ran into Athena, his assistant. The dance was now coming to an end, but not without a snapped glance back at Grace.

"Sorry, Mr. Finn, your 10 o'clock is in the conference room waiting." Athena looked down at her feet, avoiding Finn's intense gaze.

Grace was glad *she* had been promoted and no longer his assistant. Now, Athena was his latest muse, and Grace hoped she would make it. Athena was tough, but Grace hoped she would last. Finn always grew weary of his assistants. He had been through a dozen in as many months.

Grace watched as Finn and Athena were on their way to meet his next appointment. Finn's hand rested a little *too* comfortably on the small of Athena's back. It would seem natural to the untrained eye, but Grace knew better deep down. Watching them leave and walk from her view, Grace sat back and decided she was overreacting over the one gesture. It wasn't like Grace believed the rumors nor had any actual proof of infidelity. Just because Erick cheated on her all those years ago didn't mean his brother Finn was doing the same now. Finn was just overworked and was just closing another deal for his father's business, and Grace decided not to worry about this assistant.

Grace began looking through the manuscripts on her desk. She had only been gone less than two days, but there seemed to be several new files on her desk. Grace could not focus as she opened the files and the words were a blur. She put the files down and left her office. Outside the glass doors of her office, FinnLondon buzzed with people working in her department. She headed down the hall, passing cubicles and phones ringing. She saw her co-worker, Nic, leaning back in his chair while simultaneously throwing a small rubber ball against the wall and catching it. He was talking into a microphone headset and winked at Grace as she walked by. She hoped Finn didn't see him being so casual at work.

The break room had a glass door, and once inside, Grace grabbed a black and red cup from the cabinet that read "FinnLondon: Dreams come true, one page at a time." Grace frowned as she thought of her very own dream not coming true. Her mother's words haunted her, and she was right after all. Grace *was* still waiting for her book to be published. Filling the cup with hot water, Grace placed it on the table and selected mint green tea. As her tea steeped, Grace could not stop thinking about the journal. Thoughts of Aunt Raven's life seemed more like a fairytale. When Grace was growing up, she imagined her aunt having all sorts of adventures. Having read only a few pages in the journal suggested that Raven was raised solely by her father, and she had also met the man of her dreams early in life. Bringing the mug to her lips, Grace remembered another thing Aunt Raven wrote about, how the journal was for *her* and that Grace was in some sort of danger. Just then, another employee burst into the break room, and Grace headed back to her office.

A new memory popped into her head as she opened the door. Aunt Raven had told her about her wild adventures and barefoot summers running through the forest.

"Raya Sunshine, you are a princess," she said, her hands cupped around Grace's chubby six-year-old cheeks. "Always remember that princes are frogs!"

Aunt Raven opened her hands, and suddenly a toad appeared, all wiggly and brown. Grace's aunt giggled, and then her larger-than-life laugh burst free. Her wild, red, curly hair, like fire in the sun, blew in the wind. Grace touched her hair and remembered when she, too, had wild red hair. When the memory faded, Grace removed the journal from the drawer.

"Aunt Raven," Grace whispered into the journal, "There really are happy endings, and I'm living proof. I will be a famous writer one day, and I will marry a handsome, rich prince. His name is Finn."

Aunt Raven never met Finn, but she did meet Erick once. Grace never got to tell her what happened after graduation. It seemed crazy now, Grace thought, to have made such a big decision to move to New York with her ex-boyfriend's twin brother. *I just wanted to move on and get away from the past.* It wasn't her fault Daniel and Erick were in a car accident all those years ago. Finn told her about it, and he said Erick was okay, but his brother lost feeling in his legs and ended up in a wheelchair. Things were not supposed to turn out that way. Finn, not Erick, went against his father, Declan, who did not want any of his sons dating Grace. Declan had always seen Grace as inferior. But Finn still stuck up for her. Finn always chose *her* over his family.

She placed the journal on her desk. Her fingers smoothed over the etched compass on the outside, focusing on the letters and the arrows. She picked up the journal and hugged it close. As she did, a nagging feeling made its way through Grace's body. A thump on the window startled her, and the delicate journal slipped from her fingers, falling to the floor.

Grace shuttered. Something felt wrong. Her eyes focused,

and outside the window, she saw a black raven stunned but trying to fly. The raven cawed as it flew by the wide window as if it were mocking her in her thoughts. The next thought came as if it was a clear voice in her head.

If everything was so perfect, then why do I feel so out of control? Why do I keep justifying my relationship with Finn? Most importantly, why does it feel like I'm about to be cracked open from the inside?

Grace shook the thought and the bird from her mind and got up to retrieve the journal. Grabbing it off the floor, she noticed a bit of the leather was worn in the back, revealing a tiny opening between the leather and the pages. The space revealed a small folded piece of paper that had been secretly tucked inside. Grace brought the book back to the desk and held it up. Next, she carefully removed the paper, gently unfolded it and smoothed it out. Her breath quickened, and the hair on her arms stood up. Her eyes focused, and it appeared to be some kind of treasure map. The paper was yellowing, but she could make out the words *"Freedom Trail."* She could see lines with a sketched fallen tree with an "X" over it on the page. The words *"Where it all began"* were scrawled on the side in her aunt's handwriting. On the top, more writing revealed, *"The answers you seek"* with a small heart drawn. Before anyone came into her office, Grace carefully folded the map up and replaced it in the small opening, hidden once again in the back of the journal.

What did you do, Aunt Raven? What did you hide there that you don't want anyone to find? Determination and curiosity filled Grace. She would find out what Aunt Raven was hiding, but how could she even think about getting away again? She got lucky last time. Finn may not be so understanding the next time. Grace felt it would be foolish to go back to Connecticut, but at the same time, something inside her felt like she had no choice. It was as if her life depended on it.

Erick wrote notes about his nightmares inside his journal he kept on his side table. Each always started differently, but it always ended the same. It seemed counterintuitive to write down and remember something he tried for all these years to forget. As he put the pen back in the drawer, he wondered if there was anyone he could talk to about what really happened that night. His brother Finn was there, but he didn't speak to Finn much after his dad announced the sons would be running the family business. Finn had called him the next day after he ran out of the conference room.

"Dude, what happened to you?" Finn demanded.

"The business is all yours." Erick sounded resigned.

"As happy as it makes me that you would give me your share of the company, I think Dad wanted us to run it *together*."

"Not interested, man. It's what *you* were born to do. I'm going to do my own thing."

"Your own thing. Interesting. Well, then, I should thank you. There is nothing I enjoy more than taking things from you."

Erick rolled his eyes at the memory. Finn and Erick had an unspoken rivalry with everything, mainly because Finn found it impossible to let Erick have anything of his own. Some twins had a telepathic connection, but they were like oil and water. Finn was highly competitive, and if he wanted something Erick had, he would find a way to take it. So, it came as no surprise to Erick when Finn added the final jab that day, "And, now I have the girl *and* the business."

"Whatever." Erick's blood boiled with rage. "Do me a favor and don't call me again." Erick hung up.

I have the girl. Finn's words echoed in Erick's mind. Finn got the girl because Erick never got a chance to tell Grace his side of the story at the graduation party or after because she was with *him*. He didn't see the point. Grace had made her choice. Erick still doubted if she ever really loved him at all. He ran from the conference room, ran from the guilt he felt from his family, and ran from the only woman he ever really loved. He had no one else to blame but himself.

Seven

"Sometimes, you come to a crossroads in your life. The next step will determine your destiny. Choosing to ignore that path was no longer an option for me."

– RAVEN'S DIARY

Grace wrapped her scarf around her neck. A chill came through the wind as she exited the car Finn had sent for her. The leaves were brown, gold, and orange. Fall had arrived in all its New York splendor. The nights were cooler now, and it was 7:02 pm. She hurried inside the new trendy restaurant. Guests filled every white linen-clothed table; Grace could hear dinner chatter and silverware clinking on the restaurant's high-end plates. Crystal flutes, filled with champagne, were delivered to a table with a young couple when Grace spotted Finn at a table by the window. She could see the frown on his face illuminated by a flickering candle on the table. He stood up as Grace approached.

"You're *late*," he hissed in her ear as he kissed her cheek.

He removed her jacket to reveal a forest green long-sleeved cocktail dress. An older gentleman appeared in a white shirt and black vest, and Finn handed her coat to the man with one hand and placed a large folded bill in the other.

"Thank you, sir."

The gentleman lowered his head and moved on. Finn pulled out the chair for Grace. She sat down and began looking at the menu. Grace realized looking at the menu was pointless even before Finn announced,

"I went ahead and ordered the salmon for us."

Grace took a sip of champagne. She was not in the mood for fish.

"Did you work late again?" She looked down at the champagne bubbles rising to the top. "Is that why we couldn't ride together?"

"The office won't run itself, Grace. You of all people know this. The amount of work I have to do, the amount of pressure I'm under. I don't need pressure from you. Besides, I've finally come to realize, my dad may never come back. Then the company will be mine to run full time. My father always envisioned it this way, and it's what I have always wanted." Finn lifted his glass of single malt whiskey to his lips. "Dad is drawing up the papers for me to become CEO by the end of the month."

Grace took a sip of her champagne and said, "It must be bittersweet for you. To get everything you always wanted. I can't imagine my dad being sick, and it must be hard on you."

"Life comes full circle sometimes, and you must meet it where you are or die trying." Finn looked away.

"There's something I want to tell you about my trip, and there is something else I need to do." At that moment, the waiter brought out their meals.

Finn's phone buzzed. "I have to take this. It's Brooklyn Becker. She has been keeping me in the loop about my father."

Grace stiffened at the mention of the woman's name as

Finn got up from the table and took the call outside. She could see him from the window, his back to her.

Grace remembered her from high school and had successfully avoided her since. Annoyingly beautiful, Brook was from the wealthy Becker family, who owned large insurance companies in Connecticut. The Beckers and Finn family had known each other long before they had children. Grace recalled her senior year when she wrote a story for the school newspaper about the current senior class and their plans after school. Brook had agreed to be interviewed by her.

Grace had met Brook at a local coffee shop the day before their graduation. Brook spoke about her passion for the Tabitha Finn Foundation and how many people she had helped. Grace was aware of her philanthropy, but she was also aware that Brook was a force to be reckoned with, and the interview was going to be difficult. Brook was top of her class and excelled in sports. Grace also knew she had been with just about every popular guy in school, but not with Finn. Even during the interview, Grace remembered the smile on Brook's face. "One day, I will be with *a Finn.*"

At the time, Grace thought she was talking about *her* boyfriend, Erick Finn.

"Excuse me?" Grace remembered saying.

"This is how it was always meant to be, and even the Becker and Finn families have been friends forever. Besides, The Prom King and Queen deserve a happily ever after, don't you think?" Brook raised her eyebrows and laughed. "Oh, wait, you thought I meant Erick, didn't you? I mean, don't get me wrong, he's great, and you're one lucky girl, but I've always had my heart set on the other twin. You know, Finn? I've seen you two talking at a party before. I wonder if Erick knows about your little one-on-one time with Finn. *Does* he know about that?"

"What are you getting at, Brook?" Grace felt her cheeks flush.

"Nothing," Brook shrugged. "I just know the family very well, is all! You know, Grace, you should go to Lance's party. It's the last time we will all be together. You owe it to yourself to let your hair down. You have every right to be there, and I hope we can be friends after all this."

Brook stood up, ending the interview, and Grace was left there with her notes and thoughts. Grace also recalled the same party and how that ended with Brook kissing Erick.

"So, Grace? Where did you go?" Finn had returned to the table. "Unfortunately, I had to let Ryan, the intern, go. I was hoping you could finish the work that you missed when you were gone. While you were doing God knows what with God knows who in Connecticut, the rest of us were working." Finn drained the glass and set it down. "I need you at the office. Work has gotten more difficult, and now my dad wants me to handle all the high-end accounts. I have a flight out in the morning to London to meet with the partners in that office. They want me to work from there with a challenging client. Athena will be going with me." He cut a piece of his pink salmon and took a bite. The waiter exchanged Finn's empty glass with another glass of single malt. "This is cold. Bring me another piece of fish." He turned to Grace. "What did you want to tell me? I already told you what you *need* to do."

Grace took a sip of her water and decided against telling Finn her plans to return home again. "It's nothing I can't handle on my own. Why does *Athena* have to go with you?"

"I had wanted *you* to go with me, but your department is short-handed and, because of you, behind schedule. I set up some interviews for you this week for your new intern." Finn chewed his food thoughtfully. "Unless, of course, we need to hire a new chief editor to do *your* job." He looked at her, daring her to say something.

"How is the salmon, Mr. Finn?" someone suddenly asked. The chef placed a steaming new plate in front of him with ample portion béarnaise sauce.

"Chef Jason, it was cooked perfectly!" Finn responded to the chef in approval. "But it could use more sauce."

"Of course, Mr. Finn!" Chef Jason returned to the kitchen.

"It will be fine. I'll make the deadline." Grace used her fork to stab a cherry tomato artfully placed on her salad.

"That's my girl." Finn winked and smiled, getting his way. Finn continued to eat his salmon while Grace poked her fork at hers a few times.

Once the waiter cleared the plates, another appeared with a black forest cake. "This is our specialty dessert. It consists of vanilla mousse filled with brandied cherry, a vanilla crémeux with dark chocolate. These petite chocolate cakes are topped with smoked chocolate ganache." The waiter presented the artful plate in front of Grace.

"Happy Birthday, Grace!" Finn slid a small black box across the table his eyes on hers.

"Thank you, Finn."

Finn waved his hand in the air. "Can we have this to go?"

After dinner, they took the car service back to the loft together.

"You need to behave yourself while I'm gone," he breathed into her ear. He went to bed and snored softly, ending the discussion while Grace lay awake most of the night. She checked her calendar on her phone, as a plan took shape in her mind.

Erick drove to work, and he tried to escape his thoughts about his family by listening to Christian music. Erick parked and entered the building. He was surprised that Joyce was there early.

"Your 3 pm canceled," Joyce declared. "Luke is doing his college visit today. He said he would see you next week.

"Okay, that is great news that he will be moving forward with his college plans! Thanks, Joyce. You're here early!" Erick noticed.

"I have to pick up my granddaughter, Daisy, this afternoon. She is almost two and cuter than ever. Going to get a jump on the paperwork so I can leave early."

"You should bring your family to the office one of these days. I would love to see her. Oh, and leave whenever you need to."

"Thanks! Come on, Jace." Joyce patted her thigh, and the golden lab followed her into the front office.

Erick walked back to his office to finish his write-up on another patient's progress. Just then, his phone buzzed, indicating a text. *Brook*.

Erick knew Brook Becker wanted him to be by her side for this dinner or that fundraiser. He also knew he was capable of so much more than being Brook's trophy boyfriend. She did not consider that people counted on him at HigherGround. Erick did not have time to waste on his phone. He turned the phone over and kept typing the notes.

The hours spent writing in his patients' charts and looking at financial reports took him past lunchtime. Brook was calling him now, and just as he clicked the ignore button the door opened. Daniel's long-haired golden retriever, Luna, came bounding in, followed closely by Daniel rolling into the office in a wheelchair. Daniel's job at HigherGround wasn't just a therapy tech. He helped all the therapists and patients with whatever they needed. Daniel made sure each patient was set up with hot and cold packs. He did the laundering of towels, cleaned the place spotless and made sure everything was ready for the week. Daniel was very detailed in his work. Erick liked having Daniel close and kept an eye on him. Daniel had come to terms with his paralysis and had made peace with his new life years ago.

"This is *my* life. Instead of fighting it, I want to go out there and live it. Find love and purpose and not focus on my disability." How could Erick stand in his way when Daniel's mantra was what Erick wanted most. *Live life on his terms.*

"Hello, Erick! Who is the unlucky person you're ignoring?" Daniel laughed as Luna jumped in his lap.

"Guess." Erick laughed and finished his typing to look up. "How's Sky?" He cracked his fingers from the tension of typing for so long.

"She should be here soon. She has one more patient, and then she will take Jace and Luna. Where is Jace, anyway?" Daniel looked around the office for the white fluff ball.

"Joyce is giving him treats."

"Of course she is. Your dog will literally go with anyone who has treats, dude!" Daniel teased Erick. Luna leapt off Daniel's lap just as Sky walked into the room. She was barely five feet tall; her wavy blonde hair was up in a loose bun, and when she smiled, her freckles seemed to dance. Her southern accent made her pediatric patients feel at home at HigherGround.

"Dr. Erick, good morning. Can I consult with you on one of my pediatric cases if you have time this week?" Dr. Sky asked Erick.

Erick had hired her immediately after opening HigherGround. She was the one who helped Erick get into the physical therapy program all those years ago after Daniel's accident. Erick discovered her after the accident while staying with Daniel, who was doing in-home therapy at the time. Sky originally grew up on a cattle ranch in Georgia but ended up in the physical therapy program in Connecticut at UConn. At night she worked at a cleaning service. On that particular night, it was his destiny that their suite was the last one scheduled for the day. Daniel invited her to play video games, and Erick got the information he needed to start school that spring. Sky and Erick graduated from physical therapy school together.

He paid her very well, and her young patients enjoyed seeing Jace and Luna. It helped them to relax. "Of course, let me know what time is good for you." Erick noticed Daniel looking intently at Sky.

"Let's go, Lu Lu! These guys have work to do." Sky moved toward Daniel, quickly kissed him while she rounded up the long-haired golden retriever, and closed the door behind her.

"That kiss." Erick tilted his head towards Daniel. "Looks serious!"

"It *is* serious." Daniel leaned in and, with a low voice. "I'm going to ask her to move in with me, man."

"Really? Congratulations! Sky is really an amazing doctor and person. Why did she pick you?" Erick laughed.

"Because I have the better dog, of course!" Daniel jabbed his brother. "I'm also the best looking brother."

"Well, that's true, but when it comes to dogs . . . Jacey Boy is the best!" Erick said, closing up his last patient's folder and sliding the large stack to the side of his desk. "Jace and I have been here most of the day. I'm getting out of here after I finish payroll. It is supposed to rain later, and I need to get a run in."

"Do you ever work?" Daniel rolled the wheelchair closer to Erick and punched him playfully in his arm. "Lazy, just like that puffball you call a dog."

"Daniel, I checked with the boss and got the rest of the day off. Oh wait, I'm *the* boss." Erick laughed at his joke.

"Anyway, you better get out there. I'm not paying you to sit around all day." He realized his mistake. "You know what I mean."

"Well, that is what I do! But I do it better than anyone!" Daniel smiled because he loved giving his brother a hard time, even if he was the boss.

"Yeah, well, *your* therapist, Devon, was here this morning, and she told me last week that you aren't doing your exercises."

Daniel rolled his eyes.

"I'll be fine, and at least I like my new wheelchair." He began spinning and doing wheelies. "Why do I need to practice wearing the braces? It's not like I need to run anywhere. I can outrun anyone in this machine!"

"Because Daniel!" Erick sighed from frustration. "Don't you ever *want* to walk again?" The playful mood was gone.

"You're *not* my doctor. I'm perfectly happy with my progress. And, Sky doesn't care if I'm in a wheelchair or running a marathon. She loves *me* for me."

Erick could see he was getting nowhere. "How could she not? You're sooo cute!" Erick teased him and made kissing noises in the air.

"Shut up! You have your problems with your own girl to deal with!" Daniel shot back, the playful mood returning.

"True." Erick finished what he was working on and put his coat on. He followed Daniel out to the reception area. "Joyce, make sure Daniel cleans this place from top to bottom. I'm out. See you all Monday."

"Slacker!" Daniel coughed the word out.

"Have fun, Daniel, and do your exercises with Devon today, or I *will* become your doctor, and we'll see who is slacking then!" Erick felt Jace lean on his legs. "Let's go, Buddy."

Eight

Grace seized her opportunity to return home as Finn left at dawn. She honestly did not think there would be another time like this to go. Grace reasoned that it would be a quick hike, and Monday, she would arrive at work, and no one would be the wiser. She would have plenty of time to interview the new interns and finish the last of the editing. Grace quickly packed her car and drove to Connecticut for the second time. She planned to talk to her dad, find the trail Aunt Raven was referring to, and make it back to New York the following day before anyone suspected she was gone.

Traffic was light when she arrived at her parents' home that morning. Grace lifted her hand to knock on their door when she realized she had forgotten to tell anyone she was coming. Her dad answered the door wearing pajama pants and an old grey tee-shirt that said, *"Go Huskies"* on it. His eyes widened at the sight of her.

"Grace? What are you doing here?" he asked, rubbing his reddish beard.

"Dad, sorry, I just stopped by for a few minutes to talk, and then I have to go."

"Of course. Come inside." They entered the house, which smelled of woodsy vanilla. "Mom isn't home right now; she had to go into Washington D.C. for a huge case she was working on there. What is going on?"

Grace followed her dad to the living room, relieved not to have to deal with her mother. She did not have the time.

"Dad, I read part of the journal. Did Aunt Raven ever tell you of a trail that she loved to hike? Did she ever mention her favorite place? There are giant clusters of wildflowers there called white wood aster."

"I don't know. Raven never talked to me much about her most recent adventures. What else did she say in the journal?" He seemed concerned. "There is this *one* place. It's actually about a half-hour north. I'm sure she hiked a lot of places. My sister was always on some trail. Come to think of it, I think she said certain flowers grew there. I went with her once years ago. She'd always collected herbs and wildflowers, even when we were kids. And now that you mentioned it, her favorite aster does grow there. I don't know if it's the same place you're looking for, but I know she loved the views from the summit. Hang on. I will be right back."

Mr. Evans got up and left the room and padded his way to his office. When he returned, Grace was anxious to see what he had found. Grace could hardly contain herself; she was excited to get going. She didn't have much time.

"Here are directions to a place called Freedom Trail in West Rock. I'm pretty sure this is where she liked to go. But," he looked at her. "Do you have to go now? It's only 8 am. Stay for breakfast. I missed your birthday, and I have to tell you something about your aunt. It's been too long, and you have a right to know." He moved to the sink, filled up the tea kettle, and set it on the stove.

"Okay, but only if you make those special Swedish pancakes I loved as a child!" Grace wanted to get going but loved these moments with her dad. A pang of guilt filled her because she had waited so long to mend things with her parents.

Time passed, and Grace finished the last bite on her plate.

"So I was hoping to have this conversation with you when Mom was here, but you surprised me." Robin put the dishes in the sink.

"I'm sorry I left, but I'm also sorry that I didn't stay in touch all these years." Grace realized she had lost precious time.

"I just worry about you, Grace. You in the big city all alone."

"I'm not alone. Finn is there." Grace winced at the mention of Finn, and she realized it was getting late.

"Well, I know you are off on your adventure. I always wanted to tell you something about your aunt but, the timing was never right. I have been selfish in keeping it from you, but I just wanted to protect you. You are the most important thing to me in the whole world." He got up and put his arms around Grace and held her close.

"Oh, Dad," she hugged him tight. "I have to go. It's a long trail, and I have stayed longer than I can afford. I have to see what she left for me up there, and then after I get back to New York, we can talk more. I won't have another chance like this. Wish me luck. We can catch up the next time, Dad."

Robin let go of her and said, "I love you. Please remember that no matter what you find, promise me you will remember how much I love you." Robin loosened his embrace and looked at Grace. "I really don't like that you are going up there alone. Be safe. It's a very rocky trail." He pointed to the papers he printed. "It even says the trail has a high difficulty rating. *Please*, take your time." Mr. Evans suddenly ran off to Grace's old room and reappeared with an orange backpack.

"Where did you find that? I haven't seen that since high school . . ."

"Take this with you, and it could take a while to get to the summit. The trail is long, and I hope you know what you're doing. Do you have water?"

"I will be fine, Dad. I have water in the car. Thank you for my lucky backpack." She kissed him, said goodbye, gathered up her papers and shut the door behind her. When she got into her car, she plugged the information into her phone GPS and backed out of the driveway. *This is it*, she thought to herself. Grace was excited for the first time in a long time. She could not remember the last time she felt this way and began to wonder what Aunt Raven had left for her at the top of the mountain. Grace also hoped to find everything before dark. She wanted to get back before Finn called and checked in on her. Grace planned to return to the office early Monday before anyone else noticed she was gone. Her pulse quickened, and she felt herself smile for the first time in ages.

Erick exited HigherGround. The sun was high in the sky, but Erick knew he would have enough time to run the trail before the rain came. Jace wagged his tail when they pulled up to the cabin. Once inside, Erick hopped around on one foot, trying to get his shoe off. Landing in the bed, Erick took a minute to lay, arms outstretched as he stared at the ceiling. Jace jumped up on the bed and licked Erick's face. Erick laughed.

"Don't listen to Daniel. You're the best pup, Jacey boy!"

Erick quickly dressed in his running clothes and Jace followed him out the door. They were both running now on the trail. Erick found the familiar calming thud of his shoes on the ground. He looked up at the trees with their golden and orange leaves swaying slightly in the cool autumn breeze. Jace went ahead and scouted the trail sniffing everything happily as he scampered from tree to tree.

Erick sighed as his thoughts turned to Brook. He had been ignoring her texts all day, but that would only suffice for so long. Eventually, she'd find him and demand answers. The truth was, they had no business being together, and he knew he had to break it off with her soon. Even if she did run his mother's foundation, he knew being with Brook was a mistake. If he broke it off with her, would he let his mother down, yet again? Erick ran deeper into the hills of Connecticut.

Erick was tired of feeling the weight of his guilt. He decided he needed to get to an AA meeting sooner than later. Erick didn't need a drink at that moment, but the meetings were always there to comfort him over the years when it came to the next step. He didn't want to take a chance and end up like his father with a drink in hand every night chasing the pain away. Oh, if he just didn't drink that night at the party.

Tension released as he quickened his stride, crunching the fallen leaves under his feet. *How could anyone love him after what he had done in the past? What should he do about Brook?* Erick knew he could find the answers only on this trail. It was where he felt most at home, alone with God.

He ran all the way up to the top of the summit with Jace and breathed in the fall air. Peace filled him, and Erick began to pray. Pray for wisdom and what to do next, especially when it came to Brook.

Nine

Chasing after lies is the quickest way to find yourself lost in life. I prefer to find myself lost among the white wood asters and the fire-red leaves turning on the trees. But, somehow this is how I feel these days—lost and confused. How can he say he loves me, yet he cannot see the real me. Not facing the truth is a lie we tell ourselves.

In the end, I just want to matter. Love should be simple. How can a person who claims to love be so hurtful? Sometimes he can be like a stranger. It was slow at first, the disappearance of me. Do I even matter? If the wind blows a tree down, does anyone notice? Does loving someone mean you become invisible? You must go deep inside to find what really matters and fight harder than ever to stay true to yourself. Where does it start, and where does it end? What do you want your legacy to be?

— RAVEN'S DIARY

Grace drove through Connecticut's back roads after nearly half an hour of driving and a few wrong turns. Her heart quickened when she saw the wooden weathered brown sign with yellow letters spelling out "Freedom Trails at West Rock." She turned onto a side dirt road and into the parking lot. Slinging her small orange backpack over her shoulder and she remembered how it served as a good luck charm in her high school days. She always used it to hold everything when she was working on the newspaper. Grace hid her keys and wallet in the compartment between the seats.

Grace packed a few water bottles, sunglasses, and a granola bar. *No sense in overpacking*, she thought. *There will be plenty of time if I keep a steady pace, find whatever my aunt left, and be back down before sunset.* Whatever was up there, she hoped it would fit in the backpack.

Before locking her car, Grace grabbed her phone and looked at the screen. The battery had an 80% charge. To conserve battery, she shut the phone off and placed it in the pack's outer pocket. Next, she retrieved the map her dad printed and shut the door. She looked around and saw "Freedom Trail: entrance seven miles to the summit." She was glad she wore her leggings and her running shoes. She zipped up her light jacket and began her journey. Heading towards the sign, she felt a wave of excitement flow through her body as she started her journey. The trees were thick, and the trail was hard to see with all the fallen leaves on the ground. She started thinking about how far she had come in the last decade in her career and her life. So much had changed for her since high school. She could feel her heart beating faster as she continued to walk.

Grace wondered what she would find at the top of the summit. She felt sadness that she would not see her aunt again and felt the pain of lost time with her family. Suddenly, Grace stumbled on a tree root, but was able to steady herself without falling. She needed to be careful and follow the trail markers, one step at a time. Her heart quickened with each step. Fallen leaves crunched beneath the running shoes that

Finn had bought for her. They would take her to the top, and she would finally have the answers she was looking for.

Erick turned and ran down from the summit as he recalled his mother's last request before her death. It had seemed so possible then, but he had failed in the end, and it killed him inside. Erick felt her looking down on him. Her disapproval and his guilt consumed him. He had become a disappointment to everyone back then. He had also failed Daniel.

Even now, as Erick ran harder, the leaves crunching under his trail runners, he wondered what would have happened if he had not walked out of that conference room nearly a decade ago and never looked back. Jace was barking ahead, and as Erick rounded the bend, lost in thought, he saw someone on the trail. A woman with straight dark black hair held back by white sunglasses stood there gazing at papers, clearly unfamiliar with the path. As the woman came into view, it was apparent she was not looking where she was going. She was staring intently at one of the papers she held, not realizing Erick was running towards her, and she nearly crashed right into him. An excited Jace barked his hellos. The woman glanced up, and her eyes met Erick's. He stumbled back. Her eyes sparkled like glowing jewels. *Emeralds.* Embarrassed, he stopped suddenly and narrowly avoided a collision with her. He quickly looked away, realizing he was staring.

"Excuse me. I didn't see you there. Hello sweet puppy," the woman said, patting Jace gently on the head.

Not waiting, the woman turned and ran down an adjacent path. Erick froze in the spot, his chest heaving in the fall air. He regained his composure and decided to ask her if she needed help, but she had vanished by the time he turned around. He put his hands on his knees as he let his breath out. A squirrel ran by, and Jace went in for the chase. Erick just stood there thinking about the woman. There was something about the emerald eyes. He had never seen eyes so green like that before, except once. A long, long time ago. *It can't be,* Erick told himself and shook off the memories from the past, and his eyes searched for his Golden-white Labrador among the trees. Jace was always wandering off, sniffing for anything new. Erick wasn't worried, but he needed to get back before the weather changed to rain. Erick clapped his hands and shouted,

"Come, Jace! Let's go. Race you home!"

Erick started running again, but he couldn't shake what he had seen. As the cabin came into view, he prayed. The prayer he prayed over the last decade became his life mantra. *Dear God, please take these awful memories from me. Help me to forget the past and focus on the future.* Jace was there at the cabin wagging his tail, mouth open, panting— the victor of this race. As he made his way up the steps to his place, Erick wondered why he'd asked God to forget when all he wanted to do at that moment was *remember.*

Remember, the girl with the greenest eyes he had ever seen, until today.

Ten

"It is written 'Where your treasure is, there your heart will also be.' Sometimes there is a cost to freedom. The price was more than I wanted to pay. They say, 'if you love something, set it free . . .' Freedom comes at a price. There is always a price to pay for the choices we have made. For you, I would do anything to keep you safe."

— RAVEN'S DIARY

Grace's long black hair blew in front of her face as the wind picked up. She kept walking faster down the new trail. The dog had startled her as much as the man in the beard did when he almost ran into her. A few droplets of water started to fall. She realized she forgot to check the weather today and hoped that was not a mistake. She reached for a hair tie on her wrist and grabbed up her dark hair into a high ponytail. The man seemed familiar and wore a faded heather blue t-shirt that said, "HigherGround: You can learn to walk on water." Grace focused on the trail ahead because time was running out.

Two off-center painted blazes on the tree ahead indicated

another turn on a new path. Grace quickened her pace to a jog. She was so busy thinking about bears that she forgot about other people on the trail. Grace jogged faster now and was more determined to reach the summit. Through the trees, she saw a black bird flying up the path, its caws interrupting her thoughts of the stranger.

The sun streamed down, causing rays to shine through the trees. A family of deer stood still and came into view. Even though the deer blended into the scenery, Grace could see them on the trail. They were only visible by the quick swish of their brown and white tails. When they realized they were no longer alone, they took off deeper into the woods. Grace smiled at them as she took one step after another over hills and around a bend in the trail. Grace continued up the path.

Suddenly, Grace let out a yelp as the leaves on the trail directly in front of her started moving. Out of the corner of her eye, she saw the tail of a black snake wiggling his way quickly off the trail, narrowly avoiding Grace's foot. Her confident step froze in place as she waited for her heart to settle and stop banging around in her chest.

Grace's eyes darted to a fallen tree as it lay on its side cracked, broken and jagged, and separated from its trunk. Grace felt like this tree, so disjointed and out of place. She moved to the log and sat down. A new thought popped into her head. She had no business being on this trail. Grace started to have second thoughts and wished she had listened to Finn and stayed home and caught up on work or, at the very least, figured out her next step in her life—the life that she and Finn built.

Grace stopped again to look at the map and realized she was only halfway to the summit. She could not turn back now. With a renewed sense of purpose, Grace started to walk faster. The trail became steeper, and the sun was directly behind a cloud. Growing weary, Grace took off her pack and retrieved her water bottle from it. She unscrewed the cap and closed her eyes as the cool water ran down her throat.

Doubt continued to shadow her thoughts. Grace thought that whatever Aunt Raven left for her might be gone by now, eaten away by bugs or blown away by the wind. The thought of wasting her time and what could happen if she did not make it back in time nagged at her. The symphony of cicadas clicking and buzzing blared in her ears. Grace looked a few feet ahead of her, aware that she may not be the only living thing out here in the woods. She carefully looked deep in the woods for any other creatures she might come across on the path.

Suddenly, Grace heard rustling deep in the trees. A black raven burst into the sky and took flight. She exhaled, and then her breath caught again. Grace, wide eyed, looked around. She imagined a large black bear that may have caused the raven's startle in the first place. She began to feel queasy.

She rubbed her fingers over the compass necklace she felt on her neck, feeling it calm her nerves as it did years ago. As she followed the trail, and the large black raven, a smile came over her face as she realized the trees were getting sparse. She was getting closer to the summit. Up ahead would be the treasure she had been looking for, and she could not wait to find the answers to all her questions as Aunt Raven promised. The answers were just ahead at the top of the mountain.

Erick climbed the few stairs to his porch and entered his home. Jace followed him in, and Erick filled the dog's water bowl. Erick couldn't help but wonder why that woman was on the trail. She seemed so familiar, but he did not know anyone with jet black hair. It was her eyes that reminded him of someone he knew. Perhaps she could have just been one of his clients over the years. He would ask Joyce when he got back to work.

Jace laid on the braided round rug in the main room, legs sprawled, eyes closed, happy from his last adventure.

Erick exited the shower with a thick white towel wrapped around his waist. He opened his small wooden dresser and removed the clothes he wanted to wear. Removing the last shirt from the bottom of the dresser revealed a picture frame in his dresser drawer turned upside down. He placed the clothes on the bed and picked up the frame. He looked at the picture.

The memory of the girl in this picture came flooding back to him. He was barely twelve years old when a red haired girl with a splattering of freckles moved into his town. She caught his eye at the lockers that day in the 6th grade. She was putting her things in her locker, which to his delight, was right next to his. When she closed the locker, their eyes met. There stood the most beautiful girl he had ever seen in his life.

Her wild red hair fell to the middle of her back. She had on the Kings Oxford school uniform. Erick noticed the short burgundy plaid skirt, but her white shirt was untucked, and her tie hung in one loose knot. She looked straight into his eyes.

Her eyes narrowed, and the corners of her mouth turned down, "A picture would last longer!"

Erick stood frozen in place as his eyes widened. The girl slowly smiled, threw her head back, and laughed. Her hair floated around her, and he felt her contagious laughter. Erick realized she was teasing, and he smiled in relief. She closed her locker and turned so fast that her hair moved with her as she walked down the hallway.

Her emerald-green eyes sparkled like gems. The image was forever burned into Erick's mind. Determined to meet her and get her name, he waited for her at his locker the next day. She came into the school, and just as he was just about to ask her his burning question.

"Grace Evans, please come with me," Principal Stewart called out.

Erick didn't realize he was holding his breath until he let a burst of air free from his lungs. He was not defeated, because he did learn one thing, her name was Grace. He found something else out later in the second period that would change his life forever.

"Let's welcome Grace to our honors English class!" Mrs. LaMonica announced. As Grace stood at the front of the class, her face blushed. She looked around the classroom for an empty seat and found one next to Erick. This day would change the course of his life. Despite the reservations from their families, they became best friends.

Erick rubbed the framed glass removing a streak, and then he carefully placed the picture on the top of the dresser, looking into the photo closely. The emerald eyes looked back at him again. Suddenly, he realized that was who the girl on the trail reminded him of. It was Grace! *But Grace has red hair . . .*

As he got dressed, he remembered back to the hot summer night when he and Grace were up on the rooftop of his childhood home looking up at the stars. There were only a few days until they both would be starting their freshman year in high school in the new wing at Kings Oxford.

"So I was thinking," Grace began. She sat with her shoulder touching his and her tanned legs tucked under her. "We should talk about something before we start high school officially on Thursday."

"Sure, anything!" Erick said, looking into her moonlit

illuminated face. Her eyes sparkled in the night like brilliant green Kryptonite to his heart.

"You're my best friend. My person. You were there for me when I first moved, and we have been friends for years now." Grace reached for his hand. Erick didn't breathe, and his heart began to race. Her hand was so soft in his. She leaned closer, and he could feel her breath on his face. "Would it be too crazy if I said I was falling . . ." her words trailed off as Erick placed his lips on her soft mouth.

He didn't remember her snapping a picture of them that day, but she showed up the first day of school with a tissue-wrapped package celebrating their commitment. It was a photo of them on the roof that day enclosed in a frame—the same frame Erick was looking at now. Looking at this young girl's image with the greenest eyes he had ever seen, he could not help wondering if Grace might have been the same girl Erick saw on the trail. He knew she no longer lived in Connecticut, so it was doubtful it was her. She had her own life now in New York, the life she had always wanted. That life was with Finn and did not include him. He put the frame back into his dresser and dismissed the thought. The woman on the trail was not Grace. Grace was in New York now, and it couldn't have been her. Erick drove to the only place he needed to be at that moment. He needed to get to a meeting. On the way, Erick could not shake the feeling something was about to happen that would change everything.

Eleven

"Follow your heart. It will always lead you to the next step. The danger is in ignoring the truth. The path to the truth will always lead you home. Trust and believe."

— RAVEN'S DIARY

Grace came upon an overlook and found a rock to sit on to catch her breath. The trail was getting much steeper. She realized that the two water bottles were not enough for a long hike. Thoughts came at her quickly. *I have no business being on this wild goose chase. What if there was nothing up there, and I wasted time searching for nothing?* Grace thought about Athena and Finn looking longingly at each other over cocktails seated in first-class, or maybe they took the private jet. Finn would be faithful to her, wouldn't he? Or was Finn just one girl away from leaving her? *No. Finn would never do that*, she thought. Grace felt the words were flimsy at best.

Grace attempted to focus on the trail and erase the doubts with each step. A few drops of rain fell on her forehead, and the clouds gave way. The rain came all at once then, soaking her hair. She closed her eyes and just breathed. The rain suddenly stopped, the grey clouds dispersed, and the sun shone down on her.

The trail was muddy, and Grace could feel that the ground beneath her was slippery. Determined to see this through to the end, Grace continued up the steep trail, careful not to slip on the spots where rain had collected in tiny pools of dark earth. She could feel the sun as it peeked through the clouds making Grace squint and feel warmer. Suddenly a couple with walking sticks came into view. Overhead she could still hear the beckoning of the raven, her bird guide. The older couple dressed in hiking boots and trail pants smiled at Grace.

"That was a heavy shower." The woman looked up. She was wearing light rain gear. The man had binoculars that hung around his neck; he had a white beard and wore a tan wide-brimmed hat.

Grace responded simply with, "Yes, it was unexpected," and kept walking past.

"Hey, uh, be careful. It's quite muddy and a bit slippery," the woman warned.

"I will. Thanks."

Grace barely sidestepped a giant crimson topped mushroom as she followed the trail higher now to the summit. The hot sun hung lower in the sky now. Grace unzipped her damp maroon jacket and tied it around her waist. Next, she stopped and took out the map. The summit should be right up the hill and just around a bend. On her next turn, she would finally see what Aunt Raven had left for her, and she hoped whatever it was would be worth the journey. She could lose everything, but there was no stopping her now. Grace had to finish what she started, even if it meant that everything changed from this moment forward.

Erick's phone buzzed as a text came through. It was the hospital. The patient coordinator, Sherri, needed a consult.

When Erick arrived at the hospital, he showed his I.D. at the front desk and made his way into the elevator area. He pressed floor four, and he felt a sense of possibility. Erick couldn't stop thinking about the woman on the trail and her resemblance to Grace. *It couldn't have been her*, he assured himself. First of all, Grace would have recognized him, for sure. She was dating his brother, but he had not seen his twin brother for quite some time. He avoided going home on the holidays and spent his days working or at the cabin. The only family he kept up with was Daniel.

The woman on the trail and Grace had nothing in common. Well, almost nothing. She may not have had the same fiery red hair, but she had the same sparkle in her green-jeweled eyes. He shrugged his shoulders. *He was mistaken*, he told himself. Grace was in New York with Finn, living happily ever after. His wishful thinking would not make Grace the woman on that trail, no matter how badly he wanted it to be true.

The elevator doors opened, and Erick made his way to the far end of the hospital. Erick was deep in thought and felt a sense of regret. He wished he had at least stopped to talk to the woman on the trail. There was something about her that captivated him, and Erick could think of nothing else.

Erick walked to the door of the physical therapy wing. Entering the studio, he saw one patient who was working out his knee. Scars on his exposed knee suggested he had replacement surgery.

"Dr. Erick?" A woman called out to Erick. Her name tag read *Sherri* in italics. Under her name was printed, *Patient*

Therapy Coordinator. Erick had met Sherri during his clinical rounds during college, and they enjoyed working together. Sherri was married with two children. Erick remembered they ran a few charity 5ks and Sherri's husband, Kyle, in years past.

"Hey, Sherri! You need a consult?"

"Yes, a patient isn't progressing after knee replacement. I thought you could take a look. How is business at Higher Ground?"

"Pretty good. We have several therapists on staff now."

"As fall sports begin, we will likely have more patients."

"Do you have the patient's chart?"

"Right here, Dr. Erick." Sherri showed him the file.

Erick agreed he could help and signed the paperwork to transfer him to HigherGround. Next, he headed to work, but something caught his eye when he arrived.

Daniel and Sky were kissing at the ramp on the side of Higher Ground, unaware of anyone else. His heart swelled for his little brother. He was so proud of Daniel for finding the love of his life, but at the same time, Erick felt his heart ache for the girl from his youth.

Finally, Erick admitted something to himself because he could no longer deny the truth. *I miss her.* Grace was with Finn, he told himself. He wanted her to be happy. Maybe, the key wasn't to run from his past but rather to face it head-on. If he had one more chance, just one more opportunity to see her, or even talk to her, perhaps then Erick could put the past behind him once and for all.

Twelve

Grace's thoughts shifted to her father as she climbed higher up on the mountain trail. Even when she had seen him earlier, he looked older, worn-down. Now, Grace was even more determined to not only find the treasure that Aunt Raven left her but find out why her father waited so long to tell her. Grace thought about her dad again and all the secrecy surrounding this gift. And what about the cryptic map in the journal? What was she missing?

Grace continued to take step after step, crunching the leaves below her shoes. Grace recalled the look of pain on her dad's face when he handed her the journal and how it reminded her of when she left all those years ago. All young Grace wanted her father to say was, "So proud of you, Grace!"

Instead, he said, "You will always be my little girl. I love you more than life. I hope you find everything you are looking for."

He had whispered in her ear, hugging her in the driveway while Finn stood by the service car with the door open. Grace remembered what her dad's strong arms felt like around her and how she could not return the hug. At the time, Grace wanted to separate herself from her parents. She wanted to start her way in the world on her own. Grace broke free from her dad, and she walked away from the house. Her mom stood there in shock and disbelief. Grace could hear her dad stifle back tears, but she kept her feet moving and ducked into the car.

Finn shut the car door for her that day, and she did not dare look back. She buried her face in Finn's shoulder. His arms shielded her from the pain. Back then it felt good to be starting the first chapter of her new life. Now, it felt more like a mistake.

With only a few more steps to go, I will make it to the summit any minute. Grace took inventory of how much water was left. Grace had half a bottle of water, and time was running out to get back. She shuddered to think what would happen if Finn ever found out she left. Grace sucked in a breath and started running as fast as she could.

Erick tried to do the right thing when he texted Brook to meet up that night. Brook suggested he meet her at Skye Bar, located at the top of her parent's insurance building in downtown Hartford. Before going to the trendiest bar in the city, Erick planned to stop at the closest AA meeting on the way.

A big part of being in AA was to be honest, not only with others but with oneself. Erick had not been forthcoming with himself lately. He wasn't slipping up or drinking, but lies were the beginning of what would lead to an inevitable downward spiral. Especially lying to yourself. Being with Brook was living a lie. Erick needed to clear the air, and going to a meeting would prepare him for what he was about to do. Alcoholism was in his genes, and he could not take any chances. Erick had spent the last five years building his business HigherGround, but the rebuilding of his personal life wasn't going as well. He missed his family and had to admit he wanted someone to share his life with who would love him completely. His life was becoming unmanageable, once again, and the nightmares were a clear sign that he was powerless without the help of a higher power.

Erick quietly walked to the back of the room and ducked into a metal chair as the other group members nodded and murmured, "Thank you for sharing." Erick tried to slip out when the meeting was over, but he ran directly into a large man. "Where are you off to in a hurry?"

Erick swallowed. The thought of telling this stranger the truth that he was on his way to the rooftop bar wasn't going to be the right thing to say. Instead, he said, "To right a wrong, long time overdue."

The man smiled just then, "Name is Errol." He held out his hand, and Erick shook it. "Nothing changes if *nothing changes*. Think about it. Keep fighting the good fight and come back and see us again, okay?"

"Thanks, Errol. The name is Erick. Your story about making amends was truly moving, but some things can never be forgiven."

"Well, buddy, if that were true . . ." He wrapped one of his arms around Erick while simultaneously slapping his back. "We all would be wasting our time. You know that not being able to forgive is like drinking poison and hoping the other person will die."

"Yeah. I've heard that," Erick said, managing to separate himself from this friendly man. "But, what if the person you can't forgive is not another person but *yourself?*"

"Well, that's the toughest of all!" Errol looked straight into Erick's eyes. "The road is not easy, my friend, but you have to allow it to happen. Have you done step seven, asking God to remove your shortcomings?"

"It has been a while since I had a sponsor or worked the steps, for that matter." Erick put his hands in his jeans pocket.

"I highly recommend you get a sponsor." Errol put his hand on Erick's shoulder and squeezed it. With his other hand, he handed him a small card. "Call me when you're ready to do the real work. I got your back."

Errol nodded to Erick, shook his hand, and went back into the room. Erick stood there holding the card that simply read, "*Forgiveness is free. Errol Brown 555-7655 AA Sponsor.*" By the time Erick turned around, Errol was deep in conversation with some other men. He put the card in his pocket and decided he would call Errol when he got a chance.

As Erick left the brick building, he breathed in the chilly fall air. He could feel something in the air had changed. Just like the weather, something deep inside him was also shifting. He zipped up his leather jacket and pulled the collar up around his neck as the night air sent a chill through him. He got into the car waiting for him and said, "Skye Rooftop Bar, Capitol Ave, please."

Erick decided he would ask God to help him forgive himself for the past. He looked out the window into the sun. Erick gazed down at the card again and was more determined than ever to move on from his past. Returning the card to his pocket, he went over the plan in his head. Erick would be at the bar in about ten minutes and would take Brook aside. He would finally ask her one last question about that night. Then he would tell her how much he cared for her and explain that they were just two very different people. It could mean a great disappointment for her now, but they both would be free to pursue true love in the long run.

The car pulled up to the tall building. The sun would set soon, and he had a mission. A brown leaf blew in the wind, and all Erick could think about was how his past kept playing over in his life, on repeat. This would end tonight. With the help that could only come from God, he would do the right thing.

Thirteen

Grace continued walking as the trail narrowed, and her thoughts turned to Finn's brother Erick this time. Despite the sting of the last time she saw him, she felt terrible now for not trying to work things out between them over the years. She figured if he wanted to clear the air, *he* could pick up the phone as well. Grace found herself looking for Erick, but he never went to his family events. Back then, there were so many things that had kept them apart. Her parents thought the whole Finn family was evil. Grace did not think the sons were, but the dad was very controlling.

The first time she met Erick was at the lockers after transferring to Kings Oxford. Grace did not know what to think. Grace slammed the locker door that day, hoping this school would be different and would be her ticket to becoming a famous writer in New York. Far away from the disapproving eye of her mother. "Maybe *you* should go to law school . . ." was the last thing Grace said to her mother that morning. The sound the metal door made rattled her out of her thoughts, and she looked up and saw crystal clear blue eyes staring at her. She smiled, remembering the boy from yesterday in the principal's office when her father enrolled her in the prestigious private school. "You should take a picture. It lasts longer. Finn, is it?"

"Actually, Erick Finn." He looked away from her stare and then down at his shoes. Grace wondered what happened to the cock-sure attitude he had the other day. One afternoon, it all became clear. It all started when she discovered an old weathered stone wall that separated her small backyard from the enormous Finn estate. In contrast Grace's family had a modest house that her grandfather had built many years ago. Robin Evans followed in his father's footsteps and was also a carpenter. Bran Evans left both the home and business to Robin when devastating news came about his family in Wales. While Grace's mother was working as a paralegal and her father worked on wood projects in the workshop out back, Grace spent afternoons exploring the only backyard she ever knew. Grace ventured as far as she could. Where the short the short grass ended, began thick clusters of large red maples. Black birch trees looking mysterious and inviting like an enchanted forest. Her father loved these trees and carefully maintained them for use in his wood projects.

On this day, she ran through the trees as far as she could go. Hidden below heavy ivy, she noticed an old stone wall. This discovery would reveal that it was the only thing that separated the Evans' property from the infamous Finn property. There was no turning back now, and Grace was determined to see over the fence. The wall was roughly about seven feet high. Excitement flooded her as her fingers found broken pieces in the stone structure that worked as footholds. Using the ivy-like ropes, she pulled herself to the top. Grace's eyes focused, and she took in the view— beautiful cut green lawns sprawled in every direction, not a leaf in sight. In contrast, her backyard was full of leaves, while the Finn's yard was pristine and immaculate. It looked unreal, like a lush green carpet.

Grace jumped down on the other side of the stone wall

and ran to the nearest fiery red oak. The trunk was large enough to conceal a baby elephant. Like a secret agent, she ran from one tree to another and down the grassy hill. Several large topiary trees came into view. They were scattered around the patio to offset a covered pool, complete with private cabanas and covered outdoor furniture. The landscape took Grace's breath away. Colorful, Koi-filled ponds and flower beds filled the yard. Even tall shrubs were cut so evenly they looked like a maze. Deep onto the property now, the main house off in the distance, Grace heard muffled voices. Immediately, she ducked down behind a shrub and saw the back of both a blonde girl and a sandy-haired boy who wore a long-sleeved sweatshirt. They both still wore their burgundy and khaki school uniforms. Grace smiled when she recognized the boy as the one from the office and lockers earlier that week. The boy was sitting on the stone bench, and the girl sat down, her hands waving in some sort of heated discussion.

Suddenly a second boy came into view, and he walked toward them. Grace moved in closer and crouched behind one of the vast pine trees only a foot away. The second boy approaching had the same school uniform. Grace still could not hear what they were talking about, but the boy on the bench stood up and ran up to the second one. The girl rose to her feet, hands on her hips. The first boy turned around and walked back with the second boy.

What? There are two of them? Grace covered her hand over her mouth, trying not to make a sound.

"You're lying!" The girl yelled to one of the boys.

"No, I wish I was. I had to tell someone." The one boy with his shirt untucked looked at the second boy, "Erick, look."

Grace could see what they were looking at, as the first boy rolled up his sleeve and showed them his arm and hand.

The second boy examined the forearm and said, "Finn, this is bad. You need to get that looked at."

Finn recoiled and put the sleeve down. Next, he reached in his pocket and pulled a cigarette out. With his other hand, he lit it and blew smoke out. "I'm not lying, Brook. He did this to me. To teach me a lesson."

"You did that to yourself," Brook said with her hands still on her hips. "Your dad is like a father to me. He would never do that."

With the cigarette dangling from his lips, he rolled up the sleeve again and put the cigarette close enough to nearly burn his skin. "Does this look like a cigarette burn?" Satisfied, he took another drag from the glowing cigarette. "*No, it's a cigar burn.*" In a huff, he put the sleeve down again. Erick stood there in silence. "Forget I said anything. Make no mistake; I will take my father down one day. I will be the head of FinnLondon, and you all will be my servants begging *me* to take care of you. Declan is old, and his ways are *old*. You'll see. I will be the most powerful man in New England."

"You should tell someone," Erick finally spoke up. "That could get infected. No one should do that to another person."

"No one is going to tell anyone!" Finn looked nervously around. Grace crouched lower, hoping he didn't see her. "You two are useless." He flicked the end of the burning cigarette, and it fell precariously next to Grace's bare foot, and then Finn walked up the patio out of view.

"Erick, this is bad. I knew Finn was crazy, but this?" Brook reached down under the bench and pulled out a bottle of champagne. "Stay with me," she pleaded as the bottle popped.

Grace didn't wait around to hear what happened next. She quickly made her way back to the wall and avoided being discovered. She climbed the stone wall and dropped down to her side with only one thought. *What secrets are the Finn's hiding?*

Grace took a deep breath, and she continued walking on the trail as the memory of the two boys faded in the late afternoon sun. She was so sure back then that Erick would have been the one by her side. Grace's heart ached because her life would have been so different had they both stood up to their parents all those years ago. The nagging thought returned. *Maybe I made a mistake.*

Erick was immediately greeted with lights and soft jazz piano music as soon as the elevator door opened. The bar was full of well-dressed young men and women. They did not seem to notice Erick as he got off the elevator and made his way through the hipster crowd. He saw many couples paired off huddling close in deep conversation out in the cool early evening air. A group of men was clinking glasses in a celebratory way. Strung white lights twinkling created a romantic scene. Erick could see the Mark Twain building and the Regency Hotel standing tall in the clear air. He took a deep breath, and the cool air filled his lungs.

A waiter approached Erick and asked him what he would like to drink. "Club soda and lime, please." Erick always ordered the same thing when he was out, keeping life simple.

The large outdoor patio area had groups of people clustered around pub height tables. Others were lounging on white pillow top couches. A few people appeared overly drunk, staggering and talking face to face. An ebony grand piano separated the bar area from the patio.

Speakers carried the upbeat notes that Erick quickly recognized as Billy Joel's "She's Always a Woman to Me." He finally spotted Brook and straightened his posture. He could see her back. She wore a cream-colored silk suit. Brook's hair was in an up twist, diamonds dangling from her ears. Erick's breath caught in his throat at her grace and beauty. When Brook moved, people noticed. Tonight was no exception. Erick could see several men looking her way and women looking as well, wanting to be *her*. She was leaning over the piano, talking to the pianist. Brook smiled and placed a folded bill into a glass fishbowl chock full of bills next to the pianist. She had always loved Billy Joel.

The next thing he knew, a young waiter blocked Erick's view and handed him his drink. Tiny bubbles danced around a fancy green lime cut into a corkscrew twist. Suddenly Brook was standing in front of him when the waiter moved on, and the shock nearly caused him to drop his club soda.

"Look who decided to show up!" She stared incredulously at Erick. Before Erick could speak, a man in an expensive suit with wavy dark hair came up next to Brook, and with one hand, he handed her an amber-colored martini and placed his hand on the small of her back. She took the drink without taking her eyes off Erick.

"Well, I'm here now," Erick said as he raised an eyebrow at the man beside her. He was wearing a black suit, no tie, his red shirt was open at the top. He had a clean-shaven bald head. The man suddenly felt uncomfortable and removed his hand from Brook.

"We need to talk, Brook. Alone." Erick got to the point, still not taking his eyes off Brook.

"Brooklyn, I will be back and we can finish talking then." The man seemed older than her and looked like he was used to getting what he wanted.

Erick took Brook's hand and guided her to the far end of the balcony, away from the crowd and the piano, which he could hear growing quieter. The setting sun cast a beautiful orange glow.

"What is going on, Erick?" Brook's eyes narrowed.

"I have some questions." Erick tried not to sound like a lunatic. "I need to see some sort of therapist." He looked down at his drink.

"This is good, no?" Brook seemed to relax a little. "You look like you haven't been sleeping."

"I haven't talked to anyone, honestly. I have been having nightmares off and on recently about the accident. They have been getting worse lately."

"You look awful," Brook admitted. "That explains your odd behavior recently."

"I need to ask you something." Erick looked at her. "That night at the graduation party, why did you kiss me?"

Brook shifted her gaze, clearly uncomfortable. "Why are you asking me this now? It was so long ago!" She took a sip of her drink, "Why do you always have to question everything? What matters is that we belong together. I have always loved you, Erick. You loved me too. For the record, *you* kissed me back that night. Don't deny it."

"I do care about you, Brook, but," Erick said aware of her hard stare.

"But what?" Brook was getting angry again.

"I have to figure out what happened that night," Erick pressed on. "You weren't there when I woke up in the hospital."

Brook took a deep breath, "Are we really going to dredge up the past again? This is old news. Besides, you were chasing after *her!*" She nearly hissed the words, her face crimson. "I came to see you as soon as I could." Brook downed the rest of her drink.

"Listen, I don't blame *you* for what happened." Erick shifted gears because this wasn't the way he had planned it to go. He wasn't getting the answers he wanted. Brook found out later what happened, and the blame was solely his to bear. "You were right, and I was wrong," he began as Brook placed her hands on her hips. "We are just two very different people. Look around you. *This isn't me.* This is your scene." Erick caught the gaze of Brook's companion as he approached and handed her a new drink. "Look, I'm sorry, I just can't do this anymore."

Erick shifted his weight from one foot to the other, bracing himself for a slap. Instead, Brook's steely composure softened, and he felt he finally got through to her once and for all. She remained silent as her eyes held his. He felt her eyes drawing him in again.

"It's not you, it's . . ." Erick stopped mid-sentence as he was startled by a sudden splash of cold liquid running down his face. He wiped his eyes, effectively breaking the spell.

Fourteen

Grace breathed a sigh of relief as she saw the trees start to clear. Just then, she looked at her watch and started to panic because she realized she would have to walk back in the dark.

"I just need to get up there, grab whatever it is, and get back. Then I will be home, and everything will be just as it should be."

But Grace started to doubt herself again. Would she make it back in time? The sun was way below the tree line, and it was already setting.

The trees cleared, and there it was. A sign confirmed "Summit 3,000 feet." She noticed layers of volcanic basalt rock called traprock mentioned in the description of the trail her dad printed out. She looked at the printed paper again, and it read, "... *unique largest geological feature only found in Connecticut. According to Legend, two lovers in a Romeo-Juliet scenario threw themselves off the Freedom Summit so they could be together forever. They believed that the great spirit of the Raven totem resides here. She does not put down roots but goes where the wind takes her, in the hope to reunite with her one true love* . . ."

Grace knew she was at the right place when she looked up and saw the beautiful black raven spread its wings wide in the orange sky. Grace looked in awe as it flew out over the cliff, fearless and majestic over the foliage patchwork quilt below. In awe, she felt like she was now on sacred ground. Not a soul in sight, Grace found herself completely alone. The view was breathtaking. One could see all the tiny towns, cities, and beautiful trees below. Grace had never felt so alive as she tried to breathe in all the beauty. She took some steps closer without taking her eyes off the scenery and stumbled on a few rocks that crumbled under her feet. Carefully, she set her orange backpack and the map on the ground. Next Grace unzipped the pack to reach the soft journal. She opened Aunt Raven's hand-drawn map and noticed a few notations in her aunt's handwriting: "where the horizon meets dreams, where the eye cannot see nor imagine, under the black birch, where roots join together forming a nest, tucked away in the womb is where the true treasure of my heart will be . . ."

Grace looked and saw only one small tree that grew at a slant with wild roots underneath. She walked up to the side of the tree and saw a small hole beneath. White wild aster flowers still bloomed strong and were not deterred by the fall weather. Now standing slightly higher than the overlook point, Grace noticed the roots of the tree, woven together with roots did look like a large nest. It was pretty steep to lean over the tree, but she managed to stretch an arm up and reach inside, praying no animal would bite her hand. Next, Grace's fingers felt something solid, and she carefully pulled out a small dark wooden box.

The container was etched and weathered, about the size of a kitchen canister. Grace sat down on the uneven terrain and opened it. Grace felt the mechanism inside spring into motion, and a haunting melody played out of tune and suddenly stopped. She noticed a tiny purple ribbon, and she pulled on it. The music box had a cover, and when lifted,

Grace could see a small plastic bag sealed shut. She carefully removed the bag, and some dirt spilled out. Grace noticed the same dried iris flower lay inside the plastic, just like the one in the journal. Grace caught her breath as she removed the contents one by one. Her heart raced with anticipation as she pulled out the folded worn papers and a small faded photograph fell to the ground.

"Erick! Are you breaking up with me? Me? You can't break up with me! You, you NEED ME!" Brook's voice was a little too loud and sharp. She smoothed her jacket back into place, quelling her anger and embarrassment. "Hell, *I need you*. Erick, please don't break up with me. We were destined to be together since we were children. Please don't do this." Her voice was softer now, and Erick could feel his own heart breaking with her vulnerability. He looked around as her companion and others stopped talking and stared at them.

Erick steered Brook by gently taking her arm and led her inside the bar area. The music grew louder, and he could barely hear what Brook was saying.

"I'm sorry, Brook. I really am. But you'll be fine." He gazed around the bar area, and then looked up at her again. "This is *your* life. You're gorgeous, you're perfect, and there are a million guys that want to be with you."

"But not *you*!" Her voice was colder now. "After all this time, you are still chasing *her*."

"Please, don't make this harder than it is. You know we're not right for each other. Brook, you hate dogs and the cabin."

"I don't hate dogs, and who cares about that shoe box you call a cabin. You could live with me in the city."

"Don't you get it? I don't want to live in the city or go to bars, for that matter. We want different things."

"Please, Erick. Can't we just take a minute here? How about I call you tomorrow when you've come to your senses. You are being irrational from not sleeping. We can work this out!" Brook shouted over the music.

"I'm sorry, Brook. It's over." Erick put his arms gently on her arms.

"Is there a problem here?" The expensive suit guy said, seeing Brook's red face.

"No problem here. I'm leaving anyway." Erick dropped his hands to his side.

"Erick . . ." Brook pleaded.

"I have to go. I'm sorry." Erick turned to the guy, "Take care of her, will you? She's a special girl."

Erick decided to skip the elevator and run down the stairs. Running was what he did best. He had so much adrenaline coursing through his body. He ran down over eighteen flights of stairs and called for a car. Erick smelled the acrid smell of vodka on his clothes. All he wanted to do was go home, shower, and be with Jace in the woods where he belonged—not in the city, not where the chill was everywhere, not just in the wind, but in the people. Erick smiled as her driver pulled up. He quickly climbed into the back. From the safety behind the window, he looked up at the cold buildings as they faded from view—their blinking lights in the twilight sky. Erick ended the relationship, but hated the fact that Brook was hurting. Her icy blue eyes and set jaw forever burned in his mind. He realized when it came to handling relationships, he couldn't even end this one properly.

Now home, with the night washed from him, Erick climbed into bed with Jace's pink nose a few inches from his face. He wasn't closer to finding the answers to what happened all those years ago, but he knew one thing was sure, this wouldn't be the last he'd hear from Brook Becker.

Fifteen

Grace laid the backpack on the ground and placed the music box on top of it. She examined the weathered photograph and saw Aunt Raven with what looked like a baby wrapped in a pink and white blanket, the colors faded from age and the elements.

Grace rubbed her thumb over the picture, trying to smooth out the wrinkles. Next, she pulled out a small piece of paper curled around like a hospital bracelet and examined it. One end was severed, the circle broken. Grace could barely make out the faded computer-printed words. *Raya Joy Evans* on it and *Hartford Clinic* on the side and a barcode. Why would Aunt Raven have baby things? As far as Grace knew, she did not have any cousins. Even her dad never mentioned a baby. *What happened to this baby?* Her eyes narrowed to read the date printed on it. *September 25, 1992,* The date on the bracelet gave her a chill down her spine. Grace questioned herself, *did I have a twin? Why was my aunt in this picture and not my mom? Is it possible this bracelet belonged to me? What is going on?*

Suddenly a thought made its way through her brain so quick and fast like a freight train. It seemed impossible. She would have known. Could it be that . . . no, Grace was sure there was some mistake. Her dad would not ever tell a lie this big! *Is it possible?* Grace's thoughts turned dizzy in her head as the final piece of the puzzle came together. Is Aunt Raven my *birth* mother? The last question hit her like a brick. This would mean my entire life was a lie! What does this make Faith?

No, this is not possible! She would take this box and ask her mother and father for an explanation. Nothing made sense. Just then, Grace felt a stir and rustle building. The sun was sinking lower now—she felt the panic again that she needed to leave, *now!* Grace's fingers held the small faded plastic bracelet. She heard her aunt's voice in a memory, "Raya sunshine . . ." as she looked again at the name on the bracelet. Grace had to find her father and get answers, no matter what the cost would be. She could barely breathe, but she had to get back. Fear gripped her as Grace unzipped the backpack and put the music box in it. All her empty water bottles were at the bottom. There would be time later to figure out what all the items meant, but one thing was sure. She had to leave, now!

Still holding onto the baby I.D. bracelet, a large black raven flew over her head, cawing and circling her. Grace looked up and shielded her head from the raven. Just then, the wind started to pick up the leaves, making them dance in jerky zig zags. The big gust continued to billow, and dark clouds swirled threateningly above the traprock cliff, concealing what was left of the sun. Rocks crumbled under her one foot, and Grace steadied the other foot up near the tree.

Her head swam with questions. To her surprise, the wind lifted the tiny bracelet out of her hand. It spun around and then plummeted down to the ground. Grace reached for it instinctively, not wanting to lose it. Her foot sent more tiny rocks tumbling down the cliffside. Grace took a step down to get to safety, but to her horror, she realized there was no step there.

Grasping for anything, Grace held her breath and her arms flailed around her. Panic seized her. Falling through the air, she realized she would never know the truth about Aunt Raven and the baby in the photo. Her whole life was a lie. Lies from the people she loved the most. What about Erick? She missed him more than she would admit to anyone. Even now, she wished he was with her. Erick was the only one who truly "got" her. Despite both of their families not allowing them to be together, they met at the stone wall and dreamed about a life with no boundaries. He taught her about having faith and about God. Erick loved her without expectation as if they were two parts of one whole.

As her body connected with the cliff below, she would never find out the answers to what happened to her first love and why it ended before they even got started. Questions that would never see the light, forever lost, along with Grace at the bottom of the summit.

Erick's mind filled with big emerald green eyes with red hair floating in slow motion as if underwater. The way the drink felt burning down his throat. The look in Brook's blue eyes. The alcohol in his face. The refrain from Billy Joel's *"Always a woman to me..."* The loud, piercing noise of twisted metal that followed. The flash of light so bright, the tree. Red and blue lights were blinking through the prism of rain. Erick hearing Daniel. *"Hey, dumbass, are you going to answer your phone?"* Daniel was in the passenger seat. *"You better get that, besides I got this."* Daniel laughed. *"I guess I shouldn't let my brother drive."*

Erick woke with a start. His heart was racing as the images faded like smoke from his eyes. He looked at his phone and saw three missed calls from Brook. Erick put the phone down and reached for his journal. In his journal, he wrote the nightmare's details and carefully placed the book on his side table. Inside his cabin, it was dark, but the moon shone through the window. Everything was still. Jace was lying at his feet, unaware of the startle. "Jace, get up, buddy." Erick's voice was low. The dog stretched but did not budge. Erick's feet hit the floor, and he began to get socks and clothes to go for a run.

He wasn't about to go back to sleep. By the time Erick was lacing up his trail runners, Jace was by his side, the perfect companion.

Erick opened the front door, and they looked out into the night sky. The stars seemed so bright that night. He could hear the great grey owl hoot at him and see the crispy brown leaves covering the trail glowing in the pale blue light of the night. The moon was nearly full and high enough to sprinkle light on the path. Erick's feet crunched their way down the trail, widening the distance between him and the never-ending nightmares.

After fifteen minutes, Erick could feel his body relax and glide over the crunchy brown leaves. He began to quicken his pace and outrun just about anything. Erick would run and run until he could not run anymore. He would run for all the people who feared they would never run again. Erick would run *for* himself. He would run for *Daniel*, and he would run for what is right.

Daniel. Erick loved his brother and considered him his only family. His father was a disagreeable man, and after Tabitha died, he went out of his way to be cruel. Erick promised his mother he would protect Daniel. Maybe she was warning him about Declan's abusive behavior. Erick remembered the cigar burns on Finn's arm and wrist. He shuddered to think that could have happened to little Daniel. Even after the accident, Erick never left Daniel's side. Declan rented the VIP suite for Daniel to recover instead of at the hospital.

"Let's keep this private," Declan said. "Finn is a big name in town. We can't let our competitors know we are weak."

Erick was with Daniel hearing the sobs in the night. One time Erick woke up to a crash when Daniel tipped the wheelchair over. He helped his little brother get right again. Daniel became depressed, and a therapist came to the apartment.

Everything changed when a southern girl named Sky walked into the suite. She was barely five feet tall with strawberry blonde hair and an accent like Miranda Lambert came to change the linens.

"I'm so sorry. I'm late! This is my first day, and you are my last customer." She looked flustered and embarrassed.

"You can do that later. What I need right now is someone to help me defeat this soccer team." Daniel punched Erick on the arm on the sofa parallel to a big screen T.V. "My brother wouldn't know how to kick a soccer ball if it hit him in the head."

That was the last day Daniel felt sorry for himself. It was a miracle that Sky just happened to be working at the same cleaning company Declan had hired. Sky's family had money, but she wanted to pay her own way through physical therapy school.

The next miracle she brought was for Erick. It was Sky's recommendation that got Erick the last spot that year in therapy school. To this day, Sky was one of the best therapists on his team at HigherGround.

As Erick's trail runners glided over the familiar path he had run millions of times before, the pangs of guilt about his brother still nagged at him. He kept running and running away from the weight of his past and all the mistakes he had made. Erick would run a thousand miles just for one more chance to be with the girl of his youth, but only this time he would get it right.

Sixteen

Grace's teeth chattered, and chills ran up her spine as she regained consciousness. It was dark, but the moonlight cast ghastly shadows in the damp air. *Where am I?* Grace asked herself. She tried to sit up, but her body would not cooperate. A raven cawed and flew overhead, blocking the moon briefly. She tried to shield her eyes, but she could not move her arm. Her hair felt wet and heavy, and she had dirt and a metallic taste in her mouth. Caked mud covered her face. Grace desperately wanted to wipe her face, but her arms felt so heavy.

What is this place? She looked up at the stars, and tears began to flow. *How did I get here?* The chill had now reached through to her bones. She felt an ache beginning in her head, but she didn't feel much pain other than that. Grace tried to move her legs, but nothing happened. She needed help. Her heart began to beat faster as a chilling thought came over her. *Is anyone looking for me? Does anyone know I'm here?* She wondered who would miss her. No one came to mind. Panic seized her, and her chest began to rise and fall. She let out a scream that echoed in the night. Pain seared through her body just then, but Grace could not pinpoint where it started or where it ended.

She closed her eyes and surrendered to the sleep that

nagged her from the far reaches of her mind. Like a heavy wet blanket, Grace allowed herself to sink into the deep dark abyss.

Erick knew he had no chance with Grace now. She was with Finn, and he had to respect that. Finn made it clear to Erick to stay far away from her. Finn said she was happy and that if Erick cared for her, he would let her become the woman she was meant to be. Besides, he caused tremendous pain to everyone he loved. Grace was better off without him. First, his mother died, and then Daniel had his accident. Love always had a painful outcome for him. If Finn could make Grace happy, who was he to stand in their way?

Deep, loud barking broke through Erick's thoughts. He was breathing heavily now, and he was unsure how long he had been running out in the cold night air. Time did not exist out here.

Erick stopped and stared into the forest, which was illuminated only by moonlight. He looked around, trying to get his bearings; the trail looked different at this time of night. On every side, Erick could see ghost-like trees standing tall and menacing. A grey owl hooted at him. Erick thought he saw movement in the distance, perhaps a large cat, out of the corner of his eye. His heart raced as Erick thought about his beloved dog. He turned around and around, but Jace had vanished. Erick was filled with dread for taking Jace out here so late at night.

"Jace!" He cried out for his companion. Erick squeezed his eyes shut at the painful thought of losing his best friend.

Suddenly, the barking resumed, and Erick began to run towards the sound. A few minutes later, he saw Jace near the summit, barking at the edge.

"Careful, buddy, what do you see?" The ledge was steep, and rocks crumbled under them and tumbled down below. Erick dropped to his knees and held Jace's body close as it shook from barking.

Erick imagined an animal had died and was now at the mercy of the cougar and its sharp jaws. Careful not to slip on the leaves or the traprock which broke under his feet, Erick pulled Jace by his leather collar back from the edge. It wasn't easy to see anything. Erick stepped back, remembering his cell phone flashlight.

Erick removed the phone from his pocket and opened the flashlight app. The small light illuminated the mountain top, and he saw a small orange backpack and a turned-over wooden box next to it. The lid was open, and the box appeared empty when he picked it up and examined it. Erick set the box down next to Jace, who happily sniffed it. Next, he crouched down and picked up the unzipped orange bag. Erick found two empty water bottles, a small leather book, a few papers, and a cell phone inside. He tried to find out the owner of the cellphone and turned it on. A security screen indicated it was password protected. Erick put the box and the cell phone into the bag and zipped it up. He slung it over his shoulder and then walked over to the edge. Jace began barking again. He aimed his phone flashlight and shined it down the cliff. Erick moved the light from left to right until the ledge below came into view. He saw something dark, and his stomach dropped. A sick feeling took over Erick as he realized it was a *person*.

He shined the light directly at the dark mass. The light revealed long dark hair spilling out over the rock. Then he saw a face covered with dirt and maybe blood. Careful not to slip, he moved the light down more and saw a body broken and bent in a horribly, grotesque way. Erick stepped back, shut the light off, and quickly called 911.

"9-1-1, what is your emergency?" a female operator came on the line.

"I'm a doctor, and I found a body." He swallowed. "Summit Ridge near Freedom Trails. A woman fell. Hurry, she might still be alive!"

Erick waited for what seemed like forever. As dawn broke, he could see the figure below more clearly. The helicopter flew above, cutting through the morning fog. Erick shielded his eyes as the propeller spun the fallen leaves around, and a blinding spotlight illuminated the night. Two men in rescue gear and helmets swiftly repelled themselves, one after the other down from the helicopter. One took a statement from Erick. The other paramedic was getting a stretcher down from the rope leading up to the aircraft. It was hard to hear over the massive propeller. Erick's thoughts turned to the woman below. He didn't know if the woman would make it or why she was up there all night in the first place.

Erick covered Jace's ears as they huddled together, staying out of the way. The paramedics placed a collar on the woman's neck and expertly guided her limp body to the helicopter. The helicopter took off and headed to the nearest hospital.

Erick and Jace began the long run back down the mountain. No longer was he consumed with his own pain. *How long was she down there? What if he and Jace hadn't been out there or had gotten there in time? What if . . .* Erick stopped running and thought of the only thing left to do. Pray.

"Dear God, please help that woman make it. Please help heal her broken body. Thank you, God, for bringing me here tonight, and God, PLEASE save her!"

PART 2

Seventeen

Grace stayed in the operating room for hours. She was not awake, but she felt an out-of-body experience as if she floated above the doctors as they painstakingly took their time putting her back together. As they closed her up, they shook their heads in disbelief. "It's a miracle that she is even alive right now. Only time will tell the extent of the injuries. I cannot believe someone could fall that far and live to talk about it." Dr. Vicarri gave the nurses instructions and moved Grace to the recovery room. "Page me when she wakes up."

Grace could hear muffled voices. She tried to speak, but no sound came. Her eyes would not open. Grace was no longer cold. The nightmare was over, and now she could be free. *Wake up.* She told herself, but nothing happened. *What is happening to me? Where am I? Am I in heaven?* Her brain could not fill in the answers. Slow rhythmic beeping sounds grew louder, and she heard several people enter the room. Her heart rate increased; the beeping sound screamed louder. Then a faraway voice filled her ears, "Miss, you are going to be alright."

Erick's feet hit the trail in sync with the fast beat of his heart. He was a man praying for a broken stranger, a man who God placed there at the right place at the right time. *A miracle.* A man who knew all too well about being broken. Erick ran faster now than he had ever run in his life. One time, he tracked the distance to be just under ten miles from the summit. He could not run fast enough to get back to the cabin. Arriving in record time, Erick ran up on the porch and flung open the door. He filled Jace's bowl with fresh water. Next, Erick quickly showered, changed his clothes, and grabbed his work ID card. He had hospital privileges, and he wanted to get more answers about the girl they just brought in. On the bed was the orange backpack Erick found on the trail. He removed the phone from the pack and placed it in his pocket. Rezipped the bag he slung it over his shoulder.

"Hey buddy, you might have saved that girl's life back there!" Erick rubbed Jace's ears while Jace happily laid on the braided rug, tired from his adventures.

The Jeep's engine started just as the morning sun was rising. Erick placed the backpack next to him on the passenger seat. All of a sudden, a patrol car appeared in his rearview mirror, blocking his exit.

"Are you Erick Finn?" The tall, dark-haired man approached the vehicle wearing a police uniform.

Erick didn't move and kept his hands visible out in front of him. "Yes, sir. Can I help you?"

"I'm responding to a 9-1-1 call that came in earlier. I have some questions for you. Please turn off your engine."

Erick answered all the officer's questions but was impatient to get to the hospital.

"If you think of anything else, please reach out. This investigation will remain open until we figure out who Jane

Doe is and we can determine if this was an accident or if foul play was involved."

Erick had nothing to hide. As the officer pulled out of the driveway, Erick exhaled and remembered the orange backpack still in his car. Next, his hand touched the phone in the back pocket of his khakis. Guilt filled him as he realized he was withholding evidence, but Erick brushed it off as he jumped back into the Jeep. He would give it to the girl it belonged to when he got there.

Erick arrived at the hospital and realized his prints were on the cell phone. The officer asked if he knew the victim personally. Deep down, he thought it could be Grace, but he couldn't prove it. The whole interrogation made him uncomfortable. The officer implied *he* might have pushed her over the ledge. Erick would never hurt anyone, but the officer did not know that.

Erick knew in his heart that the right thing to do was to return the cell phone. He took the phone out and turned it on. The battery was at 40%, and a passcode locked the phone. He clicked it off again. He had to find out if the hiker was indeed the same woman he saw the other day. Erick put the phone in his back pocket.

Next, he opened the pack and looked at the papers, which only contained trail information. Erick returned the documents, and his hand felt a leather book. Erick carefully flipped through the pages and could not find any information, nor did he have time to read it. He surmised that it was some sort of journal and put it back and took the pack with him.

An automatic door opened, and Erick jogged into the building. At the front desk, he saw his friend Sherri. The hospital's lobby was sleek and modern, with light cornflower blue walls and wooden accents. Metallic chairs with blue cushions that lined the waiting area were mostly empty. The light wooden floors spanned throughout the lobby.

"Hello, Dr. Erick," she chirped. Her name tag read: *Sherri Wilkes, Patient Coordinator*. She wore her usual pink scrubs and white sweater and looked up at him with her eyebrows raised.

He usually would have made small talk, but he was on a mission today. "Hey, Sherri! Listen, a patient was airlifted to the hospital maybe a few hours ago? Is she here?"

Sherri always wore a smile, even if she was about to deliver bad news. Her light brown hair touched her shoulders, and her brown compassion-filled eyes peered through her black glasses. "Oh my. Yes, Jane Doe was in bad shape. We couldn't find any identification on her. She's in surgery." Sherri looked pained.

"Here," Erick said, handing her the small orange backpack. "I found this at the scene. Please call me when she is out of surgery?" Erick exhaled.

"You betcha. She is in good hands with Dr. Vicarri. Do you *know* her?"

"No, I'm not sure," Erick finally said. "Keep me posted."

Sherri opened the backpack, peered inside briefly, and then zipped it back up. Next, she placed it in a plastic bag, marked "Jane Doe" on it, and handed it to another person behind the main desk. "Save this for Jane Doe," she said to the other woman.

He left the desk as another customer entered the building.

Erick walked through the doors marked *Authorized Personnel Only*, waving his ID badge over the sensor. He went to the surgical wing and located Jane Doe's name on the sign outside the recovery room. Next, Erick walked up to the window. He saw her sleeping and connected to tubes and wires. Erick placed his hand flat on the window and prayed a quiet prayer for her.

His breathing finally returned to normal, and Erick decided he couldn't do anything more for her and left the hospital. His heart ached for this woman. Erick didn't know what she was doing up on the summit after dark, but he knew one thing as he turned the key in his Jeep. *She was alive, and God heard his prayer*

Eighteen

Grace screamed on the inside. She could feel herself floating above the clouds. *Am I dead? Why can't anyone hear me?* She drifted out of consciousness.

"*What are you doing?*" A sandy-haired boy appeared next to her. She looked up towards the clouds, her back resting against the cold stone wall.

"Watching the parade," she said her eyes looking to the cloudy sky above.

"What?" he asked.

"It is just something I used to do when I was younger. It calms me down."

"Can I join you?" The boy hoisted himself up and laid his body opposite of hers. Their ears were nearly touching.

"Sure." She smiled and then pointed, "*There!* What do you see?"

"Nothing." He frowned.

"Use your imagination and look again."

"An elephant?" he hesitated.

"Yes!"

"This is calming." The boy turned his face to her ear.

"My aunt taught me to see the world differently," she said quietly.

"My mom always taught me to see the beauty in the world. I wish I didn't have to look so hard." Erick inhaled.

"My mother hates me." She sat up.

"I miss my mother." He sat up now.

"Where is she?"

"She died when I was eight."

"I'm sorry, that is awful. Well, at least you have brothers."

"Family is complicated."

"Yes, it is. You're a good listener. I have to go," she said rolling her eyes and then shot a smile at him. "Meet me here again?"

The boy kept his blue eyes on her as she jumped down on her side of the wall; her red hair wound in two braids down her back.

"Sure."

She turned back to him. "You and me we are alike, you know." Grace smiled. The sunny afternoon suddenly turned dark, and she plunged into the deep murky water. Grace could see the little girl falling deeper, her braids rising from her head. She reached out, but the little girl vanished.

Erick arrived at HigherGround full of anxiety. He needed to know if Daniel could figure out how to unlock the phone. If he could just get into the phone, it would be the proof he needed. Erick got a text from Sherri that the patient was in the recovery room.

Erick caught up with work on the computer, left his office, and found Sky in the studio. Jace found Luna and sat by an eight-year-old boy working on building strength in his arm after a break. "Hey Sky, how was your trip to Georgia?"

"My parents love Daniel!" Sky handed the boy a small ball to squeeze.

"Where is Daniel now?"

"He will be in soon," Sky replied as she stood up.

"Sky, can you do me a favor? Can you see my last patient today? I need to head over to the hospital to check on a patient there. Jace and I found a girl on the trail the other night."

"Who is she?" Sky's ability to get to the point was one of the reasons he hired her.

"Not sure yet. I have a hunch I might know her. But it's a stretch," Erick said. "You remember Don, right? Joyce's husband? He knows his routine well. Just keep an eye on him. He likes to do *double* the reps. Did you know that they have been married *fifty-two years*? So don't let him get distracted at the front desk."

"Fifty-two years? Whoa! I wonder what their secret is!" Sky laughed.

"If you find that out, let *me* know." Erick smiled. "Thanks for holding down the fort. See ya, buddy." Erick patted Jace's head and headed to the lobby. Pumpkins of all sizes were scattered with silk red and yellow leaves on the long tables. Erick grabbed a potted plant containing two Amaryllis blooms in white and red that sat on one of the end tables.

With the plant in hand, Erick drove back to the hospital. He waved to the head nurse, rounded the corner, quietly entered the room, and slid the glass sliding door shut. His heart began to ache as he saw Jane Doe lying there with tubes running through her body. Julie, the nurse supervisor, came up to him. Erick knew her because he often worked with her when he was called in to consult on complicated physical therapy cases.

"Hey Julie, how is she doing?" he asked softly.

"Friend of yours, Dr. Erick?" Julie asked, noticing the

flowers in his hand. Her lavender hair was pinned back from her face by her clear glasses perched on the top of her head.
"I was the one who called it in."
"Then thank God you were there at the right time."
"Yes. Glad she has a chance. What do you know so far?"
"Jane Doe had several spinal injuries and was in a coma for a while. The surgeries were complicated, but she woke up for a few minutes before falling asleep again." Julie's bright eyes shone with positivity as she kept her voice low.

He thanked her, and Julie smiled as she left the room.

Erick set the pot of Amaryllis flowers on the windowsill, moved to the bedside, and sat on the chair. He noticed a large bandage covered her dark hair. Cuts lined her face, and purple bruises dotted her arms. He felt compelled to hold her hand, and then he began praying for her. Erick looked at her face and knew without a doubt it *was the same woman from the trail.* The woman with black hair. Erick wanted, more than anything in this world, to see her eyes again.

Erick held her hand, and it felt familiar. All at once, he felt a strong desire for her to recover. Whatever the prognosis was, Erick knew he had to continue to pray for her.

Erick had prayed every day since he was a kid. He had seen the miracles that happened with prayer. Erick looked at the woman and wondered why God had chosen him, of all people, to be there that night.

He got up and gently moved the ebony piece of hair from her eye, careful not to move or disturb her. He saw a small scar over her right eyebrow. It was a faded scar, something that happened a long time ago, he thought. He traced his fingers over the tiny mark.

"*Is it you?*" He whispered as he looked right at her. The sound of the machines and her breathing were the only noise in the room. *I promise to help you no matter what.* Erick was surprised by the strong connection he felt for her. He carefully removed his hand from hers and quietly left the room. The girl he saw on the trail seemed lost that afternoon and even more lost now.

Erick exited the hospital and knew better than anyone that she was facing a long recovery ahead. The weather felt warm for October in New England, and he rolled down the window.

Erick drove back to the office and felt blessed to have a career that he loved. From the outside, his life looked perfect, and for the most part, it was. If only he could forgive himself for the mistakes of the past. A beautiful sunset cast an orange glow over the HigherGround. The years there had flown by, and he felt he had a front-row seat to the power of God from all the transformational work he got to see firsthand in his patients. Erick entered the main lobby and saw Don, who was putting Joyce's coat over her shoulders.

"We are closing up, Doc. Do you want us to leave the lights on for you?" Joyce asked.

"Sure, I will turn them off. Have you seen Daniel?"

"You just missed him. He and Sky left just a little bit ago," Joyce said.

"How are you feeling, Don?" Erick reached to shake his hand.

"Better than ever!" Don shook his hand. "You are a gentleman and a scholar. Outside of that," he said with a wide smile. "I like you!" He laughed and turned to Joyce. "Let's make like a tree and leave. See you in a few days, Doc!" Joyce and Don left.

"Bye, you two!" Erick smiled at the joke and hoped to have a love like that, timeless and beautiful. Next, he went to his office, grabbed the cell phone, turned the lights off, and locked up. Erick didn't want to bother Daniel tonight. The phone could wait until morning. After all, he didn't really need proof. His heart already knew the truth about Jane Doe.

Nineteen

Grace coughed, and she squinted in the bright light. A short man stood over her, wearing a white coat over dark blue scrubs. He had a thick speckled salt and pepper beard. The surgical cap barely covered his balding head beneath.

"Hello, I'm Dr. Vicarri, your surgeon. Do you know where you are? You're in the hospital. You had a serious fall."

"What?" Grace whispered hoarsely. She instinctively tried to touch her throat, which throbbed in pain, but she couldn't move.

"You are a lucky woman!" His chocolate eyes looked intensely into hers. "Do you remember what happened? You did not have any identification on you, miss. Can you tell me your name?"

Say something, Grace thought to herself.

"I . . . I . . . don't know what happened. I don't know . . . I don't know!" Frustrated, Grace began to cry.

"All right. It's okay. You've undergone severe head trauma, and we released some of the pressure from the hematoma. It will take some time for the brain to adjust. We are in the 'wait and see' stage. Dr. Sonya will be in later to discuss the traumatic brain injury sustained in the fall."

Grace began to cry more. Her one arm had tubes and

wires in it; the other one was in a cast. She was unable to wipe her tears; they flowed down her cheeks, pooling in her ears.

"Anyone you can think of that we can call?" When the doctor didn't get a response, he placed his hand on her arm. "We will know more soon. Get some rest." With that, he nodded to the nurse and left the room.

Grace looked around fearfully as the doctor left her alone. What had happened to her? In shock, she closed her eyes, and Grace felt like she was swallowed whole as sleep enveloped her.

Erick woke up the following day, realizing he had slept all the way through the night. He couldn't even remember having any dreams let alone nightmares. Confusion and relief filled him as his thoughts went to Grace in the hospital. He was sure she was the girl from his youth.

After his run with Jace, Erick came into the office on his day off and found Daniel cleaning the free weights.

"Dude, it's Sunday! You never work on weekends."

Erick closed the gap between them, "I'm the boss, and that requires me to check on *all* my employees. All joking aside, I actually need your help." He removed the cell phone and handed it to Daniel.

Daniel looked at the device. "Nice phone."

Guilt wracked Erick as he rubbed his beard. "Listen, it's obviously *not* my phone. I can't get into it . . . Do you know anyone that can hack into this? It's for a patient who has amnesia. We are trying to figure out her identity."

"You mean that girl Sky was telling me about that you had to go see the other day?"

"Yeah, I think I know who she is. I just have to prove it.

That's why I need you. Can you do it?" Erick resisted giving too much detail.

"Yeah, my buddy Cody is good at hacking shit. You want me to give him a call?" Daniel eyed Erick. "Never thought you were the type to be involved in espionage or hacking into patient's phones. Are you in trouble or something?" Daniel smirked. "Wow, you aren't Mr. Perfect after all, are you? What else do I not know about you?"

"I'm just trying to prove it is someone I know. It could be a matter of life and death." Erick patted Daniel's shoulder.

"Who do you think it is?" Daniel looked wide-eyed.

"I don't want to say until I'm sure. You won't believe me anyway. I will explain everything later, I promise."

"Dinner is at 7 pm. Sky will be there. You're still coming, right?" Daniel continued cleaning.

"Of course, I'll be there!" Erick smiled and headed to his Jeep. There was only one person he needed to see—the girl in the hospital.

Twenty

Grace awoke to several people in her room.
"How are you doing today?" One of the doctors asked. "I'm Dr. Sonya, head of the neurology department."

"I don't know." Grace was getting more frustrated by the minute.

"The mind is a funny thing," explained Dr. Sonya. In contrast to the surgeon, the neurologist was a tall, slender woman with long dark hair perfectly braided and swept to one side. She wore a beautiful red paisley scarf. "The information is there, but the mind has protected itself from events that may be too painful to recall." She looked into Grace's green eyes, "When you are ready, the healing will begin, and then you will remember. You may or may not walk again, but that will depend on how your recovery progresses. We are putting together a team to work on your case as we speak."

"Hello, Dr. Sonya!" Dr. Vicarri came in all smiles. "How is the patient today?"

"Dr. Vicarri, I was just telling her we're putting together a team of specialists for this case."

"Yes, we'll meet to discuss the treatment plan." Dr. Vicarri looked at his tablet and frowned. "Your test results came back . . ."

Grace had been quiet long enough, and her eyes blazed with rage. "When can I get out of this bed. I . . . *can't*—" Tears burned and threatened to flow like scalding lava down her face. All she did was cry and sleep. *Enough already! I'm done.*

"I understand you want answers." He approached her right side of the bed, "There is still significant swelling around the lumbar region—more than we anticipated. We had hoped that with the treatment, it would subside, but there is a chance of infection. This infection needs to be resolved and contained before it spreads to your legs."

"Also," the doctor continued, ignoring Grace's sobs. "You had a significant thoracic injury. During surgery, we had to do an exploration of the injured nerve. Then we had to remove all injured tissue. After that, our team reconnected nerves to the brain and spinal cord. We will run more tests. Once the inflammation reduces, we hope some function in your legs returns. But there is a chance you may not walk again."

The doctor continued, but Grace couldn't hear the rest. *Never walk again* played over and over in her mind. *So, this is how it all ends.* Stuck in this bed, forever all alone. The doctors left her, and her eyes looked over at the windowsill. *When did these flowers get there?* More unanswered questions flooded her mind. There was one thing Grace did know, however. The fact that she was alone, and *no one* was coming to save her.

Erick entered the hospital and clipped his ID card to his heavy blue therapy jacket. He desperately needed to get inside to see her, or he thought his heart would explode. Erick felt like his feet were in cement and couldn't get into her room fast enough. He knew in the depths of his heart that it *was* her. The girl he saw on the trail. The girl of his youth. The girl with the sunset hair. The girl he could never forget. Without stopping to chat with anyone, he entered the floor where Sherri had told him Grace was recovering.

Erick took the stairs two at a time and entered through large wooden doors. He turned to the nurse's station, where he saw Julie.

"How's the patient?" Erick asked as his heart banged in his chest, his breath slowing.

"Oh, Jane Doe? Yeah, we still don't have any leads on her. She is awake and in room #444. but I must warn you she isn't doing well. Her surgeries were successful, but she won't speak much or eat."

"Okay." Erick barely contained himself, trying not to run down the corridor. He found room #444. A nurse was in the room taking her blood pressure and checking the IV monitor. Erick stood there and gazed into the dimly lit room. Sun shone through a small window into her room. The sound of beeping monitors was all Erick could hear as he just stood there silently. He felt like his heart might explode from his chest when he saw she was awake.

The nurse named Amy leaned over the patient. "I just replaced the bandage on your incision. I'll come back to check on you in a few minutes. Drink some of this while I get you another blanket." She poured some water from a pale pink plastic pitcher into a matching cup with a straw. Nurse Amy placed the straw up to her patient's lips. She took a few sips, clearly in pain from only lifting her head. Her long black hair hung loosely over her one shoulder.

"Hello, Nurse Amy," Erick said in a low voice. He moved toward the bed and ignored the stern look on Amy's face, "I promise I won't stay too long."

"She needs to rest. It's been a long road for this one."

Erick moved to the bed and looked at the woman. "It's going to be okay. *I got you*," he said in a low voice and moved to sit on the side of the bed. She looked up at him with her jewel-like green eyes. He noticed something behind them. He recognized it. *Fear.* Erick instinctively held her hand and said, "You can rest now if you like." Without a word, she closed her eyes. He watched her for a few minutes until sleep consumed her. Her eyes were the only evidence he needed, and he knew without a doubt that it was *her.* "Grace," he whispered, "I promise you, I will never let anything ever happen to you again. I will never leave. Not now, not *ever.*"

Twenty-one

Grace felt a cold chill worm its way up her spine. Next, a high-pitched shrill sound filled her ears. All at once, she realized the sound was coming from *her*. Wide-eyed and gasping for air, her body jerked back. It was like watching a movie in slow motion as cobalt blue eyes burned into Grace's. As her breath became shallower, her vision blurred.

Smash! Grace turned her head to see an explosion of glass against a wall. Shattered and broken pieces slid down next to her. Suddenly, his fingers were around her neck, squeezing tighter and tighter on her throat.

"*I own you!*"

His growl made Grace cower. As his fingers released from her neck, she choked, gasping to find fresh new air into her lungs. She winced from the pain and closed her eyes. Amber liquid ran down the wall. Shaking, she closed her eyes and begged for it to end. All she wanted was to be invisible and for the pain to go away. Pain weaved its gnarled winding fingers and made its way up her back. Spots danced in front of her eyes. She had no choice but to surrender to the blackness.

Now, Grace felt herself tumbling back down, down a rabbit hole, and only one thought came to her mind. *I will not die, not today.*

Grace awoke alone, and her chest constricted as the nightmare faded. She swallowed back the terrifying dream. The man's features were blurry, but he had the most brilliant blue eyes. Soon the image disappeared into the fog of her mind.

The next thing Grace remembered, she was falling, far down in the blackest of holes. Powerless to the black abyss, she continued to fall. Hitting bottom, her body shattered into a million pieces like glass. She'd woken up with a start with sweat beaded on her skin. Grace took a deep breath. Nurse Julie was back, her purple hair, a beacon of comfort like a lighthouse in a sea of nightmares and hopelessness.

She heard humming in the distance—a familiar tune. "Julie?" Grace whispered, still fogged by sleep. The moonlight shone in the window, illuminating her still small room and beeping equipment and IV bag. "What is that song you are singing?"

"Oh, *Mended* by Matthew West," she said. "I heard you screaming down the hall and wanted to check in on you, Sunshine."

"I had a nightmare. Can you stay and sing it to me, please?" Grace begged her.

"Sure." She pulled up a chair, "But close your eyes. You need your rest."

Grace felt more comfort from the song as she drifted off to sleep once again, her body lifeless like a rag doll on a shelf. *This can't be real. This has to be a dream.* Grace drifted off into sleep.

Grace opened her eyes again, and she was still in this hideous room with grey and pink wallpaper. Grace willed herself just to get up and move. Her arms ached, but she could move them around. Using her torso, she tried to sit up, but she was still too weak.

Grace lay there in deep thought when a new nurse with

silver spiked hair and a frown on her face entered the room. Grace felt scared, and her eyes darted around the room. *Where's Julie?* This new nurse was short, round, and had bright green scrubs. Grace squeezed her eyes shut and ignored her when the nurse tried to take her pulse.

"You really should just try walking; it would do you some good. Laying in this bed all day is not going to get you to walk faster." She had a white sweater on and a sharp accent. She put a fresh pitcher of water on the tray.

"Get out!" Grace screamed. "Get out of my room!" Grace reached up to the water pitcher and threw it on the floor, causing a loud clatter that broke the silence in the room.

"That's not very nice!" the nurse picked up the cup. "Now, you won't have any water." She chided Grace like a two-year-old and pressed a button. Then a man came into the room and injected something into Grace's arm. The room blurred, and tears streamed down her face.

Erick could not get Grace out of his mind. He had overheard the nurses talking about her having amnesia. He couldn't imagine waking up and forgetting everything. Erick actually did want to forget some things, but he also knew his nightmares were the mind's way of sorting through the missing pieces like a puzzle.

As Erick headed to Daniel's house for dinner, he thought Grace was sorting through a puzzle as well. Of course, he would do anything to help her recover and be there for her in any way she needed him. Erick would do things differently this time. Erick decided that *he* could be the miracle *she* needed, even if it were the last thing he would do. He was determined like never before that she would not just walk, but she would run. Just like the young girl he knew long ago. If he was honest, he also wanted her to run away from his brother, Finn.

A memory surfaced from the past when Grace was vibrant and full of life.

"Hey, I bet I can make it up that tree faster than you!" taunted a twelve-year-old Grace with red braids swaying like two cinnamon ropes down her back. She jumped from the grey stone wall that divided their two properties.

"You are on!" Erick took off and didn't look back. He ran through the yard and started to climb an enormous oak tree. Erick carefully grabbed the branches and used the crag in the trunk as foot holes. He got to the top of the tree and found her there on the highest branch. She looked at him with those eyes that glistened like emeralds in the sun.

"Wow, you really are slow!" she said, swinging her legs back and forth in victory. "You let a girl b-"

Before Erick could say anything, she fell hard and flat on the ground. She lay in a heap, face-up, her braids splayed in different directions. He immediately jumped down to the ground.

"Are you okay, Grace?"

She rolled over and groaned. Then she looked at Erick with her emerald eyes and leapt to her feet, laughing. Looking at Erick as she walked backwards. She said, "I meant to do that!"

He saw above her freckles a minor crimson scrape over her right eyebrow. She continued to take steps backwards, not taking her eyes off his. "Where are you going?"

"I gotta go home. See you tomorrow!" With that, she turned and ran away. Young Erick just stood there, his eyes on her, the late sun setting. Her red braids bounced up and down, and her jean shorts were now caked with mud. None of it seemed to bother Grace. He didn't really know this little girl well. Each day they would meet at the edge of their properties. They came from two different worlds. Neither of their parents approved of the other, but he knew one thing was for sure. This was the girl of his wildest dreams, and one day they would be together forever.

His mind returned to the present, and a plan began to take shape in his head. The fact that she didn't remember him meant she didn't remember the tragic past they shared. Erick didn't like lying, but the truth would be too much for her to handle in her fragile state. He would keep their past a secret for now. As Jace bounded to the HigherGround building, they both made their way to the side entrance of Daniel's place. He couldn't wait to tell someone about the crazy plan he was about to put into action. Just before Erick could knock on the door, the phone buzzed. He clicked the phone on. He had a message from the one person he didn't want to think about right now. *Brook.*

Twenty-two

Grace saw flowers by her window. They were white and red. It was like she was seeing flowers for the first time. Next, she looked up at the wires connected to her hand. The IV bag hung high and was accompanied by another bag this time. She recalled throwing her food on the floor and the dishes' rattling sound on the ground. She could feel her body tense and then relax as the drugs made their way through her veins. She scratched at the tape on her hand that held the port of the IV in place. Next, Grace read the plastic laminated hospital bracelet on her wrist. *Who are you, Jane Doe?* Grace's eyelids felt heavy. Grace wanted Julie to come back. She reasoned if she could just see Julie again, she would try harder and work on her recovery. Disappointment filled Grace as another nurse came in, and it wasn't Julie.

"How are you doing today?" The nurse had a southern accent and curly blond hair. "My name is Melissa. I'm filling in for Julie this week. Can I get you anything?"

"When will Julie be back?" Grace asked.

"In a few days, love. Have you seen the dinner menu today?" The nurse handed Grace the menu.

"I'm not hungry." Grace stared out the window.

"I will pick something wonderful for you. Just promise

me you will try to eat something. I will bring you an extra dessert!" Nurse Melissa left the room.

Nearly an hour passed when a young man placed the food on Grace's cart next to her bed. "Bon Appetit!" He smiled at her and left.

Grace sat up a little and winced. She moved the cart with her good arm and swung the table over her waist. She looked at the spread of food before her: fried chicken, mashed potatoes, green beans, and a cup of gravy on the side. Grace poked her fork in the mashed potatoes and took a bite. It had been days since she had eaten food and the buttery potatoes warmed her. She took another small bite.

"Bless your heart! Look what I found!" Nurse Melissa said as she bounced into the room, her pale blue eyes sparkling. She had two small clear plastic containers in her hand, one with a slice of pecan pie and one with a pumpkin roll.

"Enjoy! I will be back to check on you in the morning. Press this button if you need me."

Grace was beginning to think she must have been a terrible person, or maybe all her family had passed on. She finished the potatoes and hoped there was someone out there searching for her.

Erick knocked on Daniel's door without responding to his phone. The door opened, and Luna burst through the door. Immediately, Erick lost himself in a sea of golden fur and a slobbery tongue.

"Get back in here!" Daniel shouted from the entryway. Luna ran down the ramp and galloped back up to the house

After Daniel graduated from high school, Erick invited him to live in the apartment next to the physical therapy building. Erick lived there originally until he finished his rustic house in Connecticut's hills, a mere twenty minutes from HigherGround and the hospital. The hallway opened to a beautiful black and white kitchen with an island, and three grey cushioned bar stools. A lower table of the island displayed crackers, red grapes, and cheese organized on a serving tray. Between the kitchen and the living room were French sliding glass doors. Daniel had the doors wide open as he wheeled in and out between the porch and the living room. The weather started to cool off a bit as evening approached. A golden fire blazed in the living room's gas fireplace.

"Sky is on her way over." Daniel smiled from ear to ear. He picked up a pitcher and poured ice water with sliced lemons into a glass on the table. From the patio, you could see part of the lake and wooden dock through the trees. Twinkle and white lantern lights lit up the railing. "We will eat out here since it's not too cold tonight." Daniel set out three place settings, and then he wheeled back into the kitchen to grab more food while Erick looked out over the patio. The evening lights were coming on in town.

Erick took a sip of lemon-infused water and smiled at Daniel as he placed his glass back onto the table. "You and Sky are doing well then? How did meeting the family go?"

"They were skeptical, but I charmed them with my winning personality!" Daniel said as he put salt and pepper on the table.

"Are you sure you don't need any help?"

"Nope!" Daniel was stubbornly independent. Even as the youngest of the Finn family, he hated to ask for help insisting on proving himself.

"So, I wanted to talk about that girl we found on the summit." Erick had desperately wanted to tell his brother about Grace and his idea to win her back.

"Go for it."

Suddenly, there was a knock at the door.

"That'll be Sky. And she's just in time because she loves hearing your stories."

As Daniel wheeled his way back to the front door, Erick stood there on the patio and took in the scene before him. Daniel never let his disability have control over him. Daniel was different from the twins, a real superhero to Erick—stronger emotionally and mentally and willing to overcome any obstacle in his life.

"Dude!" Daniel shouted from the front hall, interrupting Erick's thoughts. "Someone is here to see . . . *you!*"

Twenty-three

Grace sat on top of a roof. It was a peaceful night, and she was not alone as she stared in awe at all the stars above.

"So, I was thinking," whispered Grace as she sat with her shoulder leaning on a boy's shoulder, her tanned legs tucked under her. "We should talk about something before we start high school officially on Thursday."

"Sure. Anything!"

The sandy-haired, blue-eyed boy looked at her. His eyes illuminated in the moonlight like brilliant gems of lapis lazuli.

"You're my best friend. My person. You were there for me when I first moved, and we have been friends awhile now." Grace reached for his hand, and her heart began to race. Her hand was so soft in his. She leaned closer, and she could feel his breath on her face. "Would it be too crazy if I said I was falling . . ." Grace kissed the boy as she never had before. At that moment, time seemed to stand still. All the stars above seemed to align at once. The boy's hands caressed her neck, and she closed her eyes and deepened the kiss. Suddenly she could not breathe. Glass shattered, and she was no longer on the rooftop under the stars. She closed her eyes and awoke to gasp for air.

"Bless your heart! Are you okay?" Nurse Melissa came bursting into the room. Light flooded the small room as she flipped a switch. "You were screaming!"

"Can I have some water, please?" Grace whispered and squinted at the bright light.

"Of course, darling!" Melissa poured some from the pitcher into a cup and put a straw in it. "Was it a bad dream?"

"They happen a lot lately," Grace said wishing Julie was there to sing her a song.

"Well, there is nothing like a hot cup of chamomile tea to calm the nerves. I will go get us some!"

Grace sat herself up a bit and took a deep breath. Her cast was starting to itch. She tried to rub around the part over her hand. Melissa brought back two cups of tea in Styrofoam cups.

"Don't you worry, dear! I made yours not too hot. In case you spill."

Melissa talked about her life in West Virginia and how she became a nurse while Grace sipped her tea. Eventually, Grace slouched down and felt her eyes getting heavy again. She fell asleep thinking about all the patients who had families that visited them. She wondered if anyone would ever come to see her or if she'd be stuck in this sterile hospital forever. All alone, always alone.

Erick stood in the doorway, looking at Brook. He saw her wearing dark jeans, knee-high suede boots, and a white cashmere sweater. Brook's platinum blonde hair was braided to one side and a small diamond clip held it all in place.

"Erick. Hi! So . . . are you going just to stare, or are you going to let me in?"

Erick stepped aside to let Brook walk past him. She

smirked as she walked by him. He turned to watch her enter Daniel's apartment. Erick had the front door still wide open when another girl with wavy blonde hair appeared, her hands full of containers filled with food and grocery bags.

"Sorry, I'm late!"

"Let me help you with that!" Erick leaned in to grab the handles of the bags.

"Sky!" Daniel beamed at the dark blonde girl with hazel eyes. She placed a bag on Daniel's lap and followed him inside as the door shut behind them.

Brook made her way out to the kitchen. She had brought a bottle of white wine and placed it on the counter. Daniel and Sky started to unload the bags and placed the hors d'oeuvres out on the island. Daniel handed Brook the wine opener and a long-stemmed glass.

A bell chimed, and Daniel announced, "Dinner is ready!" as Brook filled her glass with the golden liquid.

Warm steam billowed from the pan as Sky placed a lasagna on the center of the table. Meanwhile, Brook carried out the salad, and Sky returned to the patio with another new place setting.

Seizing the opportunity to be alone, Erick took Daniel aside in the kitchen. Erick spoke low so no one could hear outside. "Daniel, we haven't had time to talk."

"If this is about the phone, my buddy Cody cracked the code. I was going to give it to you after dinner." Daniel started to make a move toward the patio.

"Wait!" Erick lowered his voice again. "That's great news about the phone, but I wanted to tell you something else. Brook and I broke up the other day. She just hasn't *accepted* it." Erick fidgeted, knowing Brook was out on the patio.

"Oh, man! I had no idea. You have to keep me in the loop, dude!" Daniel wheeled over to Erick and punched him in the arm.

"What are you two conspiring over here?" Sky had come in to get a pitcher of water. The brothers froze and looked up.

"Apparently, he and Brook are no longer together," Daniel whispered to Sky.

"Oh my. I'm so sorry! I had no idea!" Sky's southern accent made everyone feel at ease. "Well, we are here now, so get outside, you two!"

Erick took a seat across from Brook next to Sky. As far as he was concerned, this relationship was over. Brook took a large sip of wine, and her red lipstick left an impression on the glass.

"Thank you for the invite, Sky." Brook nodded towards the lasagna. "Everything looks great." Erick looked at Daniel and decided he really needed to communicate better about his personal life. Maybe if he had, then he wouldn't be in this awkward situation he found himself in now.

"I don't think I have ever seen you wear jeans, Brook." Erick decided to make small talk.

"I'm capable of change, you know." She batted her eyelashes and smiled her victory smile.

"Sky," Erick replied, ignoring Brook. "If I haven't said it before, I greatly appreciate you helping the pediatric patients at HigherGround and finding a way to include the dogs in the therapy. "

"Well, of course, I love helping the kids and filling in for you and the other therapists. And you know I love animals."

"Yeah," Daniel chimed in. "Apparently, Sky was quite the cowgirl back in Georgia on her family's cattle ranch. Did you know she can even shoot a shotgun?"

"I definitely can! I keep one under my bed just in case I need to scare away any other wild animals!" Sky winked at Brook. "Yeah, and my daddy used to take me outside on the ranch and line up bottles on our fence," Sky replied.

"He would keep me out there until I shot each one down. I sort of picked up a thing or two."

"That's incredibly impressive." Erick grinned, avoiding eye contact with Brook.

"You must have been like a regular ol' tomboy in Georgia, Sky," Brook said. "We city girls are too busy running companies. As you can imagine, no time to learn to shoot guns."

"Anyway," Erick interrupted Brook before she could start an argument, although he saw Sky unfazed at the remark. "I think Sky deserves a toast for all her hard work at HigherGround, and simply for the fact that, unlike *most* girls, she can shoot a shotgun."

Daniel and Sky laughed as they held up their wine glasses and clinked Erick's water glass. Brook reluctantly lifted her glass also.

"To Sky, for being dedicated, kind, and original." Daniel gave Sky a quick kiss just then, and Erick noticed the natural connection between them.

After dinner, Brook and Erick brought the dishes into the kitchen while Sky and Daniel gave Jace and Luna some scraps.

"Erick," Brook said, cornering him in the kitchen as he washed the dishes in the sink. "I have been meaning to talk to you about something."

"Is that so?" Erick dried his hands with a kitchen towel. He was cautious. After all, what could she possibly say that would change his mind?

"I realized I need to make some changes and meet you halfway. If this relationship is going to work, I guess I can try harder," Brook said as she dried the last of the dishes. Next, she wrapped her hands around Erick's waist.

"Brook," Erick backed up only to find the island blocking him from moving far enough away. "I told you, this isn't working. I'm sorry, Brook. I just can't!" Erick freed himself and went outside to find Daniel, sitting in his chair with Sky on his lap facing the railing.

"I'm leaving," Brook interrupted. "Will you walk me to my car?" Not taking no for an answer, she turned to Daniel and Sky. "Thank you for the lovely evening, Daniel and Sky." Brook turned towards the door.

"I will be right back," Erick said to the couple.

Erick followed Brook as she walked down the ramp to the parking lot by HigherGround.

"It is over, Brook. Please let's give it a rest. We are just not on the same page, and we haven't been for years. You deserve to find someone who shares your dreams," he said as he opened the door to her Lexus.

"This is *not* over, but I will give you some time to come to your senses. We both know we can't fight destiny. I don't know why you cannot let yourself be happy for once." Then, only to drive the stake farther into his heart, she said, "It is what *your* mother wanted from the beginning. It is the only thing *my* father wanted for me. I hope you will change your mind. My father would like to see me marry while he is still alive." She turned and entered the car. Erick closed the door as Brook looked up at him through the window. He stood there as she drove away. It was too little too late for Brook, but Erick was not sad. He was smiling as he thought about Grace. Everything was going to work out perfectly this time around. It was time to put into motion the craziest idea he had ever had. If it worked out the way he planned, Erick would help Grace remember the past but help rewrite their future.

Twenty-four

Grace dreamed she was walking for miles in a wide open field. She looked up and saw a black raven on a fence looking around. Grace approached the black raven, and it spoke to her. "Everything is not as it appears," the bird said in perfect English. Then it cawed and took flight. She had to cover her eyes as the large wings unfolded and cast a massive shadow on the fields. The sun was burning hot and cast an otherworldly bright orange glow. Grace could see a Native American woman walking towards her in the shimmering waves of heat in the distance. Next to the woman was a white man with red curly hair. As the couple approached, the woman said, "You are one of us now. Daughter of my daughter." Grace smiled and watched them as they kept walking and disappeared into the horizon. Lastly, a large robin came into view; it took its wing and wrapped it around her. "I will take care of you," the bird spoke clearly. Grace closed her eyes and relaxed in the soft wing. The robin lifted her, and they flew away together into the sunset.

Erick went back into Daniel's apartment and saw his brother and Sky cleaning up the dishes. "Well, that wasn't awkward at all!"

"I had no idea you two were on the outs," Daniel said, wheeling out of the kitchen and into the living room. He opened the box revealing the white cell phone. "So, the phone is now unlocked." He looked back in the kitchen to see if Sky was looking. She didn't seem to notice. "I have to admit I looked at the contact list. I couldn't help but notice Finn's name under favorites." He extended the phone to Erick.

"Just as I thought," Erick reached for the phone frowning. "*It is her,*" Erick whispered. "Remember Grace?" Erick winced a little, hoping not to remind him of the dreadful party when both of their lives changed forever. Erick told him about rescuing her on the trail. "You have to help me get it right this time, and you cannot tell anyone, not even Finn."

"You mean the woman on the cliff is *Grace?* Your ex-girlfriend? Finn's *current* girlfriend?" Daniel was wide-eyed at this piece of news.

"Who is Grace?" Sky asked as she dried her hands on a dishtowel as she entered the living room.

"Only the girl my other brother has been practically pining over his whole life." Daniel frowned.

"Okay, sounds serious. I have some paperwork to do. I will leave you two alone." Sky kissed Daniel.

"You're staying over, right?" Daniel asked, slightly embarrassed.

"Of course." Sky winked and disappeared into the back room.

"Sounds serious to me." Erick smiled at Daniel.

"We are. But tell me more about Grace," Daniel demanded.

"It's complicated. Jace found her, and I'm the one who called the paramedics to the scene. Grace fell off the summit."

Erick rubbed his beard, thinking of all the terrible things that could have gone wrong and now the pain she must be feeling. "She made it, but she cannot remember anything, and she can't move."

"You've already seen her? Are you sure it's her?" Daniel looked skeptical. Luna and Jace were lying on the floor by the fireplace.

"It's her." Erick held out the phone. "It's all the proof here."

"Oh my God!" Daniel suddenly exclaimed. "You have to call her parents. You have to tell them she is in the hospital. They have a right to know."

"Of course, I'm going to call her parents. Tonight, I will call." Erick's eyes closed for the moment, imagining the pain they would be in when they found out.

"Call now. It's the right thing to do." Concern flashed over Daniel's face. "What is your plan after that?"

"Well, the doctors say she can't walk," Erick spoke slowly, watching Daniel's reaction to the news. "I'm going to be on her recovery team."

"This is a bad idea!" Daniel looked skeptical. "Finn is sure to find out and kill you. Brook is always around, as you can see. Plus, you and I both know how she feels about Grace."

"If there is any chance I can help her, I have to do this." Erick exhaled.

"Aw, man. This is insane. Don't you think Grace will recognize you and remember everything?" Daniel trailed off.

"She has *amnesia!*" Erick knew he probably sounded crazy to his brother.

"Of course, she does! When her memory comes back, she will kill you! Finn will kill you first. What about that?"

"I know, but if I can help her recover, I have to try!" Erick did not know what else to do. He had to do the right thing. "Finn can wait. He wouldn't understand what she needs right now."

"You are crazy to think this will work. You should call Grace's parents, at the very least." Daniel reminded Erick. "They will want to see their daughter right away. Leave Jace here. You can get him after." Jace was snoring softly next to Luna, who rested her head on his back.

"Okay, I'm going to call from the car. I imagine you are right. They will want to go to the hospital tonight." Erick got up and hugged his brother with one arm. "Let's leave Finn and Brook out of it." He shook his head, thinking about the disaster it would bring if they knew what Erick was about to do.

"Good luck. You don't have to worry about me saying anything. Sky will be discrete as well."

"Thanks, man!" Erick put Grace's phone in his pocket to look at later. For now, he had to do the one thing he dreaded doing. He had to call Robin Evans and tell him his daughter was in the hospital and the crazy idea he had to help her.

Twenty-five

Grace dreamed she was at some sort of dance. The music was loud, and a boy approached her wearing a black tux and bow tie. His hair was slick back, and he had put a little too much cologne on.

Silver and black balloons decorated the banquet room. People were dancing while others were standing on the perimeter observing or drinking punch.

"I am going to remember this day for the rest of our lives," he said. "May I have this dance?"

She had her hair pinned up in an updo with a few red tendrils that fell soft on her face.

"Y-y-you look beautiful," he finally said, not taking his eyes off of her.

The disco ball sparkled, and all at once, the image shattered into tiny pieces. Grace was all alone again in the hospital room. She squeezed her eyes shut and tried to sleep once more.

Erick closed the door of his Jeep and found the number he still had on his contact list. Erick hoped Mr. Evans would take the call. Putting himself into a father's shoes, he wasn't sure if he would take a call from *his* daughter's ex-boyfriend. Even though Erick was nervous, it was his duty to let Mr. Evans know about Grace. Dread filled him as he dialed the number. Erick held his breath as the phone began to ring.

"Hello?" a man picked up the phone.

"Hello, Mr. Evans, this is Erick Finn. Please don't hang up. I know it's been a long time, and I'm the last person you'd want to talk to, but it's about Grace. She has been in an accident."

"Is she okay?" Robin began firing questions like bullets through the phone, "What happened?? Is she alive? Where is she?"

"Grace is going to be okay. She is recovering from back surgery. I think it's better if we talk about what happened in person."

"What?" Robin breathed into the phone. "Tell me, now!"

"She was in a hiking accident, but please meet me at Saint Mary's hospital. You can see for yourself."

Twenty minutes later, Erick met up with Mr. Evans outside the main entrance of the hospital. Mr. Evans wore a dark brown jacket buttoned up and a thick red scarf. His breath appeared like white billows as he spoke into the night chilly night air.

"Erick?"

"Hello, Mr. Evans." Erick grabbed his hand to shake it, and both men walked in through the revolving door.

"What's going on? Please tell me."

"Please, have a seat." Erick gestured to the blue seat.

"What is going on, Erick?" Robin demanded, refusing to sit. "I need to see Grace. *Where* is she?! You're treating me like you're some doctor. I demand to see my daughter right now! Please!" His voice wavered.

"Actually, I am a doctor, and I was the one who found her up on the summit a few nights ago."

"Oh, God." Robin quickly took a seat.

"But she's going to be okay. I promise!" Erick insisted, taking the brown seat opposite Mr. Evans. "Listen, I know it's been a long time, and you have no reason to trust me. But I promise, Grace is important to me, and I'm going to do everything I can to help her."

"I told Grace not to go. Begged her to be safe." Mr. Evans wiped his hands on his forehead. "I thought she was back in New York. How bad is it?"

"It is not your fault. Grace will be okay, but she doesn't remember what happened or who she is. She's had a bad fall and has gone through extensive surgeries. The doctors said the back surgery was a success, but she hasn't made much progress." Erick rubbed his beard, measuring his words.

Mr. Evans squeezed his eyes shut in hopes to awake from the nightmare. He jumped to his feet just then. "What do you mean she is not making progress? I demand to see her right this minute!"

"I didn't realize it was Grace at first or would have called you right away. She looks *different* with dark hair, and she's pretty banged up. I have no doubt now it is truly her." Erick left out the minor detail about how he had the cell phone in his possession. He got up, and Mr. Evans looked sick as they headed to the elevators. "I hate to ask, but I need you to do something for me. Please do not mention that we all know each other. I promise you will understand once you see her. Her brain has suffered trauma, and her doctor warned that too much information at once could impede her progress."

"I have to see her. I won't do or say anything that could harm my daughter." Robin looked directly into Erick's eyes. "I won't let you or anyone hurt her either. You hear me?"

Erick nodded and walked silently to Grace's room.

They both saw a woman sleeping, the moonlight shining through the window. Mr. Evans immediately went to the bedside and sat in the chair, holding his daughter's hand with both of his. He sighed as tears filled his eyes.

"Pumpkin, what happened? I warned you about that trail, but I never thought . . . I *should* have gone with you." Tears streamed down Robin's face. "I'm so sorry. I just assumed you had gone home and were still angry with your mom and me." Grace awoke, startled. She jerked her hand away.

"Who are you?" Grace whispered as her heart raced.

Erick moved toward her.

"It's okay," he whispered and came to her bedside. "I'm Dr. Erick. We met the other day. You're safe." Grace seemed to calm down as she looked at Erick. "I know you have been having trouble remembering who you are. This man is your *father*. Don't worry if you can't remember him. In time you will."

Grace looked from Erick to Mr. Evans and blinked blankly. "Okay, I don't remember. I'm sorry," she whispered, the pain etched on her face.

"Grace, I'm the one who is sorry," Mr. Evans said between sobs.

"Would you like a few minutes?" Erick asked, and when he didn't get an answer, he said, "I will be back in about ten minutes. If you need anything, have them page me. Again, I'm *Dr. Erick*." He emphasized the last part hoping Robin would not tell Grace who he really was.

Erick leaned against the wall in the hallway and prayed for a miracle. The myriad of ideas flooded his mind of how he could help her. A real plan began to take shape in his mind. It was her best hope and the second chance he had prayed for all these years.

Twenty-six

Grace studied him now and saw a man who had light green eyes that looked pained. Silver flecks dotted his beard. Grace's heart ached. After being alone for days, *she desperately wanted to be his daughter.*

"Grace, I'm so sorry!"

"My name is *Grace?*" she whispered, trying to stay awake, trying to remember. Her dad would know her real name. Comfort filled her heart, but she hoped this was not just another dream. She wanted to ask him questions. Grace wanted to know all about her life.

"Yes, your name is Grace. I should never have let you go up there alone on the trail." Robin winced with guilt.

"I'm sure it's not your fault, and I most likely had a reason to be there," Grace said, assuring him. "Do you know why I was there?"

"We can talk about that later." Robin reached out ever so lightly, touching her cast, and then his hand smoothed her dark hair away from her face. "We need to talk to your doctors about getting you out of here. You should be home with your family. Not alone in a big empty cold hospital. I will build a ramp if I have to, whatever you need. I will never let anything bad happen to you again." He hugged her and sobbed again. This time Grace did not resist.

"Mr. Evans? We should go." Erick appeared and spoke in a low tone, almost a whisper. "I will set up a meeting with her doctors as soon as possible. She needs to rest."

"I will be back! I will make sure you are safe and at home soon. I promise!" Robin stood up. He wanted to kiss her forehead, but he didn't want to frighten her either.

"Okay," Grace said as she waved goodbye.

She allowed her eyelids to fall, and she drifted into sleep again, but this time she dreamed of this red-haired man in an empty library filled with books. Books with all the answers she needed, if only she read all the books in time, but the darkness enveloped her, and sleep took over her heavy eyelids.

Grace awoke the next day, but she was not happy. She wanted the man with the red beard to come back—her father. Julie was supposed to return today, but she had not stopped by yet. She had no one to read to her and no one to brush her hair. Even Melissa and the desserts were gone. Just then, a tall, slender male physical therapist came to train her. He moved and stretched her legs, but it hurt so much she screamed and told him to leave.

"Oh, Sunshine, what happened to you, love?" Julie found Grace crying in the bed.

Grace didn't look at her, but she just stared at the window, blinds still drawn.

"I'm sorry, I wasn't here love, I had to take a few days off because my mom was ill, and I had to move her in with me."

"Oh." Grace just looked down.

"What's wrong, love?" Julie sat next to her.

"My *dad* came to see me." Grace hung her head.

"Wow, that is great! Do you remember him?"

"No, but he seems nice." Grace turned to Julie, "I missed you so much. It was awful without you!"

She walked over close to Grace, who had tears in her eyes. "But I'm back now!" She pulled a brush out of the drawer and brushed Grace's hair. "You have beautiful *red* hair, you know."

"What? My hair is black." Grace barely breathed the words out.

"Look!" Julie exclaimed as she handed Grace the mirror. She could see her hair in the reflection. Some gold mixed with dark cinnamon color grew in the small part where they had shaved it for surgery. "Your wound is all closed up nicely. I will be right back."

Grace stared at her face in the mirror. She looked into unfamiliar green eyes as she studied her own face. *Who are you, Grace? What will become of you?* Grace wished that she could remember who she was. All she hoped, for now, was that her dad would hurry back soon and give her the answers she desperately needed.

Erick was at the hospital first thing the next day. He wanted to meet with both Dr. Vicarri and Dr. Sonya about Grace's case.

He found Dr. Vicarri during his rounds. "Dr. Vicarri, may I have a moment?"

"Hello, Dr. Erick. I was going to call you today." Dr. Vicarri raised his eyebrows. "We are putting a team together for Jane Doe. The nurses told me you were the one who found the patient, and you found her father."

"Yes, this is all true," Erick said. "I would like to be a part of that team. Her name is Grace Evans." Erick tried to give the doctor as much information as he could. Then he hesitated a moment to let all the information sink in.

"Jane Doe is Grace Evans? That is great news." Dr. Vicarri stopped walking and looked at his watch. "How do you know her?"

"We actually went to high school together. With my background in physical therapy, I believe Grace will be able to walk again, and I can help with her memory."

Dr. Vicarri sized up Erick. "Don't get your hopes up. She probably will never walk again." A nurse came by with something for him to sign. "You could try, I suppose, but you need to talk to her neurologist, Dr. Sonya. It's a delicate situation and a possible conflict of interest. Get Dr. Sonya on board, and you'll need Grace's parents' consent as well. I must go. Call me when you have that done."

Dr. Vicarri disappeared into a patient's room. He could convince Dr. Sonya, he thought. Grace's parents, on the other hand, were going to be more of a difficult task. He made his way to Neurology and realized he had to convince all of them that he was the only man for the job.

Twenty-seven

Grace stared at a dark-haired woman and the man with the red beard. As they both entered, Grace noticed the woman with him had her arm tucked into the crook of his arm. They both wore light coats that were damp from the rain. The man was her father, and *he had come back for her.* He rushed over and hugged Grace. His hair smelled of cedar and wood. She looked over his shoulder to the window and saw drops of rain slide down the glass pane.

"So good to see you again!" her dad said and stepped back.

"We want you to come home with us instead of going back to the city." The petite woman approached and placed her hand on Grace's shin. Grace noted the stiffness of the woman's tone. "It would be for the best. So, you can remember, in a more *familiar* environment," she added quickly.

"Are you, my mother?" Grace smiled. *They have come to get me!*

"Yes, dear. I'm glad you are okay," Faith said and hugged her quickly.

Grace asked. "What took so long for you to find me?"

"We didn't know—" Robin trailed off.

"What your father is saying," her mom briskly interjected. "Is that we didn't know you were in trouble. We just got the call that you were here. We thought you had returned to New York."

"New York?" Grace wanted to know more. "Dad?" Tears reached her eyes and threatened to spill.

Dr. Vicarri came in behind the couple and interrupted. "Hello, I'm Dr. Vicarri," he said, shaking both the man and woman's hands. "Robin, we spoke on the phone about your daughter. As the lead surgeon on this case, I need to inform you about Grace's latest developments. Our patient has suffered severe spine trauma and, at this time, she is still suffering from retrograde amnesia. As I warned over the phone, my fellow neurologist, Dr. Sonya, agree that this is an unusual case. Dr. Sonya will be here later to go over more details of the brain injury." His face grew serious. "You should know that the infection has subsided. Grace has recovered from her spine surgery, but she has been unable to regain mobility in her legs. We are running more tests, and the results of the blood workup should give us a better idea. The infection may have caused damage and, therefore, a lack of muscle response. Dr. Sonya and I also believe the brain trauma is hindering her motor skills and function. We are putting together a team and a plan of action for her recovery as we speak."

Grace just laid in her bed, tears pouring down her face. Her parents, whom she could not remember, held on to her shoulder and hand.

"When can we take her home?" Robin insisted.

"I need the neurologist to sign off on her paperwork. We need to review a few more tests, remove the cast on her wrist, and go over the phases of treatment and all therapies. Grace is an adult, and her signature will be required. Dr. Sonya and I agree that Grace will regain more of her memory if she is in a familiar place. She will need access with a wheelchair, and she will have to follow up over the next few weeks. Can we have all this ready by next week?" Dr. Vicarri turned to Grace. "If your parents can make the necessary accommodations, would this work for you, Grace?"

"I guess that would be okay." Grace was unsure, but she had nothing to lose at this point.

"Of course!" The man reached for his wife, who moved her hand to his. "Can we have a few minutes alone with Grace while we wait for Dr. Sonya?"

"Indeed," Dr. Vicarri agreed.

"I know all of this must be scary, but we love you, Grace. Please let us take you home with us. I will hire the best doctors and therapists. Please let us do this for you," Robin said sincerely.

"Anything you need, we will get it for you. When you feel better, you can leave whenever you want. We just want the best for you, Grace. What do you say?" Faith Evans pleaded her case.

Grace believed her father was telling the truth, so she said, "How soon can I get out of here?" Grace had heard enough and was ready to leave the hospital. Grace could feel things changing not only in her life, but she felt something was changing inside of her as well.

Erick found his way to the conference room and pulled Dr. Sonya aside as the other doctors filed in. "Dr. Sonya, can I please have a word? I'm Dr. Erick Finn. I work here with the physical therapy department and at HigherGround Physical Therapy. I specialize in against-all-odds cases." Dr. Sonya stopped looking at MRI scans on her tablet and looked up at Erick.

"I know you. You come highly recommended by this

hospital. Dr. Vicarri filled me in. You are the one that knows Grace from high school."

"Yes. I also am aware of her amnesia."

"You are also aware that there is a conflict of interest here? Knowing the patient can compromise your judgment."

"If everyone could find their seats," Dr. Vicarri said as he turned on the large monitor at one end of the table. "This won't take long." Erick and Dr. Sonya took their seats. Dr. Vicarri brought everyone up to speed and introduced Erick. "This is Dr. Erick Finn. He wants to handle the outpatient physical therapy for Miss Evans."

"I believe as her memory returns, Miss Evans will regain her mobility as well," Erick said. "I think there is a connection. Maybe the amnesia is affecting her ability to *remember* how to walk."

"That might be possible," Dr. Sonya interjected. "I'm going to sit in on one of the therapy sessions. A special wheelchair should be arriving today." Dr. Sonya looked over the scans again.

"Nurse Julie, you can set up some home visits starting next week." Dr. Vicarri continued. "Any questions?" he nodded toward the team.

The room emptied, and Dr. Sonya turned to Erick. "Because Dr. Vicarri thinks you'd be an asset on the team, I won't stand in your way. It's unorthodox, but as you said, it might help with her memory, and your expertise in the field of physical therapy would play a large role in her recovery."

"Thank you for your endorsement." Erick was happy with how this was going.

"You can thank me by helping that girl. I must warn you, though, to go slow with the memories. Too much too soon could cause irreversible damage."

"I will go slow," Erick agreed. "I also won't mention that we know each other, and I will keep things professional."

"One or two memories is about all she will be able to handle once they start coming back, *if* they come back at all. Good luck," Dr. Sonya said.

"Thank you, Dr. Sonya. Also, Grace's parents are here, and they want to ask you a few questions. When you can, please stop by the room to give them an update."

"Of course." Dr. Sonya peered into the scans much closer.

"Thank you, see you later." Erick left the conference room. He was so excited to be on Grace's team that he wanted to run and tell her. Erick had only one final thing left to do, and that was going to be the biggest challenge he had faced in nearly a decade—win over Grace's parents.

Twenty-eight

Grace and her parents were chatting when Dr. Sonya entered the room with a large envelope.

"Hello, I'm Dr. Sonya. I have been working on Grace's case as her neurologist. You must be Faith and Robin Evans, her parents?" The three shook hands. The doctor turned to Grace.

"How are you feeling today? I understand your name is Grace. What a lovely name!" She pulled out the MRI scans and placed them on the lighted board. "These slices are of Grace's last scan. They show inflammation of the right hemisphere here and here." She pointed to the scan. "This area shows lesions on the hippocampus where learning and memory take place. When Grace fell, it caused TBI, Traumatic Brain Injury. Her brain sustained damage to the medial temporal lobe. She also lost her semantic memory." Dr. Sonya paused to allow the information to sink in. "This retrograde amnesia could be temporary or permanent. Several studies show we can use different therapies to help Grace remember certain skills and restore abilities previously lost. Our team hopes she can restore her memory of walking." Dr. Sonya pointed out another area on the scan. "You can see severe inflammation. During her initial surgery, we made a small incision. This effectively released some of the pressure and stopped the bleeding." Dr. Sonya made her way to Grace and examined her forehead. "This is healing nicely. Do you have any questions?"

"What are the chances she will have a full recovery of all her brain function and mobility?" Faith asked.

"We're in the 'wait and see' phase. Only time will tell. I will warn you not to move too fast. We do not want to traumatize the brain while it is healing. I recommend no more than one or two memories shared with Grace per day. Too much too soon could cause permanent damage. She needs time to adjust and heal."

"When can she come home?" Robin spoke next.

"She has responded to the heavy course of antibiotics through this IV, and soon we can switch medications. We should know more after we run some more tests. She will get training for the wheelchair. Dr. Vicarri already went over the modifications you will have to have at the house. If you don't have any other questions, I will be in touch." Dr. Sonya left the room after everyone nodded.

"Grace?" Robin sat next to Grace now. "Would you like us to take care of you for a while?"

Grace took a deep breath, "I do. *I really want to remember.*"

Erick stood at the doorway of Grace's room. Not wanting to disturb their meeting with Dr. Sonya, he went to the main lobby. After a time, Robin and Faith exited the elevator and headed towards the main exit. Erick approached them.

"Mr. Evans." Erick shook his hand and turned to Faith. "Mrs. Evans," he said, holding out his hand, but Faith pulled it back.

"I *know* who you are!" Faith looked disgusted. "You may not be as bad as your brother, but you are still a Finn!"

"I apologize on behalf of my entire family. We certainly have our faults." Erick forced himself to keep his composure. "But I care for your daughter, and her recovery is important to me."

"He did save her life!" Robin surmised. "If it weren't for Erick, Grace would be . . ." He could not finish the sentence.

"I'm very thankful for all that you have done, Erick, but Grace has a long road ahead. We really are grateful, but we will take it from here." Faith put her arm in Robin's and turned to leave.

"Wait!" Erick didn't mean to shout in the lobby. "Let me walk you two out. I have something I need to tell you."

The three of them exited the hospital.

"I don't have a lot of time. I need to get back to work," Faith warned.

"I will make it quick. I'm a physical therapy doctor now. I did not join the family business." Erick's heart was pounding, and he barely could get his thoughts together. "I specialize in tough cases. I have helped many people regain their mobility and strength even if their doctors say they could never walk again. I have a large studio a few miles from here, and we have all the latest state-of-the-art equipment and an Olympic-sized pool. All the therapists we hired are at the top of their class, and our success rate is 97%. We are rated one of the best studios in New England. People travel near and far to work with us." Erick looked directly at Faith and Robin. "I want to train your daughter, and I believe she will regain not only her mobility but all her memories."

"Let's hope Grace isn't the three percent you couldn't help. You're lucky she does not remember what you did all those years ago." Faith looked over at her husband. "I'm not sure this is a good idea, Robin."

"Dr. Erick has been honest about everything thus far, and

I did research on HigherGround. He is telling the truth. They are highly rated. You're on Grace's recovery team?"

"Yes, sir, pending your approval, of course."

"I will allow it on a trial basis. But Robin and I will write you up to the medical board if you hurt her at all! If you do anything we don't like, we will make sure you never work again. Do you accept these terms?"

"You have my word." Erick exhaled. "I also need something from you both. I've talked it over with the neurologist. Grace's recall of memories must be slow and steady. I need your word that you'll not tell her who I am. More importantly, who I *was in the past*. Because it would interfere with her recovery."

"That makes sense," Robin said, nodding with Faith. "I also think, for now, we should focus on her recovery. I think the best way to do that is to make sure your brother, Finn, stays out of the picture. He will try to take her away from us again."

"You have three months, and we will not discuss your past or her life in New York until she is further along in her therapy. Until then, we will keep your identity a secret, and we all need to keep Finn away from her as well. It will be tricky, but it seems like the best shot." Faith winced at the name Finn.

They all shook hands in the parking lot. "Thank you! I will not let you down," Erick said. He would keep this promise as if his life depended on it.

Twenty-nine

"Grace, do you trust me?" Julie's hazel eyes sparkled as she opened a box and handed it to Grace. Grace looked over the words.

"Golden Copper hair dye," she read aloud, looking at the woman smiling on the box. "How is this going to change anything? Will it make me walk again?"

Julie smiled, "I got you, Sunshine. Do you want me to call you Grace instead? I thought we should get you out of that bed. What do you think?" Grace stared at Julie as she wheeled a black wheelchair into the room. Julie lowered the bed, put her arms around Grace, and lifted her gently to the chair, careful not to pull on the IV. "Light as a feather! Now for that hair!" Julie wheeled Grace into the large bathroom.

Grace let her work her magic as Julie began mixing the bottles. Grace closed her eyes when she covered her with a plastic sheet and commenced massaging the dye into her hair, careful to avoid the small healed area of the incision. Julie washed out Grace's hair and then blow-dried it carefully into soft waves. When Julie finished with Grace's hair, she put a little make-up on her and then handed her the mirror. "What do you think? Sometimes, we just need a lift. A lot of my long-term patients need a new look at life. I love showing them what they look like to me."

Grace held the mirror to her chest and asked Julie, "What if I never remember who I *really* am? What if no one loves me? I can't even . . . walk." Julie put her hand on her shoulder and gently held the mirror out for Grace.

Grace looked at herself in the small mirror. Her hair was a beautiful brick and copper color, and her skin tone seemed to glow. Her eyes seemed to sparkle brighter. *Who are you, Grace?*

"The universe loves us just as we are, Sunshine! One day you will remember how to love yourself. I'm sure your parents are excited to take you home." She winked. "I'll see you tomorrow!"

With the mirror still in hand, she felt something new. More than the hair color, Grace felt something she hadn't remembered feeling before. *Hope.*

Erick and Jace walked into the therapy studio the next day and saw Joyce, his office manager.

"Good morning, Dr. Erick!" Joyce handed him a mug of mint green tea. She wore her HigherGround cornflower blue fleece jacket as she organized files and set up for the day.

"*It is* a good morning, Joyce." Erick took the black steaming mug.

"Here are your patients today." She handed him a stack of folders. "They completed their sessions, and these can graduate today."

"Awesome!" He smiled. "Just so you know, if Brook calls, we are no longer together."

"Ah!" Joyce looked at him incredulously. "Does *she* know?"

Joyce knew Brook over the years.

"You know how she is." Erick enjoyed his talks with Joyce.

"Persistent!" They both spoke in unison and had to laugh.

"What is so funny?" Daniel entered the front area curiously.

"Daniel!" Erick smiled as Luna circled his legs and went to play with Jace. "Come into my office. We need to catch up before my first appointment."

Sky came into the office doorway and knocked. "Good morning! Where are my cute doggies?" Jace and Luna ran to her, both wagging their tails. "Good morning, Doc!"

Erick waved from his chair as he sipped hot tea. Sky kissed Daniel quickly and left with the dogs.

Daniel wheeled closer to the desk, picked up a giant tennis ball, and tossed it from his left hand to his right hand and back.

"You wanted to see me?" Daniel looked serious.

"Things look serious between you and Sky," Erick said. "If I didn't know better, I would say someone is in—"

"Don't say it!" Daniel interrupted, "Sky and I are really happy and in a good place. I'm going to ask her to move in with me. She is . . ." His face exploded in pure joy and his eyes danced. "Really *great!*"

"Good for you!" Erick caught the ball as Daniel tossed it to him and then threw it back. "So, I realized at your dinner party last night . . ."

"Brook!" Daniel cut him off and threw the ball to Erick. "Yeah, that seemed . . . heavy! I guess you two aren't going to make it down the aisle anytime soon."

Erick caught the ball and held it for a moment. "You got that right! She has some crazy idea that our mother wanted us together. She just doesn't get it. It is time for her to move on. *I* have." Erick rubbed his beard and seemed lost in thought. "There's one more thing we need to talk about before we get out there and change some lives!"

"What's that?" Daniel looked at Erick intently.

"Remember Grace?" Erick saw Daniel's eyes widen. "Her

doctors and her parents agreed to allow *me* to train her. It could be any day now. Daniel." He tossed the ball to his little brother. "Daniel, I need your help to get it right this time, and you can't tell anyone, especially Finn."

"Don't worry, Finn and I haven't really spoken much," Daniel said shrugging. "Other than an occasional holiday, we don't talk, honestly. I hate being in the middle. Sky won't say a word either. But what will you do if Grace finds out?"

Erick knew it was a risk. "I plan to train her to walk again. When I know she is safe, then I will tell her."

"If she finds out from anyone else, she may never forgive you. We don't even know if she ever forgave you!" Daniel pointed out.

"It's complicated, but I have to try, don't you think?"

"It's a bad idea, bro. But your heart is in the right place." Daniel wheeled around the office. "It could work—one thing you have to watch out for, though. The most unpredictable thing in the world!" Daniel's brow furrowed as he cringed.

"What's that?" Erick caught the ball, his eyes wide.

"Brook!"

Thirty

Grace's hope had disappeared by the following day. *No one loves me. If they did, they would already be here.* Just then, she recalled that there were visitors. She remembered that a woman visited her as well as her dad. Was that her mother? It was muddy in her brain as she sorted through the events of the last few days. She still had trouble keeping a sense of time. *Where were they now? Were they real?* Grace wondered if she dreamed the whole thing. Just when Grace was about to give up all hope, another miracle came.

Dr. Vicarri entered the room with an orange bag. He huffed and puffed as if he had run over a mile to get there. Smiling at Grace, he said, "Wow, your hair looks great! I also have good news!"

Nurse Julie came in behind the doctor, her eyes wide and hopeful.

"What is it?" Grace asked. She was ready for some good news.

"Your parents are making the modifications as we speak. You have a long road ahead of you, but we have the best support team to help your recovery." Dr. Vicarri's eyebrows lifted in delight.

"What is that in your hand?" Grace was curious. She

tried so hard to be happy and wished she could have more memories to draw from, but she came up empty.

"When the paramedics found you, you didn't have any identification. Dr. Erick brought this pack in after calling in the accident. It was misplaced in our storage facility. It could help you remember something." He handed her the bag. "I also have a necklace you were wearing when they brought you in. We couldn't save your clothes."

The orange backpack seemed old and a bit dirty and damp. Grace unzipped the top of the bag.

"Julie," Dr. Vicarri said, turning to the nurse. "Stay with Grace for a bit. I have to see another patient, but let me know if she remembers anything."

After Dr. Vicarri left, Julie headed over to Grace's side.

"This is good news, Grace," Julie assured, touching Grace's shoulder and peering into the bag. "Every little thing can help your memory, don't you think?"

Grace reached her hand in the bag which was lined in some sort of plastic, so all the contents were dry. She timidly reached in and found a wooden box. She lifted it out and opened the top. A warped tune began to play fast at first and then slow. The sound stopped, and the mechanism came to a halt. She handed the music box to Julie. Next, Grace found a leather book about the size of a journal with a compass on it. She ran her fingers over the soft leather and opened the journal as Julie peered over her shoulder.

Julie exclaimed in delight, "Do you recognize that song? It's 'You Are My Sunshine!'" She placed the box on the windowsill next to the red and white flowers. "Oh! A journal! This is so exciting!"

"*Dear Raya Sunshine,*" Grace read the first page bewildered.

"Is your name actually Sunshine?" Julie squealed as she looked over Grace's shoulder. "It must be because this journal belongs to you!"

Erick got to work seeing patients. He loved days like this, but all he could think about was Grace. Finally, the end of a very long day came, and he couldn't wait to go to the hospital.

Erick looked up at the stars, turned up the music in his Jeep, and left HigherGround and allowed his mind to drift back to the past.

Grace used to sneak over to his house sometimes when they were in middle school. She would climb up on the roof eaves below his bedroom window. That night they were looking at the stars.

"Do you see Orion's belt?" Erick asked Grace. He loved the way the moon cast shadows over her face at night.

"Of course I do," she replied. "Don't you just want to get out of this town?" Grace changed the subject. "Do you think you will run your dad's company?"

"I don't know. It's all my father ever talks about." Erick loved being this close to her. Somehow in the dark, just looking at her made him dizzy.

"But, what do *you* want?" Grace's face was so close to him, but he did not dare kiss her.

"I want to make a difference." He wanted to be with her forever, but he also respected her. "What about you? What do you want?"

"I have always wanted to be a writer. I will be one day. You'll see."

"What do you want to write about?" Erick didn't want the night to end.

"I am writing a story already," Grace said with a faraway look. "It's about a girl that finds herself at a new school. She isn't like the others. She doesn't come from money."

"Oh, this character sounds awfully familiar? Does she have a boyfriend, this new girl?"

"Not yet, but she is working on it." Grace smiled really big. "She doesn't want it to lose her friendship with him, though."

"Oh, that could never happen! You know in the story. The character. The girl. If her best friend is the one. She will know."

Grace leaned her back on Erick's chest, and he knew he wanted to stay there forever.

Thirty-one

Grace opened her eyes the following day. She saw a tiny sliver of light. Everything in her past remained blank for her. She was closer to getting out of the hospital and had no idea how long she had been there. She looked at the hospital tray table and saw the journal sitting on top. Picking it up, she ran her fingers across the soft leather top. Grace opened the cover and began reading the first few pages, which were poems about trees. She jumped at a loud tapping sound. Out of the corner of her eye in the small window, she heard a tapping noise and a "Caw caw!" A black raven had flown onto the window, and its eye turned towards her. The tapping continued on the window. Grace felt something familiar about seeing this majestic black raven. She had seen it before, but she couldn't quite put her finger on it.

Grace turned back to the journal. On the next page, she was stunned to see a pencil drawing of a raven.

"Grace?" A professionally dressed woman was wearing a cream-colored blouse with a herringbone skirt entered Grace's hospital room. She wore Her name tag read *Dr. Hopkins, L.P.C.* She approached Grace slowly and extended her hand out. "My name is Dr. Hopkins. Dr. Vicarri has asked me to talk to you and discuss your recovery plan. Is now a good time?"

Grace lifted her hand to meet the woman's handshake. She was getting more movement in her arms, and she could sit up longer now. "Hello."

"Can we take a ride?" Dr. Hopkins nodded toward the wheelchair.

"Sure." Grace put the journal back on the small table.

"Great! I know you are anxious to leave, but we have to ensure your support system is in place. I will be a part of that team." She helped Grace get into the chair. Next, Dr. Hopkins placed a small blanket on Grace's lap. "Do you want to wheel yourself or relax and enjoy the ride?"

"I'm not strong enough yet. Why don't you lead?" Grace rolled her eyes in frustration as she attempted to wheel herself with one arm. The path back to normal seemed like an endless road.

"It's no problem," Dr. Hopkins assured her. "Healing takes time. You relax, and I will drive. Then we can talk."

Dr. Hopkins pushed Grace out of the room and down the hall past the nurses' station. Grace noticed Thanksgiving turkey crafts made from various colors of construction paper lined the hallway along the wall. Suddenly Grace had a memory flash before her eyes. She saw a small hand, and with the other one, she traced around the fingers with a wide brown crayon. "A turkey!" the little child exclaimed. The memory faded as they continued down the hospital hallway.

Dr. Hopkins swiped her ID card, and they rolled down the glass-lined breezeway. Outside, some of the trees still had a few leaves with a mix of red and yellow. Most leaves had fallen, leaving the trees bare.

"Grace, I'm pleased to hear you are going to be home for Thanksgiving."

"Thanksgiving?" Grace rolled through the hospital corridors. They stopped at the door.

"Yes, do you remember the holiday?" Dr. Hopkins leaned into the scanner, and the door opened. A rush of cold wind hit them in the face.

Grace sucked in a deep breath as she rolled into a beautiful courtyard. It was evening, but she could see the leaves of all colors around. "I think I know what Thanksgiving is." She shook her head, frustrated when the memories didn't come.

The stars were visible in the night sky despite the lighted walkway. Two hospital employees walked past them with coffee in their hands.

Dr. Hopkins placed the brake on the wheelchair and sat on a bench facing Grace. "What do you remember today?"

"Not much." Grace looked at Dr. Hopkins. "I have parents, and a journal from my aunt and a music box." A stray leaf landed on the bench, zig-zagging its way down. "I know my name!" Grace began to tear up.

"I can imagine how frustrating trying to remember must be. Not only that but depending on others to do even basic things. You seem like an independent woman." Dr. Hopkins looked off into the distance. "In a way, you are experiencing a huge amount of grief, losing independence, not remembering, feeling incapacitated. You must be gentle with yourself and acknowledge that you are in the midst of this grieving process. Truthfully, Grace, the only way out is through." Her pale blue eyes looked into Grace's tear-filled ones.

"I'm so angry and so tired!" Grace sobbed. "I have nothing. Even if I had something or someone, I can't remember."

"Anger is one of the stages of grief. You have been through extensive physical and emotional trauma, Grace. I really want to help you make sense of this. I want you to know you are not alone, and you are not going crazy!" Dr. Hopkins pulled some tissues out of her pocket and handed them to Grace.

"I can't control anything that is happening to me." Grace blew her nose, and the anger returned. "I feel so helpless. I can't even walk, and all the doctors say there is a chance I may never . . ."

"One day at a time, Grace. How do you feel about going home?" Dr. Hopkins stood up and released the brake on the wheelchair.

"I'm afraid, actually," Grace admitted that much. "I'm afraid to remember something bad. Honestly, I'm also terrified that I won't remember *anything* at all."

Dr. Hopkins stood behind Grace now and leaned over, "You have a long road ahead of you, but you can always talk to me. Day or night." She pushed Grace back inside. "Your memories will come back like pieces of a puzzle and may not make sense right away. Some may come all at once and may be overwhelming. When that happens, I want you to focus on your breath. I promise you'll feel a little more relaxed. Trust the process. Do you have any questions for me?"

"I guess not. Not yet anyway." Grace shook her head.

Back inside the hospital, Dr. Hopkins helped Grace back into bed. Nurse Julie came in smiling, her hair clipped to one side.

"Hey, there, Sunshine!"

"Julie, I'm going to sign off on the discharge paperwork now for Grace." Dr. Hopkins turned back to Grace. "I will do a home visit in the coming weeks. Here is my card. Call me anytime. Remember to breathe."

"Thank you," she whispered as the doctor left. It would be good to have someone to talk to when she got out of the hospital—someone to help her navigate through the memories that might come up and give her a chance to sort it all out in the coming days.

It was time to go home, and she was ready to be finally free of these four walls.

Erick parked the car, still lost in the memory when his phone buzzed. Brook's name flashed on the screen. He decided to just answer it. "You really need to stop calling me. It's ov—"

"It's your dad, Erick. Hear what I have to say, please!"

"Okay, go ahead," Erick said as he looked out the car window. He wanted to be *with Grace*. Instead, he was on the phone with Brook. It was as if his father was conspiring against them yet again.

"Your father has been undergoing tests. They found a mass on his heart," Brook hesitated. "He is having surgery today. Finn and I are heading to the Saint Mary's this evening, so we can be there when he wakes up."

"Okay." Erick could not find any other words to say.

"You should be there. Don't you think?" Brook persisted.

"I don't know, Brook." Erick rubbed his beard. "It's been a long time."

"I would expect a praying man like yourself to be there." Brook knew how to get under Erick's skin.

"Fine, I will see what I can do." Erick ended the call. As he stepped out of the car, he looked up at the Saint Mary's sign that hung out front. He had no choice but to see his father. If for no other reason than to keep all of them away from Grace. No one was going to ruin his chance this time to make things right.

Thirty-two

Grace counted down the hours when she could finally go home. She finally saw some progress. She could sit up and move her torso a bit now. Her legs were another story. Julie came into the room suddenly with giant scissors. "Today is the day!"

"What?" Grace was nervous as Julie waved around the silver scissors in the air.

"It's time to cut it off!"

"Not my hair!" Grace thought Julie had lost her mind.

"No, silly! Sit still." Julie inserted the scissors into the cast and began cutting it carefully.

Grace could feel her arm loosen from the cast, and she wiggled her wrist around very carefully. Next, Julie unhooked the IV.

"What is this?" Julie lifted a small plastic bag with a necklace inside. "A compass?" Julie pulled the long black rope out with the tiny gold compass dangling from one end. "Can I put this on you?"

"Sure." Grace loved it when Julie was there.

"It is beautiful," Julie said, admiring the compass.

Suddenly Grace heard a voice in her mind of a young boy. "This will help you know what direction to go even if you're lost." Then the memory dissolved.

"Where did you go?" Julie asked.

"I get these flashes that come and go so fast sometimes. Maybe it's a memory. I'm not sure. This room is making me crazy. I need to get out of here!" Grace would even crawl her way home if she had to. *Wherever home was.*

"They always drag their feet with the paperwork," Julie replied as she helped Grace into her wheelchair. "Let's at least get you out of bed, and I'll see what I can do to speed things up."

Erick entered Grace's floor of the hospital. He walked into her room, but to his surprise, the hospital bed was empty. *She was gone.*

His stomach dropped at the thought of losing her again. He wasn't about to let that happen. Not this time. All those years ago, he was trying to keep the peace with his family. He never expected to lose Grace in the process. All he wanted to do was remember what really happened. If for no other reason than to never make the same mistake again.

"I wish I just could remember," he said as he looked out the window. He noticed the Amaryllis flowers in the same place he had left them on the windowsill. They were withered after all this time.

"Remember what?" Nurse Julie's voice startled Erick. He turned around and could not believe his eyes. He had to blink several times because Erick thought he was in a dream.

"What?" Erick whirled around and stammered. His mouth gaped open at the woman in the wheelchair whose jewel green eyes sparkled. A woman who had stolen the heart of his younger self. A woman with hair the color of a sunset on a late August night.

Thirty-three

Grace squinted, "Erick?" She was confident it was him.

"You remember me?" Erick asked.

"I *do* remember you!" she spat the words, her face frowning. Grace looked away from Erick.

Concerned, Erick stammered, "I can explain . . ." he trailed off.

Grace seemed to surprise herself with the outburst. Quieter, she spoke again. "Yes, I remember you. You're the one who brought my dad the other day!" Her eyes blazed as she turned to him. " I know what you are up to and why you are here. There is nothing you can do. There is nothing anyone can do. I'm going home soon."

"Okay, Grace, I'm going to get you into this bed now." Julie tried to console Grace. She noticed Erick was watching her as Julie helped her return to the bed. Grace wore leggings and an oversized t-shirt that read "Saint Mary's Nurses Fun Run." Grace pulled the covers up to her crimson cheeks.

"You can do it, Grace. You just have to give yourself more time." She touched her arm and then turned to leave. "Your parents should be here shortly."

"That's great news." Erick moved towards the bed. "So, Grace, your hair . . . it looks amazing!"

"It is lovely!" Julie gushed, pleased with her part in the transformation of Grace.

Erick forgot how beautiful she was. Even now, with her hair like it was all those years ago, he was stunned. Sherri had texted him that Grace was getting discharged to go home. The last thing he wanted was for Brook, and especially Finn, to run into Grace. Erick rubbed his neck nervously.

The timing was uncanny. Grace would be leaving around the same time Finn and Brook would be arriving to see Declan. He had to make sure no one knew about Grace. Erick's plan would never get off the ground if that happened.

"I won't keep you. I just wanted to stop by and let you know I'm on your recovery team. I will be your physical therapist once you get settled at home. I know therapy wasn't your favorite."

"You have your work cut out for you," Grace sighed. "No one here thinks I will be able to walk again."

"What do you think, Grace?" Erick leaned in closer and caught Julie's eye.

"Me?" Grace shrugged. "I'm not a doctor."

"Do you *believe* you can walk again?" Erick rephrased the question.

"Honestly, I just don't know." Grace looked down.

Erick gently touched her arm as she looked back up at him. "It's going to be okay, Grace. I can believe for the both of us." Erick was confident. "I will check in with you after you've had a few days to settle in at home."

Grace nodded, and Erick left the room. He headed to see his father with one thing weighing on his mind. It was going to be a miracle, keeping this secret and the fact that Grace was was just one floor away.

Thirty-four

Grace reached the point where she could go home. She officially signed the discharge paperwork, and she sat in her new high-tech wheelchair. Faith held the orange backpack in one hand and a sunflower bouquet in the other. Robin held a thick folder and a bag with Grace's jacket and sneakers she had worn the night of her fall. Nurse Julie was there pushing Grace around in the wheelchair.

Earlier, Julie had surprised Grace with tan leggings and a black sweater for the ride home and everything else she thought Grace needed for her departure from the hospital. Julie helped her shower and dress. Grace's hair was shiny like a new copper penny.

Grace looked around the room. This place was the only home she knew. Now it was time to get out of there once and for all. Grace looked at Julie, who had brought in her ukulele and played "Over the Rainbow" until her parents arrived. She was very grateful for Julie and would never forget their time together.

As Grace's parents entered the room, Julie stopped playing the tune and hugged Grace. "I will never forget you," Grace whispered in Julie's ear.

"Call me anytime, Sunshine. Plus, I'm part of your

recovery team now, and I'll come to visit you as often as I can. You can't get rid of me!"

Grace's parents wheeled her to the elevator and out the enormous main central doors to their van. Taking one last glance at the hospital building, Grace realized she was finally leaving. Instead of joy, however, Grace felt sadness. Grace was leaving the only home she had ever known. The only home she could remember.

Erick took a deep breath as he went to the front desk and asked if Declan Finn was out of surgery. As the receptionist gave him the room number for his father, Erick looked around the hospital and exhaled. Grace was not in sight. Just then, the automatic doors in the main lobby opened, and Daniel wheeled himself up to Erick.

"Brook called me about Dad. Sky dropped me off," Daniel said. "Do you know what is going on with Dad?"

"Nope, I have been kept in the dark as well, Daniel. I have the room number. Let's see what we can find out."

"Where is Grace?" Daniel whispered as they made their way to the stack of elevators.

"Leaving soon, hopefully." Erick looked around the hospital. Next, he pressed the elevator button, and the door opened. The brothers entered together. Erick pressed the button for the surgical floor, and he was glad it was not the same floor where Grace was now.

The doors re-opened to the waiting room in the surgery wing. Erick remembered being here when they brought Grace in. His eyes darted around, half expecting to see Grace appear. His heart thudded in his chest. Brook was standing there huddled next to Finn, coffee cups in their hands.

Brook jumped up and hugged Erick. He was confused because he couldn't believe she was still acting like they were together. "I knew you would come," Brook gushed.

"Finn," Erick said, ignoring Brook.

"I didn't know you were going to be here." Finn glared as he raked his hand through his hair. He wore a thick red scarf over his long black coat. Erick used to think looking at Finn was like looking in a mirror. They could not be more different today. Erick wore his hair relatively short and had a thick beard that he had kept since his college days. In contrast, Finn had longer hair slicked back and a clean-shaven face.

"Well, he is *our* father," Erick said, squinting at Finn.

"Hello, Finn," Daniel said finally. Finn hugged his younger brother just then. "Any news on, Dad?"

"Hey, Daniel!" Finn awkwardly released the embrace. "We were waiting to see how the surgery went."

"What exactly is wrong with Dad?" Erick persisted.

"Let's wait for the doctor to tell us," Finn insisted.

Brook sat down and peered into her paper coffee cup.

"Seriously, what is going on, and why have I not been kept in the loop?" So much for small talk, Erick got to the point.

"He was doing fine. There was nothing to tell. He has been getting severe spells of fatigue. They have been monitoring him but have yet to give us a direct diagnosis. Something wrong with the heart." Finn shifted his feet. Erick felt he was not telling everything he knew.

"So, when are you going back to New York?" Erick finally asked, relieved Grace's name did not come up.

"First thing tomorrow morning." Finn looked directly into Erick's face. "You and Brook should come by for Christmas Eve. FinnLondon is throwing a big party again this year."

"We aren't—" Erick began when Brook interrupted.

"*We* have plans, but maybe we will see you at the Finn Manor on Christmas Day. Will you be bringing Grace?" Brook narrowed her eyes at Erick. Brook wasn't the only one fishing for information.

Finn looked down at his feet, visibly uncomfortable with the question. "I'm not sure I can be there. I may go back to London for business. Grace and I—"

"Excuse me." A surgeon spoke to the four of them. "Your father's surgery went well. You can see him now, but only two at a time."

Daniel and Erick entered the room first. Declan was connected to several monitors and was sitting up, demanding the nurses bring him a drink. Nothing had changed.

"Hello, Dad." Erick was filled with concern.

"Erick? Is that you?" Declan's voice boomed.

Erick walked over to the bedside, "Dad, what is going on?"

Declan looked from Erick to Daniel. "Are Finn and Brook here?"

"Yes, but the doctor said only two at a time."

"Send them in!" Declan never followed the rules.

Brook and Finn entered the room. "Hello, Declan," Brook spoke from the doorway.

"Brook, tell your father we both are beating the odds. Nothing can keep us old geezers down for too long! I'm going to live!" He chuckled.

"I'll tell him. It is probably all the whiskey keeping you both preserved!" Brook surmised. "He should be back in town for the holidays."

"We have a bet who will live the longest. Doc says I can go home in a few days." Declan turned to Erick, "So, Erick, are you ready to come back to the publishing business?"

"Well, the whole gang's here!" The doctor entered just in time and eyed everyone in the room. "The surgery went well, but we are going to keep Declan here while we wait for the tests to come back. The tumor, we suspect, is benign. The location is a concern, and we have to monitor the atrium. There is a possibility the heart will fail. It is unlikely we can get you on a heart transplant registry considering your history. Your liver isn't functioning as well as it should, either. We should know more in a few days." The doctor nodded and left the room without waiting for questions.

Erick finally broke the silence. "Well, it was good to see all of you!" Erick finally broke the silence. "I'm sure Finn and Brook need to talk business with Dad. I have to see a patient tonight, so I can't stay long." Erick averted his gaze from Brook. "Daniel, do you need a ride?"

"Sure," Daniel said.

"Finn, it was good to see you." Erick wished it were true. "Dad, I hope you get better soon. I will check on you tomorrow if I can. You do have my number. Brook, thanks for the phone call," Erick said and left the room. Daniel said his goodbyes and followed Erick out. Once in his Jeep, Erick looked at his watch and then at Daniel. "Well, that was crazy!" He said after placing the wheelchair in the trunk.

"I texted Sky that you are giving me a ride." Daniel narrowed his eyebrows toward Erick. "What patient are *you* going to see?"

"Don't worry. I'll drop you off first!" Erick had a grin on his face at Daniel as he dialed Robin Evans.

PART 3

Thirty-five

Grace fought the tears back. Getting into the car was humiliating. She felt lost as the door latched automatically, and she leaned her head on the glass and gazed out the window as they drove home. The now bare trees lined the roadway and looked jagged against a blue sky.

Grace sat in the van and noticed it was spotless and must have been new, just like the wheelchair. Grace suddenly felt guilty about putting her parents out like this. The drive was uneventful, and no one said a word.

Robin and Faith shared a look with one other, and she imagined them thinking the same thing she was. "*What will she do? What will she become? What does the future hold? It doesn't look good . . .*"

Grace knew she had been in the hospital for several weeks and maybe months. It all ran together in her broken mind.

Julie had warned her by saying, "You know the world will look different now. Enjoy the new world through fresh eyes. Let your parents have a chance to know the *real* you, and you know, *I* think you are extraordinary!"

Her words haunted Grace. *What did she mean by letting them get to know the real me?* She looked forward to Julie's visit once she got settled.

It was getting hot in the car, but Grace said nothing, not wanting to talk. The trees in Connecticut were turning brown, and most of the leaves had fallen. The roads were not familiar, nor were the houses and steep hills. Even the parks they drove past with beautiful mums planted in burgundy and yellow looked unfamiliar. Frustrated, Grace wanted to scream because it was like being in a foreign country.

The sun disappeared behind a cloud, with a slight glow peeking through as they turned on Amaryllis Lane. Robin suddenly announced, "Almost there, a few more minutes, and we will be home."

Large houses came into view in various colors tucked back from the street with sprawling lawns and long driveways. Tall, thick trees separated neighborhoods. Children bundled up in coats in their expansive yard threw a frisbee to an anxious German Shepherd who was jumping up and down. The van pulled up to a driveway just as the sun was setting. It cast a warm orange glow over the house.

Grace observed that the house was modest compared to others on the street. It was set high up on a hill and surrounded by trees. It was only one story with a long stone walkway leading up to a large oak wooden door. The beautiful wooden etched door was like something out of a storybook. All at once, she wanted to remember everything that happened beyond the door.

Her dad parked the car, and he and Faith got out. The van door clicked and opened automatically. Robin got the wheelchair out and came over to assist Grace into the wheelchair. As he leaned in towards her, his beard touched Grace's face. Grace breathed in the scent, and her nerves calmed as he put his arms around her. Her father's touch was gentle and felt somehow familiar. She closed her eyes, and suddenly she was five years old.

Grace wore a bike helmet and lay on the driveway. The pink two-wheeler was on its side, white ribbons on the handlebars were splayed on the pavement. Grace had scraped her knee, and tears streamed down her face.

"Daddy, Daddy!" She cried. He hurried over to her and held her tight.

"Dad?" Grace finally spoke and opened her eyes.

Robin gently put her in the wheelchair and released his embrace.

"I remember," Grace whispered. Tears pooled in his eyes, and he hugged her again, leaning down to the chair.

Faith was now carrying the bags to the door, unaware of the exchange

He pulled back and said, "What do you remember?"

"I remember you teaching me to ride my bike." Then another memory flashed into Grace's mind as she gazed down the long road across from her house. She remembered looking at the end of a road as a bus came for her. "And meeting me at the bus stop when I was little." Grace trailed off and looked down the road once more. Faith came over to them and smiled at Robin. "Mom! I remember you as well! I remember growing up here!" Faith hugged her, and each had tears in their eyes.

Grace put her hands on the wheels and pushed herself a bit. Robin came behind and helped her roll up the steep sidewalk to the door.

"Well, this is new!" Grace sighed as they rode up the ramp built over the front wooden doorsteps.

"Your father made that door for our anniversary. Seven years ago." Faith smiled at her own memory.

"The door is quite beautiful! The doctor said my memory would return when I was ready, just not all at once. I just don't remember where I went to high school. Did I go to college? What work did I do? Why was I hiking on that trail?" Grace spoke so fast, and when the answers didn't come, the tears came again.

"All of those questions can wait," Robin said and opened the door to her room. "Let's get you settled first."

Grace didn't know much, but with these new memory pieces now in place, she knew she was finally home and for now, that was all she needed to know.

Erick's phone connected the call after it rang several times. "Mr. Evans? It's Dr. Erick."

"Please, call me Robin."

"Robin, how are you and Faith holding up?"

"Well, Faith and I are excited to have our daughter home. We never got to thank you for everything," he said getting choked up.

"Of course, anyone would have done the same! Listen, I need to talk to you. Can we meet the day after tomorrow? We should talk about Grace's treatment." Erick felt a sense of relief fill him as he waited for a response.

"Of course! Do you remember where the house is?" Robin did not hesitate.

"Yes, you still live in the same house after all these years, huh?" Erick smiled. He knew that house well. His childhood home was directly behind the Evans' house, separated by extensive woodlands and opulence.

"Yes, I have done some improvements recently to help Grace, but this house holds a lot of memories. Grace has already gotten some of them back. Just a few from when she was very a child." His voice choked again.

"That's great news! I will be by in a few days." Erick hung up the phone and drove Daniel home.

Thirty-six

Grace struggled to remember bits and pieces of her childhood and family life the next day. She was also aware that she was meeting Dr. Hopkins today.

Faith and Robin opened the door and stood next to Dr. Hopkins, whose dark blonde hair was pulled back into a clip. The doctor wore a casual light-blue sweater. Grace wheeled herself into the foyer.

"Hello, again," Grace said hesitantly.

"Hi, Grace! So nice to see you again. Sorry, I'm late. Your place was a little hard to find back here. The front yard and lane really capture the beauty of New England."

Dr. Hopkins walked over to the white couch, and she sat on the corner as she said, "Do you mind if we get started?" She nodded at Grace's parents, and they disappeared to another part of the house.

Dr. Hopkins crossed her legs in her black straight-leg pants. She started the session by asking Grace about what she remembered so far. Grace could only recount her childhood up to about age twelve, a neighborhood boy and her parents.

"So, you can only remember the earlier years?" She clicked her pen a few times.

"I remember moving here as a small child. I remember both of my parents. School is a little hazy. It's as if I have pieces, but they are scattered. I can't remember what I did in high school, where I went to college, or what jobs I had. I don't remember driving, or friends or anything important about that time." Grace exhaled some of the frustration.

"Grace, is it possible that your mind isn't ready to remember that? Perhaps something traumatic happened, and your body is trying to protect itself while it heals." She added quickly, yet unconvincingly, "You are moving around well in the chair compared to when we last spoke!"

"Really?" There was no reason to hold back as Grace's eyes burned with rage. "I would be doing better if I could remember my life. The life I had. The one where I could walk!" Grace screamed at the doctor. She knew it wasn't her fault, but Grace was so sick of everyone saying she was doing *great*.

"I'm sorry," Grace whispered as her parents rushed into the room. Grace wheeled away as they were making amends on her behalf. Once the door was closed, Grace could hear their voices but didn't hear the words. Grace took all the rage and used it to lift herself into the bed. She ignored all the knocks and pleadings to eat dinner. Grace closed her eyes and realized there was only one answer that could fix her. No therapist, no doctor, no spiritual guru, not even her parents could save her now. Only one person could save her. That person had the power of a miracle to change everything. This person was her only hope. Unfortunately, that person had been locked away deep inside. That person was *Grace*.

Erick got into the Jeep the following day with Jace and drove to HigherGround. Daniel was there to greet him.

"Wow, I can't believe you are late today!" Daniel enjoyed joking around.

"Daniel, you know I *am* the boss. Besides, I have the best reason," Erick said, laughing. "Hello, Joyce." She handed him a cup of tea. "Joyce, do you have time to meet up? I need to talk to you both about my new VIP client." Erick looked over at Daniel. "You need to meet with us as well."

"Let's meet over lunch," Joyce said. "I need you to sign these forms, and you have an evaluation at 2 pm."

Erick signed the papers and then headed back to his office, followed by Daniel.

"So, I need your help with something," Daniel spoke to Erick as they walked. "Sky wants me to go to her sister's wedding on Saturday. Do you have a tux I can borrow?"

Erick placed his jacket on the coat tree. He loved seeing Daniel this happy. "Dude, *who are you?* I have never seen you this happy!"

"She might just be the one!" Still beaming, Daniel wheeled around the desk. "So about the tux, we are about the same size."

"Of course, Daniel! You can have whatever you need. You could just buy one, you know." Erick reminded him.

"I'm saving my money, but if I ever did get married." Daniel's eyes sparkled with possibility. "Would you be my best man?"

"Of course!" Erick jumped up in his seat just as Joyce popped her head into this office.

"Lunch is here, boys!" Joyce interrupted. They brought their sandwiches outside on the patio, where the weather was sunny and cool. Luna and Jace chased each other down the ramp to the dock by the lake, barking in delight.

"So, I have some news." Erick put his sandwich down on the wax paper. "I have a new client."

Daniel took a bite of his turkey sandwich and chewed, knowing what Erick was about to say. "Here we go!" he said with his mouth full.

Erick continued ignoring his brother, "Joyce, there was a girl I met in the sixth grade."

"What Erick is leaving out is that she was the love of his life!" Daniel teased.

"That sounds complicated." Joyce took a bite of her salad.

"It is. Remember I was telling you about the woman that fell off a cliff on Freedom Trails?" Erick took a sip of his water. "The doctors say she can never walk again because of spinal and brain trauma. Her surgeries went well, but her brain forgot how to walk."

"I see where this is going, and I believe there is a conflict of interest here. You could lose your license. You don't actually think you could be Grace's therapist, do you?" Concern filled Joyce's voice. "This is not one of your better ideas." She shook her head.

"I know." Erick took a bite of his sandwich and swallowed. "Joyce, it is risky, but honestly, I have never felt more moved to do anything in my life. Her parents believe that I can help her remember who she was. *They* need me. *She* needs me."

"Won't she recognize you?" Joyce continued the questioning.

"She has amnesia, and it's been over a decade since we have spoken. I'm not the same person as I was back then." Erick looked up from his sandwich. "This is my *calling*, Joyce. You know that better than anyone. God put Grace in my path again. I have to see it through."

"It is quite risky. It could lead to more trouble." Joyce stabbed a grape tomato with her fork.

"I know, and I will be careful. The only way this will work is if we keep it professional and we keep our past relationship a secret," Erick said sincerely. "One day, I will tell her, and she will remember, but I will have her walking by then."

"The end doesn't justify the means. Lying is never the right choice, especially for you! Have you thought about how she will feel when she does find out?"

Erick cringed at the thought as he remembered how she looked at him at the party all those years ago. At the time, he thought she would be better without him. "She needs me now, and I owe her a chance at a better life. I feel that my entire life's work has prepared me for this. I *owe* her this much. I'm willing to give her everything I have even if it means I lose everything."

"I won't say anything," Daniel replied, supporting his brother. "When will you start training her?"

"I'm going on record saying this is a bad idea, but all these years working with you, Erick, I trust you know what you are doing. I won't blow your cover." Joyce picked up her salad. "I'm going back inside, and I have a lot of paperwork to do. Be careful. I just want to see you happy. You are like a son to me." Joyce stood up and collected the trash from the table. "You have a 2 o'clock, Erick. Oh, and Brook called." Then she left.

"Really, now you have two girls after you?" Daniel punched his brother's arm.

"Daniel! Brook is Brook, and I will deal with her later. I'm going to start working on the plan."

"The plan to win Grace back!" Daniel laughed. "Don't forget tomorrow is a day off. Thanksgiving at my house."

Erick loved being with his brother. Now that the nightmares were gone, he was getting sleep, and he felt like he could do anything. The wheels were turning in his head, and he knew no matter what happened, one thing was certain. There was no turning back now.

Thirty-seven

Grace started feeling better and joined her parents at the dining room table for Thanksgiving dinner. Robin had removed a chair to accommodate her wheelchair. "Is your sister coming?"

Robin froze and looked at Faith. "You remember Aunt Raven?"

"You mentioned her the other day to Mom. I forget what it was that made me want to ask about her." Grace squeezed her eyes shut, trying to remember.

Faith brought in the knife for Robin to cut the turkey and handed it to him. "Dear, it is just us this year. Your aunt passed away just before your accident. I'm sorry."

"Oh. Do I have any other family? Like grandparents or siblings?" Grace asked as Robin sliced the turkey and placed a piece on her plate.

"Your grandfather moved to Wales some years back. I was hoping to take a trip with you after you graduated high school." Robin sighed but quickly added, "Sorry, Grace, your grandma died when your aunt and I were born."

"I didn't mean to upset you," Grace said, then slowly chewed her food and stared at her plate.

"It's normal. You are trying to remember what you can," Robin said, trying to encourage Grace.

"It is so nice having us all together, don't you think?" Faith asked everyone at the table.

Grace remembered being a young girl having dinner at the house as she placed the potatoes in her mouth. She also remembered having mashed potatoes at the hospital. Grace was wondering how Julie was doing. She missed her friend.

"When does my physical therapy start?" Grace suddenly asked.

"We could go tomorrow if you feel up to it," Robin said as he cut a piece of turkey.

"I have to work," Faith said to no one in particular.

"You're scheduled for tomorrow. I just need to confirm with Dr. Erick." Robin took a sip of his apple cider. "Does that sound good?"

"That sounds good," Grace said and looked at Faith. "I remember making gingerbread cookies with you. Would you want to do that again?"

Faith paused for a moment. "I will try to make time, and that does sound like fun. It's been ages!" Faith said thoughtfully. "I have a box in the attic that we saved for you from your high school days. I can get that down for you when I get the Christmas decorations in a few weeks."

"That sounds great."

Grace knew it was going to be a grieving process. She was ready to stop being angry and start physical therapy with Dr. Erick tomorrow. Grace was happy that some memories were coming back slowly. Most of all, she was delighted she could remember her family.

Erick could not believe he stayed up the entire night researching Grace's injury and other cases of amnesia. Instead of going back to bed, he got up from the desk and made himself some tea. Jace wagged his tail and gave Erick a big lick in the face. "You silly dog! Let me guess. You are looking to go out."

Jace ran towards the door as Erick left the warmth of the bed and opened the front door. A rush of cold air blew across Erick's face. He shut the door, and he pulled on a long-sleeved shirt, running pants, and his trail runners. Before he went outside, he threw on his North Face fleece. Erick knew the best place to sort out his thoughts.

The sun was shining, but the cold wind swayed the snow-covered trees back and forth. As Erick's feet hit the trail, he began thinking about how complex the brain is. To help Grace, he would have to get the brain communicating to the legs again. He thought about it like a bridge in the brain being out. The broken bridge was not allowing the messages from the brain to reach the legs properly. He had to find a way to mend that bridge. Then he would get the nerves and the muscles to receive the messages. He also needed to challenge the leg muscles to get them to respond.

He looked at things scientifically, but he knew miracles defied science. Jace bounded up to him on the path and then ran past him. "God, if there is any chance I can help her, please give me the knowledge. Show me the way."

Erick ran all the way up to the summit and back again. He had a plan, and it had to work. Erick showered, put on some dark jeans, and pulled on a tan long-sleeved sweater.

"Jace!" Erick called his companion, who came running into the room. "Are you excited to see Luna, Sky, and Daniel?"

Jace responded as he rubbed his head against Erick's hand. Erick grabbed both of his ears and stroked the soft fur around them.

Erick got his coat and returned to the kitchen to retrieve mashed potatoes. Erick removed the covered dish that he made the night before. It was his mother's recipe. His phone buzzed as he locked the door to the cabin. Jace jumped into the Jeep. Then Erick jumped in. A text message flashed on the screen.

> *You have to come over. It's Thanksgiving, babe!*

Of course, it was Brook. He stared at the phone as he started the engine. What is her problem? He decided to text her back.

> *How is my father?*

> *My father and I are sitting with him at Finn Manor right now. He is recovering nicely and gaining his strength back. Declan asked me to invite you and Daniel over for dinner.*

> *That is good news. Thanks for the invite, but Daniel and I have plans. Please let my dad know I will visit soon.*

Erick hoped she would get the message.

> *Ok, I will let him know, but we really should be together.*

He turned the phone off and placed it back in his jacket. He was looking forward to spending Thanksgiving with his brother and Sky. They were his *real* family. It didn't matter what Brook thought, but he knew he couldn't avoid her forever. She would inevitably be a problem. For now, he had to focus. He had one chance to save the only girl he ever really loved. Brook had ruined everything all those years ago, but Erick would do everything he could not to let that happen again.

Thirty-eight

Grace felt grateful the next day to be outside again as she looked out the van window. They were driving out to the lane that led to the main road.

"The van is pretty nice, Dad," Grace stated. "I miss the old truck, though."

"You remember that old thing?" Robin seemed to be enjoying the banter between them. "I sold the old work truck when I found out you were in the hospital. I hoped you would come home and besides, this van fits your chair really well. It's not a bad upgrade!"

Grace looked out the window and thought about getting a job one day and repaying him. The thought was gone as soon as she remembered no one would hire her in a wheelchair. Grace thought about what would happen if the doctors were right about her never walking again. Would she ever be capable of working a job? She didn't want to burden her dad, but she was unsure how the rest of her life would unfold. It felt good to remember growing up in this neighborhood. She loved reliving her memories with her dad and how good it felt to be truly loved by someone. Grace felt more like herself every day. She couldn't wait to go through her box from her high school days and remember more. Dr. Hopkins, however, had warned not to press too much at once. Grace was ready for more.

Robin pulled into the parking lot, and Grace saw a tall brick building with rows of windows. It looked to be about four floors. Grace wondered what it would be like inside. Robin parked and went to get the wheelchair. Grace was getting more defined arms and stronger each day. As getting in and out of the wheelchair became routine, she wondered if there would ever be a time when she would no longer need it. Hope filled her as she wheeled herself to the entrance and noticed the giant sign on the door. "HigherGround, where YOU walk on water." She smirked as she read it out loud.

"Ready, Grace?" Her dad asked as the automatic doors opened to the building. They made their way to the large doors on the left. Another Logo of a mountain and HG was on the summit. There were waves below the mountain image. Robin pushed the button, and the doors slid open. Plants and potted trees were around the front desk where a woman met them in a pale blue HigherGround fleece.

"Welcome to HigherGround. You must be Grace." A woman greeted her wearing a name tag that read *Joyce, Office Manager.*

Grace wheeled to the lower table, "Yes, I'm Grace Evans." She spoke the words, but they felt unfamiliar.

"Here are the forms that need to be filled out by you and your father. This one is for the insurance." Joyce looked at both of them and handed them each a clipboard and a pen. Once they completed the paperwork, the second set of doors opened, and a young man in a wheelchair came out. Suddenly a large golden retriever burst through the door and licked her hands. Grace began to laugh.

"Daniel, this is Grace." Joyce introduced them. "By the way, do you know when Sky is coming in?"

"She is coming in soon. This girl is Luna!" Daniel introduced his dog. "Luna! come up!" Daniel commanded his dog. Luna jumped on his lap. "Follow me, Grace."

As the doors opened again, Grace took a deep breath. She watched Daniel as he seemed very proficient with his wheelchair. Robin stood behind Grace, and they both followed Daniel as he entered the waiting area. The room was large with wood flooring, and rows of chairs lined the back wall. A teenage boy sat on a chair next to his mom. He had brown hair with freckles splattered across his cheeks and a boot on his foot. Across from them, Grace saw a grey-haired woman with a walker trying to take her seat with incredible difficulty. Grace continued to wheel herself between them and eventually came to a small table with a sign-in sheet.

"Sign here, Miss Evans; this is consent for treatment." Daniel showed her the clipboard. "Dr. Erick will be with you shortly," Daniel said. "We are happy you are here!" His smile was big and full, showing his straight white teeth.

Grace returned a partial smile, narrowing her eyes at him, surprised by his enthusiasm. Perhaps he was covering the fact he had a dog in a medical office.

A woman came out a side door. "David?" She wore purple scrubs with a long-sleeved pink shirt underneath. The boy with the boot hobbled over towards Grace, who moved to allow him to pass. He followed the nurse through a pair of French doors with opaque windows. The door shut behind them.

Robin took a seat near Grace. A large fish tank spanned the opposite wall. Orange and white Clownfish and indigo angelfish swam around happily. *They are the lucky ones,* Grace thought. Robin reached for her hand, "Just give it a chance, Grace. Promise me you will?"

"Okay. I will try." Grace wanted to make him proud, but she wasn't sure what to expect. She hoped her new therapist would not be like the last ones she had at the hospital.

The door opened, and a man with a dark blue and grey collared shirt and khakis came out carrying a tablet in one hand. Grace looked up, along with the rest of the patients waiting in the room. His brown hair parted to the side. He looked at Grace with the most striking blue eyes she had ever seen.

"Miss Evans?" he didn't take his eyes off hers.

No sound came from her throat. They both seemed to be locked in a trance.

"Yes, this is she!" Robin interrupted the staring contest. "Would you like me to go with you?" He nodded to her to go on ahead.

Grace felt unsure if she wanted to go by herself. "I want you with me just this one time," she said, not taking her eyes off the doctor. "Have we met?"

Erick froze, and Robin turned pale.

"No, seriously. I remember you!" Grace pleaded her case. "I may have amnesia, but I would never forget you, Erick!"

"How . . . ?" Erick stammered, looking at Robin, who just stood there.

"You're the doctor that came to the hospital. You're the one who found my dad!" She cut them off. "Are you my trainer?"

Both men relaxed, and the color returned to their faces. "Yes, you are correct. I am your physical therapist. Come, I will show you around."

Robin exhaled and followed Erick and Grace down a corridor into a large office.

"Can I get either of you water before we begin?" Erick stood by his desk, and Robin took one of the blue seats facing the desk.

"No, thank you," Robin answered.

"How are you feeling today, Grace?" Erick leaned back on the edge of his desk, holding her folder and flipping through the pages.

"I guess I feel okay. I have some pain every day. I can live with some pain, but I really want to get out of this wheelchair!" She twisted her hair mindlessly around her finger. "If it's even possible. I just don't want to waste your time. You should know the doctors all said . . ."

"Do you believe in miracles?" Erick interrupted her. He had to take control of the situation before Grace spiraled. When she was in high school, Erick remembered she overthought everything.

"Um," Grace replied, not knowing how to answer the question. Instead, she went with what she knew. "I might believe in miracles, but I don't remember." She rolled her eyes, frustrated with being asked this question.

"No worries, Grace. I got you," Erick said softly. "*I believe* with hard work, we can get you out of that chair once and for all!"

"That is the goal!" Robin finally spoke.

"Maybe we can help you remember some other things too?" Erick looked directly at Robin. They both knew this entire ruse was insane. What they were trying to pull off would be a miracle. But, Erick was confident he could get her to walk again. The feeling grew as he turned and looked straight into Grace's green eyes. Erick knew deep in his heart that there was no place on earth he needed to be than right here, right now, with *her*. His second chance was here, and he was not going to waste one more second.

"I hope you are ready because this is your *second chance*, Grace. I will be with you every step of the way. Are you in for an adventure of a lifetime?"

Thirty-nine

Grace was skeptical at first when she arrived at HigherGround. She didn't actually believe that physical therapy would work. Grace owed it to her dad to try, though, because he bought the new van and modified the house to be more accessible.

Dr. Erick looked the same as when she saw him in the hospital, but he seemed more relaxed here without his white coat. Grace thought it was strange he introduced himself as though they had never met. She didn't have time to analyze his peculiar behavior. *Focus!* All she could think about were those striking blue eyes. *I wonder if his beard felt soft or scratchy.* She shook the thought away, and she felt her stomach flutter. *Get a grip, Grace,* she said to herself.

Her gaze fell on the large mahogany desk that was in the middle of the room. Along the right side was a padded table, and next to that, a small computer laptop lay open on a rolling table.

A prestigious award for innovative physical therapy was engraved and placed on the side of the desk. Behind the leather chair on display was a photo of a beautiful woman with tawny-coloured hair and blue eyes. On the far wall were multiple certificates bearing the name *Erick Finn*. A poster hung above the padded table read, *"It is not the mountain we conquer, but ourselves."* Erick sat on the edge of the desk.

Grace looked at her dad once again and wondered if Erick was selling them a line of crap. *How could he promise she'd walk again?* She also realized she had nothing to lose. Grace wasn't getting any better sitting at home, wishing she had legs that worked. Besides, she could feel his passion for wanting to help her. It was like a fire on a cold night, and it made her want to be near him. She felt like her own fire had gone out, and she wanted to feel whole again.

She felt strangely comfortable around him as he squatted in front of her and asked his final question, "Are you in?"

Erick was waiting for her response, and he felt the electric air around them.

"Yes," Grace's whispered, her eyes sparkling.

Erick had always imagined asking Grace a life-changing question. *Get it together. You are not proposing! Dude, focus and keep it professional!* Erick laughed at himself.

"Before I do an evaluation, let me show you around this awesome place we have here. I call it 'The Sanctuary' instead of rehab because I want you to feel like you are on a healing journey. We believe healing is also spiritual like you are on sacred ground."

Erick beamed as he led Robin and Grace to the main studio with the large automatic glass doors. Windows surrounded the room, and the sun shone through the glass, causing the machines to gleam. The trees surrounding the property made it look like a spa retreat more than a medical facility. Erick explained to Grace the types of clients they had over the years. Daniel was getting an older man an ice wrap for his shoulder in one corner of the studio. In the back, a woman in her twenties was working out on a stationary bicycle. Erick pointed to the cardio equipment and the weights. "We will do the evaluation, and I will put you on a program that works for you. We will spend some of our days here and over there." He directed Grace to the parallel bars and the mat. A man with a steel prosthetic working on balance with a therapist.

"We have the highest success rate in the country," he said to Grace. "All of our therapists are top-notch, but I will be working exclusively with you. Do you have any questions at this point?"

"Doctor Erick?" a petite blonde came up to them. She wore a light blue collared shirt and khakis, but she had a pink fleece jacket over her shirt. "Joyce said you needed me?"

"Yes, Sky, this is our new patient, Grace, and her father, Robin," Erick said, introducing them. "Mr. Evans, it is time for Grace's evaluation. Do you want to join us, or would you be more comfortable in the waiting room? Our session should take about forty-five minutes, and I have asked Sky to be there with us."

"I have some phone calls to make. Will you be okay if I step outside, Grace?" Robin had his hands on his hips.

"I will be fine, Dad," Grace assured him.

"Sky, do you mind showing Mr. Evans the way to the waiting room and then meeting me in my office?" He asked Robin, "After the session, I will bring Grace out, and we can go over any questions you have."

"Right this way, Mr. Evans." Sky showed Robin to the waiting room.

Erick moved behind Grace. "Would you like a ride back to the office?"

"Sure," Grace said as she placed her hands on her lap.

Back in the office now, Erick was careful to leave the door open. Sky bounced in and looked at Grace.

"Hey, girl!" Sky closed the door behind her. Erick hoped Daniel had filled Sky in on the plan to keep his true identity a secret. "I'm just creating your chart, Miss Evans." Sky clicked away at the computer at the stand-up desk. "Dr. Erick will evaluate while I document the results. I'm also a therapist. I may ask you follow-up questions as well."

As much as Erick wanted to be alone with Grace, he was grateful Sky was there to keep things professional. Erick put the brake on the wheelchair. "I can help you get to the table. I will need to place my hands on your waist. Is that okay?" Grace nodded, and Erick scooped her up. She was so much lighter than he had remembered. He became a little dizzy as he lowered her down to the table. His face inches from hers. He ignored Sky, who coughed a warning. *Daniel told her the plan. Good!*

"I'm going to move you to your side. Please let me know if anything hurts," Erick said to Grace.

The session ended way too soon. Erick had Grace in his arms again and helped her back into the chair. Sky gave her some water and left to get Mr. Evans. Erick was relieved that the evaluation was over but loved having Grace so near. He was aware they were alone now.

Mr. Evans suddenly entered the room and went over to Grace. "You okay, Grace?"

"Yes, Dad." Grace looked tired now. "I *can* do this." She was confident.

"Doc, I will send you some notes later today," Sky returned. "It was a pleasure to meet you both!" She waved and left the room.

"Great!" Erick shook Robin's hand. "I won't let you down, sir."

Robin smiled, but his eyes said, *If you hurt her son, I will break you!*

"Mr. Evans, she has all the muscle response needed.

Now we just need to get them to reconnect with the brain and remember what to do! I will come by tomorrow and go over the details of the treatment plan. Let's do this!" Erick high-fived Grace and then watched as Mr. Evans and Grace headed out the door. He was determined to make Grace walk again, even if it was the last thing he did on earth.

Forty

Grace wondered why her dad had trusted Dr. Erick so quickly. "Dad?" Grace looked at her father. "What do *you* think of Dr. Erick?"

"He seems okay." Robin kept his eyes on the road.

"You seem oddly comfortable with him." Grace looked out the window.

"Do *you* feel comfortable with him?" Robin glanced in Grace's direction.

"He seems um, enthusiastic!"

"He was, wasn't he?" Robin laughed.

"He said I would walk again soon, and he also said, 'With God, all things are possible!' What do you believe?" Grace looked at Robin just then.

"My sister was the spiritual one in the family. I haven't really thought about God in quite some time, Grace. I'm just glad you are home safe."

Grace looked out the window and realized that her dad only wanted the best for her. She didn't want to admit the truth. The truth was that this was her last resort, after all.

As they pulled into the driveway, her thoughts went back to the evaluation with Dr. Erick. He had his hand on hers, and she wondered if he had felt the electricity too?

"*I can help your body and your mind remember what is*

important. Our training will focus on healing your mind as well as the body connections." Erick's voice echoed in her mind.

Erick was going to train her to walk again. He also promised to be with her every step of the way. Grace was sure of one thing as they drove to her home. She could not wait to get started.

Erick went for a run with Jace after work. The sun was setting as he ran back down the mountain. Doubts started to creep in. Could he really fulfill his promise to Grace? She was bound to remember who he was eventually. When she did find out, he could only imagine the disaster that would be. He had to make sure that didn't happen. At least not before he could help her walk again. He wasn't a hundred percent sure if he could help her walk again, but in theory, it could work. As with all his patients, the odds were against him, but he was sure God was involved each time they all could walk. If they believed they could, he'd witnessed the miracles unfold one after another. Grace's treatment was going to be no different. Physical therapy was more than just exercise. Erick knew the mind played a huge role in recovery. If Grace could *believe* she would walk again, she surely would. It was his job to help her genuinely believe. If nothing else in his life had taught him this, faith always won in the end. He would help her remember their past one day. At least remember the good things and show her the man he had become.

Jace and Erick stepped off the trail and entered the small cabin as the sun disappeared behind the horizon. The wind had taken the last leaves, and the tree branches swayed in the evening air. Once inside, Erick opened his drawer and lifted the framed photo, and looked at the picture of the beautiful young girl in it. His heart swelled for the chance to make things right again. As he put the picture back and remembered Daniel had unlocked the phone. In all the excitement, Erick had forgotten he still had the phone. Curiosity beckoned him, and he pressed the power button. Several notifications came up as the phone came to life, indicating several missed calls and a text message. He tapped on the notification, and his heart sank. It was from Finn.

> *How dare you ghost me! I gave you everything. We are done, and you are fired! If you show up, security will be called, and you will be removed. I warned you, Grace!*

Next, Erick noticed over ten missed calls from FinnLondon, and finally, his eyes landed on the voicemail box. He tapped the icon, and the messages started playing.

> *"Hey, Grace, it's Lauren. I'm calling to give you a heads up. Since you left, they cleared your office, and now Nic oversees the editing department. Finn was throwing things and yelling at everyone. His dad took a turn for the worse and is now back in the hospital. Finn has been out of town. I just thought you should know. You didn't hear it from me. I hope you got far, far away from here. Miss you. Call me if you need anything." Then click. Message saved—next unheard message.*
>
> *"Grace, I hope you are happy! Damn it! You destroyed everything. This is all your fault. I got rid of all your stuff from the loft and your office. You should have seen that book of yours. I toasted to you being out of my life as I threw it in the fireplace, and it went up in flames just as our relationship did. You're dead to me, Grace. You were*

> never a writer, and you never will be. I felt pity for you in high school, and I never loved you. It was just revenge on my brother Erick. Everyone was in on it, even Brook. The look on his face was worth it. I made sure of everything. Sure we had fun when we got to New York, but baby, it was over a long time ago. I warned you not to cross me. You were not special. No, I'm glad you are gone. I don't have to sneak around anymore. You thought you were the only one. Goodbye, Grace. You never belonged here. My dad was right about you all along, and I should have listened to him. You are nothing to me and good luck getting a job anywhere again in publishing. The message clicked off mid laughter.

The following message was also from Finn. It was dated the following evening.

> Would you please come back? We were good together. I'm sorry for . . . everything. I can be a better person. You make me a better person.

The message ended, and it sounded like sobbing. Erick wondered how Finn could be so all over the place with his moods. At first, Erick burned with fury. He wanted to throw the phone and smash it to pieces, but instead, he shut it off and put it back under the framed photo. Erick never thought that Finn would become such a terrible person. Finn may have ruined things all those years ago, but one thing was for sure, Erick would never let him near Grace again, even if he was his brother.

Forty-one

Grace was sleeping soundly but awoke when she heard a knock on her door. Her room was just off the foyer, and she could hear everything. The large wooden door creaked as it opened.

"Hello? Can I help you?" Faith asked.

"I am, Julie. Grace's nurse from the hospital."

Grace heard them talking and slowly got out of bed and into her wheelchair. Then she wheeled herself to the bedroom door and peeked out.

Julie stood there wearing a grey winter hat and a long cream-colored winter coat. A thick patchwork scarf was wrapped around her neck. She had a red and white rose bouquet and a leather book in her hand.

"Oh, yes, that's right. Julie, so good to see you!" Faith looked at her watch. "Grace is not awake yet. Do you want to come in and stay? She should be getting up soon to prepare for her therapy lesson."

"Oh, that's okay. I can't stay long. Do you mind if I leave these for Grace? The hospital said Grace left behind this journal, and I think she would want it. It seemed important to her."

Faith set her coffee and briefcase down on the table by

the door. Julie handed Faith the journal and the roses. "I will make sure Grace gets this."

"Thank you! I promise I will come back and visit soon. Merry Christmas," Julie said and left. Grace wanted to see her friend but hesitated while she observed the exchange. She could not shake the feeling that her parents were keeping something from her.

Grace peered through the door and saw Faith place the book in the table's small drawer next to the front door. Next, Grace could see her mom disappear with the flowers to the kitchen. *Why would her mom put the journal there? What was she up to?* When Faith returned to the foyer, she grabbed her briefcase, stainless steel coffee thermos, and left for work. As soon as Grace was sure Faith was gone, she wheeled herself over to the small table. Grace looked around to make sure her father was not around and then carefully opened the drawer. The leather book was the same journal she had started reading in the hospital. Grace put the journal in her lap and wheeled back to her room. She opened the journal to the first page. Grace flipped through the pages and remembered reading a few short diary entries while in the hospital. Grace's eyes landed on the next page, and she froze. Her name was there in black and white.

> *Grace, this is our story. I have to start at the beginning, but keep in mind that these are the stories told as their parents remember them. So this is what my father, your grandfather, told me.*
>
> *A few minutes after my brother, I was born on a hot summer's night in the village somewhere in Central Connecticut where my mother grew up. She was Native American. The tribe she belonged to was called the Sequin tribe, and it was part of a more prominent tribe known as 'The people at the bend in the river.' I have tried to*

find and connect with my people over the years, but most of my mother's tribe relocated to New York or blended in with other tribes.

I didn't get a chance to know my mother because she died in childbirth, but what I do know is that she taught me how to love fiercely. She gave me everything she had, including her own life, to bring my brother and me into this world. I was told I got my free spirit from her. My father raised us away from the tribe, assuming he did this because the tribe did not accept us. Years later, he confessed that he had fallen in love with an indigenous woman and got married against her family's wishes. They had planned to leave the reservation as soon as we were born. It was the early '70s, twenty years from Connecticut passing laws to preserve the land heritage. My mother's name was Alo, which means spiritual guide. My mother's parents were traditional. They forbade her to date outsiders, a custom they held onto long after many other tribes allowed it.

My father's heritage is Welsh. He told me his name Bran means 'Raven.' I lived with my father, and Robin, in a small two-bedroom apartment near Farmington. We eventually moved to Amaryllis Lane when Robin and I started school. The same house that you grew up in as well. My father built Robin's woodshop so he could stay close to home. He even had hand-carved a large cradle for the both of us when we were little.

He was always there for us. Ironically, my father never remarried.

My earliest memory is walking with my dad deep into the woods. We searched for the suitable timber needed for the current projects he was working on. We were careful to use only fallen trees to preserve the trees as much as possible. My dad taught me about poisonous plants and

> *how to tell the time by the sun's position versus using a watch. When Robin and I were older, we were allowed to explore on our own. We would rush home by sunset, and Dad would make us a wood fire pizza, a Welsh tradition. I was always reading books while Robin liked to use his hands to build things. Eventually, we had to get an education, and Robin did well at school. I wanted to be outside and not confined to a chair. I always got into trouble for staring out the window and dreaming about the wild white aster fields.*
>
> *I promised myself I would live in the woods when I was grown up, and my dad and Robin eventually built a house for me. One day, my uncle called urgently from Wales, and dad had to fly out and help with the farm.*
>
> *My dad did his best to raise us to be respectful to the earth and people. I don't think he was prepared for me when I discovered boys. I befriended several at school. I had two close girlfriends at the time. Davina's birthday was the day before mine, and she had shiny blonde hair and all the boys swooned over her. My other friend Tammy was pretty and funny. She became my friend first since we were the only two redheads in our class. I had the gift of words. Most boys chatted with me to find out if either Davina or Tammy were available. Both of whom were too shy to talk to boys. I liked my role, but I had my eye on one boy.*

Grace looked at her watch and panicked at how much time had passed. She decided to put the journal on her side table by her bed, determined to read it later. For now, she would need to get ready because Dr. Erick would be here any minute.

Half an hour later, another knock came at the door. Grace finished getting dressed to answer the door, knowing her dad was most likely working in the back shed. Robin had shown Grace the beautiful cradle he was making the other day. He had hand-carved it out of walnut for one of his clients that had just become a grandfather. Robin entered the house from the back door and came up behind her. Grace was already at the door, dressed in her workout clothes. The front door opened, and Erick was standing there on the other side of the door. A cold wind blew in, and he zipped his jacket tighter. Grace and Erick didn't say a word.

"Ahem, won't you come in, *Doctor* Erick?" Robin emphasized doctor.

"Mr. Evans." Erick reached for Robin's hand.

"Make yourself at home." He shook Erick's hand quickly and then looked away." I have work to do, but I will be in the shop out back if you need me. Help yourself to coffee or tea in the kitchen."

"We need to start in the bedroom." Erick blushed and turned to Mr. Evans. "Please join us? Then I can explain what we are doing."

"Of course." Mr. Evans looked as Grace led them both to the bedroom.

The three of them entered Grace's room, which was off the main entrance. Immediately, the photo collage caught Erick's eye when he saw pictures from high school pinned to a corkboard. He looked at Mr. Evans and then to Grace.

"I have reviewed the case. I won't waste time using medical jargon, but honestly, Grace has all the proper muscle responses. The surgery she had on her back should have completed connections between her brain and her extremities by all counts." Erick continued. "To start, we will work on building what connections and skills she already has. We'll keep building on her skills and use her legs more each day. I will need to see her as much as possible. Today she will be running me through her daily routine, and this will be the starting point. Each session, Grace will have homework to do as well," he said directly to Grace. "I want to see how you get in and out of your bed and to the other areas of the house. I will observe mostly today. Any questions?"

Robin and Grace shook their heads, and Grace got back into bed and then out of bed. Her arms shook, and her face was rosy.

"I don't want you to get into any bad habits," he chided gently. "I want you to use more of your core as you lift from here." Erick placed his hands gently near her hips and abdomen. "Great, now let's see you move about the house,"

"Doc, she is all yours. I trust you will take care of her," With that, Robin went out the back kitchen door.

Next, Grace spent the next twenty minutes showing Erick how she wheeled all around the house, and they ended up in the kitchen.

Grace opened the fridge and removed two water bottles. Then she handed Erick a water bottle, and they went into the living room. He sat on the chair next to the fireplace, writing notes. "This is great, Grace. Now I want you to get out of the chair and walk to me."

The air seemed to leave the room. "What?" Grace's confident smile vanished. "You're joking, right?" Her mouth hung open in disbelief.

"Nope, not joking," He put his pen down. "Your back has healed completely, and your muscles are just a little weak. I have looked at both your x-rays and your MRI. There is no reason you *can't* physically walk. You just need to remember *how* to walk." Then Erick asked, "Do you *believe* you can walk?"

Grace opened her mouth, but nothing came out. *Who do you think you are?* She wanted to ask. Anger started to rise from a place she had been ignoring. All this talk about believing was getting on her nerves.

"I thought . . . What the hell is your problem? I thought . . . Is *it not your job* to teach me how to?" Tears burned her eyes, and she wanted this session to end. Why would he make her do this now? She didn't want to fail on her first day.

Erick stood up. "Yes, I *will* teach you to walk again. But you aren't ready. Not *today*." He looked as uncomfortable as a raccoon in a trash can with a flashlight on him. "That's enough work for today, Grace." He walked to the front door.

What was his problem? Grace thought. *How dare he come here and give me hope and then just leave!* As Erick reached for the door, Grace followed behind him. He opened it and turned. "I will see you tomorrow, Grace. Your homework will be to truly *believe* you can walk. I want to help you, and I can help you, but you *have* to believe in yourself." Erick knelt in front of her, "Spend ten minutes before you go to bed and ten minutes in the morning visualizing yourself walking. Can you commit to that?"

"I guess." Grace could feel her anger seeping out like a balloon with a slow leak. Today had not been what she expected at all.

"Tomorrow, I will pick you up. I will take you to HigherGround, and we will work on the next step." He laughed, breaking the tension, "See what I did there? Next *step* . . ." He smiled a full grin.

His eyes crinkled, and Grace could feel the corners of her lips turn upward. Despite her best efforts to conceal it, she was amused by the joke. Being this close to him, she could smell his cologne, and her eyes caught small dimples trying to peek out from behind his beard. Grace felt the warm familiarity again. Like she had known him her whole life. At the same time, he was getting under her skin, and Grace could not figure out why. Confused about the rushing feelings that felt like heaven and hell all rolled into one. It made her want more.

Erick left, and later Robin came in for lunch. He asked Grace how the session went, and he didn't understand why Erick would push her so hard the first session.

"Grace, at any time you want to stop, we can. I just want you to be happy. By the way, these flowers came for you this morning. I got a text from Mom saying they're from Julie, the nurse from the hospital. It was early, and you were probably still sleeping."

Grace opened the red envelope that came with the flowers. The card read:

> *You are on the right path Sunshine.*
> *Love Always, Julie*

"I wanted to ask you, Grace," Robin said, lifting his eyebrows for the question on his mind. "Do you still have the journal that I gave you from Aunt Raven?"

Grace put the card back in the envelope. "Well, actually, Julie brought it over, and Mom put it in the foyer table drawer. Why would she do that?"

"Your mother gets so focused on her cases and probably didn't want to be late. These flowers are beautiful." Robin scratched his nose and got busy emptying the dishwasher. *Why was he acting so weird? Why does everyone act weird about the journal?*

She wanted to read more of it. Suddenly, Grace remembered her days with Aunt Raven at the little house. They ran through wildflowers, ate lavender vanilla cookies, and drank tea from small cups.

"Where did you go?" Robin put the last dish away and faced her again.

"I just remembered when you used to take me to Aunt Raven's house for tea and cookies. She was so magical. I miss her." Grace was happy she could remember, but sad at the same time because she knew her beloved Aunt Raven was gone. "How did she die, Dad?"

"Well, that's a story for another day. I will tell you, though, it was a hiking accident. She was always traveling to faraway places. She was on the Pacific Coast Trail in California. She said she needed to find someone out there. I really don't want to talk about it right now, Grace. It's too painful for me, honestly. Besides, I have a present for you," Robin said, handing Grace a wooden box. Robin had carved a message on the top.

> *"Your story is yet to be written. You're braver than you believe, stronger than you seem, and smarter than you think." —Christopher Robin*

"Winnie the Pooh?" Grace smiled at the memory. "It is so beautiful, Dad." Next, she removed the top of the box, revealing a shiny silver pen.

"You know," Robin said, smoothing his beard in deep thought. "You used to write all the time. You could write about your recovery and new memories. I think it'd be good for you."

"Thank you, Dad!" She hugged him quickly. They ate their lunch in silence. Robin got a phone call from a new client and excused himself. Grace climbed out of the wheelchair and into her bed and began writing in an old notebook she found in the kitchen.

Memories of her growing up in her house were easy to recall now. Of course, she wrote about Doctor Erick with his mysterious blue eyes and abrupt behavior. She tapped her pen and wrote about how she could not shake the feeling that she knew him somehow. Then she decided what she needed to do was lay down and rest. Trying to sort the puzzle out was exhausting.

Grace got comfortable in her bed and dozed off thinking about her next session with the doctor.

Erick sat in his Jeep, and he punched the steering wheel in frustration. "You are so stupid!" he yelled at himself. "You pushed her too hard! What is wrong with you?" He continued the tirade as he jerked the keys out of the ignition. Erick reviewed the entire morning in his head. Then it hit him like a ton of bricks. *It was the picture that spooked him.* The photo of the two of them from high school was hanging in the bedroom. Back when they were still *together*. It shook him. The tack was right in his eye over his face in the worn yellowing photograph. The photos were from a mall photo booth. They made serious and silly faces, and the small images were dispersed on a small page, a few at a time. Grace had shared some with him, and she kept the one that was on her bulletin board. It was a great photo, even now with the large push pin right through Erick's face. There was nothing funny about that, especially since their relationship ended in heartache. It was a mistake to go to her house. He shook his head, hoping it would erase the mistake.

Tomorrow will be better, he promised himself. He would not push Grace so hard. He was going to have to treat this patient differently than the others. He thought about training her in the pool and making sure it was *just* the two of them. He remembered Grace as a little girl, and she was all about competition, but more importantly, she wanted to have fun. He knew her better than anyone else. He didn't have that advantage over his other clients. For Grace, he decided he would make it fun. He jumped out of the Jeep and walked into HigherGround.

"Well, how did it go with Grace?" Joyce looked down at the computer.

"Not as well as I hoped, but she is coming in tomorrow. We will need the pool," Erick said exhaling.

"Oh, do you now?" Joyce looked over her glasses. "You better take it slow." She gave him a warning.

"I could have used that advice earlier today. Where were you this morning?" Erick laughed.

"The first session was that bad?" Concern filled Joyce.

"Yeah, but it is what it is. Does anyone need me this afternoon?" Erick asked her.

"You wanted your schedule cleared, remember?" Joyce tilted her head quizzically.

"True. Okay, I have some calls to make," With that, Erick left for his office. Just then, Sky popped in with Jace.

"Jace wanted to come to see you. Daniel and I are heading out for some lunch. Do you want us to get you anything?" Sky asked.

"Jacey-boy," Erick said, leaning over to rub Jace's white and golden ears. "I'm not hungry, thanks anyways."

Sky left, and Erick picked up his buzzing cell phone. "Mr. Evans?"

"What the heck happened today?" Robin sounded impatient.

"I lost my nerve, honestly." Erick had to admit it finally. "I saw an old picture of us in her room and didn't think I could pull it off. Let's start the training off here at HigherGround, in a more neutral place where I'm less likely to run into our past."

"We are talking about the most important person in my world, *my daughter*. Your ONLY job is to help her to walk and remember some things. That was the deal. That's what I'm paying you for. You will get one more chance."

Robin hung up before Erick could thank him. He put the

phone down and did the only thing he knew to do. Erick prayed. He prayed that he could get out of his head and out of his own way. Erick prayed for ultimate healing for Grace. He prayed that the treatment ahead would help her. Erick prayed a prayer of gratitude for his second chance to make things right. He prayed he would be the man he needed to be. After everything that had happened all those years ago, Erick felt like a failure and an impostor, posing as an unknown doctor. *What was I thinking?* He didn't deserve a second chance, but he had to try. Helping others got him out of a dark place years ago. He couldn't just quit now. Helping Grace wasn't just going to change her life. Erick knew helping her would only be the beginning, and he knew it was bound to change him forever.

Forty-two

Grace awoke with a start. The clock read 4:44 a.m. The wind blew outside, and a bare winter tree tapped against the window. A black raven flapped its wings and flew off. Grace's heart pounded. She willed herself to close her eyes. She was torn between trying to forget and desperately remember her dream. She rubbed her throat, remembering a man was *choking* her. He had the bluest eyes. "*I own you!*" He spat the words. "*You are nothing without me.*"

Grace tried to remember his face. "*Walk!*" he slurred. She remembered getting up, barefoot, and running down the hallway, narrowly avoiding shards of glass on the floor.

A horrible thought popped into her mind. What if it wasn't a dream but an actual memory? Grace remembered the earlier entries in Aunt Raven's journal were warning her of something. What if her aunt was warning her about a relationship she had? A connection Grace couldn't remember. She kept going over the words the blue-eyed man kept saying. *Walk!* As the words echoed in her mind, she recalled Dr. Erick had said the *exact* words in the same tone. What was happening here? Is this why Erick seemed so familiar? Was Aunt Raven trying to warn her about Erick? Nothing made sense. She had just met Erick.

Next, Grace remembered her training with him yesterday.

What happened to make him *so* aggressive? He seemed to snap for no reason. *Is it possible I could have met this man before the hospital?* She shook the thought away because she liked Dr. Erick and believed that he could help her walk again. *My parents would have said something.*

Dr. Hopkins told her that dreams were sometimes are jumbled with facts and fantasy while the brain sorted through events. In her case, the events were jumbled and confusing as it was. Besides, there was no way her parents would lie. They never would. They had done nothing but be supportive, and they cared for her deeply. *It was just a nightmare.* It wasn't a memory. It was just her fear getting the best of her. She pulled the covers up to her chin and hugged herself. Grace recalled that the next session with Dr. Erick would be at the HigherGround studio. To be successful, she'd have to surrender to the process. That process included believing that her body would be strong enough. Grace decided then that she did believe, and eventually, she would remember everything, including what happened to her. She closed her eyes as she visualized herself walking around and even dancing in a field of wildflowers. Then she opened her eyes and pulled the journal out of her end table. Opening it to the next page, she continued to read.

> *It was the dead of winter. I was in middle school at the time and in Algebra class. I remember looking out the window wanting to be outside even though large drops of rain slid down the classroom's windows. I remember feeling trapped inside and wanting to go out and feel the rain on my face. Winters in Connecticut were typically heavy with rain and snow. My daydream of dancing in the rain was interrupted when a mysterious boy sat down next to me. His name was Jack Stone. Jack had very*

dark curly hair and piercing eyes. Each day after that, my need to escape into the outdoors faded, and I found myself looking at him more and looking out the window less. One day he invited me over to study. I could never have boys over. Living with my dad and brother made it nearly impossible to do much of anything. They were so protective of me. Looking back, I should have appreciated their concern. I have always been stubborn and wanted to do my own thing. Very slowly, like a frog in lukewarm water, I lost that free spirit. All in the name of making Jack happy, and I was completely unaware at the time. I began to disappear little by little. I see this happening all the time, and I see this in your current relationship, Sunshine.

Jack seemed different from the other boys at school. Although he was dark and broody, he was handsome. Jack was interested in discovering the world, and he read many books. We had that in common. His mother said to me once, which I thought was peculiar, "He didn't have many friends growing up. His friends were books. He just needed to meet the right person."

I believed that I was 'saving' Jack, and the evidence was that his grades improved. I loved just being near him and having him all to myself. It was quite intoxicating. We would take walks in the woods, and I taught him which plants he could eat and which to avoid. He seemed fascinated with the medicinal plants and enjoyed being out in nature. It was there he told me his innermost thoughts.

Then one spring day, I saw the red flags. We were going for a long walk in the woods. Robin wanted to join us. I insisted Robin stay home. I really wanted to be alone with Jack because I was looking forward to sharing our first kiss. I'd find out later that Robin had secretly followed us when he confronted me about what happened.

> *After a long winter, the trees were budding, and flowers began to bloom on the trail. Jack told me that his parents weren't actually his biological parents.*
>
> *"What do you mean?" I asked him while I skipped along the trail, hoping Jack felt the same way I did. I was smitten and wanted to know more about this mysterious boy.*

Grace fell asleep with the journal open and dreamed about walking through the woods herself and twirling around in a long flowing white dress. When she woke up, she was thankful for not having any other bizarre nightmares. She closed the journal and placed it in the drawer.

Next, Grace hoisted herself out of bed and wheeled into the walk-in shower. There she found a plastic chair to sit in as the water ran down her face and hair. She visualized herself standing tall in the shower one day soon. Grace didn't want to spend her life confined to a chair. She was tired of being angry all the time, and she was no longer in denial about what had to happen next. She dried off and dressed in her gym clothes. It was still winter in Connecticut, and they were predicting some heavy snow. Her mom was out of town, but she promised she would be home after her big case was over. Faith would undoubtedly have the answers about her days in high school and beyond.

Robin helped her get into her heavy winter jacket and zip it up. She felt like a little girl heading off to school when Robin handed Grace her gym bag.

"Good morning, Grace!" Erick looked tired when they opened the door. "Mr. Evans." The men nodded at each other. "I will have her back early in the afternoon."

Grace almost felt like she was going on a date instead of a physical therapy session.

Erick helped Grace get into the Jeep and then loaded the wheelchair in the back. Once in the Jeep, he looked at her, his face inches from hers. "I'm so sorry about yesterday. I wasn't thinking. Most of my clients need a direct approach. I have never treated anyone with amnesia before. I promise I will not push you more than you are ready ever again, no matter what. Can you forgive me?"

"Just treat me like all your other clients. I can handle it." Grace decided she needed to stop focusing on him and start focusing on herself and her recovery.

As Erick pulled out of the driveway, Grace stared out the window. She was unsure about this man. One part of her trusted him with her life. Another part of her wondered if her nightmares were some sort of omen.

Grace shook her head and focused on the path she was on. She had to get through this training. If the nightmares were a warning and an actual memory, Grace knew this was her one chance to be able to stand up for herself and run far, far away. She decided, for now, she would trust her trainer.

"Of course, there is nothing to forgive. You are simply my doctor, and I'm the patient. I'm responsible for my *own* recovery. You are just showing me the way." She snuck a glance at his face as they pulled into the parking lot. "Of course, my dad, on the other hand, will kill you, and *that* should scare you. Nothing can save you from that!" She laughed at the thought, even if it was probably the truth. She was going to do this, not for the doctor and not for her father. This journey would be the start of something good for *her*, and no one could take that away, not even a handsome doctor.

Erick had to reign in his feelings if he was going to make this work. He helped Grace into her wheelchair and allowed Grace to hold her gym bag in her lap as they entered HigherGround. They met up with Sky outside the door to the women's locker room.

"Good morning, Dr. Erick. Grace, so good to see you! How are you today?"

"I'm ready to work," Grace said, determined.

"I will be helping you get ready for training today if that's cool with you?" Sky's southern accent soothed Grace.

"Okay," Grace said, relieved to work with Sky again.

"We will train in the pool today. Don't worry about remembering how to swim. I will be with you the whole time," Erick reassured Grace. "Sky is going to help you get dressed before our session."

Erick left and entered the pool area, turned on the lights, and placed the pool weights, noodles, and boards by the shallow end. The pool had windows along the far wall that had condensation covering them from the heated pool. When Grace emerged, she had on a one-piece black bathing suit, and her red hair was swept up and held in a loose bun. Sky helped her out of the wheelchair and onto the top step of the shallow end. Slowly, with the help of Erick, her legs entered the water. Erick tried not to get sidetracked as he stared at the freckles on her nose. He took a deep breath. "Thank you, Sky."

"I'm off, but I will be back before your session is over." Sky nodded toward Grace.

"I'm going to give you this board." Erick turned to Grace and placed a blue oval-shaped board in front of her." I will use my hands to keep you steady. Ready?"

Grace nodded as she leaned her chest on the board, and Erick held her waist. Grace's face lit up as Erick moved her around the water. "How does that feel?" he asked, noticing her green eyes dancing in delight. Christian rock music played over the speakers. He silently thanked God for showing up to the session today. Erick could *feel* the difference when he got out of the way and let *Him* do the magic.

"Liberating," she said. Erick wore a light blue rash guard and black swimming trunks. He showed Grace how to float and move her legs some. He could tell she was relaxing when she laughed at his jokes. "We are in the deep end now!" He laughed because it was only waist deep. "I want you to let go of the board now."

"What?" Grace's smile evaporated. "I'm not ready."

"I know," he said softly. "Do you trust me?" Erick was confident but careful not to push her too far again. She nodded. She released the board, and her legs dangled to the floor of the pool. He supported her with one hand under her armpit. She was weightless. "You are standing, my friend!" Erick noticed Grace was smiling wide.

"I'm doing it!" Grace exclaimed.

"Now, using your arms, try to walk. I promise I will catch you! He backed up a little, and she tried taking a few steps. As she began to sink, Erick caught her. "You did it! Now, take my hands." It seemed natural as they held hands as she walked towards him without sinking. Their eyes locked, and Erick found himself getting lost in the moment.

He would never forget one late summer night when they were kids. They'd decided to go swimming in the lake. They'd left their outer clothes on the shoreline. Just wearing their underclothes, they ran into the cool dark water together. He'd wrapped her in his arms, and he vowed never to let her go. He closed his eyes, but instead of her moving in for a kiss, she splashed him instead.

"Race you to the shore!" Grace splashed her way to shore, determined to win. He caught up with her, and they both fell onto the sand.

"Hey, Doc! Adult swim is over!" Daniel shouted playfully behind Erick, breaking through his memory.

"Daniel!" Erick led Grace back to the stairs as Daniel wheeled himself over to Grace's wheelchair. Erick picked up Grace, wrapped the towel over her, and gently placed her back into the wheelchair. Erick stared at Daniel, silently reminding him *not* to blow his cover. "You remember my patient, Grace?"

"Ah, yes. Grace! Nice to see you again. I have heard so much about you."

Erick furrowed his brow in warning. "Daniel is also is my little brother. Hey, is Sky in the locker room?"

"Yeah, she just went in there," Daniel replied.

"You can go on and change in the locker room now. Great job today!" Erick observed her maneuver her wheelchair to the locker room. Sky opened the door, and then it closed behind her.

"Daniel, she is *still* a patient. She won't be if you blow my cover, though." Erick lowered his voice, and his eyes grew wide.

"I was just trying to be friendly. If anyone is going to blow up this charade, it will be you, dude. You are in *way* over your head!" Daniel spoke the truth, even if Erick didn't want to hear it.

Daniel wheeled away. As Erick grabbed his thick blue towel, he realized one thing was certain. The entire training hinged on her trusting him, and he needed to be careful. Otherwise, this would be over before it even started.

Forty-three

Grace woke up the next day encouraged for the first time in months. Even the darkness outside her window seemed to be moving on. She looked out into the bright world and saw a blanket of white snow had fallen overnight. She inhaled the new day. *Today was going to be a great day!* She had enough of feeling sorry for herself. Today she would use the anger to fuel her determination and get back on her feet. Robin gave Grace a ride to HigherGround.

"Are you okay?" Robin asked once they pulled out of the driveway. He drove carefully over the salted road.

"I feel better than I have in days, Dad. I just hoped more memories would have come back to me by now. When will Mom be back from D.C.?"

"Christmas Eve. I was going to ask you if you feel like celebrating this year. Mom and I haven't done much celebrating since you left." Robin rubbed his beard thoughtfully and kept his eyes on the road.

"Whatever you and Mom want. I just want to spend time with you guys. I do have some questions about my childhood. Specifically, the relationships I may have had. I can't remember much at all." Grace stared out the window at the snow that looked like pure cane sugar sparkly and smooth. She pulled her coat around her tighter.

"We can get some photo albums when Mom gets home. You can always ask me anything you want," Robin said. He turned on the wipers as a few flurries collected on the windshield.

"Was I dating anyone?"

"You liked a few boys. Of course, I didn't like any boys dating my daughter," Robin said. He got quiet, watching the traffic ahead.

"That's okay. I need to focus on therapy today. The past can wait," Grace said as he turned into the parking lot. She was confident that he knew the answers to her past, but she was still a little afraid of the truth.

Shutting the engine off, Robin hopped out, got the chair out and around wheeled it to Grace's side. Grace admired the ease with which he did things. Her love for her father grew more and more each day. Robin helped her get in the chair and followed her into the building. "Thank you, Dad."

"Of course, you know I will do anything for you!"

"Hello, Mr. Evans and Grace! There's something different about you today!" Sky's curiously greeted them.

"*I'm* different," Grace said simply. She felt herself sit up straighter. Today was going to be about action, not words, and Grace offered only this. "Let's just say it's time to ditch the chair sooner than later!" The automatic doors closed behind them.

Robin kissed his daughter's forehead just then. "Text me when you need a ride back." He handed her a cell phone.

"Ok." Grace was thankful for all he had done for her. Robin left through the same doors they came in.

"You'll meet Dr. Erick in the therapy room. Do you remember how to get there?" Sky asked.

"Yes, I can do this. Thank you." Grace took the brake off the chair and rolled down the hallway towards the therapy room. Sky waved and turned right as Grace wheeled herself to the next set of double glass doors.

As the door opened, Grace rolled her chair in and looked around. Erick had called this, *a sacred place*. She was going to get her life back, and she would be a *new and improved* Grace. Whoever that was. Maybe both Julie and Erick were right when they had said God had a plan for her. This thought comforted her. She was ready to train, and she was prepared to do whatever it took to walk again.

"How is my girl today?" Erick's eyes looked right through her. *He must say that to all his patients*, Grace thought, but she didn't care. His nice words were not going to distract her today. She looked away, avoiding his gaze.

"Let's do this!" Grace spoke with some otherworldly confidence she didn't even know was there. Grace glanced again in his direction and noticed the fine lines around his eyes. She wondered about his life.

Suddenly, Erick pumped his fist in the air and did some awkward little dance that made the air feel lighter. He stopped and took a breath. "Ok, we are burning daylight! Wait here." Erick lifted his hand and high-fived her. His enthusiasm was contagious.

Next, Grace's eyes followed him across the room as Erick walked alone over to the parallel bars.

From there, he cupped both hands and shouted to her. "Ok, I want you to wheel yourself over here and get started on your own! I will be right back."

Wait, what? Where is he going? Isn't he going to help me? Grace thought. She could feel her confidence fading. *What was he thinking?* She swallowed, determined to keep her promise to herself. Grace wheeled herself to the back of the room.

Grace could hear instrumental music over the speakers as she approached the bars. She put the brake down on the wheelchair while visualizing how she would pull herself up to the bars and eventually take steps independently. She had no idea where Erick was.

Suddenly, the music shut off, and Grace could only hear the hum of the fan. She felt awkward in the silence and looked around nervously. *What kind of therapist left their patient all alone? What if she fell? Where did he go?* He had not returned, so she decided to focus on the bars. She imagined walking like a beautiful model on the runway. She sat up straighter and closed her eyes as she had done every day for homework. The music changed, and she opened her eyes. Heavy rock beats pumped through the speakers, and her heart began to beat to the same rhythm. The band began to sing lyrics that filled her with courage. Next, Grace pulled herself up.

"Have you ever heard of *Skillet*?" Erick came up behind her and seemed to be amused by Grace's change of attitude.

"No," Grace said quickly and shrugged. "You know, amnesia and all." Distracted, she sat back down in her chair.

"Place your hands here." Erick's hands touched hers, and she felt electricity flow through them as he guided Grace's hands to the bars. He nodded. "Now, lift yourself again."

The music filled Grace's ears. She wanted to feel invincible. She stood firm, all her weight supported by her arms and hands.

"Look at me," Erick said gently. Grace's eyes focused on his. It was as if there was nothing else in the room. Her mind wondered who was there for him? *Oh my God, Grace! Focus!* She told herself. Her arms shook. Then shooting pain made its way up her back. The feeling was almost more than she could bear. Instead of giving up, she kept focusing on him. Next, she slowly dragged her foot forward while holding her knee bent. Her foot felt like it weighed a thousand lbs, but somehow, it slid her foot forward an inch. Tears threatened to spill from her eyes as she realized how hard relearning to walk was. Grace's hands still shook under strain.

"You got this, Grace! Doesn't this remind you of that one time we . . ." he trailed off. Awkwardly he scratched his nose and broke eye contact with her.

"What?" She asked as she caught her breath and focused on the next leg.

Erick stepped back, clearly uncomfortable as he stammered. "Nevermind, I was thinking about another client. Stay focused."

The shaking muscles in Grace's arms did all the work. She looked down and whispered, "I'm . . . walking." Grace took more slow steps, one after the other. She made it to the end. Exhausted, Grace closed her eyes, and she collapsed onto Erick, who caught her in his arms. Grace surrendered to tears and sobbed on his shoulder. It was then she realized two important things. The other doctors didn't have a clue about her, and this man somehow knew her better than she knew herself.

Erick's heart leapt as he saw the joy explode on Grace's face as her feet made it to the end of the barre. With more training and time, her legs would become stronger and do the job independently. He felt her sobbing as she held on to him. He never wanted to let go. *Keep it professional.*

"That is enough for today, Grace. Well done!" He helped her to the wheelchair, and her breathing slowed to normal. "Do you have any pain right now?"

"A little, maybe just soreness," Grace admitted.

"I want you to drink lots of water. Your muscles did a

lot of work today, and they need to stay hydrated," Erick said as he handed her a cup from the cooler. "Is your dad coming to get you?"

"I need to text him." Grace took a big gulp of water.

"If it's easier, I can take you home," Erick suggested as he typed in the notes from today's session.

"You don't have another session?"

"No. Let me know." Erick placed some ice on her back and set a timer.

"That's fine. You can take me. Let me just text my dad." Grace said.

Erick left to get Jace. Erick came back as her timer went off, and he prepared for their departure.

Once they were in the Jeep, Jace hopped in his spot, lying down on his blanket in the back seat.

"Your dog is really well behaved." Grace looked back at Jace. Then, she asked, "Do you really think I will be able to get rid of the wheelchair soon?"

Erick kept his eyes on the road noticing the giant snowbanks from freshly plowed snow. "Of course, you will! Your muscles will build up in your legs quickly, and then it will get easier. It'll take time and practice." Erick's eyes were forward, but he was keenly aware of Grace sitting beside him. At stoplights, he would glance over at her while she looked out the window. "You warm enough?"

"Yes," Grace replied. They rode in silence as they drove to Grace's house. Erick cut the engine in the driveway. He helped her get into the wheelchair and followed her to the door. "Do you want to come in?" she asked, looking up at him. He noticed her eyes were greener than ever in the afternoon winter light.

"I don't think that is a good idea," Erick said, putting his hands in his pockets and shifting his weight from one foot to another.

"My dad is out back in the woodshop for another hour. I really don't want to be alone right now," she persisted.

"Ok, I'll come inside for a little bit. Do you mind if Jace comes with us? It's too cold for him out here. He won't hurt anything."

"Of course." Grace wheeled up to the front door.

Erick let Jace hop out. Then he retrieved something from the glove box. Grace waited for him by holding the front door open. Once inside, Erick took her coat and put both on the coat tree. Jace bounced in after them.

"Do you have a DVD player?" Erick asked as they entered the living room.

"We might. Why?" Grace stopped the chair and turned to see what was in his hand.

"Part of your training is in your mind, right?" Erick began. With his eyes on hers, and he held up a DVD. "Peaceful Warrior" It's about a guy who was an Olympic athlete." Erick walked over to the TV and turned on the DVD player. "Do you know how to make this work?" He crouched low over the entertainment center.

Grace looked unsure as they both took a look at the remotes. They were huddled there, focused and unaware someone had entered the house.

"Grace?" Faith startled them.

"Mrs. Evans!" Erick stood up straighter, blushing.

Faith wheeled a white square suitcase and had a bag on her arm. "Doctor Erick?" she set the suitcase upright and shook his hand.

"Mom! You are home. How was your trip?" Grace put the remotes in her lap and hugged her.

"We won a tough case, so I thought I would come home early and surprise you!" She narrowed her eyes at Erick.

"I walked today, Mom," Grace said quietly.

Faith looked at Erick and then back to Grace. "Really? That is wonderful, sweetheart!"

"Is it okay if Doctor Erick stays over for a little bit and we can watch this movie?" Grace asked.

"Of course. Do you need help with the DVD player?"

"Yes. I can't remember even how to use a remote." Grace handed Faith all the remotes. Grace wheeled herself to the couch and lifted herself out of the chair onto the cushions. "Thanks, Mom."

"Do not let that dog on the furniture, please!"

"Jace is a therapy dog, and he'll stay on the floor," Erick said reassuringly.

"Fine. I will be in my office if you need me."

Faith left the room, and Erick found his way next to Grace. He was conscientious not to sit too close to her. Faith returned with two water bottles and a large bowl filled with popcorn a few minutes into the movie. Erick could hardly believe he was with *her*. Jace curled up between their feet. Here he was sitting with Grace after all these years. A dream come true.

Forty-four

Grace couldn't help feeling like she was on a date. Here was a handsome man, sharing a bowl of popcorn with her. It felt so natural to steal glances in his direction. She almost felt normal except for the wheelchair. She still felt strangely comfortable around this man. He seemed so calm and at home today compared to the first day he had come over and left abruptly. Since then, he had been nothing but gentle with her. Grace looked toward the window. She could see it was raining again, and the dark clouds dimmed the late afternoon sun. Jace was next to her foot, snoring away, separating Erick from her. The movie was good, but Grace couldn't keep from being distracted. She and Erick reached for popcorn at the same time, and their hands touched with such electricity that he pulled back as if the contact burned him. On a whim, she threw a piece of popcorn at him while he stared at the TV just to see if he was into the movie or not.

"What the . . .?" Erick jumped back when the popcorn connected with his forehead. The jolt caused the popcorn to fly up in the air and land on the floor. Jace woke up instantly, and his nose found the wayward buttery popcorn.

Grace couldn't help but laugh. Their eyes met, and she knew the fireplace wasn't the only thing that warmed the room. For a few moments, they just stopped and looked at each other, no longer hearing the movie. Grace looked at his face, detecting a hint of sadness in his blue eyes. She suddenly wanted to touch his face. The was so much electricity between them. The rain tapped the window harder, and the lights flickered. Suddenly, the room plunged into darkness. There in the dark, she hoped he couldn't hear her heart pounding in her chest as his hand moved on hers.

A loud noise broke through the darkness, and Robin came bursting in through the front door wielding a large flashlight, and his face wild.

"Mr. Evans, the power is out." Erick jumped up, shielding his eyes.

Robin narrowed his eyes at the unexpected guest, "What are you doing here?"

Grace could only imagine what was going through her father's mind. Faith came running in and stopped by the side of her husband. The light illuminated Jace as he continued to help himself to the upturned bowl of popcorn. Grace watched the scene play out, trying not to laugh, and felt something she had not felt in a long time. She finally felt safe and finally home. Eventually, the power came back, and Erick said his goodbyes, and the moment became another memory in Grace's mind. Her parents didn't chastise her or ask her questions at dinner. When Grace went to bed that night, she could not help but smile, thinking of Dr. Erick. Next, she pulled out the journal and continued to read her aunt's words.

> *What Jack said next surprised me. He took a deep breath, and I knew it was going to be a significant concession.*
>
> *"I was adopted." Jack stopped in his tracks, waiting for my reaction. "I was in many foster homes over the*

years. When Jeremiah and Sarah adopted me, they tried to give me a stable home when no one else would. My biological mother left me at a firehouse. She was a drug addict and didn't love me enough to be with me." Jack began walking again.

I didn't know what to say. Somehow my heart swelled for this boy even more.

"Social service called and told me my mother overdosed. I think I was seven." Jack kicked a stone with his foot. "So, I began acting out, and most foster families could not handle me. I had even tried even to end my own life. Then Jeremiah and Sarah came into the picture. They didn't force anything on me, but they were adamant about working. I guess I owed it to them." Jack had a faraway look on his face, but he did not shed a tear.

Before I could say anything to Jack, a bird fell out of a tree just then. I ran over to it and saw that it was a raven. Its wing was bent backwards and possibly broken.

"Jack! We have to save this bird!" My heart broke when I ran over to the bird. Jack was on my heels and grabbed my arm hard.

"Don't touch it!" Jack hissed at me and released his grip. Small purple dots appeared on my arm where his fingers grabbed me.

"Ow! Why?" I rubbed my arm.

"Let it die in peace. Leave it!" Jack was serious, and then he did the unthinkable. He pulled his foot back and kicked the bird. I felt a chill up my spine and cried, and Jack held me. He told me that the bird was in a better place now and put out of its misery. Jack pulled his face back and looked at mine, now tear-stained. He kissed me just then, and I forgot about the bird until I got home, and that's when Robin confronted me about it.

"I saw what Jack did to that bird. He murdered it, and

you didn't stop him!" Robin pleaded with me. "Please stop seeing that guy. Jack is bad news. I heard he was in juvie and beat up a kid at his last school."

"Jack is misunderstood, but I can help him."

The pleasant feeling Grace had earlier was fading, and she knew she needed to get some sleep. She hoped Aunt Raven could save Jack Stone, but she wasn't sure that would be the case. Her aunt shared this story to help Grace. She was sure of that. Grace had a sinking feeling that the message of this story was about her life before the amnesia. She couldn't do anything about her past, or the news Aunt Raven was trying to get to her. For now, Grace had to focus on only one thing. Learning to walk again.

Erick could not believe the irony of the situation as he felt so much like a teenager when they were together. Erick had to remind himself that the reason they were together now was for professional reasons. He remembered the feeling of when Mr. Evans suddenly burst through the door. Erick could swear Grace's hand was on his, and it felt electric. Of course, that all went away when Robin took him aside as he was leaving the house.

"May I have a word, son?" Robin had lowered his voice as they stood at the door in the foyer. "You better know what you're doing." Robin's eyes narrowed. "I hope this doesn't backfire on us, or we both will lose her."

"I'm aware, sir. Please just ask her about her day today, and you will know she is on the right track," Erick said goodbye. He promised himself to be more careful next time and not get too close to Grace on the drive home. Keeping it professional was the only way to make this work.

The next afternoon, Erick and Grace worked on more exercises at HigherGround to strengthen her legs. Erick could not help but notice that Grace always had her eyes on him as if he had the answers to the universe. He loved working with her. It was something he could have never imagined happening in the last decade, let alone now.

Grace laughed at all his physical therapy humor. They were more like puns. *One step at a time.* All the while, he deflected her questions about the past.

"Do I know you?" Grace was serious. "You seem so familiar to me."

"Okay, you got me! I'm your long lost '*step*brother.'" He laughed nervously, sidestepping the question. Humor seemed to be the best way to keep her questions at bay and keep their past secret.

The next few weeks flew by in a blur. Erick noticed Grace was not only getting stronger, but they were getting closer. She had warmed up to his style of inspirational yet unconventional Christian music. Grace was also doing her visualization homework and included doing meditations each morning. Her mind was getting sharper along with her body.

Most clients he would see two to three days a week, but with Grace, he tried to see her every day. The days passed at lightning speed, and he decided that there weren't many days Erick could stand *not* to be with her. He called the sessions outside of HigherGround, 'life skills.' Grace used the wheelchair for most days, but on others, he held her hands for support, used a cane or the help from a walker. Everything was going according to plan, but the lie about their past weighed on him. Erick was relieved the nightmares were gone, but now he would lay awake at night and wonder if he was doing the right thing by her. If AA had taught him anything, it was that lies were a slippery slope.

"Grace, I have something I need to tell you," Erick said as he put the ice pack on Grace's back after their session. He handed her a cup of water.

"I wanted to ask you something as well," Grace said and drank the cool liquid.

"Ladies first." Erick finished typing notes on the computer, shut the laptop, and looked into her green eyes.

"I need your help," Grace said, looking into his blue eyes now. "I need help with some Christmas shopping, and you should come over for Christmas dinner. Unless," Grace said and drank some more water. "You have plans, of course, with Daniel or your girlfriend."

Was this really happening? Did she ask him out? "Well, you're my only client. I don't have a girlfriend," He said quickly. "You're ready for some more *training*, and shopping would be a great way to do just that."

"Great," she blushed. "Your turn. You wanted to tell me something?"

Erick couldn't tell her now. Grace had more training to do, and just because he was in moral crisis didn't mean she was ready. She was so close to walking, and Erick wanted more than anything to spend the holidays with her. He could wait, but not too long. "Never mind, I was going to ask *you* if you had plans for the holidays."

"It'll be fun!" Grace couldn't contain her smile. "Plus, my mom promised we would get out all the old photo albums and the box with all my things from high school. Wouldn't it be great if I could remember *everything*? That would be perfect!" Grace's green eyes danced. Her phone buzzed, and she looked at the text. It was her dad. She looked up again, "My dad is on his way."

"That's great. Remembering *everything* is what you have always wanted."

Erick's smile faded. He realized part of him wanted to

be there at Christmas dinner by her side. The other part of him suddenly panicked about her taking the trip down memory lane. Where he knew there was only one thing at the end of that road. The road of lies always ended in heartbreak.

Forty-five

Grace couldn't deny the feeling like Erick was hiding something but shrugged it off.
"I will see if your dad is here." Erick disappeared.
She seemed confused, and she didn't want the moment to be over so soon. She waited there with the ice, just listening to the music. Someone must have switched the playlist to Christmas music. *"Rocking Around the Christmas Tree"* piped through the speakers.
All at once, the music seemed to grow louder. The room became dark. Grace blinked as memory began to surface in her mind. The song flooded her mind. She was no longer in the therapy studio, but she was transported in her mind to an office party. She was no longer in the wheelchair, but she sat on a dark burgundy chaise lounge in the middle of a large hotel lobby. Grace's feet, tucked beneath her while she gazed down to see strappy silver shoes placed next to each other. A giant Christmas tree was in the center of the room. The tree was expertly adorned with large pink and silver balls. Poinsettias on a few cocktail tables draped in a silver cloth lined the far wall. Several people dressed in cocktail dresses and suits moved all around the lobby with crystal glasses in their hands. Grace could hear music coming from the banquet room down the hall as two large

white doors remained open. She smoothed her white dress down, trying to cover her knees, suddenly self-conscious.

Faceless people laughed around her. Grace squinted to see who the people are, but their faces were blurry. In her hand, she had a crystal martini glass with a bright pink liquid. Grace sipped the contents and tasted the bitter drink with the sweet cranberry taste. The liquid went down smoothly, and she emptied the glass. A server brought her another before she even finished the last swallow. Suddenly, Grace winced from a sharp pain coming from her forearm. A faceless man wrapped griped her arm tightly. He squeezed harder, causing Grace to drop the glass on the marble floor, and to her horror, the glass shattered, scattering shards of glass across the marble lobby floor. The pink contents splattered over her, pink dots stained her white dress. She reflexively jumped off the lounge knocking her shoes over. Grace yelped, trying not to cause a scene as a piece of glass cut into her foot. The staff rushed to clean it up as she looked up at his blurry face and then to his mouth. He smiled sardonically with his perfect white teeth, and the hair gelled into submission.

Next, she felt him pull her closer, his breath in her ear, "What the *hell* do you think you are doing? Who the hell was that guy you were talking to?" The voice was raspy. She limped barefoot as he squeezed tighter on her arm. He forcefully pulled her through the crowd of people and into an open elevator to her embarrassment. Grace reached down and removed a jagged piece of glass from her foot as the doors closed. The pain was searing. The elevator door opened, he pushed her through the doors and into the hallway. They stopped at a room and swiped the hotel key. The bolt made a loud click as the room unlocked. Next, he pushed the door open, and Grace through it with such force she fell hard to the ground.

"Get up!" he growled. "I saw you were talking to that guy! Don't try to deny it!"

Grace quickly noticed the red blood on her foot and jumped towards the open door. Adrenaline ran through her body as she tried to escape. She lost her footing and fell, her body now in the hallway. The carpet burned her knees as Grace scrambled to get up, but he had his hands around her ankles now. She screamed as he pulled her into the room in one swift move and slammed the door. Grace sobbed because knowing her escape was futile. Resigned, she watched his feet walk from her to the desk. His face was still blurry.

Next, he took off his suit jacket and lay it over the chair neatly, and that was when she noticed a tattoo on his hand, but it too was blurred. Next, she heard him place a bottle on the desk and unscrew the top. He laughed as he put the bottle to his lips as the contents poured down his throat. She sat there on the floor, paralyzed with fear in her stained, ripped dress. Her foot throbbed, and her mind raced with questions. *Who was this man? Why was he pushing me around, and why was he yelling?* How could she be with a man who was so cruel? Tears burned her eyes, and Grace wished she could remember. She squeezed her eyes shut as pain filled her head, and the scene faded in her mind.

A loud beeping noise brought Grace to the present. Was this just her imagination running wild? But it felt so real. Could it be another flashback or repressed memory?

The physical therapy timer continued to beep incessantly for attention. Daniel arrived in the room, wheeled over to her, removed the ice, and took her empty cup.

Grace blinked and looked at the garland decorations around the studio. She took a deep breath and realized she was back at HigherGround.

"Are you okay? Where did Dr. Erick go?"

"I'm okay. He went to check on my ride."

"Well, you're free to go." Daniel stared at her. "Your dad is here to pick you up. Would you like me to accompany you to the parking lot?"

"No, I know my way."

"Merry Christmas, Grace." Daniel followed her only to the lobby.

"Merry Christmas, Daniel." She wheeled herself to the front lobby, retrieved her coat, and headed to the large glass automatic front doors.

Grace spotted her dad across the parking lot. She couldn't shake the feeling that something was very wrong down to her bones.

Erick tried not to appear like he was ambushing Robin even though that was what he was doing.

Robin looked exhausted as he closed the door to the van.

"Robin," Erick said, getting to the point because he didn't have much time. "Grace has invited me over for Christmas dinner. She wants to go through the photo albums and her memory box, and I am concerned about the plan falling apart."

Robin rubbed his beard and pulled his jacket closer. His breath was like steam in the winter air. The sky was white and grey. He placed his hand on Erick's shoulder. "We can't turn back now. The progress Grace has been making is remarkable."

"I agree, sir. Maybe you could look through the albums and the boxes, so there are no surprises?" Erick suggested.

"I will see what I can do." Robin stood up straighter and suddenly shook Erick's hand while his gaze moved over Erick's shoulder. "Grace! Are you ready to go?"

Erick turned to see Grace. She wheeled over to them, and she had a frown on her face. He wanted to ask her what was wrong, but he decided to say goodbye instead. "See you tomorrow?" Before she could answer, his phone began to buzz, and he waved good-bye to them, mumbling he had to take this call. He went back into the building, phone in hand, and the name Brook flashed on the screen. Once inside the building, Erick answered the phone, but it was too late, and the call went straight to voicemail. Erick stood there in the glass doorway and watched the Evans' van leave the parking lot. He needed to be more careful. Grace had several weeks of training left, and if he was honest, he didn't want the training ever to end. The phone buzzed once, indicating that the caller had left a message.

"Erick, you need to call me right away. It's urgent." Brook's voice sounded serious, but the last thing he wanted to do was call her back and get involved in her drama. In the past, her 'urgent' meant losing a donor for her fundraiser or the caterer canceling. Brook would have to wait. For now, all he wanted to think about was where he would take Grace shopping and what he would bring to Christmas dinner.

Forty-six

Grace did not sleep well that night. She kept getting flashbacks of the violent scene at the Christmas party hotel. Dr. Hopkins had told her that Grace will have dreams that do not make sense because the unconscious mind is still working and sorting things out. She woke up thinking about the man. The only thing Grace could remember was his expensive suit, blue eyes, and some sort of tattoo. Who did she know with a tattoo? Grace sat up in her bed and looked at the clock. She had over two hours before Erick would be there to take her shopping in town. Grace knew she could not sleep, so she took out the journal. What would happen with the mysterious Jack Stone?

I should have known then, but I ignored the signs. One time in high school, a new boy named Creed slipped me a note in Biology since we were lab partners. The message said, "Are you single YES, or NO?" with boxes to check. Jack found out declared me as his girl. Then Creed didn't come to school for three weeks because he was sick. Robin found out the truth that Creed was in the hospital. Robin assumed it was Jack. It was just easier to believe he was fighting for me. One wrong decision led to another. We both started drinking and experimenting with drugs which made him seem more exciting and dangerous. At the time, Instead of hiking, our days blurred together in his room, getting wasted. This was when I started to lose myself.

After high school, Jack continued to work in the family business and supported us. My father didn't like him, nor did he understand why we had to move in together quickly. I stopped talking to my father and my brother when Jack said he was all I needed. Jack and me against the world. When we were together, I felt alive, at least I thought we did. It seemed more comfortable just to put my focus on Jack and ignore the rest of my life. But Jack began to change and expect more from me. I needed to try to be better because Jack let me know if I made a mistake. The first time he hit me across the face, he apologized. He insisted he still loved me, and he surprised me with a diamond bracelet. After that, it was earrings or a weekend away in the Hamptons. It felt amazing that he cared about me so much. I got better at concealing the marks with make-up. I knew I deserved more, but I loved him. I thought I could save him. He gave me pills to help me with my anxiety that seemed to get worse. I was in a fog most days. Over the next five years, I lived a blurred life, and I forgot who I was. It was easier to ignore than to make the changes I knew I needed to make. Just after the holidays, he told me he was going on a business trip. I begged him to take me, but he refused. He left me alone for two whole weeks. I did not go to college or get a job as he said, "I have enough money for the both of us, no need for you to work." Just look great at all the business parties was all he had asked me to do. At the time, it sounded like a dream come true.

Two whole weeks with only myself, and I did not know what to do. I was lonely. I looked for my pills and could not find them, and I didn't want to call Jack and tell him *that he forgot to leave my medication out for me. It was then I realized that I had relied on Jack for everything, and he had done all the thinking for me. I decided to get outside the apartment, and everything changed when I found the hiking trails. It had been years since I walked Freedom Trails. I forgot how much I enjoyed walking, even in the winter. I got lost that day, but it didn't matter. I found the summit and watched the sunset without worrying about when to be home or if Jack would be in a bad mood. I set out on my walk and walked down the summit filling my lungs with the clean winter air.*

It was well after dark when I finally came home and got Chinese food delivered. I ordered the fried rice and Moo Shu pork. Without the drugs and alcohol, I could see clearly and make my own choices. Magically, my anxiety dissolved without medications. That is when the shift occurred, and I discovered something important. I was finding my way back to me.

Grace's alarm went off, and she closed the journal. She got up and wheeled herself to the bathroom, and showered, excited to begin her day with Erick. She closed her eyes and let the warm water cascade over her face.

In an instant, Grace opened her eyes and saw the sun sparkling over the waves. The smell of saltwater and the sounds of seagulls and children laughing filled her ears. Grace lay back down and felt the sun's warmth, and closed her eyes.

A shadow fell across her face blocking the warm sun. Grace opened her eyes and squinted to see a young boy with sandy hair standing over her. She could not see his face because the sun darkened his tan face and caused a significant halo effect around his head. Grace tried to see the face more clearly and blinked. In an instant, he jumped next to her, landing on her towel and kicking up sand as he straightened his legs. She looked over at the boy. He looked back at her with eyes as blue and deep as the ocean that roared only a few yards away. He laughed as he propped his head up with his hand. "You're getting burnt, Grace. How about some lotion?"

Grace looked down at her young self, wearing a two-piece bathing suit. She felt herself laugh with delight. "Sure!" Grace rolled over on her stomach. The sandy-haired boy then poured an entire bottle of ice water down her back. The shock sent her to her feet, and adrenaline pulsed through her veins.

The chase began as she took after him and tried to run in the deep and hot sand. Grace nearly caught him as he turned and ran backwards, keeping his eye on her. When Grace reached the water, she splashed him until he begged her to stop. His hands gently pinned hers to her back. They stood there like that for a few moments as the saltwater around them clapped their backs. She closed her eyes, and he leaned his face toward hers. Grace was sure he was going to kiss her.

Instead, a short and unexpected wave crashed over her, and she gasped for air. Saltwater filled her nose and burned her throat. As the next wave crashed over her head, she went under, and her legs burned from the coarse sand, cutting her when she hit bottom. Grace surfaced again looked around, but the boy had vanished. She tried to regain her balance but stumbled and went under the water. Grace tilted her head above the water, scanning the beach for anyone she could see. Grace went under the water again, and before her lungs burst, she surfaced and gasped for air. The good feeling from earlier was gone. She scanned the beach, but all she saw were a couple of kids building sandcastles. The sandy-haired boy was gone. Tired, she went under again as another wave crashed. Grace felt something lift her, and she noticed tan arms around her.

"Do you trust me? You'll be okay! I got you," the voice

spoke into her ear. "Riptide is dangerous out there. Do you trust me?" he asked again, and she nodded, still scared. "Swim this way with me. Now, try to stand." He looked sure of himself. Her feet touched the sand below, and together they reached the shore to safety. He smiled, and she could see dimples on both cheeks. The memory faded, and she felt tired. The memories were coming faster now, and she was unsure how much more she could take.

Grace exited the shower wrapped in a towel and wheeled herself to her closet. She stood up and reached for her clothes. After carefully choosing a nice sweater and jeans, she got dressed as the phone rang in the kitchen.

"Grace, it's Erick. Doctor Erick," he clarified. "You still want to go shopping together today?"

"Of course! I should be ready in about twenty minutes." Grace could not wait.

The doorbell rang after Grace fixed her hair and make-up. She opened the door and saw him standing there, his eyebrows raised in anticipation of the day. He wore dark jeans and a black leather jacket with a grey scarf wrapped around his neck.

"I have a great day planned for us!" Erick stood in the doorway. Grace realized that she may not remember everything yet, but she smiled at the sight of him. She had no doubt the day Erick had planned for them would be nothing short of an adventure.

Erick had the whole afternoon planned out for them. They would start at the town center with the outdoor markets and boutique shops. They would end up at The *Café Bella*, a very upscale quaint spot known for its exceptional hot chocolate.

The door opened, and Grace was there in her wheelchair. Her red hair hung in loose curls under her white knit cap. "Come in. I just need my purse and jacket." Grace stood up and reached the hooks, put her coat on, zipped it up, and grabbed her purse. Then Grace sunk back in the wheelchair.

"You are getting more mobile by the day!" Erick was pleased with her progress more and more with each passing day.

Grace hoisted herself up into the car without any help from Erick. Next, he placed the folded wheelchair in the back, knowing full well she would not need it for much longer. Once seated in the Jeep, she spoke up. "I need to get something for my dad, and I have no idea what to get my mom. How do you buy gifts for your family?" Grace was looking at Erick now.

"Other than Daniel, I don't see my family. My mom died from cancer when I was young."

"Oh, I'm sorry. I didn't know. Did you grow up around here?" Grace looked out the window. The sky was white, and the ground was a mix of fresh and dirty plowed snow.

"Born and raised!" Erick parked the car and helped Grace get out. "Let's start here for your dad," he said, changing the subject.

Erick held the door open to an antique book shop as Grace wheeled herself inside. The store had books lined up on shelves and hand-carved wooden figurines. "My family is complicated. Daniel and I are close. I like to keep an eye on him. He and Sky have been dating now for over five years."

"That's so sweet," Grace replied. "How did they meet?"

"They met when Daniel was a senior in high school. Sky's the one who helped me get into therapy school. She uses the dogs to help her pediatric clients feel more comfortable."

"She seems cool."

"She is a great doctor. My brother Daniel adores her. He is going to ask Sky to move in with him. It's weird because I used to take care of Daniel every day, but lately, Sky seems to be taking over that job. I'm really happy for him, but it's like he just doesn't need me much anymore." He handed Grace an oversized large wooden rook chess piece. "Does your dad play chess?" Erick let the words out before realizing his mistake. "Sorry. Do you have any memories of him playing chess?" He loved having someone to talk to about life. With Brook, she was always talking about herself and the city. In contrast, everything was so natural with Grace.

Grace felt the rook with her fingers, smoothing over the carvings. Her fingers found their way to the price tag. Looking at it, she replied, "I can't afford this, and since he makes things out of wood, he might be particular." Grace continued to look around, and then they left the store.

Outside, the wind was picking up, and her eye caught a cashmere scarf blowing in the wind. A vendor had many different varieties and colors hung up on display. She wheeled over to the pastel scarf and felt its soft material against her skin.

"*This!* I want to get this for my mom. It will go with all the business suits she wears when she travels." She opened her wallet and handed a $20 bill to the older woman, who wore one of the colorful scarves around her neck. The woman expertly wrapped the scarf in tissue paper, placed it in a box, gift-wrapped it, and handed it to Grace. "Thank you!" Grace's face lit up, and Erick could tell she was having a good time.

Erick felt the pain of the lie that was like a black cloud over them. He needed to tell her the truth. The longer it took made things harder for him. "Can I see your wallet please?"

"Why?" Grace looked confused.

"Do you have a driver's license?" Erick regretted asking.

"Here." Grace handed him her purple leather wallet. "My dad gave it to me this morning. I'm sure he put money in there for me. When he learned I was in the hospital, he went looking and found my car. My wallet and keys were inside. It's parked in the garage now until I'm ready to drive again." She looked down at the wheelchair. "I hope I can remember how to drive."

Erick took the wallet and found several bills, a credit card, and her driver's license. He pulled the driver's license out and looked at the New York address and her photo with dark hair. Knowing the answer already, he asked, "So, are you from New York?"

"My parents said I was, but they seem like they don't want to talk about my life in New York. Every time I bring it up, they shut down. Besides, it's not like I'm ready to drive, let alone take a road trip down memory lane. Maybe *we* could go there and see what's there," Grace said unexpectedly.

"Let's get you out of this wheelchair first." Erick handed her the wallet back and smiled as he took the back of her chair and started running down the sidewalk, "Then we can plan a road trip! One *step* at a time."

Grace moaned. "No more jokes!"

He pushed her to the cafe on the corner with a sign out front that read *Café Bella*. Once inside, he wanted to kick himself for not remembering that this was the same cafe Grace frequently used to go to in high school. She could easily have a flashback, and their perfect bubble would pop. Erick reasoned she would be suspicious if he suddenly suggested they leave. How would he explain that? Erick pushed her inside and parked her wheelchair at a table in the back. He quickly looked around the café, and then Erick took the seat next to her. From where he sat, Erick could see everyone who entered and left the small cafe. A young waitress wearing a pink *Café Bella* shirt chewing gum came over to take their order. Erick ordered two hot chocolates with extra whipped cream. The waitress looked from Grace to Erick, then gave him a sultry smile and a wink.

"Looks like someone has a crush on you," Grace teased.

"Nah," Erick replied, blushing.

"Well, it was quite obvious by that smile and wink the waitress gave you."

"Well, she's not my type." He was uncomfortable with this subject. "So, how did you get here from New York? Do you have any new memories yet?"

"My dad said I came here for my aunt's funeral and then after that to hike the trail I was on. I do remember Aunt Raven. She always was nice to me. My dad said she disappeared to hike the West Coast for a while, and I hadn't seen her in over ten years. I can't remember the last time I saw her since my recent memories are blurry, but she left me a journal that I've been reading."

Grace smiled when the hot chocolate came in a large round cup. The cup was more like a bowl with a generous amount of whipped cream and cinnamon sprinkled on top. Grace was about to take a sip when Erick shouted.

"Wait!" Erick grabbed the cup of hot chocolate, sending some of the velvet liquid sloshing over the side. "You can't have cinnamon!" The words tumbled out of his mouth. *Another mistake!*

"*What?*" Grace looked at him. "How did you . . . how do you know that? *I* don't even know that."

Erick gave her his hot chocolate, which did not have cinnamon on top. "It was on your patient paperwork your dad filled out the first day at HigherGround." *Would Grace buy his story? Why should she?* It was another lie. He felt an ache at the bottom of his stomach. The lies piled up and threatened to bury him. The longer he kept this charade going, the worse it would be in the end.

Erick felt her eyes on him, and he braced himself for the fallout. Grace took the cup Erick gave her, put her finger in the cream, and dabbed it on his nose. "You really are quite thorough for a doctor!" Grace took a sip of the hot liquid and placed it back on the table. She smiled at Erick as he wiped the cream from his nose.

"You have no idea!" His eyes shifted from side to side. "Can't break the streak now," he joked.

"What streak is that?" Grace asked playfully.

"I haven't killed a patient yet!" He let out a sly laugh, and she laughed too. He loved looking at her and wished he had a photo of her smiling. Then he got serious. "Maybe I could take a photo of you, for your dad's present. You could buy a nice frame. I bet he would love to see you this happy. Do you have a cell phone?" He shook his head again. *What is wrong with him? He* had her cell phone tucked away in his dresser drawer along with all the terrible messages from Finn.

"No, my parents only lent me an old one for emergencies and to get a ride from therapy. Since you have been driving me most days, I don't really need one."

Erick removed his phone from his pocket. "Here, let me take your picture, and if you like it, we can go back to that store and get a nice handmade wooden frame. I'm sure your dad only wants *you* for Christmas this year." Erick could relate to this and found spending time with her intoxicating.

Grace blushed and smiled as Erick took the photo. He didn't want this day to end. After Erick paid the bill, they returned to the first store, where Grace purchased a nice mahogany frame.

"It's still early, and if you're up for it," Erick suggested. "We could go back and watch a movie. You can pick one this time."

"That sounds great," Grace said, and he loaded her chair back into the Jeep.

Erick's phone buzzed as he turned the ignition on, starting the car. It was Daniel, but he let it go to voicemail. As he shifted the Jeep in reverse, Erick saw something out of the corner of his eye. Another car pulled in next to him.

A fire-red Lexus pulled in the parking space, and a tall blonde got out. She looked straight at him and then at the red-haired girl in the passenger seat. All at once, Erick panicked and hit the gas hard with his right foot. The Jeep lurched backwards, and the tires screeched in protest. Another car swerved and honked. Erick took a deep breath looking behind him, and avoided eye contact with the blonde woman standing there, hands on her hips. Erick's heart raced, and he could not get out of there fast enough. He shifted into gear and squealed the tires more. The one person in the entire world that could blow everything up for him: *Brook Becker,* was standing right in front of them. Erick didn't know if he could talk himself out of this one.

Forty-seven

Grace gripped the door handle nervously as Erick sped out of the parking lot. Grace noticed Erick's mood was all over the place. They had a lovely afternoon shopping, and he had helped her pick the perfect gift for her dad. He was even going to print out a picture of her and put it in the frame they picked out together. She was impressed with his ability to remember small details about her. Everything was perfect, but suddenly Erick seemed very distracted.

"Are you okay?" Grace broke the silence. He turned onto the highway.

"I'm fine. I just hate driving in the city." Erick kept looking out the rearview mirror as though someone was following him.

"Are you wanted by the FBI or something? Also, that was *not* the city." Grace chuckled. "When you told me you lived in the woods. I thought you were joking. You really should get out more."

"Should I now?" Erick loved the easy banter between them. "I'm surprised you even remember the FBI."

"I watched a lot of crime shows on television," Grace said.

Erick pulled into Grace's driveway. He got the wheelchair out, and then they both headed to the door.

"Is anyone home?" Erick asked.

"Mom and Dad went to the mall, but they will be back later." Grace wheeled up the ramp, and at the door, she exclaimed, "Damn it! I didn't take a key." Just then, as if on cue, snow began to fall gently from the sky.

"Maybe you should check in the flowerpot or under the mat?" he said quickly. "I watch TV too," he insisted as snowflakes collected on his beard.

"Well, look at that!" Grace held the key up to Erick suspiciously. "You are full of surprises today! Are you sure you're not a secret agent?" They entered the house, and Grace put her packages in her room.

Erick met up with Grace in the kitchen.

"Grace, the snow is coming down out there!" He removed his jacket and placed it on the bar stool. "Want me to make some tea?"

Grace stood up and reached for the large plastic bowl, and placed it on the counter. "Sure, and popcorn!" she added and sat back down in the chair and reached below to get the popcorn box. Then she stood up again to put the bag into the microwave. Within minutes Grace had a large yellow bowl of popcorn in her lap. She laughed at Erick.

"Impressive moves!" Erick beamed at her and moved to the outside of the island to allow her to roll past him.

"Well, I made the popcorn. The next event is a round of snowboarding? You better keep up!" Grace thought about how easy it was to talk to him.

"There's my girl," Erick said, filling up the tea kettle with water.

"You say that to all your patients," Grace shot back.

He placed his canvas bag on the island and pulled out what looked like DVDs, and spread three of them on the table. "So, don't judge me, but we have some serious chick flicks here. Sky, let me borrow these. *Me Before You, The Vow, and The Upside.* You choose."

"I never heard of these. Well, I can't remember truthfully." Grace grabbed each DVD and one by one and read the summaries. "Hey! All these movies are about either amnesia or a person who is in a wheelchair! You have got to be kidding me!" Grace punched Erick playfully.

"Well, it's all part of your *therapy*. You have made so much progress. Why stop now?"

Grace looked over the movies once again. She was focused intently on the film in her hand because she wanted to pick the right one—the right one where she and Erick would feel like they were on a *date* instead of training. *Always with the training*, Grace thought. *I wonder if he will see me as anything other than a patient.*

Grace was so focused on reading one summary, that in one swift move, Erick snatched up the popcorn bowl from her lap and ran around the room with the bowl high in the air, yelling, "Too slow, G, too slow!"

Grace froze. *He called me 'G.' He never called me 'G.'* Without any warning, a memory surfaced and transported her from the kitchen to gym class.

Grace was dribbling the basketball towards the net. She could hear her sneakers squeaking across a wood floor. The smell of polyurethane and sweat was strong. Grace heard, "Go, G! Go! And you got this, G!" Then, as quickly as it came, the memory faded.

"Are you okay, Grace? Where did you go?" Erick sounded far away. Grace's eyes adjusted and Erick came into view with the popcorn bowl like it was a trophy.

"You called me 'G.'! I swear I just had a flashback. Someone from middle school or high school called me that." She squinted. "I thought I remembered something, but it's gone now." Grace noticed Erick, who was grabbing handfuls of the popcorn and eating them.

"We better watch a movie before you eat all the popcorn."

She waved the DVD. "Let's watch *Me Before You*, and if you're nice, maybe I will give you a ride on the wheelchair like this picture." She said as she pointed to the back cover. The picture was of a woman sitting on the lap of a man in a wheelchair. They were on the dance floor dancing at a wedding. Grace didn't care that it sounded unprofessional. She was having one of the best days of her life. She wheeled closer to Erick, winked at him, and grabbed the popcorn bowl in one quick movement, sending some kernels flying.

"Too slow!" She was laughing in front of the fridge now. "Do you want a beer?" She opened the door.

"No thanks. I don't drink." He avoided her gaze

"Mr. Doctor goodie-two-shoes doesn't want a drink?" She teased.

"Let's just say I didn't have a good experience when I was younger," Erick said, averting his eyes from hers. He went to the cabinet looking for mugs. "Tea is my favorite beverage anyway."

"How did you know where we keep the mugs?" Grace narrowed her eyes.

"If I tell you, I will have to kill you." He frowned and fidgeted while selecting two mugs.

"All the lies!" Grace continued the teasing. Grace was about to ask more when the tea kettle whistled loudly, breaking the mood. Erick found two suitable cups and placed them on the counter. He carefully poured the steaming water into each. He turned off the kitchen light and took both mugs with the steeped tea into the living room.

They ate popcorn in silence as the movie started. Grace and Erick both laughed at all the funny parts. They got quiet by the end of the film as it ended differently than she expected. Grace tried not to cry at the end, and she was sure Erick was choked up as well.

"How can you do all that for someone, and it's still not enough?" Grace asked him after the movie ended.

Erick pondered the question for a while. "You have to have faith," he said finally. "Sometimes you meet someone for a reason, and that alone can change everything." His blue eyes held hers a moment longer than Grace could take.

"I just would be crushed to find out that I . . .was . . . not enough," Grace said, struggling to speak the words and noticed the mood turn somber.

"Grace, any man would think you were more than enough. You have nothing to worry about," he said very softly.

"Even in a wheelchair?" Grace challenged him.

Erick leapt up from the couch in one quick motion, lifting Grace simultaneously, and the two of them landed on the chair together. Erick was sitting in the wheelchair with Grace on his lap. They both couldn't stop laughing. Then he spun them around the living room while Grace gasped for air through giggles. She loved the feeling of being so close to him.

"You mean this old thing?" He spun Grace around at a dizzying speed and doing wheelies on their way to the kitchen until she was breathless. They stopped just before crashing into the island in the kitchen. Then she looked down at him, and he looked up at her. A position they have never been in before. Time seemed to stop. It felt like a dream, his blue eyes looking through hers.

Finally, Grace could feel her breathing even out, but the electricity was still sparking all around them. The kitchen light was off. The TV had a black screen. The only light was coming in through the windows from the grey sky outside. Outside, a blue-grey hue cast a glow on the two still sitting there in the dark. Erick had his arms around Grace to keep her from falling off his lap. The heat was rising in the air despite the fact it was bitter cold outside. Erick was so close to Grace's face she could smell the buttery popcorn on his breath. His head moved closer to hers, and she felt her eyes close. Erick's lips moved over Grace's mouth. Grace jumped as the front door creaked open.

"I think we have gotten more snow in the last few days!" Faith said to Robin as they entered the kitchen and flipped on the light switch illuminating a strange scene of two people in a wheelchair.

"Grace! Doctor . . ." Robin frowned as his eyes landed on the two of them. What a sight they must have been with her on Erick's lap in the kitchen in the dark.

Erick lifted Grace, and she supported herself against the counter. "We were just goofing around in the wheelchair," Grace said, her cheeks crimson. She was a grown woman, but at that moment, she felt more like a child.

"It's late, and I should go." Erick exited the wheelchair and began cleaning up. It seemed like they had found themselves in a compromising position for the second time.

Grace returned her body to the wheelchair and followed Robin and Erick as they moved to the front door.

"Grace, I want to see you first thing tomorrow at Higher-Ground. It's time we get you out of the chair, once and for all." Erick raised his voice as he got his jacket on. "See you tomorrow. Mr. Evans. Mrs. Evans, always a pleasure." He waved to them and headed to the door.

"Okay, well, it's late, and I'm going to bed. Good night!" Grace hugged her parents.

"Goodnight, sweetheart," Faith said.

"Be careful." Robin kissed her forehead with a peculiar expression on his face. "Don't get too attached to Doctor Erick. You have more work to do, and this is your time to focus on yourself," he warned her as he gently moved a stray hair away from her face.

"I'm fine, Dad. I'm happy for the first time in forever. I just wanted to enjoy the moment. I promise I will keep my focus on me."

Robin nodded, and Grace wheeled her way into her bedroom. She reached for the gifts she had bought her parents and hid them under the bed. Grace could have floated from the wheelchair to the bed. She had only one thing on her mind as she got into bed, and it had everything to do with the kiss. She closed her eyes and sighed at the blissful feeling. Then she remembered her Aunt Raven, how in love she had been with that boy, Jack. Her Aunt Raven had lost herself in that love. Grace could sympathize with Aunt Raven as she opened the journal and continued reading. A man didn't cause her to lose herself, but the accident made her forget who she was.

The next day I went again to Freedom Trail Summit, and I stayed there for hours. Each day, I felt more and more alive, and I would stay up at night doodling in my notebook I bought at the bookstore to walk from my apartment.

I loved the smell of books, and I found a pink notebook with a bird on it the first day Jack was gone. He would call each night at 9 p.m. to see how I was doing, and I listened to his tale of endless business meetings. I heard a woman's laughter in the background, but I didn't dare ask him about it.

The next day, I went back to the bookstore and looked at the hiking section. I tried to reach a book called Connecticut's Guide to Hiking the Appalachian Trail, *but my fingers only grazed the bottom of the book. Determined to get the book down, I leapt in the air, nearly falling backwards. Falling is a funny thing. It's so quick, the body sends alarms off in the brain, and then relief comes, especially when you catch your breath. What happened to me was even more exhilarating. A handsome stranger with solid arms caught me.*

"Do you need help?" *This man looked close to my age with shoulder-length brown hair. He looked at me with hazel eyes. Next, he released me and reached up quickly to hand me the book I was trying to get. He wore a "RESERVOIR BOOKS" shirt with his name tag "Stephen". His skin was deeply tanned, and I could see a tattoo of a compass on his forearm with the words, "Those Who Wander are not lost."*

"Can I help you with anything else? I hiked the AT last summer. It was amazing!" *Stephen grinned from ear to ear.* "Do you like to hike?"

Words filled my mind, but they wouldn't surface. I coughed instead, embarrassed. "I love to hike." *Finding my voice again, I asked,* "Have you been to the Freedom Summit?"

"I love to trail run there because most people don't know all the side trails up there. I prefer to hike alone," *he said, looking at me just then.* "Of course, I could make an exception for the right person."

Was he flirting with me?

"That sounds fun, actually. I will be up there tomorrow when the sun comes up."

"Oh, you need to go earlier than that! I can meet you there at 4 a.m. It will still be dark, but I won't let you get lost."

"I don't even know you!" *My heart raced.*

"That's true. May I have the book, please?" *He walked over to the counter, paid for it, and took off his name tag. Then he grabbed his jacket below the counter and returned to me.* "I bought your book, and now you can spring for coffee. Then we can get to know each other better."

Grace closed the book. Was her aunt crazy? How could she just run off with a stranger she just met? He could have been a serial killer for all she knew. Another detail stuck out in Grace's mind. Freedom Summit. Wasn't that where her dad said she had fallen? It had to be the same place. As soon as she could walk, Grace decided she would have to go there again.

So many questions about Aunt Raven's life flooded Grace's mind. She realized there were still so many questions she could not figure out about her own life. One question bothered her the most. What was the connection between Aunt Raven's story, the freedom trails, and Grace's life?

Erick drove his Jeep home in the snow. He planned to meet Grace the next day at HigherGround. His thoughts about being with her made him more confused than ever. The shopping, the cafe, and the movies had really muddled things between them. His inability to stay professional, mixed with his feelings for Grace, was getting out of control. He was getting more attached than ever, especially when her lips ended up on his. He couldn't believe he kissed her! He checked his phone and saw that he missed three calls from Brook. She did not leave a message. Erick rolled his eyes and called Daniel. Jace climbed up on the bed, resting his body against Erick's foot. Erick stared at the ceiling as he waited for his brother to answer the phone.

"Hello?" Daniel picked up on the third ring.

"Daniel, I'm in trouble," Erick began.

"What is it?" Daniel sounded concerned.

"I just spent the whole day with Grace, and something happened."

"She remembered you?" Daniel guessed wide-eyed.

"No, worse than that maybe. We kissed at her parents' house," Erick said while exhaling.

"Are you crazy? If her parents find out, you could lose your license!"

"Daniel, it gets worse. I'm a terrible person. Grace is ready to walk. She's been ready for weeks now. I should have told her the truth about us."

Spending time with Grace all these weeks was like heaven on earth. Erick decided that it was time to tell her the truth. Erick imagined that he would first explain to her how he knew her. Then he would reveal to her what really happened all those years ago. He would tell her what he could remember. Erick would say to her the other thing that never left his mind. The one fact that brought him to help her today. The truth is that he had not only loved her back then, but he was still in love with her today.

"So, Erick? Listen, I have been trying to get ahold of you for days!" Daniel broke the silence. "I'm at the hospital."

"Daniel, are you okay?" He jumped to his feet. The sudden movement startled Jace. Erick wanted to kick himself for being so consumed in his life and not looking after his brother.

"*I'm* fine, but Dad is in the hospital again. I know you have been busy, but you should come and see him, seriously today."

"Ok, Daniel. I will be right there!" Erick started getting dressed.

"Sky gave me a ride. Joyce and I closed HigherGround early. It is Christmas Eve, after all."

"Okay. I'm on my way." Erick got his keys. "Sorry, buddy, I'll be back soon." He scratched Jace's ears, grabbed his coat, and made his way to the hospital.

Erick saw Daniel first. Sky was standing by his side.

"Daniel! How is he? The last time I was here, they sent him home."

"Dude, follow us, and we will explain."

Erick followed the couple down the hall into the VIP section of the hospital. They entered the room, and Brook was there seated next to his dad. Erick could feel his body tense up.

"Hello, Erick. I was just leaving." She glared in Erick's direction, frowning.

"Sounds like a good plan." Erick was not interested in dealing with her right now.

"What was up with you the other day? Racing off like a lunatic! I've been trying to reach you. Were you avoiding me?" Brook's eyes blazed, and her arms were folded over her chest. "I know what you're up to!"

"Now is not the time, Brook. I'd like to talk to *my* father." Erick refused to engage or make eye contact. *"Alone."*

"Fine, but I saw her. How long has this been going on?" Brook stood up and glared at Erick. "Does Finn know?"

"Oh my God, Brook! This is none of your business or the time and place for any of this! You're not even *family*, and you shouldn't be here." Erick sat in the now empty seat. Brook flipped her blonde hair behind her shoulder and brushed by Daniel and Sky, who stood at the doorway in disbelief.

"Trouble in paradise? You just missed Dom. He just left," Declan spoke in a raspy voice. Declan looked small, and his skin looked grey. He owned the largest publishing company and had been larger than life. He looked sad and lost here and now.

"Finn was here?" Erick looked around nervously.

"Yeah, he had to get back to the office. I just appointed him CEO of FinnLondon."

"How are you doing, Dad?" Erick tried to distract himself from what was sure to be a disaster up ahead.

"Well, son. The doctor says I need to step back from the stress of work permanently this time. I guess it's time I retire." Declan took a deep labored breath. "They told me my heart condition is worse. There isn't much time left, I'm afraid. I guess this old guy had a good run."

"Sorry, Dad. Sorry I wasn't there for you. When can you get out of here?" Erick reached for his dad's hand, thinking about how much time he wasted being angry at his family. God would have wanted him to show his family that love was the way. He could see that now. Sometimes love requires one to do the thing he had been avoiding.

"I'm not getting out of here alive." Declan frowned.

"None of us are, Dad. What's the treatment plan? Can you get on a list for a new heart?" Erick was concerned.

"Not for an old guy like me. It is my time. There are no treatment options at this point, son. I asked to go home and be with my family. I was hoping that would include you. I never got to tell you how *proud* I am of all that you accomplished. The world needs more people like you. I should not have insisted you run the business. I saw HigherGround on the internet, and your therapy practice is one of the *best* in New England. You have not only turned into an exceptional doctor, but you really are a great person and a good son. You didn't get any of that from me." Declan coughed.

"It's okay. I get it. It must have been hard raising three boys on your own." Erick felt a weight fall from his shoulders. After all these years, he finally received his father's blessing.

"Your mother was the love of my life, son. I did the best I could after she left us. There isn't a day that goes by that I do not think about your mother. I hope one day you find that kind of love, son."

"I found it once, Dad. I ruined it all those years ago in high school, after Daniel's accident. I still have questions about what happened exactly all those years ago."

"Some things are better off NOT knowing, son. I took

care of that problem years ago. You should not be worrying about that now."

"It's been *ten* years! It was *my* fault. Wait, what do you mean *you took care of it?*" Erick was sitting by his father's side, and he followed his father's gaze. Daniel and Sky were getting coffee. It was just the two of them.

"It was not your fault at all, and I made sure it was no one's fault."

"What does that mean? How is it not my fault? I was the one drinking. I was the one driving."

Declan shook his head and started coughing when the nurse came in.

"You have to go. Your father needs his rest," the nurse said sternly and was not taking no for an answer.

"Dad," Erick could barely breathe himself. "What happened that night, and what did you do? I have to know!" He raised his voice, and the nurse frowned at him. Erick stood up and moved away so the nurse could adjust his medication.

"He can't have *any* stress right now. You'll have to come back later." The nurse ushered him out before he could ask another word.

Erick reluctantly left the room, and his mind was racing. He was glad that Brook was gone, and he found Daniel and Sky in the lobby waiting.

"What are you going to do about Brook?" Daniel asked him.

"Pray for a miracle." Defeated, Erick waved to them both and returned to his Jeep. Questions fired at him like bullets. *What secret was Dad keeping from me? Could I have been wrong about everything?* How much time did he even have left with his dad? The last question pierced him in the heart. Now that Brook knows about Grace, it won't be long before she tells Finn. Erick was running out of time.

Forty-eight

Grace woke up late on Christmas Eve and found a note her mom left for her saying Erick had canceled their appointment because of a family emergency. Grace hoped everything was okay. She thought about calling Erick from the house phone but decided to give him time.

Her parents were out, and Grace had the whole house to herself. She was looking forward to working with Erick today and seeing him after they shared their first kiss. Would he lie about the reason he had to cancel? Grace didn't think he would lie to her, but he might have been spooked after the kiss. She went over the details in her mind savoring the memory. When he put his mouth on hers, she felt like they had always fit together. Grace was confident he kissed her back. She knew it was dangerous to start something, especially with her doctor and maybe he thought it was a mistake.

A knock at the door broke through her thoughts. Grace wheeled herself to the door, hoping it was Erick and opened it.

"Hi, Sunshine!" Julie stood there on the other side of the door with a bouquet of light purple Amaryllis flowers.

"Julie!" Grace exclaimed. "Come in! I'm so happy to see you."

"I'm so happy to see you! The flowers are so pretty," Grace said as Julie handed her the bouquet. "Thank you!"

"I thought you might like these." Julie beamed.

"Sorry I haven't called. I have been training so much. I've been making so much progress."

"I heard you were doing amazing. I've known Erick for a long time, and he is the best. You're in good hands with that one!"

Grace could agree with that. *His hands were undeniably good.* She shook the thoughts from her head, trying not to think about his hands around her waist.

"So, what's going on with you? Have you been out in the world yet or just cooped up here?"

"Well, we went to the center of town in West Hartford the other day and had hot chocolate at the cafe."

"That sounds more like a *date* than training!" Julie hung up her coat on the foyer coat tree, followed Grace into the living room, and took a seat next to the fireplace.

"It's not like that," Grace replied but realized it exactly was like that. She couldn't lie. "I don't know, Julie. I'm so attracted to him. It's crazy! I don't even know who I am. How could I start a relationship with someone when I don't even know where I live?" Grace frowned. "Actually, I do know where I lived."

"What do you mean?" Julie leaned closer. "Did you read the journal that I dropped off the last time I was here?"

"Oh yes! I have been reading it nearly every day when I'm not training, of course. I want to tell you all about it! How long can you stay?"

"It's my day off, and I just have to be home for dinner with my mom." Julie's eyes sparkled.

"I'll be right back." Grace wheeled herself into her room, found her purse, and took out the wallet. "Look," she handing Julie the NY state license.

"Whoa. This is a clue!" Julie stood up. "Where is your computer?"

"I don't have one, but my mom does in her office. I have never been inside the office, though, I don't think." Grace felt her chair move. "Wait, what? What are you doing?"

"Come on. Let's see where you lived before. It'll be fun." Julie followed Grace out of the living room. "So, lead the way to the office."

Once inside, Julie found the laptop, turned it on, but password protection came up. Julie moved her fingers over the computer and figured out a way to sign in as a guest. When the search engine came up, Julie typed in the address on the license. *111 Central Park West.*

As Grace wheeled her way around the large oak desk when Julie let out a shriek.

"What is it?" Grace peered at the computer screen.

"Oh my God! Grace, this is *your* apartment?"

Grace's mouth fell open, and she gasped when she saw what Julie had up on the screen. Julie continued to click through the images one after another. Grace then saw the value of her apartment was over *seven million dollars.* Julie continued scrolling through and found the owner, *Declan Finn.* Next, Julie did a search on Declan Finn.

Owner of FinnLondon in NYC and Hartford, CT. Declan Finn's net worth is 27 million.

A photo came up on the screen of a man in a suit. He had grey hair and a stern look. Julie was still talking, but Grace could no longer hear her.

Her mom's office morphed into another office. Long floor-to-ceiling windows wrapped around a white room. Grace heard yelling outside the glass walls of her office. Two men were talking, their faces close to one another. One was Declan, and the other man was blurry. She couldn't hear their words through the glass as it muffled it. Grace walked closer to the men to make out their words.

"You need to get it together, son."

"I'm doing the best I can, Dad."

"It was a mistake thinking you could . . ."

"That was a long time ago. Stop holding that over my head."

"Don't think I won't fire you. That girl isn't one of us, you know."

"Grace?" Julie was standing over her now. "Where did you go?"

"Julie, I—," Grace stammered. "I keep getting flashes of memories. I have seen that man before! There was another man with him. There were glass offices, but I can't remember anything else. It's too much to process, and my head hurts. I need to get some water. When you're done, will you meet me in the kitchen?" Grace was more confused than ever.

"You are *not* going to believe what I found out!" Julie exclaimed, running into the kitchen a few minutes later.

"I just can't right now," Grace implored her as she took a sip of water. "My memories are coming faster now, and each time I get a memory, my head hurts. I need to lie down on the couch."

"I understand." Julie put her hand on Grace's shoulder. "Can I get you anything?" Julie frowned and followed Grace into the living room. Grace left the wheelchair, climbed onto the couch and stretched her legs out. Julie sat down next to her. "Do you want me to go?"

"No. Please. Just stay. My headache will go away soon enough. Can you read the journal to me? Your voice was always so soothing to me in the hospital."

"Okay, where do you want me to start?" Julie asked.

"So, my aunt was in some crazy relationship with a guy named Jack Stone. He controlled everything she did. She met him in school, and Jack must have been super cute, I guess, and he was adopted. I can't imagine being adopted and not knowing who my birth parents are. I guess her dad, my grandfather, and her brother, my dad, did not like him at all. She didn't realize how much she had disappeared into the relationship with this guy until he went on a business trip for two weeks. Then my aunt remembered everything she loved to do, like going hiking and going to her favorite bookstore. So, while Jack was gone, she got a glimpse of life without him, and then suddenly she met a mysterious guy at a bookstore. The part I left off on was her deciding if she was going to go hiking with him before dawn." Grace handed Julie the book and put a pillow under her head. "I wonder if she goes with him."

"That sounds crazy. Did your aunt ever tell you this story before?" Julie raised her eyebrows.

"No, but what's really crazy is that she keeps referencing that my life is on a similar path. Get this! She goes hiking at Freedom Summit. The *same* trail I was on when I fell. Okay, just read. I'm dying to know what happens next." Grace closed her eyes.

"Well, that *is* crazy!" Julie began to read.

> *This man I hardly knew just paid for my book. I followed him to the cafe adjacent to the bookstore with an entrance through the mystery section. "I would prefer tea, actually," I said, suddenly finding my own voice as if I was used to choosing what I wanted.*
>
> *"Tea it is! 'Getting coffee' is just an expression. I believe you should have only what you want. Never settle for what you think someone else wants." Stephen's words rang true more than he realized about what my life had become. "So," Stephen took a sip of his black coffee and looked at me. "How often do you hike?"*
>
> *I took a cautious sip of the herbal tea and looked up at Stephen. "I used to live to walk in the woods. My brother and I used to walk every day."*

"How many siblings do you have?" Stephen asked. I realized how much I missed people asking about me. Had it been that long since I had a live conversation with another human being?

"Just one brother, but we are twins, actually." I lowered my eyes because I did not want to admit I missed my brother.

"You look sad. Is that one of those phenomenon things where you can feel what the other twin is feeling?"

How is he reading my mind? I looked away, "It's been a while since Robin and I spoke, so . . ." I looked back at this man. "The twin thing is real, and we had it once."

"So, what is your name?" Stephen suddenly asked, and I realized I never said.

"Raven." I felt my cheeks flush because my name embarrassed me. My name never bothered me until Jack told me he thought ravens were scavengers and the memory of him kicking one made me cringe.

"Whoa, that is a great name!" Stephen's hazel eyes sparkled. "Did you know in my culture, the meaning of the raven symbol signifies that danger has passed and that good luck will follow? The raven is a highly adaptable creature. According to legend, the Raven is the bringer of light. The legend states that on one night, a raven escaped from the darkness of the universe to bring light down to earth for others." Stephen paused and sipped his coffee, not taking his eyes off me. "The raven is the bringer of light where only darkness lives. It's also a messenger from the spirit world. Ravens who fly high above to the heavens bear actual prayers from mortals. Once they deliver the messages to the spirit world, they can sometimes bring a message of hope back from the spiritual realm."

"You sure know a lot about ravens." I was pleased with Stephen's thoughts about ravens.

"Well, I'm fortunate my grandparents passed down their wisdom to me. My heritage is ¾ Native American. Cherokee, to be exact. I'm also surrounded by a lot of books." He waved his hands toward the bookstore. "I have only been written up once for reading on the job." He laughed, and his long dark hair swayed over his shoulders. "I love my job."

Who was this guy? I found myself just wanting to listen and hang on to his every word. Hours had passed in mere minutes, and we talked about how the forest could heal a broken soul. Although he did not tell me his story of healing yet, I was fascinated with the idea that the forest could heal us. He said that trees emit energy, and when we absorb that energy, we are transformed. And just like that, I agreed to meet him the next day.

At 4 a.m., I was more nervous he would come to his senses and not show up than I was spending time with a stranger. He was waiting for me, just like he said, and he wore a large grin on his face. We drove to Freedom Summit and hiked up to the top without saying a word as the sun rose behind us. Once at the top, I saw the most beautiful sight I had ever seen. We sat there and took it all in. I got lost in his hazel eyes, and I never wanted to leave. We made plans to see each other again.

Stephen would take me to many places that week. He taught me about which plants were healing and which ones were toxic. He gave me a small field guide, another gift, no doubt from the bookstore.

I spent every minute of my free time with this man. When he worked, I went home and wrote in my journal. I collected wildflowers and herbs that he would show me how to steep in tea. He told me about his dream to travel and how he would take months off at a time to hike the longer trails. Stephen preferred the less-traveled places.

I felt like I had stepped into a movie where I was suddenly the main character. At the end of the week, I felt like anything was possible. I did speak to Jack a couple of times. I told him I was working on projects and reading books. I left out the part about Stephen because I knew he wouldn't understand.

The second time we went to the summit at Freedom Rock Trails, we sat on the same rock, but we watched the sun go down this time. He confessed to me that he was going to leave soon to hike the Pacific Coast Trail. I knew our time would run out because Jack would come home, and Stephen would return to the life he had before me. The fantasy would fade just like the sun setting before us. We walked down the summit in the dark, but I wasn't afraid. I had learned the secrets of the woods. I actually felt like I re-learned them as if they had died inside me long ago. Stephen called this a rebirth.

The night before Stephen left, I wanted to thank him. He invited me over to his studio apartment and wanted to cook for me. He had his hair pulled back in a hair tie and an apron tied around his neck and waist. Stephen had mentioned he was a vegan when we met. He said that we ingest the energy from what we eat. Stephen asked me that day in the cafe, "Do you want to feel alive or dead?" I felt dead inside until the day I met Stephen, and he opened my eyes to the whole world of wonder and aliveness. I stopped eating meat after that day. I wanted to feel alive. We went out on his small patio deck after a homemade dinner of portobello mushroom paella and cornbread. Stephen confessed that his birth name was Pala. He shared that this name means Guardian. He was the guardian of the forest, and I believed that he was too. The moonlight flooded the patio, and Stephen looked like an angel.

"I'm leaving tomorrow. My lease is up, and it's time to move on to my next adventure."

Julie closed the book. "How dreamy is this story?"

Grace smiled, her eyes still closed. "I know, right?"

Looking at her watch, Julie said, "Listen, I got to stop by the hospital. Let's do this again soon. Let me know what happens next." She got up and hugged her friend. "Are you going to be okay?"

"I will be fine, Julie. Thank you so much for coming by. It means so much to me!"

"Of course!" Julie embraced Grace and headed out the door. Grace drifted off thinking about her aunt and Pala.

Erick and Jace set out for a run. It didn't matter that the snow had turned into rain. He needed to get out there. He put on a heavier vest, hat, waterproof trail runners, and gloves to keep warm and dry. As his feet rhythmically hit the ground, he thought through that fateful night in high school. *What was he missing?* How he had arrived with Finn and Daniel, Brook's kiss, the look on Grace's face, and the drinks. He went through every detail about that night. What was still coming up blank for him was what had followed. As Erick kept running, he looked at the soft white snow covering the trail.

It was Christmas Eve, and all he wanted to do was see Grace. It was only a matter of time when she would find out the truth about him. Erick needed to be the one to tell her. If she found out from someone else, it would end badly for him for sure. The same outcome as it was all those years ago. He thought about the look on her face the night she saw him with Brook at the party. It pained him that she would look at him again like that, but Grace deserved to know the truth.

As he approached the cabin, Erick slowed his run. Once inside, he removed his snowy clothes and took care of Jace. Erick had plans to meet up with Daniel and Sky that night. Erick showered, got dressed and left for the hospital. His dad was getting released today, and he wanted to be there for him.

Erick pulled into the hospital parking lot. He walked in and waved to Sherri at the front desk. Next, Erick looked to see if Brook or Finn had arrived. He rubbed his neck and ran his hand through his hair when he heard his name. His heart stopped.

"Erick!" a woman called from behind him. His pulse quickened. He turned around and was happy to see Julie, the nurse who took care of Grace.

"Hello, Julie." Erick stood there rocking from one foot to another, hoping this would be a short conversation. He had to get to his dad before he got discharged.

"Erick, I need to talk to you. It's about Grace," Julie said frowning.

They walked over to the corner of the waiting area for more privacy. "What's going on? Is Grace okay?"

"I *know* who you really are!" Julie looked at him sternly.

"What?" Erick stared at her, confused.

"You are Erick Finn, one of Declan Finn's sons. Grace and I were on the computer looking for clues to her past and at her New York apartment. Your family knows Grace! Plus, I saw a photo of Dominic Finn and Grace. She is your brother's girlfriend, Erick! You know her, don't you? You've been lying to her this entire time!" Julie placed her hands on her hips, daring him to deny it.

Erick took a deep breath. This situation was getting worse. "Listen, Julie. I'm not a criminal or anything. I just have family issues. Yes, I know Grace from high school. My intentions are pure, and I just wanted to give her the best chance of walking again."

Julie softened a little. "It's bad enough she can't remember her past, but I think she is falling in love with you."

Her words filled him equally with hope and sadness. The weight of what she was saying meant that it would only be a matter of time before Grace found out the truth. "Did you tell her? Does she know?"

"No, but I almost did. We put the address on Grace's driver's license in the search engine. Your father's picture came up as the owner of the seven-million-dollar loft, and Grace had a flashback of something that happened to her at the office. I was able to figure out everything about her past in under five minutes online."

"Thank you for telling me, Julie. I promise you I have Grace's best interest at heart. I'm protecting her from my brother, and I'm going to tell her soon. It's complicated." Erick ran his hand through his hair again. "Her training is going so well that tomorrow I'm going to give her a cane for Christmas. She is ready, Julie. She is walking!"

Tears of joy replaced the angry feelings on Julie's face, "Really? She can walk?"

"Yes, she can! Please just give me two more days. Please let me be the one to tell her about our past. We were a couple in high school and broke up over a complete misunderstanding. I loved her! God, I haven't stopped loving her. Please give me a chance. I can see you care about her as much as I do."

"Please don't hurt her, Erick." Julie suddenly hugged Erick. He knew it was hard to understand. He wasn't sure if he understood all of it.

"I love her so much, Julie. I will make it right. Trust me." He pulled away from her and handed her a tissue. "My dad is here, and he is going home on hospice. I need to go. Please don't say anything!"

"I won't, but please tell her soon. She is going to freak out, and lies can only hurt people. Make it right!" Julie implored him to do the right thing. "Sorry about your dad."

"Thank you, Julie," Erick said. "Going to see him now." He waved to Julie and left to find his father. He was relieved to find him alone in the room.

"Dad!" Erick saw his father signing papers on the table. Declan Finn wore jeans and a flannel shirt. One wouldn't know he was sick the way he carried himself.

Declan looked up over his reading glasses. "Son!"

Erick hugged his dad just then. Just because they had different ideas about Erick's life didn't mean he didn't love him. Erick suddenly realized how short life really was and decided he wouldn't miss any more of it.

"Dad." He took the seat next to him. "Are you leaving the hospital soon?"

Declan nodded.

"That's good. I want to be there for you and help you in any way I can."

Declan put the stack of papers down on the hospital tray table, sighed, and looked deeply into Erick's eyes.

"Erick, I have people to do that for me. If you're by my side, it's so we can mend our relationship. I love you, son."

"I love you too, Dad," Erick said, trying not to get choked up. He really wanted to ask about the accident, but he wasn't sure the timing was appropriate.

"I know the accident is still on your mind, Erick. I know how it's tortured you. But I just want you to be happy. I don't want secrets between us. Secrets will kill a person."

"I know, and that day has defined my entire life. If there's a chance, just one chance, that I can come to some sort of closure with it, it'll be the greatest gift you could ever give me."

"Son, you were *not* driving the car that night. You are not responsible for Daniel's accident, as I have told you many, many times before. I paid a lot of money to protect the family. I tried telling you years ago to stop blaming yourself. Sometimes you are so much like me, son. Stubborn to a fault. I also want to tell you something else." Declan looked tired suddenly. "I don't blame you for leaving the family business. You were more sensitive than your brother, and I wished we had spent more time together. I should never have punished you for choosing your life calling. I have so many regrets, especially with Dominick." Declan's eyes watered. "I only have a short time to make it up to all *three* of my boys."

Erick stared into his father's eyes, trying to hold the tears back. "Dad, I love what I do. God put me here in this life to help others who have no hope."

"I'm sorry it took me this long to have this conversation with you. All that matters now is the relationships we hold dear, son. If I could go back and do it and do it all over again, I would. You are so much like your mother. I wanted to give you my blessing before . . . you know." Declan shrugged off any display of emotion.

Erick moved closer to his dad and hugged him. "I forgive you, Dad." The tears flowed, and they held each other for a moment. "I was only trying to protect—"

"I'm sorry to interrupt," the nurse said as she moved the wheelchair in the room. "Let me know when your ride is here," she told Declan. "You are ready to go."

"Talk to Dom, Erick. I fear I've made such mistakes with him that it might be too late. I can't help him, but *you* can. You have a way about you, just like your mother. He should be here soon. It would be best if you cleared the air with him, too. No one knows how long we have on this earth."

"I will talk to him one day soon. I'll see you as soon as you're settled. I promise."

"Your ride is here," The nurse announced. "It's time to go."

"I will see you soon. I love you, Dad." Erick got up with a sense of urgency. He did not want to see Finn. Not yet. There was too much at stake, too much to lose.

"Love you, son." Declan hugged him and got into the wheelchair. "I'm not a cripple!" He snapped at the nurse, and Erick cringed.

"Hospital rules!" The nurse was not going to take no for an answer. She winked at Declan, and he softened.

Erick walked down the stairs and exited through the surgeon wing to avoid seeing Finn. Seeing his dad revealed so many things, including what really happened that night. He could not believe how long he was wrong about everything. He was not the driver that night, and he was relieved.

The wheels in Erick's mind began to turn. He would get to the bottom of who really was driving that night. Then that chapter of his life could close once and for all. For now, he was happy to finally have his dad's blessing. After all these years, he felt the guilt leave his body. It was like a heavy weight was lifted off his shoulders. He got to his Jeep and did the only thing he knew how to do. He prayed for what to do next.

Forty-nine

Grace had fallen asleep on the couch after Julie left. She awoke and looked around, not sure where she was. Grace saw the familiar fireplace and an undecorated tree by the front window.

"Hey, Mom," Grace said, still groggy from her nap. "Did you know I lived in New York?"

Faith looked at Robin, who was sitting in the easy chair by the fireplace. "Robin, we really need to tell her about her past. Don't you think it is time?"

Grace sat up and rubbed her eyes. "My wallet," Grace began once Faith sat down. "I found my license. I know I lived in New York. Julie looked up the address, and it's a million-dollar loft near Central Park. I'm not the owner, but do you know a *Declan Finn*?" The words tumbled out. She couldn't understand any of it. "*Why* did I live there?" She asked.

"Yes, Grace, it's true you worked and lived in New York the last decade or so." Pain etched across Robin's face.

"Why did you wait so long to tell me?" Grace was hurt.

"The doctors said not to push your memories, that you had to remember on your own, or they would bury themselves too deep. Your amnesia could be permanent if we told you too much too soon." Robin rubbed his beard and sighed. "I wanted to tell you all of it."

"Grace!" Faith grew impatient. "Did you read the journal?"

"I started it. Aunt Raven seemed to have relationship issues. I'm still unsure why she gave me the journal and why I was up on the mountain that day. I also want to know why I was in a million-dollar loft in New York. My head." Grace started crying. "I just don't know what is going on. I feel like everyone knows, except me. I need to know!" Grace held her head and cried. Robin moved to the couch and hugged her tight.

"You will in time. Please be patient with us," Robin choked the words out. "Do you want us to call the doctor?"

"No, I'm going back to bed. I can't talk. My head hurts too much." She climbed into the wheelchair, wheeled herself back into her room, and shut the door. She felt something was terribly wrong, and she was going to figure out why with or without their help. Even if it were the last thing she ever did, she would find out the *truth*. Grace stared at the ceiling and blinked. *"Did you finish reading the journal?"* Faith's words echoed in her mind. All Grace wanted to do was rest. The journal must be the key to everything. She grabbed the journal and opened to the part where she left off. *Aunt Raven, I really could use some answers right now.*

"I have taken you as far as I can. You cannot come with me. I'm sure your boyfriend is a great guy, and your life is here."

I couldn't speak because his rough hands on my face pulsed with electricity. Stephen never touched me when we were out. He never tried to kiss me or even hold my hand. Yet now, I felt the rush of all my cells alive and magnetized to his fingers. If I didn't kiss him, then I thought, I'd burst into flames. Every cell in my body felt like the fourth of July. He pulled back, "I should take you home." His kind hazel eyes looked deep into mine. He swept my wild red hair off my face as the tears came again.

He was like a breath of fresh air breathed into my half-life. I told him this and how thankful I was that he held space for me to become something else. I told him I was lost, and I forgot who I was. He had awakened me, and now I saw in color.

He told me he saw darkness in my eyes and wanted to help, and he expected nothing in return, and he didn't want to get between Jack and me.

I whispered, "I really want to be with you—one time. No strings attached. I will not complicate life for you. Just let me give you this, please. I know you feel it too."

In the morning, he left me a note.

> You are the author of your own wstory. Raven.
> Fly high. my friend.
> You are a life bringer.
> Your next adventure awaits.
> I will never forget you.
>
> Pala

Erick slept in and was thankful for another nightmare-free night. It was Christmas Day and sunny for the first time in days. He went for a run with Jace that morning, and he was excited about what he had planned the day. The first part of that plan was to stop by Daniel's house early.

Sky opened the door laughing with a glass of orange juice in her hand. Jace barreled in past her looking for Luna.

"Hey, Erick!"

Erick had wrapped presents in his hand as he entered the apartment. Daniel was making pancakes in the kitchen. Erick noticed that Daniel and Sky had matching red and black buffalo plaid pajamas. He felt joy watching the two of them as if they had been together their whole lives.

"Merry Christmas!" Erick exclaimed.

Daniel waved the spatula. "Merry Christmas. Any word on how Dad is doing?"

"He is home now. The doctors said he could live a few more months. Still, he is stubborn enough to hang on longer." Erick had already decided he would spend more time with his dad once he faced the current problem at hand and told Grace the truth.

"How is Grace doing?" Daniel flipped a pancake over to reveal a golden-brown top. Erick handed Sky the presents.

"She is doing well. I'm going over there for dinner." Concern filled Erick's face. "I'm going to tell her tomorrow. The truth about our past. It's time. Besides, she can walk now."

Sky put a steaming plate of pancakes on the table. "Join us for breakfast?" Luna and Jace immediately perked up at the word *breakfast*. "You two! None for you. Go *play*." They did not give up. Instead, the dogs sat down, their eyes looking up as if they were saying: *We're starving.*

"Sure." Erick followed them to the table. "*No*, Jace," Erick said sternly. Jace and Luna laid down, just in case.

After breakfast, Erick was sitting in the living room drinking green tea, looking at the flames in the fireplace. Luna and Jace were lying by his feet.

They exchanged presents, and before long, it was time to leave. Erick got to his feet, and just as he put his jacket on, he noticed Daniel give Sky the last present under the tree. He backed up to let them have this moment. Pure joy filled his heart as he knew what was coming next.

Sky unwrapped and opened the box only to find another wrapped box inside. After opening the next box, she laughed and found another box. Four more boxes lay on the floor, each smaller than the next. Finally, that revealed the last one, a small red velvet box. Daniel wheeled himself closer to her, and Erick froze where he stood. He watched the scene play out as Daniel slid down off the chair to be on both knees. It was more beautiful than Erick could have imagined. Sky shrieked, "YES!" and Daniel put the sizeable sparkly ring on her finger. They kissed, and Sky helped him back into the wheelchair. Daniel pulled her onto his lap and spun Sky around in a victory lap.

"She said yes!" he exclaimed.

"Congratulations to you two! Merry Christmas!" Erick waved, and Jace followed him out as he closed the door behind him, and he couldn't help feeling pride and love for his brother. Finally, someone was getting their dream come true. Erick looked over to the present in the back seat: a simple long pink ribbon wrapped around a beautiful wooden cane. He hoped Grace would love it, but he secretly wished he was giving her a velvet box and a promise for the future. Erick figured the gift of walking without a wheelchair would be the next best thing.

Fifty

Grace woke up to the familiar black raven tapping on her bedroom window. Frost framed the window. Fresh snow fell overnight, and the sun was rising. Grace pulled herself out of bed and noticed that standing was getting easier. She picked up Aunt Raven's journal and placed it on the nightstand. Grace sat in her wheelchair and looked out the window. *How strange*, she thought, *that a raven would visit me every night. Could it be a sign from Aunt Raven?* She loved Stephen's description of ravens bringing her light and messages from beyond.

Grace tapped back on the window, and the bird flew away. Silence filled the room, and still in her pajamas, Grace wheeled herself into the kitchen. Faith was sitting at the island typing away on her computer. Smells of browned butter, pancakes, maple syrup, and coffee filled her nose. Robin was plating up a few pancakes and placed them in front of her.

"Merry Christmas, Pumpkin!" Robin smiled as he tied an apron over his flannel shirt and dark blue jeans. It read, *"I might be Robin, but I'm the hero of this kitchen, not Batman!"*

Faith peered over her black reading glasses at Grace, closed the laptop, and hugged her daughter close with one arm. "How does your head feel today?"

"It's much better now. Thanks, Mom."

"I will be back." Faith took her laptop and went into her office. When she returned, Grace had finished her breakfast and had her hands wrapped around a steaming cup of tea. Robin was clearing the island as Faith spread out a stack of photo albums.

"Are you feeling up to looking at some photographs?" Faith asked gently.

Grace nodded and put the mug down as she reached for the photo albums.

"This one first, honey." Faith handed her the large one. Grace opened it and saw a younger Faith and Robin sitting on a couch holding a tiny infant with a pink hat. Fascinated, Grace rubbed her hand over the pictures hoping the memories would connect with her brain. Turning the pages revealed more photos of her in kindergarten and more school pictures through sixth grade. There were a few holiday pictures and one of her making a snowman with her dad. One picture was of Grace in her burgundy and yellow uniform, her arms folded across her chest.

"Private school? I look thrilled in that outfit," Grace said sarcastically without taking her eyes off the girl in the yellowing photo. "That must have cost a fortune!"

"We were lucky to find a scholarship for you to go to Kings Oxford. They had a better writing program than most public schools." Robin dried his hands on the towel and moved between them

"When did you become a lawyer?" Grace asked Faith, now looking up.

"When I met your father in college," Faith said, grinning at Robin. "I knew he was the man for me. When you came along . . ." Faith wrung her hands, trying to come up with the right words. "You were a surprise, honey. I postponed my Bar exam and decided to focus on you until you were old enough for school. Once you started at Kings Oxford, I went back and took the test and eventually became a partner at the firm I am with now.

Grace looked back at the photo albums and flipped through all the pictures. Most of them were of Grace and her father. Faith was not in many photos. Grace wanted to ask why, but she didn't want to ruin the moment, and it was possible Faith was probably the one *taking* pictures.

"When Dr. Erick comes over, you too can go through the box from high school in the attic. I will bring it down after we open presents. Then I will go for a run." Faith left Robin and Grace in the kitchen.

Faith returned with her running clothes on and found Grace and Robin looking at the small Christmas tree in the living room. The sparse tree was about three feet tall and had only a few ornaments.

"Sorry. We don't decorate much anymore since you left." Faith took the seat by Robin near the fireplace.

"This one is from me," Robin said while leaning over and passing a small red and silver-wrapped box.

Grace opened the gift, carefully removing the wrapping paper. Inside was a black velvet box, and when she opened the lid, she saw a beautiful gold chain. As Grace lifted the chain from the box, a locket tumbled out with it. Grace opened the locket, and inside was a picture of the three of them he had taken in the last few weeks. "It's beautiful," she whispered, and there was an inscription on the back. *"Life takes you to unexpected places. Love brings you home."*

She wheeled closer to her dad and held her hair up as he put the necklace on. It rested just below her collar bones over her heart.

"This one is from me!" Faith handed her another gift wrapped in green and gold. There were two gifts. One was in a small rectangular box, and the second one was in a large thin box. Grace opened the little box on top and discovered a cell phone.

"Oh, Mom! This is too much!" Grace gushed.

"This way, you can take *new* pictures or text us if you need anything. This one is all yours, and we can always stay in touch no matter where you are." Faith wiped a tear from her eye.

"Thank you, Mom!" Grace set the phone aside and opened the large gift. "You didn't have to . . ." Grace's eyes widened in delight a few minutes later. Inside the box was a soft case. She unzipped it and removed a brand-new laptop. "*Mom!*" Grace had tears in her eyes. "This must have cost a fortune!"

"You deserve it, honey. Your father and I agree you have been working so hard. Even Dr. Erick says you will be out of that chair in no time." Faith and Robin both looked on proudly.

"I will be right back!" Grace wheeled to her room, removed two packages, and returned to the living room. "This feels like my first Christmas, and until I remember, it *is* my first!" She handed Faith a long rectangle box with white and red wrapping paper.

Faith opened the wrapping paper to reveal a beautiful cotton candy pink cashmere scarf and wrapped it around her neck. "Honey, it's beautiful!" She blushed. "Cashmere. Thank you!"

Grace smiled as her dad winked at her. "You are next, Dad." She handed him the next box, and Robin unwrapped a beautifully carved wooden frame. He seemed to appreciate the detailed work and rubbed his fingers over the smooth wood.

"*It's beautiful*, Grace," Robin whispered. He looked at the photo of his beautiful daughter. "When did you take this?"

"Erick helped me. It is recent. I didn't know what to get you, Dad." Grace shrugged.

"No, Grace, this is perfect!" He stared at the photo.

The doorbell rang, and Faith got up to answer it.

"Hello, Dr. Erick!" Faith's voice carried into the living room.

"Mrs. Evans, Merry Christmas!" Erick took his snow-covered shoes off on the rug in the foyer. Erick handed Faith two wrapped gold and red presents and followed her into the living room.

"Merry Christmas, everyone! This is for you!" Erick handed Grace the cane. "It's time for you to say goodbye to the chair, once and for all!" He backed up to give her room as her parents looked on.

Everyone was silent. All you could hear was the jazzy instrumental playlist of Christmas songs playing on the speaker. Without taking her eyes off Erick, she placed the cane down and stood up. Grace's hand shook slightly, but she smiled wide as she slowly took a few steps toward Erick.

"You got this," Erick whispered. His eyes locked on hers.

Grace took several confident steps until they were face to face. She wrapped her arms around him, and Erick did the same, and she hugged him. He had followed through on his promise that Grace would walk again. Tears streamed down her face for the forgotten life she had left behind and for this new life. Even now, as Grace looked up at Erick, she realized that no matter what happened next, she would never forget this moment. Not ever.

Erick was in awe of Grace. Seeing her standing with him now and the steps she took to move *toward* him, holding her, after all these years, was almost more than he could bear. He didn't want to let go. He looked over to Grace's parents, who held onto each other full of pride and gratitude.

Erick pulled back from her and exclaimed. "That's my girl! And no," he laughed. "I don't say that to just anyone!"

Grace smiled and seemed to relax a bit.

"Thank you, Erick. For helping me *remember* how to walk again," Grace said shyly.

"You did all the work," Erick laughed. "But go easy, on walking around too much. Work up to walking longer or farther each day. You will need the wheelchair less and less. I want you to practice as much as you can with the cane. Honestly, you will need the cane only in the beginning. Eventually, you may not need the cane at all as your balance improves. Take your time. You don't want to fall rushing it."

Grace sat on the couch and placed the cane across her lap. "I'm not taking the ribbons off," she laughed. The sound of her laughter was more than Erick could take, and he took the seat next to Grace. *It's a Wonderful Life* was playing on the television. They sat together in peaceful silence and watched the movie while Faith went for her run and Robin went to the kitchen.

Erick allowed himself to imagine a future with Grace in their own living room one day, perhaps with their children. They would tell their children about how God brought them together again and all the miracles that followed. He noticed the photo albums on the table. The familiar ache of pain from the lies churned his stomach. "I need to tell you something important, Grace." She leaned her head on his shoulder.

"Let's not ruin this moment with words," Grace whispered, and he felt her hand slide into his. Erick closed his eyes and wanted to bottle this feeling forever. He swallowed down the guilt and prayed she would be okay after hearing the truth tomorrow. Only then could they be together forever, just like he imagined so many years ago.

Fifty-one

Grace didn't want the day to end. It started with her taking steps away from her past and into the future with Erick by her side. Grace would never forget this day and how her hand fit perfectly into Erick's hand. He did not pull away, and she knew he felt the same.

At dinner, they talked about her training. Erick was going to pick her up tomorrow. He had something to tell her. She wondered what it could be. She hoped it would reveal his feelings for her, and she wanted to share her feelings for him. After dinner, they drank hot cider by the fire in the living room while admiring the lights on the tree. Even Jace had a new red knit sweater on and was fast asleep on the rug.

"I have to go," Erick said reluctantly. "Tomorrow, you'll graduate from the program. You did it!"

"Put my number in your phone, and you can text me later," Grace insisted.

"Okay, I can do that." Erick nodded toward Grace. "Rest up. I have something special planned for tomorrow to celebrate." He turned toward Robin and Faith, who stood there smiling. "Merry Christmas, Mr. and Mrs. Evans." They returned the sentiment.

Grace loved every minute of the day, but she realized she had forgotten to look at the memorabilia box from high school when Erick left. She gazed at her dad standing there in the kitchen with her mom feeling the warmth of their love, and she could not imagine leaving this place.

When she had first come home from the hospital, she remembered being afraid. All she could feel now was love. The love they had shown her and the love she felt for them. At this moment, that was enough. She hugged her parents and wheeled herself back to her room with the cane resting on her lap. She climbed into bed and allowed herself to think of what life would be like without the chair and maybe even without the cane one day. Grace heard the familiar tapping of the friendly black raven in the window as she charged her new phone.

Her phone lit up, indicating a text message. She looked at the phone and clicked on the message.

>   *Erick: Merry Christmas, Grace!*
>   *Grace: Thank you for the best gift ever!*
>   *Erick: What gift was that?*
>   *Grace: Following through on your promise that I would walk again.*
>   *Erick: That was all you!*
>   *Grace: I really appreciate all that you have done for me.*
>   *Erick: It's been great working with you. Get some rest. We have a big day planned for tomorrow. Good night, Grace!*
>   *Grace: Good night.*

Grace wondered what would happen when Erick was no longer officially her doctor. She wished Aunt Raven was there today to see how far she had come. Part of her felt her aunt was always there, mostly when the black bird was at her window. There would be time to look at the old photo box tomorrow after Erick told her the words she longed to hear. Tonight, all she wanted to focus on was her future. For the first time in months, she was no longer interested in her past but more excited about her future. A future that hopefully included the handsome doctor named Erick.

Erick climbed into bed, reliving the day. The best day he ever had in all his life. Surprisingly, Grace's parents even seemed to be happy he was there. The nightmares were long behind him now, and he felt a weight lifted about his past. It was time for him to tell her the truth—the truth about *their* shared past. He wanted to explain everything. He was sorry primarily for not standing up to his father. He wanted her to know that he never stopped loving her even after all these years.

Once he told her the truth, he hoped she would understand why he had to keep this secret from her. His motives were pure, but he could not move forward with a relationship based on lies. He had two things he didn't have before. He had faith she would forgive him, and he had the courage to tell her the truth. For the first time, he felt worthy of her love.

Morning came quickly, and Erick was grateful for the good night's sleep. He managed to get in a quick run with Jace that morning. After his shower, Erick looked at himself in the mirror. He knew he would have to come clean today. With his hand, he wiped the steam off the mirror and got a good look at himself.

It was time for a change, so Erick took out the scissors and a new razor. The beard was now gone. "No more hiding now," Erick said to his reflection. He noticed his hair was longer now, and he gelled it back. He dressed and texted Grace that he was on his way.

Once he arrived at Grace's, the front door opened, and

all was well in the world. She had her cane in her lap and a smile on her face. "Whoa, what happened to the beard?!" Grace commented on the fact she could see his face now. "You clean up nice! Soon, I will trade these wheels in for some great walking shoes."

"That's my girl," he said while getting lost in her eyes. He was on a mission. He prayed during his morning run that he would have the right words to say. He didn't want this feeling to end, but he was sure everything would crumble like a house of cards if he didn't tell her today.

"Have fun!" Robin called out from behind them with a warning. "Be careful. There's some weather coming in. Ice storms and thunderstorms are in the forecast today."

"I will take good care of her," Erick called out as he followed behind Grace to his Jeep. Once they were both buckled in the car, they were off. Jace barked his approval from the back seat next to the cane with the pink ribbon.

The electricity filled the car, and Erick put on contemporary Christian music on the radio. He was so excited to finally be free of the lies, and he hoped she would want to be together forever. He could hardly contain the beating of his heart in his chest as they pulled into HigherGround. The parking lot was empty. Erick jumped out with Jace and got Grace into her chair.

"I want you to take the chair because it is slick outside. I need to get something inside first, okay?" Erick suggested.

When Grace nodded, she wheeled her way with him into the dark facility and back to his office. Erick flicked the switch on and held up a portable speaker. Erick suddenly was worried that after today things might change. He could not go back after he revealed the truth. Erick didn't know how she would react to the news, but was confident of one thing. He never loved her more than he did at this very moment.

Fifty-two

Grace followed Erick into his office, reminiscing about their first days together. She recalled how afraid she felt just a few months ago. Her gaze landed on the wall behind the desk. The pictures of the smiling former patients seemed to smile at her. Grace was part of a unique club now.

Next, she saw Erick's doctorate from the University of Connecticut. Her eyes looked at the name written in script: *Erick Finn.*

Where had she seen that name before? Grace's brain would not give her the answers. Wasn't Julie saying this name when they were searching her past on the computer? Grace shrugged it off. All she wanted to think about was Erick saying the words out loud she desperately wanted to hear.

"You ready?" Erick had the speaker in hand and broke through her thoughts. "Let's go out the back." Erick led her out the back door. Jace bounded ahead of them into the wintery terrain.

Grace had only seen the lake through the window. Her wheelchair bumped along the wooden path behind the building and through a small patch of woods to a beautiful frozen lake.

The dock spanned one side of the lake's length, and at one point, they walked out on the boat slip a few feet over the frozen water. The air felt unusually warm for the end of December. The trees rustled from gusts of wind. Erick put the brake on and helped Grace get out of the chair at the far end of the dock. Jace ran around chasing a bird.

"Come sit with me," Erick said. Grace eased down next to Erick, using the cane and his arm. Both of their legs dangled over the edge. They both looked out over the lake, their shoulders touching. The lake was frozen thick in places, and it looked like hard cut glass. Birds flew overhead with their morning song as snow-covered pine trees hugged the perimeter of the lake. It was a picture-perfect display reflected in the glassy water. Erick breathed it all in. "What did you picture your life to be like, Grace?" He turned to look at her, placing his arm now across her back and his hand steady on her. He could feel her exhale.

"Wow," Grace said. She sighed at the weight of the question. "You know I still have holes in my memory."

"I know," he whispered. "I just want to know what you think. Here and now, I guess." Erick looked at Grace. He gently wrapped one arm around her, and she could not imagine being anywhere else right now. Just like the lake, she wanted to freeze this moment in time and savor it forever.

Grace loved the feel of Erick's hand on her back. She felt safe for the first time in forever. The lake was so beautiful, and here and now, being so close to Erick made her dizzy.

"I wish I could remember more. Honestly?" She looked out over the frozen glass. "I remember wanting to write." Grace surprised herself with how strong she felt about this revelation. It felt right. "I remember writing things as a child and my dad reading them." Grace smiled as memories became more manageable now.

"What about your mom?" Erick pulled Grace closer as a gust of wind came through the open space. "Did she support your writing?"

A raven flew high into the grey clouds. It seemed to dim the sun a bit. Grace took one hand and covered her eyes, trying to find a memory. "I don't have a ton of memories of her. I can remember my mom making dinner once, and she always encouraged me to prepare for the next day the night before." Grace realized how simple her life was now. She remembered a younger version of herself busy with school and writing. She suddenly remembered clearly a sandy-haired boy she was hanging from trees with every afternoon after school.

Several minutes passed. "Where did you go?" Erick finally asked

"I remember having a friend. Some boy with sandy hair. I just cannot remember his name." She concentrated hard. "My mom was always after me to have girls as friends. Oh! His name was Rick, I think."

Erick looked uncomfortable. Standing up, Erick handed Grace her cane and helped her to stand. Grace's legs shook less, and she focused as he helped her get up. He made sure she was steady, and he took his phone out. "Our last lesson is *dancing!*"

"What?" Grace thought he could say many things but never thought those words would come out of his mouth. "*Home*" by Daughtry played through the speaker after Erick clicked a few buttons on his phone. She started laughing and thinking he had lost his mind. She looked him straight in his blue eyes and realized he was not joking as he moved closer to her. Grace liked the song but loved being in Erick's arms the most.

"I have something to tell you, Grace," he whispered into her ear and wrapped his arms around her. Her heart began to beat faster, and she could feel his heart doing the same. She dropped the cane and placed her hands over his shoulders, and they both began to sway to the music. "I have always imagined this."

Grace closed her eyes and breathed in the mango scent of his shampoo. His face was so smooth. She didn't want this moment ever to end, and Grace knew she was falling for him, and she was falling fast. She loved the feeling of being in his arms, but she was also terrified. Grace pulled back and looked into his blue eyes, hoping that he, too, was falling for her. Instead, she heard him sniff. He had tears in his eyes. "What's wrong?" She was confused.

"Actually." Erick stopped swaying and stood still. His arms remained around her. "Everything is *right*. For the first time in forever." His voice was low and barely audible as he held her cheek. The music faded into the background. "I need to tell you something important. I should have told you a long time ago, but I was afraid. The truth is that this is *not* the first time we have danced to this song." His eyes held hers.

Grace waited as his words sunk in. Up until now, she had only one burning question that smoldered in her heart. Was he in love with her, too? Now another question took over her brain. *What did he mean we danced to this song before?*

Erick held Grace close as the wind picked up Grace's hair and blew it over her eyes. He pushed the stray red hair from her face, but his hand stayed on her cheek. He wanted nothing more than to kiss her just then, but he knew he had to keep going. The sky grew darker, and rain began to fall gently.

"Grace," he paused as tears filled his eyes. "This isn't the first time we danced to this song. This was the song we danced to at our prom when you were my *girlfriend*. I have loved you my *whole* life and even more now." The wind was blowing harder, but Erick held her hair back, waiting for her to say something. His eyes were locked on hers, and he felt like they were the only people on earth. Jace began to bark loudly in the distance, but neither Erick nor Grace moved. He searched her eyes, looking for a sign that they would be okay. The wind was howling so loud now he couldn't even hear the music anymore. *Please, say something, anything! Can she even hear me?*

Suddenly a loud shout came across the wind, followed by a loud crack. The dark clouds rolled fast across the sky and lit up like fire as lightning cracked. Lightning bolts exploded and illuminated the sky, and then everything was dark again. Grace and Erick's faces were now inches apart and unaware of everything happening around them, including the dangerous impending weather.

"I'm so sorry it took this long for me to find you again. My life has been so empty without you. I can't bear to lose you again!" Erick shouted now. The rain poured buckets of water down and drenched them. The roar of the storm grew louder like a train rushing by them, carrying someone else's words across the lake. They were not alone.

"She was never yours, *brother!*" A deep voice boomed from behind them. "What the *hell* did you think was going to happen?"

Fifty-three

Grace was still processing what Erick was saying. She stepped back as Erick tried to support her. The dock was flooded with rain now. Jace's barking grew louder, and a man was shouting as he approached them.

The strange man stopped several feet from Erick on the dock. Gusts of wind blew a few wet strands across his face. Grace could not help but look at the mysterious figure as he approached. She noticed intense blue eyes like sapphires.

His face. It looked just like . . . Suddenly Grace felt an alarming fear run through her body. Her mind was playing tricks on her. *There are two of them?* Her mind screamed for her to run. Instead, she looked closer at the man. His eyes blazed in anger. Erick gently let go of Grace, and fear ripped through her along with the wind.

Erick left Grace and walked toward the man as she tried to keep herself steady. Her eyes darted around, looking for the cane, but it was too hard to see with the rain coming down in sheets. *Where was my wheelchair?* It seemed even farther away. Her legs began to shake as panic seized her. The men were shouting now, but the wind made it impossible to hear the words. The world grew darker as black clouds rolled in. A thunderous boom and then another crack of lightning illuminated the dock. Erick and the stranger flashed into view and then plunged into darkness again. In another flash, Grace saw Erick's head fly backwards as the stranger's fist connected with his jaw.

"Erick!" Grace screamed into the wind as she took a step towards them. Grace saw both of the soaked men but was unsure which one was Erick was as they both had similar drenched coats.

Come on, feet, move! She wanted to run to help him and leaned forward. Adrenaline coursed through her veins, and she took off, her feet hitting the dock. The men seemed like they were miles away. Her left foot hit the dock and then her right. *She was running!* Jace barked louder by her side as she took each step. The next thing Grace felt was floating through the air. She slipped, and her feet were no longer on the ground. The dock came at her quickly, and yet it seemed like an eternity at the same time. The two men wrestled on the ground now, and Erick seemed to be losing. She wanted to save him.

Grace watched as she fell the rest of the way down. The force of the dock hitting her head was something she could not stop. She wanted to save the man she loved. Everything that happened next was faster than her mind could register. Memories flashed before Grace's eyes like an old-fashioned movie reel at the highest speed. All at once, she knew everything, but it was all too much to handle. Grace surrendered to the pain and closed her eyes. She allowed the blackness to swallow her whole. The last thing she saw was a white blur of Jace. As the relentless rain pounded her body, Grace lost consciousness.

Erick was in the fight of his life as the rain made the dock even more slippery. His arms pushed Finn down, and Erick was on top of him.

"What did you think was going to happen?" Finn sneered, and his face contorted. The sky darkened as it rained heavier. Finn swung a fist toward Erick's face, but Erick moved his face out of the way, which seemed to make him angrier, and he pushed Erick off. This time, Finn got up, and his fist connected to Erick's freshly shaved face sending Erick falling on his back. Before Erick could get up, the man jumped on top of him this time. Thunder clapped again, and lightning flashed, which intermittently illuminated the dock. The men continued to fight.

"You do not deserve her!" Erick screamed at Finn, "You are pure evil, Finn. You should be locked up!"

"I may be evil, but you are a *coward*. You are hiding behind your stupid religion. Where is your God now? He can't save you. Grace will always be mine!" Another crack of lightning, and now Finn's hands were around Erick's neck. "You are nothing, Erick. You are dead to me! Daniel is my only brother now, and he is no threat to me. I'm the only one to inherit the family fortune. I will finally get everything I deserve!"

"Leave Daniel out of this!" Erick gasped for air. "You are not my brother, and I will make sure you do get *everything* you deserve!" Still wrestling on the flooded wooden dock, Erick could barely see two inches in front of him. Finn punched Erick's face, one blow after another. Rage filled Finn's face, and Erick had no more fight left in him. Erick closed his eyes, and prayed for strength.

"*Nothing* will stop me!" Finn battered Erick's bloody face. Erick could smell the sour stench of whisky on Finn's breath.

"*But those who hope in the Lord will renew their strength. They will soar on wings like eagles; they will run and not grow weary. They will walk and not be faint,*" Erick said calmly between the blows. He read that very scripture that morning in Isaiah 40:31. Blood poured from his nose, mixing with the rain.

"You have no idea what lengths I will go to win. I let you suffer all these years. The accident and me taking the one thing you loved most in the world was the best punishment. You cared more about Daniel than you did your twin brother!" Finn's fist hit Erick again.

"I know who was driving that night when the car ran off the road and into the tree. Dad knew as well and didn't tell you either. We kept this secret from you all these years! It *wasn't* you! You were so messed up from the drugs we slipped in your drink. It was too easy, and you liked kissing Brook. While I was convincing Grace to run away with me to New York, Brook followed through on her part of the plan. She wanted you so much that night she took a risk driving the mile home. Daniel getting hurt wasn't part of the plan, of course. I tried to tell you once what happened to me when we were kids, but you didn't even believe me. You never cared about me. Now, there's only room for one of us in the world!"

Erick, tired and bloody, closed his eyes and kept praying. Finn came at him with all he had. The final blow to his side made Erick cough, and blood sputtered from his mouth. Finally, Erick pooled all his strength and got one leg loose, kicking Finn with all his might. Gaining momentum, Erick pushed Finn off, and he got to his feet. The slick ice on the dock caused Finn to slide off the wooden dock and into the frozen lake below. The ice cracked under the impact, and Erick saw Finn disappear into the lake.

Darkness was all around, making it difficult to see. Lightning continued to flash like a strobe light. Erick staggered up on all fours. The rain was hitting him in the face like bullets; he looked over the dock, but Finn was gone. A large broken hole with black water lapping the sides of the ice was all Erick could see. Next, Erick crawled over to Grace and saw his phone as well on the dock. Using everything he had left, he picked it up. Erick lay there next to her, holding her. Blood poured from where she had hit her head as he dialed three numbers. 9-1-1. Erick lay next to Grace as fatigue set in.

"911, what is your emergency?"

Erick could barely speak as the spots grew darker before his eyes and the rain poured down over them. He mumbled to the operator their location and that his brother had fallen into the lake. The sound of Jace barking was the last thing heard before passing out.

Fifty-four

Grace opened her eyes and looked around a dark room. *Where am I?* The only light was the glow from the moon shining through a window. This was not her bedroom at her parents' house, but somehow still familiar. Her head ached, and she reached up to scratch the tiny itch on her head. Her fingers touched a bandage.

Grace suddenly recalled being about thirteen and meeting Finn and Erick at Kings Oxford private school. All the feelings stacked one on top of each other, making her head pound. Her breathing became rapid as she recalled her relationship with Erick and the devastation of him ghosting her. She felt a pang in her gut as she recalled Erick kissing Brook at the graduation party. She remembered Finn smoking on the porch and Finn's offer to give her everything she had ever wanted. Then her fallout with her parents as she ran off with Finn to New York.

Flashes of New York, the grandiose loft, her job at Finn-London popped into her mind next. Grace's manuscript sat abandoned at the bottom of a desk drawer, along with her dream of becoming a published author. She remembered Finn's dad getting sick and the excessive drinking and violent mood swings. She recalled the day Finn shattered his glass when he threw it against the wall. All the rumors of his cheating and, ironically, his terrible jealousy. Grace closed her eyes and felt tears burn them.

Next, the memory of the night at the hotel he accused her of cheating on him filled her mind. An intense feeling of fear overwhelmed her. Her mind went to the hiking trail, the journal, and the map.

Finally, she remembered how much fun she had training with the grown-up doctor version of Erick. Grace relived the magic of the kiss and the dance out by the dock. He had *tried* to tell her the truth, she also recalled. But it was too late. The people she loved the most had *lied* to her. Then Finn showed up during the storm and called Erick "brother." Grace racked her brain. Finn had two brothers. *What was the other one named?* Grace tried to remember. Then she thought about the nice man at the physical therapy studio. *Daniel.* That was his name, and he was the youngest Finn brother.

"Oh my God!" Grace clasped her hand over her mouth. It would explain why her dad and Erick were always secretive. Everyone was in on the joke but her. Grace could not help but feel the rage building inside her.

Just then, Robin and Faith walked into the room with the nurse. "We are keeping her overnight for observation, but you can visit with her now that she is awake," the nurse informed the Evans and left the room.

"Oh, Pumpkin! What happened?" Robin came to her bedside, and Faith followed him.

"*You knew everything.* I trusted you. How could you?" Grace spat the words. "How could you not tell me the truth?" Her words were like daggers aimed at the heart. "Oh my God, are you even my *real* parents!" Tears burned down her cheeks.

"I'm so sorry," Robin whispered. "I just wanted you to be safe with us. We love you more than life!" Robin held Grace's hand tight. Faith tried to hug them both.

Finally, Grace pulled away. "Not enough to tell me the truth. When I get home, I want all the truth, and I do not want you to leave any details out!" She told them and took a deep breath. "Then, I will be *leaving*. Please respect my decision. If I'm going to survive any of this, I will have to do it on my own."

"I understand, Grace. We did not mean to hide any truth from you. We just wanted only the best treatment for you." Robin's shoulders slumped. "We just wanted to help you. We love you. That is the truth!"

"The truth is all I want from you. Let me rest, and you can get me tomorrow morning, and then we can sort it all out. I need you both to leave." Grace folded her arms.

Robin kissed Grace's forehead, and Faith squeezed Grace's hand. Grace wasn't sure if she remembered every detail as to why she was on the mountain in the first place. She had a feeling that the truth about her past would change all their lives forever. Grace felt that they at least owed her that much.

Erick climbed out of the hospital bed and got dressed. "I need to get out of here!" Erick had one arm in a sling and a bandage over his nose and eyebrow. "I need to find Grace!"

"You need to stay in bed. Miss Evans isn't taking any visitors, sir," the nurse told him. "You really need to stay."

"I have a dog that needs me." Erick pulled out his IV and began putting his shoes on.

"Hey, Erick," Daniel said, entering the room in his wheelchair. He wheeled closer to Erick, and they both embraced.

"Ouch, my ribs are broken, dude. What are you doing here?" Erick asked.

"Man, I can't believe you were out in that storm. Jace would not stop barking. It woke Luna up, and by the time we got down to the dock, the paramedics were there. They said the firemen would come out in daylight to comb the lake for Finn. Jace is with Sky at the apartment."

"*Finn* did this to me. He told me what happened that night ten years ago. The night of the accident. They drugged me at the party!" Erick scowled and paced around the room, collecting his things.

"What are you talking about?" Daniel asked.

"He was the one . . . you . . . that night." Erick could hardly get the words out as he got dressed.

"Wait. Do you mean the accident?" Daniel rolled back to give Erick room to gather his things in the room.

"Yes. The accident. Finn and Brook had a plan. A plan to get me out of the way so Finn could steal my girlfriend."

"*Are you serious?*" Daniel looked alarmed. "What did Finn say?"

"Even Dad said I wasn't driving. He said he had paid to have the records sealed to protect the family. Finn drugged me, and while he made off with Grace, *Brook* ended up being the one to drive us home!" Erick could not move from where he was standing as he looked into Daniel's eyes.

"I don't remember who was driving," Daniel said, confused. "I mean, the last thing I remember is the valet pulling up. The next thing I remember is waking up in the hospital. The following year I was just trying to finish high school and learn how to navigate this wheelchair. I just assumed you were driving. I never blamed you, though," Daniel said sincerely. "It was an *accident*."

Erick couldn't believe what he heard. "What Finn said makes no sense. I don't think she ever drove back then. Her dad never let her get her license when we were kids because they had a car service. Brook only got her license recently,"

Erick said, stunned. "Was he lying and blaming Brook to get himself off the hook?"

"That doesn't sound right. Have you ever known Finn to *not* take credit for winning? Maybe he is telling the truth. They are the most diabolical duo, and they will pay the price one day! Honestly, it was so long ago, and my life is so much better now." Daniel shrugged, and Erick was amazed at his composure.

"Aren't you mad at her? At what she did to you? At what happened? They are both psychopaths!"

"No, not mad. It was an accident. Brook probably didn't plan to crash the car, Erick. Besides, I have come to terms with losing the use of my legs. I may have lost the ability to run, but I have everything I need in life. Not many people can say this. Besides, I found Sky, and she is the greatest girl on the planet, and I wouldn't have if it weren't for the accident. I wouldn't change a thing about my life! My life is *perfect,* just the way it is. You know more than anyone that living with unforgiveness is not a life. My life is full, and I get to help others. Having Sky by my side makes life worth living!" Daniel continued as Erick sat down, feeling the weight of it all. "You no longer need to blame yourself. Just let it go and forgive yourself, brother. It was never your fault. Think of all those people you have helped to walk again!"

Erick rubbed his face, forgetting he had shaved his beard, and let the tears flow. "I love you, man. I do regret, though, that I couldn't be the one to help you walk again."

"The accident took my mobility away, but as I said, I gained more than I lost. If I didn't meet Sky that day during my recovery, things would be different. Dude, she helped you get into Physical Therapy School! God works things out better than we both expected. You, of all people, know my injuries were impossible to fix. There was nothing you could have done to change that. Our lives became *better* that night, believe it or not. Sky is an extraordinary girlfriend, and we have amazing careers. Besides, I get to work with the best brother anyone could ask for! Even though he and his dog are a pain in the ass!" Daniel hugged Erick close. "Enough drama, Erick. Now, get Grace back! When we find Finn. You both need to make up too."

"Why should I make up with Finn?" Erick, confused, broke the embrace. "Grace won't even see me. Besides, I have to get out of here, and I need to find out if Finn is even alive."

"What did you do?" Daniel looked concerned.

"He fell into the frozen lake. If he is alive, I'm going to *kill* him!" Erick got up. "He is going to regret the day he . . ."

"There were firemen all over the lake this morning. If he is there, they'll find him," Daniel said quickly. "I can call a car to pick us up, and then my buddy who works with the fire department can give us more information."

"No one should be going anywhere." The nurse walked between them, frowning. "As a doctor, you should know better, but I can't stop you. You are signing yourself out against doctor's orders." She placed the paperwork in front of Erick. He quickly scribbled his name and exited the room. He and Daniel went to the hospital's main entrance and asked if a *Dominic Finn* came in by ambulance.

Fifty-five

Grace frowned as she realized she was back where she started, in a wheelchair again and about to be discharged from her short stay in the hospital. Her dad pulled up to the entrance and handed her a cane. Not the one with the pink ribbon. That day seemed so long ago now. Grace skillfully used the cane to get into the car. Robin closed the door as Grace sadly looked out the window. She saw the nurse return the wheelchair to the hospital and made a promise to herself she would never use one again.

The last time she took the road home from the hospital, she had so many questions, and the autumn foliage lined the drive home that day. In contrast, she looked out the car window at the stark, lifeless bare trees and felt the bite of the bitter cold, harsh winter. Grace remembered just about every memory now, but not why she was on the mountain that day. The details were blurry except for the broken music box. She hoped her parents and the journal could fill the final few blanks in her memory. *What kind of parents keep secrets from their children?*

Robin pulled into the driveway, and Grace looked at the house differently now. All the memories in that house returned combined with the new ones of the last few months. She remembered the fight the day she said goodbye to her parents. She remembered Finn waiting in the car for her. Grace remembered all the gifts he gave her and how he treated her like a princess and then remembered the drinking, the fights, and the shattered glass. She wondered how she could have trusted someone like that.

Even the people Grace loved now had held back so much of the truth. Her hand covered her mouth in shock. Instantly she made the connection. *Finn* was the man Aunt Raven was warning her about in her journal. Finn was just like Jack Stone. Her thoughts were interrupted when Robin turned the car off and jumped out. He opened the passenger door of the vehicle.

"I need you to know that I wasn't trying to hurt you," Robin said as they walked to the door. Grace didn't respond as she used her cane and walked with her dad, who watched her every step of the way.

Faith opened the door, and Grace continued to balance on her cane to get into the house. She was walking better, but she still needed the cane for balance, and she still limped a bit. Grace was free from the wheelchair, and it was time for her to get on her own two feet once and for all.

"I'm so sorry, Grace." Faith held her tightly. "It was wrong for me to have kept the truth from you the whole time. I just wanted you to have a chance at a better life. It has been all we've ever wanted for you."

When Grace walked over to the couch and sat down, Faith sat with her. Robin hung up their coats and entered the kitchen to put the tea kettle on.

"Mom, what happened? Why was I up there on the mountain? What was I looking for? Do you know what I found? I still can't remember all of it," Grace said, tired of the lies. "Please just tell me the truth."

Faith sighed.

"Your Aunt Raven passed away last fall, as you already

know. She left you the journal and the trail map years ago, but we didn't give you the journal until you returned. This is the reason why you were there."

"What did she want me to know?" Grace needed to know how this mess all started.

"The truth is," Faith said, looking like she was going to be sick. Robin gave them each a cup of tea. She took a sip as he sat down in a chair across from them. "I couldn't have children." Faith looked down.

"You mean you couldn't have children after me? I thought you just wanted to be a big-shot lawyer." Grace looked confused.

Faith pushed a strand from her black bob behind her ear. "You were *adopted*, Grace. But you must know I grew to love you as if you were my own. I never . . ." She trailed off, looking into Grace's green eyes, and pleaded with her own.

"Dad?"

"Yes, Grace. We adopted you." Robin hung his head.

"But I look like you!" Grace squeezed her eyes shut from the pain in her head. "I . . . I . . . you lied to me! Again! Oh my God!" She got her cane, walked to her room, opened a suitcase, and started putting her clothes in it. Grace could hear her mom sobbing on the couch. *She is not my birth mother!* Grace was trying not to cry when Robin followed her into the room.

"Grace, please don't go. I have made some big mistakes, but please forgive me. We *saved* your life. Twice actually." He reminded her.

Grace continued packing, ignoring him. "Whatever, Dad, or whoever you *really* are!" She stopped what she was doing and turned around. "Who are my real parents?"

"Your mother was Aunt Raven," he said and sat down on the bed. "I am not sure about your father. Have you finished the journal?"

"Not all of it." Grace was trying to piece all the clues together in her mind.

"She was protecting you from a man named Jack. Please just read the journal. The whole story is in there. When Aunt Raven came to us, she was afraid for your life. There was a chance Jack Stone was your father, and he was an evil man. Faith and I realized you were a blessing from God. We filed all the paperwork and had the social worker seal the files so no one would ever know. We were going to tell you the day you graduated, but you left with Finn before we could. Then when you came back for the funeral, I wanted you to have the journal. You had the right to know."

"Oh, Dad!" Grace could not hold it in any longer and held him close and cried. She never considered how awful it must have been for Faith. "It must have been a terrible secret to bear. So, you are my uncle?" She shook her head.

"It changes nothing about how I feel about you, Pumpkin. You will always be *my* daughter!" Robin kissed her on the forehead, careful not to touch her bandage.

"There is more," Faith said, entering the room. She handed Grace a key. "Raven left you money in a safety deposit box. Don't be mad at her for putting you up for adoption. She was afraid for her life, and even more so, she was afraid for your life. For your safety, we kept it a secret. We just want you to be safe even now after everything you've been through."

"Mom." Grace hugged her. Everything made sense now. "I need you both to be honest from now on with me! I can't believe my *ex-boyfriend* helped me to walk again." Grace would deal with that later. "The reality is I need to take the next path and be on my own. Away from all of this." She held up her phone. "You have my number, but please give me the space to figure out what I need to do next."

"Grace, I know you have every reason to be mad at Erick, then and now. I hate to admit it, and trust me, it's painful for me to say, but Erick is a good guy. Whoever he was back in high school is not who he is today. I'm sorry I deceived you about him. We just wanted you to have a chance, and he was the perfect choice to help you. So where will you go?"

"I just want you to know I love you both. My leaving this time isn't like the last time, I promise. I clearly have never lived life on my terms. I need to find out who I am. I will let you know I'm safe. I can walk better now, and I will resume my training with someone else other than Erick. I'm not mad at you guys. I'm not mad at *him*. Well, maybe a little, but it's time to go. I'm sorry it has to be this way." Grace hugged her parents close, but this goodbye was different than before. This time she was not angry with them anymore. Determined to face all that was yet to come, Grace would do things differently this time and on her own terms.

Erick left the hospital and took a taxi to HigherGround. Today, the sky was clear and white. The only evidence of yesterday's storm was scattered trees and debris everywhere. Sky opened the door when Erick and Daniel arrived at HigherGround. Jace and Luna come running out down the wooden ramp to greet the men.

"Hey, buddy!" Erick kneeled to scratch Jace's head. His heart raced as he wondered what he and Daniel might find at the lake. He was still angry with Finn, but he didn't want his brother to have drowned in the lake deep down. Turning to Sky, Erick asked, "Can you stay with the dogs? Daniel and I are going to go look for Finn." His voice quivered, still shaken from the events of the night before.

"We'll be here. Be careful!" Sky kissed Daniel. The dogs followed her back up the ramp to the apartment.

Daniel and Erick followed the wooden pathway to the

dock. As the lake came into view, Erick saw yellow caution tape around the area. A police officer was taking photos at the dock.

"I don't have a good feeling about this," Erick said to Daniel as they approached the dock.

"This area is off-limits while we conduct our investigation," a large man in a long coat and police hat warned them. His Boston accent was thick.

"I'm the owner of HigherGround, and this is Daniel. He lives on the property. Our brother Finn may have fallen through the ice in the storm yesterday. He and I got into an argument, and it came to blows." Erick's hand went to his swollen face. "I just got out of the hospital." Erick could see the officer was glaring at his facial bruises and small bandages. "I called 911, and Grace Evans was also here. She slipped and hit her head." Erick's eyes darted over the lake, looking for any signs of life.

"So, *you* are the one who called 911? I'm Officer Thomas, Zak Thomas. We sent an officer over to the hospital to get your statement." The officer's eyes narrowed, "Guess you left the hospital in a hurry."

"My brother attacked me, and during the fight, he fell over the edge. Have they found anything?" There were too many footprints in the snow to be sure of anything.

"What were you two fighting about?" The officer sized up Erick. "A girl, I presume?"

"Did you find our brother or not?" Daniel spoke up, impatient.

"We could not get a crew in until this morning with all the trees down from the storm. Show me where you saw the victim fall exactly." The officer walked with Erick to the edge on the far side of the dock.

"He fell there. It was dark, of course, but I'm pretty sure this is the spot." Erick pointed to the ice below.

"Our search team did not turn up any bodies. Do you see the ice there?" The officer pointed, "No one could have fallen through that ice. Other than the small hole there, it's as thick as the Bruin's hockey arena at the Garden! What is your brother's name again?"

"Finn. Dominic Finn," Erick replied. His eyes scanned the frozen lake, expecting to see something, anything that could be a clue.

"You're Declan Finn's boys?"

"Yes, sir." Erick looked down at his feet.

"What does your brother look like?"

"He is my twin, so he looks like me, but he has a shark tattoo on his hand."

"Do you want to press charges or get a restraining order?"

"Not yet. I want to find Finn first."

"Well, he didn't fall through the ice, that's for sure. There isn't much evidence here because the storm pretty much cleared the area. We can't charge him with assault unless you press charges."

Erick thought about it for a moment and decided to do just that. He couldn't let Finn get away with whatever he wanted, and it would keep him away from Grace. Erick agreed and told the officer every detail he could, hoping they would find him sooner than later. Filing assault charges sped things up versus filing a missing person case.

"I will file the report when I get back to the station based on the evidence. It might not stick because it sounds like a domestic quarrel over a girl to me. We will get a statement from the witness, Grace Evans, at the hospital. The assailant could return to finish the job." Officer Thomas handed Erick a card. "Call me before things get ugly next time."

Erick nodded and watched as the officer took down the caution tape and headed back towards HigherGround.

Daniel and Erick remained at the scene staring at the lake in silence. Erick breathed in the cold air as one question came to mind. *Where did you go, Finn? Even if it's the last thing I do, I will find you! You will never be near Grace again. Not now, not ever.*

Fifty-six

Grace was packing up her things when the police came to the house to get her statement.

"I don't know what happened to either of the Finn brothers since the incident on the dock." Grace saw the look of fear on Faith's face when the officer said they hadn't found Finn's body yet.

After the police left, she zipped up her bags. She looked over at the corkboard and removed a picture of her and Erick. This picture covers another photo below. The photo was a younger version of her and Erick, and Finn was in the background. Erick and Finn were practically identical in every way except their personalities. She looked closer and examined the identical dimples and the blue eyes that looked like they had been poured from the same ocean.

The doorbell rang, and Faith went to answer it. Using her cane, Grace walked out to see what the commotion was. Robin was right behind her.

"You've caused enough trouble, don't you think?" Faith was blocking the man at the door.

Robin opened the door wider. "You need to leave. The police are looking for you as we speak."

Grace looked at the man, his face swollen with bruises.

"Erick! Oh my God, are you okay?" She reached out and held him.

"I'm okay," His blue eyes looked at Grace and then her parents. "Finn is presumed dead. I saw him fall into the lake, and no one could have survived that."

"Oh, no!" She pulled back from the hug and pushed him away. "Wait, you *lied* to me!"

"What?" He shoved his hands in his jean pockets. He looked so much younger without a beard. Grace stared at him until she came to her senses.

"You lied to me about the past and who you really are!"

"Oh. That's the real reason why I'm here. To see if you were okay, and I was hoping you could take a drive with me so I can explain!" He begged for a second chance.

"Why should I trust you?"

"Because I have always loved you!" He clasped his hands around hers as her parents just stood there, unsure of what to do next.

"Where is your Jeep?" Grace asked next, not seeing any car in the driveway.

"It's at the dock, where we left it yesterday. I came straight from the hospital. I wanted to make sure you were okay. Can you drive? I can explain everything on the way to HigherGround. Please let me explain, and then I promise if you still are angry, then I will never bother you again."

Grace had a sick feeling in her stomach, but she owed him at least a chance to say why he did what he did. Maybe none of this mess would have happened if she had allowed him to explain things long ago. She took a breath and asked him to put her suitcase in the car.

"I will take care of her. You have nothing to worry about!" As they left, he winked at Grace's parents. Grace could hear the familiar "caw-caw" noise as the black raven flew over her head as she opened the car door. Ignoring the pit in her stomach, Grace got into the driver's side, hoping she could remember how to drive as she backed out of her parent's driveway.

Erick called Grace several times, but her phone went right to voicemail. He left a message. "I love you, and I'm sorry." There was nothing he could do but drive to the Evans' house. He turned on Amaryllis Lane and remembered the last time he was there at the beginning of her training. Grace had opened the door that day, sitting in her wheelchair, with her vacant yet hopeful eyes. He parked the car in the driveway, and he and Jace jumped out and rang the doorbell.

Faith answered the door. Her eyes are red and swollen. "Hello?"

"Are you okay?" Erick looked concerned. "Is Grace okay?"

"You have some nerve showing up here like this, Finn. I am calling the police!"

"What? Wait! No! *I am* Erick!"

Faith stared at him. "You *can't* be! That would mean—Robin!" She started screaming, and Robin came to the door.

"What the *hell* is going on?" Robin had his phone. "I'm calling the police!"

"*Where* is Grace?" Erick asked

"Show me some ID, son." Robin demanded.

Erick immediately pulled his wallet out handed Robin his license. "Here. Now tell me what is going on."

"She's gone!" Faith's hand was over her mouth in horror.

"What do you mean she's *gone*?" Erick asked in a panic.

"Finn!" Faith blurted out. "He said he was *you*!"

"What?" Any shred of compassion Erick had for his brother turned to pure rage at that moment. "I'll kill him!"

Faith went inside and called the police.

Robin grabbed his coat and said, "Not if I get to him first!"

Fifty-seven

Grace had not driven in a long time, but she was able to remember what to do. It wasn't too difficult because now her legs were stronger than they had been in months.

"I still don't remember much, so what was the deal with you and your brother Finn?" Grace did not tell Erick she had recovered her memories. *Two can play at the deception game.*

"Oh, Finn? We've had disagreements for many years and kept our distance. I did see him at the hospital visiting my dad the other day."

"Oh, I'm sorry to hear that. I didn't know. Actually, I do remember something about that!" Grace kept her eyes on the road and remembered that was what had changed Finn. The pressure for his father's approval was compounded by all the work of running a large publishing company. It had all started with Declan's health problems. They drove in silence for a few minutes. "So, why did you lie to me?"

"About what?" Finn asked.

"Seriously? About all of it. You were pretending *not* to know me from the past. Not telling me about my life with Finn. Were you pretending to have feelings for me the whole time, too?" Grace tried to fight back the tears. She was afraid of the answers, but she sat a little straighter as they pulled into HigherGround. The building was closed until after New Year's Day, but three cars were in the parking lot. A Lexus, a BMW, and a van. Grace looked straight into his eyes and said, "I just can't trust you."

"It will all work out the way it should, Grace." He exhaled. Grace couldn't shake the bad feeling in her stomach as she parked the car.

"We should stop seeing each other, personally and professionally." Grace looked directly at his blue eyes. It will take her some time to trust again.

A knock on the window made Grace jump. A woman with blonde hair pulled back in a diamond clip about Grace's age was standing there. She had a long cream-colored coat and a baby blue scarf wrapped around her neck. She rolled the window down for the woman. "Grace! Glad you could make it."

"Wait, do I know you?" Grace looked from the blonde woman and then around the parking lot. Erick's Jeep was nowhere to be seen. The town had plowed snow into deep piled high banks on the parking lot's perimeter, along with a few scattered tree branches leftover from the storm.

"You remember me? I heard you had amnesia." The woman flipped a strand of blonde hair behind her shoulder.

The sick feeling grew exponentially inside Grace as she suddenly did remember who Brook Becker was and the terrible things she had done in high school. She looked to the man she thought was Erick to help her, but he was smiling, almost as he approved of the woman. "I know who you are," Grace said under her breath, and the memory flashed before her eyes again. Once more, she relived Brook inviting her to the party where she witnessed Erick kissing Brook. Not willing to keep the charade up any longer, Grace looked up at the blonde woman. "It's you! *Brook Becker.*" Grace's anger returned. "What do *you* want?"

"You do know Brook then. I understand that you and

Brook have some catching up to do," he said sardonically. As Grace watched him remove his gloves, her stomach dropped. There, on his hand, was a shark fin tattoo.

Grace froze and then jolted out of her seat, releasing the lock on the door, but her heart stopped when she realized her cane was in the back. She flung the car door open and jumped out. Grace wobbled a bit and tried to find her balance. Her legs gave out when she tried to run. Brook's laughter grew louder. Grace's knees stung as she landed on the stone parking lot. Tiny stones bit her knees sharply through her leggings. Grace pushed through the pain as she crawled away. Her heart hammered in her chest as the pieces of the puzzle came together clearly in her head. *Finn had pretended to be Erick, and trusting him again, put me in danger!*

Suddenly a loud *BOOM* pierced through the thoughts in Grace's head. Grace slowly crawled to the sidewalk to see what had happened. Her ears rang, and fear gripped her heart. She relaxed as she looked up and saw Sky. Sky stood there with a shotgun expertly aimed at Brook.

"I called the police! Don't you dare move a muscle!" Sky's accent was no longer sweet. Another loud *bang* signaled a warning shot in the air. The shell casing pinged as it landed on the ground as it rolled by Grace.

Defeated, Finn took sat down next to Grace on the sidewalk. He looked so much like Erick that her heart ached. Grace chided herself for trusting this man again. After everything she had been through, she still was too trusting. Grace looked at the shark fin tattooed on his hand, and it was glaring at her now. She remembered when he showed it off at a party during high school. Now the shark fin taunted her and made her doubt herself even more.

"Please, Grace, it's not what you think. I didn't bring you here to hurt you. I just wanted to convince you to come home with me," Finn said. It was his pattern when he felt he lost. He would sound sweet and caring. "We can start again. I can be better this time. *You* make me a better person." Finn looked at her. "What happened to you all those months ago?" he asked, feigning concern. "I thought you left me, but now I know that wasn't the case."

"I'm no longer part of your concern. You treated me awful. Please leave me alone and never come back! We are *not* together, and I do not need you now or *ever* for that matter," Grace spat the words, finding courage in her rage.

Finn's mouth opened and shut. "I'm a changed man. You have to believe me. I'm so lost without you. Since you left, my life has not been the same." He moved closer to Grace. "We can move past this. We can start over. I'll get therapy and couples counseling. I still love you, babe!"

Just then, Sky stepped between them. The shotgun still pointed at Brook, who was slowly backing away from the scene. "Don't you dare leave!"

Brook froze.

Grace glared at Finn. "I remember everything you said and did! You kept me from my family. You told me not to go to my aunt's funeral and that you were my *only* family! Who does that? I am sure the rumors are true about you cheating on me with your assistants. You are a sick man! Honestly, I wish you died on the lake. You are dead to me, and you'll pay for what you have done!" Grace's focused on something beyond Finn. The flashing lights of two police cars pulled up. Finn looked hurt and confused as one of the officers quickly jumped out of the vehicle, pinned Finn to the ground, and placed handcuffs on him.

"You're under arrest Dominick Finn for assault and battery!" The officer read him his rights. "Anything you say can and will be used . . ."

"You will regret this! No one will ever love you the way I did. When I get out, I'm coming back for you, and you *will* come back to me. We will finish what we started!" Finn shouted.

"You don't know me at all!" Grace challenged.

"Everything can and will be used against you, Mr. Finn." The female officer handcuffed him, and the male officer pushed his head down and into the police car and drove off.

The officers took their statements, and then they left with Finn. Grace stood there and watched his face as they drove away.

"You never give up, do you?" Brook spoke up now that Sky put her gun down. "You couldn't just stay away."

Grace lifted herself to her feet. She leaned back, not taking her eyes of Brook. Grace brought back her fist with all the strength she could muster and punched Brook's face. The tall blonde was caught off guard and fell to the ground as her diamond clip flew from her hair.

"You hit me!" She screamed, rubbing her cheek.

"Stay away from me! You haven't changed a bit!" Grace stood her ground, even though her legs shook. Grace planted herself there, ready to kick Brook's ass if she had to. Sky smiled in approval.

Everyone looked up just then as a car door slammed. "Get away from Grace!" Erick shouted while running to the scene, Robin Evans on his heels. Jace ran over to Brook, who was still on the ground. He barked incessantly in her face.

"Get this beast away from me!" Brook cried.

Erick turned toward Brook while Jace continued barking at Brook. He saw the diamond clip sparkling on the ground. He remembered the shiny object from his bad dreams when all the pieces came together. It was time to end the nightmare once and for all.

"It's ok, Jace. I got this." Jace moved away, and Brook stood up. He continued. "It *was* you! How could you let me be tormented all these years?" He shouted at Brook.

Robin ran over to Grace. "Are you okay?" Grace nodded.

"Get your *stupid* dog away from me!" Brook tried to kick the dog with her designer snow boot. Daniel came out to the scene, wheeling his way over to them. Jace sat by Sky, still holding the gun now pointed at the ground.

"What the hell is going on? I heard gun-shots!" He looked concerned as Sky held the gun, ready for action.

"Brook Becker is at the center of all of this!" Erick glared at the blonde woman, his eyes blazing. "She is the reason I lost everything. She set me up all those years ago at the party and has been a thorn in my side ever since" He took a breath and lowered his voice. "Did you ever care about me at all?"

"Of course, I cared about you, but you refused to see me. You were always going on about *her*. Whatever, it is time to move on." She glared at Grace.

"Good, you can stay away from me, or I will make sure my father removes you from the Tabitha Foundation," Erick warned.

"You and your father aren't even speaking!" Brook did not believe a word of it.

"You're wrong about that!" Erick snorted. "My dad and I are doing great, no thanks to you! You never cared about me then or now. You only care about yourself!"

Robin spoke up while he kept his arm over Grace, prepared for anything unexpected that might happen. "You need to leave!"

Brook looked at them. "All of you! You aren't even worth my time."

"Just leave, Brook!" Grace shouted. "You lost. No one wants you here. Stay the hell away from us!"

"Whatever," Brook rolled her eyes and opened her car door. "You all deserve what you get." She looked at Erick. "I'm glad Finn and I spiked your drink and ruined your life plans. I didn't plan on driving or crashing the car, but you had a bad reaction to the drugs. I admit I crashed the car that night, but it was an accident. You all think you're better than me. You are *nothing*!" She got into her car and drove away before Erick could say anything.

Erick walked over to Grace. Robin eyed him cautiously at first, but he stepped back. Grace collapsed in Erick's arms and heaved heavy sobs. "I got you," he whispered in her ear. His stubble rubbed her face. "I am so sorry!"

Suddenly, Grace pulled back, "Don't think you are off the hook!"

Shocked, Erick's mouth flew open. "Okay, what I did was wrong. Just know I did it for the right reasons."

"You lied to me. In fact, the lies started nearly a decade ago, back in high school. We had plans, Erick. We were building a life together. We had plans to move in together!" Tears streamed down Grace's face. Erick looked into her emerald eyes, and he winced at the years of hurt he caused still etched in her face.

"You *remember*!" Erick sighed, "I was just a kid, Grace. I didn't feel worthy of your love back then. I listened to my dad. I got spooked. Then the accident happened, and I blamed myself. I thought you deserved better." Erick wiped her tears with his hands and pushed her hair back. "The truth is I never stopped loving you! Not then and not now."

"You were kissing Brook at the party! What was I supposed to think??" Grace backed up away from Erick. Robin stood straighter and crossed his arms.

"That was . . . an accident. You heard Brook just now.

She drugged me, and she just admitted that she planned the entire thing!" Erick looked down at his feet. "I never meant any of this to happen."

Grace frowned. "I know you made mistakes. I have as well. But I cannot go down this road again. Too much has happened. I have to go."

"I believe my daughter has made her decision, son," Robin said, now standing between them.

"Wait! What? Where? Why?" Erick tried to keep up.

Grace allowed Erick to close the gap between them one last time. She closed her eyes as his forehead leaned into hers.

"Please don't go," Erick whispered and fought back the urge to kiss her. "I have waited a decade for this moment."

Grace pulled back. "I'm sorry, I have to go. I have so much I need to do, but I appreciate all you have done for me. I just have to do the rest on my own. I can't see you anymore. I'm sorry."

Grace walked over to the car. She had a slight limp, but her balance had returned. She stood straighter now. "I won't ever forget you! You were the miracle I needed. I just wish it didn't take a decade for you to tell me the truth. I won't forget what you did for me, despite the lies around it. Good-bye, Erick."

Erick stood there frozen, hanging on every word.

Robin turned to her. "Grace, if you need anything, please call." He hugged her. "And, can I get a ride home?" Robin's shoulders slumped as he broke the silence.

"Of course, Dad. I will say bye to Mom as well. She must be worried sick," Grace said with tears in her eyes.

Erick just stood there and watched the tail lights of Grace's car as it pulled out of the parking lot—just like all those years ago at the party. Daniel and Sky stood by Erick as they watched the car lights get smaller. The three stood there in solidarity.

"Been here before," Erick said, defeated. Erick's heart dropped to his stomach as he watched the car turn out of sight. Hope vanished as Erick realized his greatest fear happened. He lost the girl forever this time—the girl with the sunset hair.

Fifty-eight

Grace drove to the only place she could think of after saying goodbye to her parents and retrieving the rest of her things. No matter what the truth was, they would always be her parents.

"Hey, it's me. Can I come over? I need your address." Grace spoke after a woman answered the phone.

Ten minutes later, Julie answered the door, and Grace, leaning on her cane, walked in. Grace removed her coat and sat down. Julie sat down beside her. "No more wheelchair? Look at you, girl! Are you okay? Tell me everything!"

Grace told her about remembering everything and about Finn. "Erick shaved his beard, and the two are twins, so it was hard to tell them apart." She continued to explain how she finally remembered the shark fin tattoo, but it was too late. How Sky, who looked like she was in an old western movie, blasting the shotgun. How crazy everything was that happened. "I was so stupid!"

"Oh, Grace. You are *not* stupid. How could you know?" Julie reassured her. "You are done with the doc, then?"

"I can't be in a relationship right now. I need to figure out who Grace is. My real name is Raya."

"Ray of Sunshine!" Julie chimed in.

"My dad named me Grace, and actually, he isn't my dad.

Since I don't have a middle name, I am keeping Raya. My name will be Grace Raya Evans. I'm going to spend some time figuring out who *she* is. I will always love Erick, but I can't be with him. At least not right now."

"Would you like to stay here? I have an extra room," Julie asked. "My mom moved back to her apartment a few weeks ago. So, the room is all yours!"

"Yes, for a little while. I can pay you. Apparently, I have money my aunt er- my *mother* left me." Grace frowned. "I may need to hire another therapist to help me to walk better. Then, after the training, I need to go back to the top of the mountain." Grace was determined. "Can you help me with that?"

"I got you! I have some colleagues in mind who can help you." Julie nodded.

"This time, make sure the therapist is *female!*" Grace laughed. Julie laughed too. It felt good to laugh, Grace thought. She convinced herself she could do this. Grace was stronger now than ever. Today would be the first day of her new life— a life where she called the shots. Grace would *not* end up like Raven. She would do the next thing and take back what she lost all those years ago— her power.

"What happened to Raven and that guy Jack Stone? Did they say who your dad was?"

"No, no one knows the answer to that question." Grace pulled the journal out of her bag. We can read some more of this. Maybe my aunt knows who my real father is."

"I can order food for us while you get settled."

"Sounds like a plan!"

Grace was glad, and she wanted to get to the bottom of what happened. Did Raven stay with Jack or run off with Stephen, a.k.a. Pala? Grace felt the missing pieces would just be the beginning of her finding her way back to her true self.

Jack came home at 5 p.m. two days later. He noticed the apartment was clean, and I had gotten rid of some of my things.

"You cleaned?" He looked confused. "You know we have people to do that."

"I needed to get some things cleared out." I hesitated. "My brother, Robin, called, and we talked for a while. I want to go see my dad and Robin this weekend."

"I'm your family now. You don't need them. Besides, I might be working, and I can't go."

Suddenly the phone rang, ending the conversation. Jack looked furious as he slammed the phone down.

"There is an emergency at work, and I need to go."

Without explanation, he left the apartment. I took a shower, and afterwards, I put the television on, and the news blared.

"Three victims found at a local construction site . . ." The reporter stated.

My eyes looked over at the decanter of whiskey on the coffee table. I wanted a drink, but then Stephen's voice came into my head, "Alcohol is poison to the body. It keeps us asleep."

I turned back to the television when the reporter said, "CEO Jeremiah Stone and his wife Sarah are among the casualties. Rebekah remains in critical condition."

Oh my God! It was Jack's family! I froze in place.

"Police suspect arson . . ."

Jack burst through the door. "They wouldn't listen! My parents are gone. My sister is in a coma. I need to get out of here. The walls are closing in around me. Everyone leaves me. First my birth parents, now my adoptive parents are dead, my sister, and now you want to leave!"

His eyes were bloodshot now. I could do nothing but feel sorry for this man. I know he wasn't the best boyfriend, and I know I had awakened in his absence to a whole new world. It was going to be harder to leave now, though. Another feeling came over me. I felt guilty that I had found a path to happiness, and he was on the path to misery.

Jack exploded in rage, "Please don't leave me."

"I'm just going to my family's house for the weekend."

"You're not going anywhere!" He grabbed me by the shoulders.

"Jack, please, you're hurting me!" I was mustering all the courage I could get. "I can't live like this anymore. I need more—" I pleaded with him to just let me go.

Next, he pushed me down on the couch. I tried to fight back, but I knocked the lamp over, shattering the bulb. The sound seemed to make him even crazier.

"You aren't going anywhere," he said, pressing his body on top of me. He pinned me down and ripped my shirt. I do not remember what happened next. I escaped into my mind, and I closed my eyes. I was in a field wearing a white sundress among the wildflowers. My mother Alo was there with flowers woven in her hair, and she gave me a crown of white aster flowers. I ran barefoot in the rich earth into the dark forest. Pala called out to me. His hair was braided, and his arms were open to me. We ran off together into the woods. There we lived happily ever after in a beautiful house with a round door.

Jack slammed the door and brought me back to the present. I found my way to the shower. There I let the warm water wash over me. I scrubbed my skin raw. I sat on the floor of the shower clutching my knees and let the tears come. I dried off and put my pajamas on. The phone rang, and I went into the living room to answer it.

"Raven?" a shaky voice came over the phone.

"Who is this?"
"It's R-r-r-Rebekah,"
"Beks?"
"Yes"
"Are you okay?" I was grateful for a chance to focus on another person's pain.

"I need to tell you something about Jack," she said sobbing on the other end of the line. "Jack was at our building. he started the . . ." Rebekah started coughing, "the fire that killed . . ."

Abruptly, the phone dropped, and she heard people shouting. The phone went dead.

I stood there holding the receiver, paralyzed. I wanted to run. I wanted to cry. I thought about calling call the police. I tried to pray for Rebekah.

Too numb, I went to bed. I woke up hours later, but I could not get out of bed. My body ached, and my head pounded. Sunlight became a knife that sliced through my eyes and head. I stared at the ceiling, hoping whatever disease or sickness I had would win. Somehow dying seemed better than living. Dying seemed easier than staying and way better than trying to leave again.

I had a fever, and my teeth chattered. I could not get warm. There was a tap on the window, and I could see a black shadow of a bird. Its 'Caw-Caw' woke me out of my dizzy sleep. I slept during the day and was awake at night but could not move.

The phone rang, and I couldn't answer it. The machine played the message. It was the hospital informing me that Rebekah was being discharged today. I racked my brain. Did I imagine the conversation with Rebekah? It all came into my consciousness all at once. Could Jack have been responsible for the death of his parents? He always spoke highly of them. Saying they were the only ones who wouldn't let go. All the other foster families could not love him the way Jeremiah and Sarah had. I shuddered at the thought. My hands were shaking as I wobbled my way to the kitchen and got a glass of water. I was in no condition to do much of anything.

My head throbbed so much that I dropped my glass in the sink. The sound frightened me. It was not coming from inside my head but the front door. Bang. Bang. Bang. Someone kept pounding on the door.

"Who is it?" I squeaked. The pounding came again as I made my way to the door. "Hello?"

"Hello, open up. It's the police!" I opened the door and leaned on it to keep myself from falling over. "Ma'am? We are looking for Jack Stone!" I collapsed on the floor.

I woke up the next day in the hospital. I saw Jack's arrest on the news channel when I woke up. "Murder and attempted murder," they said.

"Miss Evans?" a young doctor said, entering the room. "Our test results have come in. There were traces of Scopolamine in your system. Do you take any medications or supplements?"

"I haven't taken anything for a few weeks now, but I was taking vitamins. What is Scopolamine?"

"It's an illegal substance used to make victims compliant. It's known as a date-rape drug." The doctor reviewed her chart. "Your blood work showed you are severely dehydrated," he said. "Are you in any sort of trouble?" He was looking at the bruises on my arms.

"Not anymore, I guess. What caused me to blackout?"

"You had a virus, but your fever is gone, and your blood has returned to normal. There is one other thing." The doctor looked at me seriously, and I braced myself for more revelations about what had been done to me.

A woman walked into the room just then. "I'm Dr. Cudnik." She had beautiful curly black hair and brown eyes. "I was called in to examine you because your blood test came back positive. Did you know you are pregnant?"

Erick poured himself into his work over the next few months and helped Daniel and Sky plan their wedding for next summer. Declan Finn passed away just after the new year. Every night until his father's death, Erick would spend time with his dad reading the bible. Their relationship grew day by day.

"I'm so proud of you, son! You have become a good man," his dad said one night. "I'm sorry it didn't work out with you and Grace. She always was a spitfire of a child, but she really did bring out the best in you. I'm sorry I let my judgment get in the way."

"It's okay. Grace must figure things out for herself. I respect that. Anyway, I don't have time to date anyone now that I am running the Tabitha Foundation. It was quite the undertaking when Brook resigned. It's been keeping me busy along with HigherGround. I'm training more therapists so that I can eventually just do research and fundraising for innovative therapies and new mobilities, like prosthetics. People need to know they aren't alone, and I can show them how to become the best version of themselves. It's a whole approach to healing," Erick said and sat on his dad's bed. "I'd rather be here with you, though. Honestly, Dad, it's been great spending time with you."

"I don't have much time left, son. I can't tell you enough how proud I am of the man you have become! I hope you can forgive me for my mistakes. I was too hard on all my sons, especially Finn. Maybe you both can reconcile once and for all. Don't ever doubt yourself again. You remind me so much of your mother! I have been lost without her. Give Grace time, but then go to her, son. You only find a love like that once," Declan said and hugged his son. These were the last words he spoke to Erick as he died the next day.

Brook paid her respects at the funeral, but she wore a large black hat and refused to make eye contact with Erick. James Becker and Finn stood by her side. Finn reached out his hand to her when they lowered the casket into the frozen ground. Daniel and Sky were by Erick's side during the entire ceremony. After the guests dispersed and made their way to their cars, Finn approached Erick.

"Listen, I know you will never forgive me, but I'm getting help now. I hired someone to help run FinnLondon Publishing, and I spent the last few months in rehab. I'm working on getting my life together, and I'm going to AA. The court ordered counseling for me, and I'm taking it seriously now." He turned to Daniel, "I'm so sorry I wasn't there for you after the accident. I could have been a better brother. All I wanted to do was please Dad. He didn't make it easy. Then the very thing I fought for years overtook me, and I became *him*. I'm glad he had time to change before he passed. Now, I have to do the same." Brook stood by, wearing dark glasses. Finn squeezed her hand, "I did care for Grace, Erick. She made me a better person, but I hurt her, and I will pay the rest of my life for that. I'm sorry I wasn't a good brother. I will make it up to all of you. It's up to me to start a different legacy for our family. We really don't know how much time we have left."

Daniel nodded and finally said, "We can be a family again. I think Dad wanted that most of all."

Erick closed the circle. "Brothers for life. Brothers look out for each other. Let's be *that* kind of family."

"All these years," Brook spoke from behind Finn, tears flowing. Her voice cracked. "I have been carrying the weight of all of what we did, what *I* did. Erick, I'm so sorry that I kept secrets from you when you were hurting the most and for kissing you that night. I barely knew how to drive, let alone in the rain. I'm truly sorry, Daniel," Brook said, looking down at her feet.

Sky moved closer and was protective of Daniel. He simply said, "It was an accident, and honestly, I wouldn't have changed any of the events that have happened. I'm getting married to the most amazing woman in the entire world!" Sky looked at Daniel and hugged him because it was true! Only time would tell if they all could be a family again.

Finn and Brook followed James Becker to his car. Erick was surprised at how healthy Brook's father looked and how he managed to out-live Declan. Erick followed Daniel and Sky to their vehicle. He was thankful for the time he had with his father. He imagined that his parents were finally together again.

Fifty-nine

Grace stayed with Julie, and when she wasn't training with her therapist, she was writing on her new laptop. When Julie wasn't working, they had dinner together, and they read the journal.

> *It's crazy how the body keeps score of what it has been through. Now my body was carrying another life. Was it Jack's child? Perhaps it was Pala's. What had I gotten myself into? I left the hospital the next day.*
>
> *Once home, I packed only a few things and drove to Robin's house. We stayed up all night talking about Jack and the fire. I could tell Robin anything, even about Pala. Robin told me about his upcoming wedding to Faith, a girl he met in college whose dream was to become a lawyer. He would joke, "A carpenter and lawyer; could be complicated!"*
>
> *Our father was set to return to Wales to take care of a family matter. The three of us had one last supper together as a family. After everything that had happened, I wasn't looking forward to being without my father again.*
>
> *I tried not to think about Jack and hoped he would rot in jail forever. I hoped Pala was safe while he was hiking. I wished I had run away with him instead of going home*

and trying to make things work. I felt you growing inside me, and I wasn't going to let anyone harm you.

I sang, "You Are My Sunshine." I named you Raya Alo Sunshine, but if you were a boy, I would name you after my father, Bran, and your middle name would be Robin.

The months passed, and the seasons changed, and the day you were born came. It was late September in Connecticut, and Robin met me at the hospital with Faith, and as soon as I saw your green eyes, I was smitten.

After a few months, we visited my brother Robin and Faith. The television was on, and the news reporter told a story about the fire that claimed Jeremiah and Sarah Stone's lives. They were interviewing Rebekah, and they were talking about mental health being a national issue and the problems with the foster care system. Children were falling through the cracks. They interviewed Jack next, and to my horror, he was not in jail. He was in a psychiatric facility in New York. "Do you want me to turn it off?" Robin asked gently.

"Jack Stone, what are you looking forward to the most when you are released at the end of the month?" The reporter asked him.

"Being with my girlfriend and becoming a family. I know what I did was wrong, but I finally got the help I needed. It will be my mission to help others who suffer from the same disease."

His eyes stared through the screen, seeming to pierce through me.

"He's getting out, and . . ." I couldn't finish the sentence. "What do I do then?" I paced around the room. "He will find me. He always does!"

The doorbell rang, and I froze, imagining Jack was on the other side of the door, but it was a delivery man with two packages addressed to me. I opened the first box.

"It's from Dad!" I exclaimed, feeling relieved. I opened the packaging to reveal a tiny music box. I lifted the box out of the cardboard packaging and opened the lid. "You Are My Sunshine" chimed from the box, and I smiled as it played while watching you fall asleep in Robin's arms.

"Wow, I bet he made that! Open the next one." I was excited to see what was inside until I opened the box. Inside was a small box. As I pulled the box out, a piece of paper floated to the floor. Robin picked it up while I started opening the envelope. The next thing I knew, Robin smacked it out of my hand, screaming, "Don't open that!"

I was annoyed at first, but I saw the brown powder pour from the envelope when he took it to the trash. Robin came back in, "Cinnamon!" He handed me the note. "Read this."

"You can't run. I know where you are. When I get out, I will find you, and then our family will be back together."

I was so afraid. What you might not know about me is that I'm allergic to cinnamon, just like you. If I eat it or even breathe it in, I have to rush to the emergency room. This was a warning that I was still not safe. You were not safe. I decided then to make the hardest decision I had ever made.

"Robin, you and Faith need to take Raya. I can't keep her safe!"

"But this little girl needs her mother, not her uncle, to raise her!" Robin persisted even though Faith was pleading with him as well.

"I have to go. If you don't take the baby, I will have to move far away and change my name. I will never be able to see you again until it's safe. If you take the baby like it's yours, no one will know, and she would be safe. She would have . . . all of us."

Robin and Faith decided to adopt you. It was the hardest thing I ever had to do. Faith asked if she could name you Grace, and I agreed.

I remained a prominent figure in your life, and I was glad you were safe even if you thought of me as your aunt. I loved you more than myself.

I hoped that when you read this journal, you would understand why I did what I did. You should have found the map by now that is concealed in the back so you can finally learn your real identity. I also left a key with Robin and Faith. The key is to a safety deposit box containing your inheritance money for your future.

I wanted to tell you myself, but if something happens to me, well, that's why I have written it all down. If I never get to say to you in person, know that I'm so proud of the woman you are becoming. You have my spirit Grace, and even though you and I both made unfortunate decisions in the past, you see the truth now and can choose your new path, the path back to your true self.

We can be stubborn, but we'll always find our way back home. You are worth more than you know and never feel like you are not enough. Know that I love you now and always, and I hope you will find it in your heart to forgive me for not keeping you. Robin is one of the best men I know, and I know he'll give his life for you. I hope someday you will get to meet your grandfather. I love you, Raya Alo Sunshine. You truly are my heart. I will love you to the moon and back. I will always be your Nokas (Mom). I can't wait to be together again soon!

Love Always,
Nokas

Sixty

Grace managed to avoid Erick all winter, and she was grateful he did not text or call her. Her training was complete. She now ran every day to build up her strength. She lifted weights and changed how she ate by adding more plant-based foods to her diet. Grace visited her parents often, and to their delight, she still insisted on calling them, Mom and Dad. She collected the inheritance Raven had left for her and the key to her house in the woods. Julie helped her clean the place up and move in.

The weather started to warm up, flowers bloomed, and leaves budded on bare winter branches. Grace knew it was time to return to the Freedom Summit, where it felt like her life ended, but it was actually where it all began.

Grace stepped out of her home, and her feet hit the trail. She recalled her journey the last time she found herself among the trees. Grace allowed herself to think about all the events that led up to this one with each step on the path. Her limp faded, as did the fear about what her life would become. Things now had come full circle for her.

Grace found the turn and hiked toward the summit. She suddenly stopped in her tracks and remembered seeing Erick at this exact spot. The spring wind picked up Grace's long red hair and swirled it around as she continued down the trail alone.

Her memory had pretty much returned, and she admitted to only herself that Erick would always take up a large portion of her heart. She hadn't spoken to Erick since the day at HigherGround, where she confronted all of them. Being away from the drama and focusing on herself gave her freedom. Grace was in the best shape of her life. She picked up the pace and ran through the trees, a backpack light on her back. *I got this! Please don't let me run into Erick today. I'm on a mission.* This time she was no longer seeking answers from Aunt Raven, but she would conquer the same path to the summit to fulfill her destiny. Unlike the last time, today, she knew who she indeed was. This is what Aunt Raven wanted for her. She wanted Grace to not disappear into her life and not disappear into a man's idea of how her life *should* be.

Grace knew what she wanted from the next chapter of her life, and it was only a matter of time before she reached the summit. Grace sat on an old stump overlooking the city below. She breathed in a warm breeze and unzipped her jacket. Next, Grace retrieved the map just before. After examining it, she looked around, remembering the photographs she found that day. Grace hoped she could see them as she scanned the terrain near the edge.

A small piece of paper caught her eye by the tree, and she picked it up. It was very faded, and she was sure she had never seen this photo before. It was of younger Raven with a dark-haired man in the picture. Grace curiously flipped it over. In faded ink was written, "Jack Stone."

Grace took the backpack off her shoulder and placed the photo inside. She spotted another smaller photo crumpled next to the tree. It was a Polaroid photo of Raven, and a bearded man with long, dark brown hair fell to his shoulders. His eyes were on Raven, and Raven's head was on his shoulder, her eyes closed. Her red hair filled half the picture. Wild and free. Grace flipped the photo over and saw writing in the same faded ink. *My Pala.* Next to that was a small heart.

Grace felt around the ground moving dead branches out of the way but didn't find anything else. Disappointed, Grace looked over the side of the cliff to the ledge below. The baby picture and the bracelet were long gone. It didn't matter who gave birth to her. What mattered were all those who loved her and kept her safe. She also knew that one of these men in the photos was her biological father. Grace promised herself that one day she would solve that mystery.

For now, her mission was to tell others her story and hoped it would help other women find themselves. Grace thought about all that she had been through in her life. Never again would she give all of herself away. Not to anyone.

Forever changed, Grace knew the next step in her journey. She would write about her story and share Raven's. Grace stood up and descended the mountain and decided she would guide others to this trail and work with women who sought the same freedom she found. It would be her most meaningful work to date. As Grace ran down the mountain, she realized something she never thought about before. *Someone's life may depend on it.*

Grace created a foundation called Healing Hikes, which helps women worldwide overcome significant obstacles and gives them a second chance to heal their lives.

Grace was no longer broken but forever *mended.*

Erick was Daniel's best man and watched as Daniel married the woman of his dreams. Jace and Luna were the ring bearer and flower girl, respectively.

Over the months, he thought of Grace often and kept in touch with Robin and Faith. Erick kept himself busy researching new therapy techniques, and he opened another studio for HigherGround.

At AA meetings, he helped Finn work through the twelve steps. Finn and Brook married that spring. All the brothers were now married except for one. Erick thanked God for all his time with Grace and hoped she was doing well. He missed her but loved her enough to give her the space she needed. Erick left his guilt behind, no longer tormented by a crime he didn't commit. He was glad to be free from his past once and for all. He lifted his eyes to the heavens and gave all the glory to God. He had seen miraculous healing beyond his wild dreams occur for Grace and all of them. He was determined to help others. After this year, Erick knew that all things were possible with God, who ultimately has the power to take a broken heart and mend it.

Epilogue

Grace walked past the sea of people seated in chairs and made her way to the front of the room. She stood behind the podium. She loved this bookstore appropriately called The Written Word, located just outside the city in Farmington, CT. Large posters honoring her debut novel, *If You Only Knew,* were strategically placed in the small front window and on the side next to where Grace stood.

"I walk alone now, but with every memory that I carry, I carry the memory of you," Grace read from her book. She was on the final leg of her book tour for her NY Times best-selling novel.

"Sometimes love stories can be second chances, but sometimes you must find your own way. Take another look at your life. Really dig deep and look around. What do you see? There is always another step you can take. Don't give up on yourself. You are worthy of the magical journey. You can always change the path you are taking. The Universe gave me a miracle when I needed it most." Grace paused as she heard a commotion coming from the audience. She looked out to the crowd.

A man moved through the people towards Grace, but she could not see his face. He shouted. "*She* was the miracle, and I will always be changed by *her*. *She* mended his heart, and time nor circumstance could keep them apart."

Grace's mouth flew open as the man read the passage nearly word for word. She looked up from her book. This person must be a fan because he knew the line by heart and added a new twist. Grace could only see a glimpse. He was of average height, and his face had a neatly trimmed beard. As soon as she saw his sapphire blue eyes, she knew who it was. *Erick.*

"I think *I* should have a say in how this love story ends?"

Just then, he closed the space between them, gently placed his hands around her face, and brought her lips to his.

Grace could not deny the electricity that still existed between them, and everyone clapped in approval.

"Meet me at the *Café Bella* in fifteen?" Erick took her hand in his. "Please?"

"Okay," Grace agreed, offering him a smile. "I just need to pack up here first, and then I will meet you there."

"Hot chocolate, extra marshmallows?" Erick offered.

"Sounds perfect." Grace could not wait to catch up with him.

"No cinnamon!" Erick laughed.

"Right!" Grace nodded, and Erick let go of her hand and left the bookstore.

After the crowd dispersed and Grace packed up the last of the books, an older man approached her.

"Excuse me, miss?" his voice was soft.

"Yes?" Grace turned around and saw an older gentleman's face with long grey hair pulled back into a ponytail.

"I was hoping you could sign my book for me. I traveled across the country to get here and missed the initial signing." The man's soft hazel eyes implored Grace.

"Of course," Grace said, honored. "Who should I make it out to?" She took the book from the man and picked up her marker.

"Pala," he continued as Grace stood there wide-eyed. "I think you and I have a lot to talk about."

Made in the USA
Middletown, DE
15 October 2021